MW01138745

To Bria,

A TALE OF TWO CITIES

A HOLIDAY NOVELLA COLLECTION

ALEXANDRA WARREN

Enjoy this trip through
the holiday season :)

Alexandra Warren

A Tale of Two Cities: A Holiday Novella Collection
Copyright 2019 Alexandra Warren
Cover Art by Visual Luxe

Included Works

A Tale of Two Cities: A Halloween Novella
Copyright 2018 Alexandra Warren
A Tale of Two Cities: A Thanksgiving Novella
Copyright 2018 Alexandra Warren
A Tale of Two Cities: A Christmas Novella
Copyright 2018 Alexandra Warren
A Tale of Two Cities: A New Year Novella
Copyright 2019 Alexandra Warren
A Tale of Two Cities: A Valentine's Novella
Copyright 2019 Alexandra Warren

All rights reserved. This book or any portion thereof may not be reproduced or used in any manner whatsoever without the express written permission of the publisher except for the use of brief quotations in a book review.

This is a work of fiction. Any similarity to real locations, people, or events is coincidental and unintentional.

A TALE OF TWO CITIES COLLECTION:

CUTE & SWEET MILLENNIAL MEETS OVER A HOLIDAY, ALL WITH ONE THING IN COMMON; CITIES.

HALLOWEEN EDITION
FOR LINCOLN, NEBRASKA & SAVANNAH, GEORGIA.

THANKSGIVING EDITION
FOR ORLANDO, FLORIDA & ASPEN, COLORADO

CHRISTMAS EDITION
FOR MADISON, WISCONSIN & DALLAS, TEXAS

NEW YEAR EDITION
FOR CHEYENNE, WYOMING & BOSTON, MASSACHUSETTS

VALENTINE'S EDITION
FOR AUSTIN, TEXAS & BROOKLYN (NYC), NEW YORK

A TALE OF TWO CITIES

A HALLOWEEN NOVELLA

SAVANNAH

"LANI, are you all packed up? We really, *really* need to get going so I don't miss my flight."

The pressure of the clock had me staring at my carry-on suitcase with my hands on my hips, trying to figure out what I was missing because I knew it *had* to be something. It always was - *usually, something small* - that I found myself needing at the last minute and overpaying for at the hotel. And while I could thankfully afford whatever it was at the moment, the last thing I wanted to be spending my vacation money on was something I already had at home.

Unfortunately, my quick review of the checklist I had in my head got interrupted when my *already-taller-than-me* teenaged daughter came in my bedroom, typing away on her phone with her overnight bag over her shoulder as she insisted, "It's fine, Mommy. Dad said he's about to pull up to get me now."

My face scrunched. "*Dad said, what?* I thought I was dropping you off at your friend's house on my way to the airport so you two could go to the volleyball tournament together in the morning?"

She knew how much I hated changing plans at the last minute. But of course, she still made it sound like no big deal when she plopped down on my bed and replied, "Nah, I'm gonna hang out with Dad tonight. Then he'll take me to the tournament, and I'll stay at her house Saturday night with the rest of the team while you're out playing slot machines or whatever it is people do in Las Vegas."

"Well excuse the hell out of me," I groaned, rolling my eyes as I tried to brush off how annoyed I was even though her father picking her up from here really did work in my favor since it saved me a trip.

Lani immediately picked up on my little attitude, giggling as she looked up from her phone to say, "Mommy, chill. It's just a little change of plans that'll only give you more time to get ready for your big trip with Auntie Jen and her friends. Which, *speaking of your trip*, don't forget to bring me back something good. Or at least be prepared to share some of your winnings."

While I shouldn't have been surprised that my baby girl was trying to talk her way into my purse per usual, I was still quick to tease, "*Mmhm.* I'll think about it, Little Miss. Change of Plans," moving to my dresser to grab another few pairs of panties - *because you can never have too many pairs of panties on vacation* - just as the doorbell rang.

"Is that your father?" I asked, though the way Lani took off towards the door pretty much answered my question.

Still, she couldn't help doing a little teasing of her own on her way out when she tossed over her shoulder, "Yeah, it's your baby daddy."

"*Girl…* just get the door," I called after her with a laugh, abandoning my overpacked suitcase to follow behind her. And by the time I made it down the staircase, she had already let her father inside, his smile proud when he asked her, "You all ready to go, baby girl?"

She nodded. "Yep! *Oh, wait.* I forgot my backup, *backup* phone charger. Be right back. Talk to Mom."

Once he noticed me, he offered me a smile too, shaking his head as he said, "These kids and their damn electronics. Couldn't rip that phone from her if you tried."

"I swear it's superglued to her hand at this point," I joked, making him chuckle as he pulled me into a quick hug.

I was glad we had gotten to the point of his unexpected visits not turning into an argument and his friendly hugs being the norm considering Lani's early years had been everything but. We were young - *really young* - when we had her; trying to navigate the world as we approached our twenties and find ourselves while also being first-time parents.

It was a mess.

We were a mess.

But now that we were both comfortably into our thirties, living separate lives and thriving individually while always keeping Lani at the forefront, everything was all good.

"How you been, Vanny? Feels like I haven't seen you in a minute," Russ said once he pulled away, slipping his hands into the pockets of his jeans; the jeans that were almost long enough for me to disappear behind since his ass was so tall. But it was his height that made me notice him all those years ago at the state track meet, when he high-jumped his way into the history books and I hurdled my way into records that still stood back at my high school.

Yeah, we were *that* couple.

It was a match made in high school cuteness heaven until we called ourselves being grown and having *loads* of unprotected sex. And well, let's just say that decision cost the both of us a lot.

Thankfully, it had also given us a lot too in our baby girl; the same baby girl who I worked ridiculously hard to give a comfortable life which meant I was beyond exhausted when I sighed to reply, "I know. I've just been so busy with work and keeping up with your daughter's crazy schedule. This trip is right on time."

I could pretty much assume Lani had given him the details of my vacation since he knew enough to ask, "Jennifer finally found a man to deal with her crazy ass, huh?"

"Yeah, deal with her crazy ass by spoiling her rotten. I mean, only someone who loves her as deeply as Derek does would agree to a joint Halloween-themed bachelor-bachelorette weekend in Las Vegas."

I had never understood why Jennifer was so infatuated with what my churchgoing grandmother thought of as the devil's holiday. But it was her wedding which meant it was her world, and I was happy to support whatever would give me an excuse to drink more liquor than usual.

Russell was sold on the idea as well, chuckling when he replied, "Lowkey sounds fun, though. I'm sure y'all will have a great time."

"If nothing else, I'll eat good at all the buffets while I'm there," I told him, already looking forward to matching my liquor intake with some of the best cuisine the city had to offer.

"Yeah, you look like you could use a good meal. *With your skinny ass*," he teased, earning himself a push to his arm that was damn near as skinny as mine which meant he had no room to talk.

Still, I was quick to groan, "Shut up, Russell. You loved this skinny behind back when it was even skinnier than this."

"And I always will, Vanny. You know that," he gushed, brushing a hand against my chin that made me smirk and roll my eyes as I muttered, "*Mmhmm*" just as Lani finally made her way back downstairs.

"Got all your chargers, and gadgets, and whatever else you carry on a daily that you claim you can't live without?" I asked teasingly, Russell's chuckle backing me up as Lani rolled her eyes.

"*Like mother, like daughter*," I thought as she replied, "It's just a phone and a charger, Mom."

"And you have everything you need for your volleyball tournament?" I asked, tempted to have her pull everything out of her bag so I could double-check for her.

She must've sensed it was coming since she wasted no time whining, "Yesss, Mommy. Now stop worrying about me and focus on your trip. Dad and I got this." To emphasize her point, she wrapped her arm around her dad's and gave me a smile that was damn near identical to his.

It made me sick.

I mean, how dare she come out looking like his butterscotch twin with thick, curly hair after cooking on three-hundred and fifty degrees in my body for thirty-eight weeks?

With a quick kiss to her forehead that I *guess* made my pregnancy worth it, Russell agreed, "Damn right. Can't wait to watch my baby girl dominate all those little weaklings at the net this weekend."

Snorting at his confidence, I asked, "Did you really just call your daughter's peers, weaklings?"

He shrugged. "Competition is competition, and my Lani is the best. Ain't that right, baby?"

Lani looked up to her father and gave him a blushing smile, their relationship always making my heart swell since it was almost identical to the one I had with my own father before he passed. Just like my father, Russell was always front and center at whatever Lani was participating in; from volleyball, to musicals, and even the occasional robotics competition.

Yeah, my baby girl did it all. And she loved having her father there to cheer her on no matter how embarrassing he could get.

Before I could get caught up watching them interact, I snapped out of it to tell her, "Well, be safe. And have fun. I'll be back Sunday evening. But if you need anything before that, don't be afraid to call me, Lani."

With a frown, she insisted, "Mom, I'm almost fourteen and my dad is *right* here. Relax."

While I wanted to check her on what sounded like her getting smart with me, I could only pout my lips when I whined, "When the hell did we get an almost fourteen-year-old, Russ?"

Shaking his head in disbelief, he replied, "Man, I swear I was thinking the same thing. Time flies, for real."

I nodded to agree, glancing at my watch before I told them, "Okay, okay. I gotta get going. But I'll see you guys when I get back. Love you, Lani."

My arms were already around her neck for a tight hug by the time she groaned, "Love you too, Mom." And when I pulled away, I hardly recognized the young lady now in front of me who looked every bit of thirteen going on thirty-two like I was.

Damn, that means we're both getting older.

"Aye, where's my love?" Russell asked, interrupting my thoughts and making Lani laugh.

I was pretty sure she had given up on the whole *"seeing her parents as a couple"* concept since she had already been a witness to the both of us seriously dating other people. But she still got a kick out of us going back and forth with each other, making it easy for me to smile even when I scolded, "*Boy*… get out of my house talkin' that mess."

He chuckled, giving me an innocent kiss to the forehead similar to the one he had given Lani when he said, "Nah, for real. Have fun, Savannah. I know you've been bustin' your ass down at the shop lately. You deserve the break."

"Thank you, Russyyyy," I sang with a grin, the use of his childhood nickname making him chuckle even harder as Lani took off towards his truck in the driveway.

"Ahh, you got jokes," he replied before ducking out of my front door to follow in his daughter's footsteps, the two of them covering so much ground faster than normal people would thanks to their extra-long strides.

"At least I can take a little bit of the credit for Lani's," I thought as I called after him, "Don't forget to send me some footage from her games!"

"I got you, Mommy," he shouted back before he got in the truck, Lani giving me another wave from the front seat as they pulled off. And after watching them disappear down the street, I got my ass into gear and rushed back upstairs to triple-check my suitcase cause now it was the only thing standing in the way of my much-needed vacation.

LINCOLN

"NIGGA, WE MADE IT!"

Staring out the window of the penthouse suite my cousin, Derek, had copped for his bachelor party, I couldn't have agreed with his sentiment more; the panoramic view of the Las Vegas Strip tempting me to snap a few pics for the 'Gram when I told him, "Yeah, you did your thing with this one, D. This view is fire."

"Shoutout to Wifey for that. We had a regular suite, but somehow she finessed this one. You know how women do."

While I had only met Jennifer a handful of times, I knew she had probably raised hell about something simple that ended with us getting a major upgrade for her trouble. But I certainly wasn't complaining, deciding to do a quick video of the view instead as I asked, "Her and her crew are staying here too, right?"

Derek shook his head, pouring himself a drink as he answered, "Nah, they're down the street at the *MGM Grand.* Jen said something about wanting to do a joint thing, but still keep some parts separate so we can have our individual fun with our friends or whatever."

Twisting my lips into a grin, I teased, "Now you know good and well your ass will be sleeping at the MGM tonight. Quit playin'."

Derek laughed, taking a quick sip of his drink before he

replied, "Nah. But I do plan on dropping in on their little girls' night to hit it and dip while I still can."

Since I probably would've been on the same shit, I could only laugh right with him as his friend, Rod, joined us and added, "Well if you're droppin' in, we *all* droppin' in, cause all of Jen's friends are bad as hell. I mean, you got Jasmine, Ariel, *Savannah…*"

I cut him off. "Wait. Who's Savannah?"

While I recognized the other two names from Derek and Jennifer's surprise engagement party, the third one was unfamiliar. And of course, Rod had to make a big deal about it, his face scrunched in disbelief when he asked, "You don't know Savannah? Man, she might be the baddest of the whole crew. No shade to your fiancée."

Derek smacked his teeth. "Nigga, shut up. I know my Wifey is fine as hell."

Rod rolled his eyes. "*Anyway*. Savannah is like… Kelly Rowland without the vocals. At least, I don't think she can sing. But I know for a fact she's the only one out of all of 'em who's sing-le."

"Yeah, singularly focused on securing the bag. She ain't checkin' for you, Rod," Derek commented with a chuckle that only seemed to amp Rod up even more.

His ass was naturally loud for no reason, but he seemed to be even louder than usual when he defended, "Man, she knows good and well she wants me to play stepdaddy."

"*Stepdaddy*? She's got a kid?" I asked, surprised that Rod would even be interested in adding another woman with kids to his roster considering he already had a crazy baby mama of his own back home.

But it was clear he had done his research since he knew to answer, "Yeah, she has a little girl who's probably taller than her now thanks to her baby daddy's crazy genes. That nigga is a skyscraper, for real. If he had a high-top fade, he'd be touching the clouds, bro. I'm tellin' you."

Derek and I both started laughing as Derek said, "Rod, you a fool."

"Am I lyin', though?"

Derek shook his head. "Nah, that nigga is tall as fuck. Their daughter, Lani, is too now. Savannah posted a picture of the three of them on *Instagram* a couple days ago when Lani got some award for killin' it in volleyball, and those two together damn near made Savannah look like a dwarf."

Even though I didn't know any of these people, the way they spoke about them had me intrigued enough to say, "Pull it up. I wanna see."

Rod and I waited patiently as Derek pulled his phone out, typing and scrolling until he found what he was looking for. And once he handed it to me, I totally understood why Rod was so pressed on both accounts since ol' boy's head was almost cropped out of the picture by accident and Savannah was… *damn.*

Savannah was gorgeous.

Smooth chocolate skin, bright eyes, and a tight little muscular body that almost made it seem impossible for her to have ever given birth.

Definitely Kelly Rowland-like...

I found myself trying to memorize her screen name so I could look at her profile by myself later on as Rod leaned over my shoulder and asked, "Do you think it'd be weird if I *Photoshopped* his face out and put mine in its place so she could see the vision?"

I turned his way with a scowl. "*Nigga.* Yes, it'd be weird. The fuck?"

Instead of being offended, he only shrugged. "Sometimes you really gotta see it to believe it, Linc. You don't know nothin' about that."

While I definitely knew all about envisioning whatever you wanted in life, I wasn't about to throw my support behind Rod's crazy ass. And luckily I didn't have to, the knock on the door grabbing all of our attention since it was so unique.

Well, maybe not all that unique considering there wasn't an ear in the room that didn't recognize the classic, *Grindin'* beat from the Clipse that we used to do on the lunchroom tables back in the day. But the fact that it wasn't a traditional knock told me everything I needed to know about who was on the other side of the door.

It definitely wasn't housekeeping.

For whatever reason, Rod thought it was a good idea for him to answer it. And to no surprise, Jennifer's excited smile fell flat once she saw it was him and then heard him announce, "Don't worry, ladies. Rod has plenty of rod to go around."

"*Eww.* Move, dusty," Jennifer replied, muffing his face as she blew past him with two of her friends behind her and went straight to Derek.

Once she got close enough to do so, she threw herself into his arms and gushed, "There's my fine ass husband-to-be."

Derek immediately wrapped her in a tight hug, burying his face into her neck and finding greedy handfuls of her ass when he groaned, "And there's my fine ass Wifey. Look at you, girl. *Mmm.* Can't wait to make you mine in a few weeks."

Jennifer giggled, and I was reminded that I wasn't the only witness once I heard Jasmine say, "I can't remember the last time Rich grabbed my ass so lovingly like that."

Ariel was quick to point out, "It was earlier today at the door when I picked you up to go to the airport. In fact, his exact words were, *"This ass is mine the second you get back in town, Miss. Jasmine"*."

Jasmine only rolled her eyes when she replied, "That's how we got two and a possible now." And while Ariel shot her a look over the *"possible"* part, Jasmine continued on like it was no big deal as she turned my way to say, "Hey Lincoln."

With a nod, I acknowledged, "Jasmine. Ariel. It's good to see y'all again."

"And you as well, though I'm a little annoyed you haven't offered us a drink yet," Ariel replied, serving me a mean side eye that I was sure she used to whip the employees at her promotions company right into shape - *her man included.*

Holding my hands up with a smile, I made my way to the bar as I replied, "My bad, my bad. I was just… aren't y'all missing somebody?"

It could've very well been Rod's mistake to have included a third person in his list of Jennifer's friends who were joining us.

And I assumed that was the case until Jasmine tossed a hand towards the door and explained, "Savannah is out there on *Facetime* with her daughter. Something about needing new knee pads for her volleyball tournament or something boring like that. *I don't know*. All I know is, I'm kid-free for the weekend so I should *not* be completely sober right now. What kind of dry ass bachelorette party is this, Jen?"

The question fell on deaf ears since Jennifer was nowhere to be found - *and neither was Derek.*

It only took a few seconds of complete silence amongst the four of us to figure out exactly what they were up to in one of the nearby bedrooms. And while I made the quick decision to mind my own business by pouring Ariel and Jasmine a drink, Rod couldn't help himself when he shouted, "Damnnnn! They ain't waste a second, did they?! I feel my nigga!"

Jasmine immediately punched him in the arm for being so loud, his pained face making Ariel and I laugh as Ariel added, "Jennifer better quit playin' before she ends up needing to alter her wedding dress to hide a baby bump underneath."

Before any of us could respond, there was a knock at the suite door. And while it was a lot more traditional than the one from earlier, the fact that we were waiting on one more made it easy for Jasmine to answer the door without even looking through the peephole.

"Damn, she looks even better in person," I thought as Jasmine announced, "There's Mommy Dearest. You definitely look like you could use a drink now, Vanny Van."

"Please," Savannah begged, letting out a heavy sigh as she followed Jasmine over to the bar. And that's when she noticed me. Or rather, we noticed each other. Cause for a second, I swear it was only us two in the suite's living room as she held my gaze and started to smile.

Matching her smile, I extended my hand. "How you doin', Savannah? I'm Lincoln, Derek's cousin."

"It is… *very* nice to meet you, Lincoln," she replied, biting into her lip after I brought her hand to my mouth for a little kiss.

Real G shit.

Our audience was forgotten until I heard Jasmine tease, "*Ooh.* Is that a love connection I detect, Ariel?"

"Definitely looks like a love connection to me, Jaz," Ariel replied, the both of them sipping from the drinks I had thrown together as Rod watched on with a frown.

Clearly he wasn't as convinced of what they were saying - *and what I already felt from just looking at Savannah* - since he was quick to insist, "Y'all two are always tryna start some shit. All they did was introduce themselves to each other."

"Stay in a child's place, Rod," Jasmine scolded, making us all laugh again as I finally dropped Savannah's hand.

I gestured towards the liquor to ask without words if she was serious about needing that drink, and her enthusiastic nod encouraged me to make a third glass for her and a fourth for myself as Rod said, "Girl, what you mean? I ain't no damn kid. Shit, I got a kid."

Jasmine and Ariel's eyes flashed to each other before they simultaneously groaned, "*...tragic.*" Then they broke into a fit of giggles that had Rod real salty as he started to defend himself.

Since Savannah seemed just as disinterested in their bickering as I was, I handed her a glass as I kicked up a conversation between the two of us. "So, Savannah. You must not be from the same place as us if I've never met you before."

After a quick sip, she piped out, "*Guilty.* I actually met Jen during her stint with *Teach for America.* I was a track coach at the same high school she was placed in and we became fast friends when she decided to volunteer with the team after school."

Jennifer being interested in track was news to me. But with a second look at Savannah's frame, her being affiliated with the sport made a lot of sense.

I mean, between the lean muscle tone in her arms and her legs, I wouldn't have been surprised if she would've told me she was actively competing in the sport as a professional. Still, learning about her interest made it easy for me to continue our conversation by asking, "Track coach, huh? Is that what you do now?"

Shaking her head, she sighed. "I wish I still had the time. But owning a hair salon and raising a teenager doesn't exactly leave much of that to spare."

While I was impressed to learn she owned her own business, I still couldn't help teasing, "A hair salon *and* a teenager? Yeah, you're *hella* booked up, shorty."

Chuckling, she nodded to agree, taking another sip of her drink before she admitted, "Like I told my child's father, this trip was right on time. I'm in desperate need of a break."

In conjunction with the information from Rod earlier, I could pretty much assume that her referring to him as her, "child's father" meant they weren't together. But I also knew how tricky those types of situations could be to navigate, keeping me at a respectable distance when I replied, "Well I'm glad you're joining us. We're gonna have a lot of fun this weekend."

With her glass near her lips, she served me a sexy little grin that made my mental distancing feel silly as she purred, "I'm looking forward to it, Lincoln." And while I knew it was probably in my best interest not to engage any further, I had a feeling I wouldn't be able to help myself as the night went on.

SAVANNAH

THE PLAN for our first night in Las Vegas was to grab a drink, walk the strip, and find one of the hotel clubs to hang out at. But somehow that got turned into grabbing *multiple* drinks and skipping the club to pile into two separate *Ubers - one for the girls, and one for the guys* - that were taking us off the strip to a haunted house.

I *hated* when plans were changed at the last minute, and I *especially* hated haunted houses. I mean, I just never understood the concept of giving someone my hard-earned money to be scared shitless. But leave it to the Halloween Queen to have our tipsy asses going to one of the top-ranked scare experiences in the area as a part of her bachelorette party celebration.

"This is gonna be so funnn," Jennifer sang as we pulled onto the property that was home to not one, but three different haunted houses.

"I know she doesn't think we're going to do all of these, does she?' Jasmine whispered near my ear, my eyes too fixated on our surroundings as I stared at a man holding a chainsaw who boldly stepped right in front of the car to stop it with his hand up. Then he walked over to the side of the car and instructed our driver to roll down his window.

"Get out here," he demanded, the lull of the chainsaw's motor telling me everything I needed to know about what we were getting ourselves into.

This was some bullshit.

Of course, Jennifer hopped her happy ass right out of the front seat, leaning back into the door frame to say, "Y'all heard the man. Let's go!"

The three of us with right minds looked between each other before finally obliging, our steps slow and steady since the whole environment was spooky as hell. I mean, the area was littered with devils, and zombies, and corpse brides, *and…*

"Is that man really over there breathing fire?" Ariel asked.

We followed her line of sight and sure enough, there was an angry clown breathing fire into the air that earned an enthusiastic cheer from the other fools who were waiting in line.

Jen's type of people.

Before I could excuse myself to the bathroom and not come out until they were done, I heard the chainsaw rev up right behind me, scaring me enough to take off sprinting. But of course, my fear only encouraged him to continue after me, the sound alone making my heart pound as I whined, "Leave me alone!"

The chainsaw man gave an evil laugh in response as he chased me back to my friends who had finally been joined by the guys, all of them laughing too as Rod teased, "Damn, Savannah. If I ain't know any better, I would've thought you were Flo-Jo reincarnated as a part of the haunted experience."

"Shut up, Rod," I groaned, jumping again when I heard the rev of the chainsaw scare someone else a few groups down. And while this whole thing was already turning out to be my personal hell, it was clear Jennifer was in heaven as she looked between the three options.

"Okay, which one should we do? If it were up to me, we'd do all three. But I don't wanna be selfish."

While I could appreciate her at least trying to be considerate, that concept pretty much got erased when Derek encouraged, "Be selfish, baby. It's your world."

"*Our* world, Derek," she corrected, planting a quick kiss to his lips that would've been adorable if my livelihood wasn't on the line with this whole haunted house thing.

I waited with bated breath to learn my fate as Jasmine suggested, "Well, how about y'all take y'all's asses to that R-rated one and we'll keep our asses out here with the food trucks? Since y'all have y'all own world and what not."

"*Jasmine...*"

"What, Ariel? I'm just sayin'. This shit already has me shook and we haven't even gone inside yet. Savannah's ass is about to fuck around and need an oxygen tank in a minute. Rod's ol' childish ass is probably gonna get in there and pee on himself. *And Lincoln...*"

He excitedly cut her off. "I'm ready. Let's do this shit."

The deep baritone in his voice only reminded me of the thick, muscular frame he had to match it - *and how fine he was* - prompting me to turn his way and suddenly feeling a little safer about it all as Jennifer said, "See. I'm in, Derek is in, Lincoln is in, and Ariel is... *mostly* in. So y'all are outnumbered. Now stop being scary."

"Isn't that the point?" Jasmine asked, earning herself a stiff side eye from Jen before we headed towards the information board to learn more about the different selections.

While Jennifer was immediately sold on whatever was deemed the scariest, the fact that my adrenaline was already pumping had me eager to bargain, "Can we at least do an intermediate one? It says here that they can touch you in that R-rated one and I can't guarantee I won't try to fight back."

Wrapping a protective arm around my shoulder, Lincoln insisted, "Don't worry, Savannah. I got your back. This shit will be a breeze."

He claimed it would be a breeze, but his touch alone had me feeling warm all over. I mean, Derek was handsome, sure. But his cousin Lincoln was fine in the worst way with his dark umber eyes and syrup brown skin coating a body built for strong hugs... *and stronger strokes.*

Though his stroke game was none of my business, I couldn't help imagining just how powerful it surely was as Jennifer finally agreed, "Fine. We'll do the intermediate one since *somebody* is being a fraidy cat."

Jasmine wasn't fazed by the jab, shrugging when she replied, "I'll take that if it means staying alive. I have a law practice, a husband, and two kids to go home to."

"And a possible," Ariel chimed in, Jennifer gasping in surprise since it was clearly news to her - *news to all of us.*

Jasmine was quick to squash any rumors, rolling her eyes as she said, "That was just a joke, Ariel. I'm not *really* pregnant."

Considering Jasmine had already had a few drinks tonight, I could assume she was telling the truth. Though Ariel wasn't as quick to jump onboard when she countered, "You thought the same thing with your first child and we all saw what happened with that."

Jasmine rolled her eyes again, tossing a hand Ariel's way as she rattled, "*Yeah, yeah, yeah.* Write a book* about it, why dontcha?"

Watching them go back and forth served as the perfect distraction to keep us from having to go into any of the haunted houses. But really, it was only delaying the inevitable which was why Jennifer interrupted, "Enough, you two. If we're picking this *kinda*-scary one, we need to go get in line." Then she led the way as we followed behind her like her pitiful little soldiers, passing by the fire-breathing clown on our way to doom.

While the desert heat had cooled some with the night, I knew my chattering teeth had nothing to do with the weather and everything to do with my nerves since even an intermediate level haunted house was out of my comfort zone. But I held it together, falling into place in line behind Ariel and in front of Lincoln since I damn sure wasn't going to be last.

That was too vulnerable of a position.

Still, my "safer" spot in line did nothing to keep the paid-terrorizers from picking on me the second we coughed up the admission fee and made it inside since it was obvious I was the most afraid. But just when I thought about chickening out and turning around while I still had the chance, I felt Lincoln's hands against my waist as he leaned in to whisper in my ear, "Relax, Savannah. I told you I got your back."

Even though I was already scared shitless, something about his words - *his touch* - helped to calm me just enough to at least keep my feet moving. But when the first monster jumped out at me, I wished I wouldn't have been so easily trusting since...

"Oh, shit!" I squealed, a hand to my chest as whatever the hell it was started growling at me.

Lincoln laughed right into my ear. "Come on, Savannah. You had to see that coming."

"How?! He didn't even look real," I defended, though I suppose I should've been prepared for it *all* to be real.

As if he had read my mind, Lincoln advised, "Stay ready so you ain't gotta get ready, shorty. Now keep moving."

Since I really didn't have much of a choice other than to do just that if I wanted to make it out of here any time soon, I continued behind Ariel who was handling things like a boss. Meanwhile, my ass was jumping at the smallest of things, on high alert for anything that made a sudden movement.

Making our way into the second room, I immediately recognized the corpse bride from outside who was now standing at the altar with her skeleton husband; making her a little less intimidating, especially once Rod teased, "Aye, y'all. There goes Jen and Derek in a few weeks!"

We all started to laugh - *Lincoln's still against my ear which made me tingle* - as Jennifer shouted from the very front of our line, "Shut up, Rod!" Then she led us into the next room that was pitch black, coming to a sudden halt once we were all inside.

"Does anyone have their phone out? I can't find the door," Jennifer whined as my skin started to crawl because I already knew some shit was about to go down. And sure enough, before anyone could respond to Jen's request with their phone's flashlight, the room went crazy with loud rock music, and walls of fires, and live demons, *and*...

"Is this floor moving?!" Ariel shouted, grabbing onto Rod who was positioned in front of her for support. And now Lincoln was the one groaning, "*Oh, shit,*" laughing as he wrapped himself around me to keep us both still as the fire-filled LCD flooring continued to vibrate and the demons started chanting.

"Grandma might've been right about this being the devil's holiday," I thought, holding onto Lincoln's arms as one of the tinier demons got right in my face and growled a warm welcome to hell on earth. And with that, I couldn't but laugh myself since under that costume and all that makeup, I had a strong feeling he was probably just a child.

In fact, they were all just people; having fun scaring the shit out of others and getting a check for it.

I could survive this.

Now that I had psyched myself out of being utterly terrified, it was a little easier going from room to room of fright and gore; though I still couldn't help myself in jumping at everything that moved my way. But with my new mental approach and Lincoln's comforting support from behind, the whole thing became a lot more fun… *until that damn chainsaw man showed up again.*

Just the sound of the motor had me trying to turn back around, bumping right into Lincoln's chest since he was so close behind me. But instead of letting me completely chicken out, he urged, *"I got you,"* wrapping me in a hug that allowed me to bury my face into his chest as he slowly guided us into the next section of the haunted house.

I didn't open my eyes again until I couldn't hear the chainsaw any more, Lincoln pulling away just slightly with a smile to ask, "You good, shorty?"

Our new location was dim, but the heat in his eyes was still potent as hell even in the darkness when I gazed into them and nodded yes. In fact, I started to wonder if we were back in the hell on earth room since I suddenly felt warm all over, Lincoln brushing a gentle hand against my cheek as he said, "Come on. I think we're close to the end."

Somehow, staying in the haunted house a little while longer didn't sound so bad. But once I heard that chainsaw rev up for the group that was coming behind us, I hauled ass out of there, catching up to the rest of our group who were already waiting outside.

"Man, I just *knew* that chainsaw man had finally got your ass,

Savannah," Rod teased, making everyone laugh as I playfully rolled my eyes.

"Nah, it wasn't the chainsaw man. It was the Lincoln man," Jasmine sang, making me gasp since I didn't think anyone had even noticed how close Lincoln and I had gotten in the back of the line.

I mean, it was a haunted house, so we were bound to invade a little of each other's personal space if we wanted to keep all the scary people from getting between us. But staying close together didn't necessarily mean lowkey cuddling up. And, *well*… let's just say I wasn't complaining about that part.

Lincoln played it cool enough for the both of us, shrugging when he defended, "She was scared. I was just being helpful."

"You mean, helping yourself to some Savannah," Ariel joked, her and Jasmine still pressed to play twin cupids while simultaneously embarrassing the hell out of me.

Then again, what was there to be embarrassed about?

I was attracted to Lincoln, he seemed to be attracted to me, we were on what was supposed to be a fun vacation to celebrate love. There was no reason to back away from whatever was happening within just a few hours of knowing him if it meant increasing the enjoyment of my time away from home. In fact, not being at home made it all the more likely that I would take full advantage of whatever this was while I could since it wasn't like we'd run into each other again outside of the wedding in a few weeks.

So when Jennifer asked, "Are y'all tryna go to the R-rated one or not? Derek and I can catch our own ride back to the strip if y'all really don't want to," I was quick to bargain, "I'll go if Lincoln goes."

His eyebrow piqued as if he was surprised by my invitation, making me wonder if I had read his attraction all wrong. But then his lips turned upwards into a grin, making me feel all warm and fuzzy again as he agreed, "Let's do it, shorty."

LINCOLN

IT WAS THE NEXT MORNING, and she was still on my mind. Let her tell it, it was because we had survived a near-death experience together by going through that damn R-rated haunted house with Derek and Jennifer. But I knew it was more than just that that had me laying in bed alone, scrolling through Savannah's *Instagram* to learn more about her before we linked up with them this afternoon.

When she told me she owned a hair salon, she hadn't mentioned that it was the top-rated one in her city. When she spoke about her daughter, she hadn't mentioned that little mama was only a freshman and already had a college scholarship offer to play volleyball at one of the top programs in the country. And when she mentioned previously being a high school track coach, she hadn't shared that she'd also had a record-setting high school career in the sport herself.

Should've known from how effortlessly she ran away from that damn chainsaw man.

It was crazy to me that she had all of this going for herself and played humble when it was clear she was on her shit, and I honestly couldn't wait to gas her up about it. Though I was sure my fuel would also have Jasmine and Ariel on that love connection bullshit again.

Sure, I found Savannah wildly attractive. But I also knew she lived in a completely different part of the country than I did which meant the chances of us having something real were slim to none.

Still, that didn't mean we couldn't have our fun for the weekend. And I assumed that was exactly what Savannah was on when she invited me into that second haunted house; the haunted house that was on an entirely different level than the first one and had my ass screaming just as much as she was.

Shit was fun as hell, though.

Truthfully, Savannah was just fun as hell. Sweet, and fun, and finer than fine which made it easy to get wrapped up in whatever she was putting out. But I also knew to remind myself that this was as good as it was going to get with us. At least, that's what I assumed as I finally pressed the button to follow her account.

She followed me back immediately.

The fact that she was on her phone the same way I was this early in the morning had me quick to slide in her DMs.

@TheRealLincolnN: "Everybody over at the MGM still sleep too?"

It didn't take long for her to send a response.

@VannyMarie05: "Yes. And the time zone change in combination with the fact that I'm so used to already being at the salon by now is really throwing me. I'm already dressed and everything."

Doing a quick glance back at the location on her profile, I was reminded that she currently lived in the central time zone which meant being in Las Vegas was two hours earlier than usual for her. And with her owning the shop, I could imagine she was used to being there bright and early to open the doors for a busy Saturday. But since she wasn't and we were the only ones awake, I quickly came up with a better way for us to pass the time.

@TheRealLincolnN: "Wanna do breakfast?"

@VannyMarie05: "Are you asking me out on a date, Lincoln? ;)"

While I hadn't thought of it as such when I originally sent the message, now that she had brought it up, I wasn't backing down from the idea when I typed out a response.

@TheRealLincolnN: "Yeah :). Come to breakfast with me, Vanny Marie. *Hash House A Go Go.*"

@VannyMarie05: "You're in luck. Eating one of those face-sized pancakes they have was already on my list of must-haves."

@TheRealLincolnN: "So you're saying you would've said no to my offer if it wasn't?"

@VannyMarie05: "Does it matter? ;)"

Smiling at my phone, I quickly decided I wasn't ashamed if she was only using me to check an item off of her foodie bucket list. I mean, I was hungry and I was getting her company, so it was giving me the best of both worlds regardless.

@TheRealLincolnN: "Nope. See you in thirty. I'll send you an Uber."

I figured it was the polite thing to do since the restaurant was a lot further from her hotel than it was from mine. But I shouldn't have been surprised when her athletic ass suggested an active alternative.

@VannyMarie05: "I just looked it up on Google Maps. I can walk from here."

@TheRealLincolnN: "Uhhh… that's like a twenty-five-minute walk for you, ain't it?"

@VannyMarie05: "Or a short fifteen-minute walk to your hotel, so we can do the last ten together. ;)"

@TheRealLincolnN: "Who said I wanted to walk, though?"

@VannyMarie05: "LOL! Don't be lazy, Lincoln! I'll meet you by the fountains outside of your hotel in fifteen."

@TheRealLincolnN: "Aight, bet. See you then, shorty."

I had a feeling those fifteen minutes would fly by, so I wasted no time hopping out of bed to brush my teeth and wash my face, grateful to have taken a shower the night before since it saved me a little time. Then I quickly got dressed in a pair of jeans and a t-shirt, completing my look with a ball cap since juicing up my close-cut curls would have to wait until later when I had a few more minutes to do so.

The second I emerged from my side of the suite, I expected to find the living room empty. But to my surprise, Rod was sitting in the middle of the floor with his legs crossed in a meditating position, his eyes closed when he asked, "Yo, where you sneakin' off to?"

Since I wasn't exactly ready to have him in me and Savannah's business, I lied, "Uh… just going for a little walk. You know, do something healthy before we spend the rest of the day clownin'."

His eyes snapped open. "*Bullshit.* Where you goin', for real?"

Now that he could see me, I would've felt too guilty lying to his face. So I sighed before I answered, "To breakfast. With Savannah."

He was slow to climb from his zenful seated position. But once he did, he got right in my face to groan, "*Wow.* Nigga ain't waste no time pushin' up on my woman. Homies phony, cuz. I'm tellin' you."

Knowing Savannah was the furthest thing from his woman, I could only laugh. "Chill, Rod. It's just breakfast."

That didn't calm him down a bit, his voice unreasonably loud like usual when he replied, "It starts with breakfast and it ends with butt-naked sex. You know that's what the BNB in *Airbnb* really stands for. Breakfast n' Booty."

I laughed even harder. "*You know what*… you might be onto somethin'. But, look. I gotta get going. Tell Derek I'll be back in time to hit the pool with y'all."

Grabbing a poolside cabana at the hotel's day party and chillin' out for the afternoon was the only solidified plan I knew about since Derek and Jennifer were still unsure of which Halloween party they wanted us to get all dressed up for. But of course, even the mention of that put Rod in his feelings when he replied, "I'll think about it. Since you wanna take a nigga's girl on the sneak and shit."

Shaking my head with another laugh, I finally made my way out of the hotel suite, taking the long elevator ride down to the lobby and then walking towards the strip where Savannah was already waiting looking like sunshine in her strapless yellow dress and flat sandals.

The smile she gave when she noticed me only added to her glowing aura as she sang, "Good morning, Lincoln."

Pulling her into a quick hug, I replied, "Mornin', Vanny Marie. You lookin' good."

Good was honestly an understatement. I mean, really she looked spectacular, *radiant*, unfairly good for me to only be dressed in jeans and a t-shirt with dry ass curls under my cap.

Still, instead of fully absorbing my compliment or putting me on blast about looking like a peasant next to her, she only smirked. "I do what I can. I'm just happy to be out of that hotel. The longer I laid in bed, the more it felt like the walls were beginning to close in on me. I mean, I'm just so used to being on the go that sitting still for so long felt… *uncomfortable*."

"Is that why you wanted to walk instead of *Uber*?" I asked as I started doing just that in the direction of the restaurant.

She matched my stride as she answered, "Exactly why. That and the fact that the walk back to the hotel will help me burn off some of the calories from this pancake I'm about to devour."

Considering it was her second time bringing it up, I couldn't help but chuckle when I asked, "You real hyped about this pancake, aren't you?"

"*Beyond* hyped. A pancake the size of my face and a few mimosas will make for a *very* happy Savannah," she replied with a twinkle in her eye and excitement in her tone that had me quick to hop aboard the pancake train.

"Well, shit. The way you talkin' about it already got me wanting to order the same thing so I can be a *very* happy Lincoln."

Instead of agreeing with me, she offered an alternative. "I'll share my pancake with you if you order the sage fried chicken and waffles to share with me. That was my backup meal choice if, *for whatever reason*, I wasn't feelin' pancakes today."

Since chicken and waffles was usually my go-to brunch meal whenever I could get it, I told her, "You got a deal, shorty."

Satisfied with my response, we made the rest of the walk to the restaurant over small talk about Jennifer and Derek. And that conversation continued up until a waiter came by our table to take our drink orders, Savannah ordering the mimosa that was supposedly going to make her *very* happy as if her ass wasn't already naturally bubbly.

Adorable as hell.

"I'll just have a water," I answered when the waiter asked for mine. And for the first time since I'd met her, I saw Savannah look slightly disappointed.

Somehow, even her pouty face was attractive as she whined, "Oh, come on. You're really gonna make me drink alone?"

Just that easily, she had me changing my mind, telling the waiter, "Aight, fine. I guess I'll take one of those little mimosas or whatever too."

Savannah pepped right back up, giggling when she asked, "Why'd you say it like that?"

"Like what?"

Mimicking my voice, she repeated, "*Little mimosas or whatever*, like you don't know what it is?"

"Because I don't."

You would've thought I told her I didn't know my ABCs considering how hysterical she got when she asked, "What?! *Shut up*. Are you serious, Lincoln?"

Shrugging, I defended, "Not everybody gets drunk over breakfast food like you do, Vanny Marie."

I don't know why I had a thing for calling her by her *Instagram* handle, but that shit had a nice little ring to it and she didn't seem to mind. In fact, according to the smile she wore in response, she seemed to like hearing it just as much as I enjoyed saying it.

Keeping her smile intact, she explained, "It's just champagne and orange juice."

"*Sounds*… not that great, honestly," I admitted, lowkey regretting letting her talk me into ordering one.

Still, even with my less than positive reaction, her support behind the drink didn't waver as she leaned into the table to insist, "Well be prepared to have your mind blown because it's fuckin' amazing when done right."

Watching her pretty lips spew profanity had me smiling just as hard as she was, licking my lips before I told her, "I'm glad you took me up on my offer."

It may have only been breakfast, but something about being in Savannah's presence just put me in a good ass mood; the light air about it all making me wish she really did live in our city so I could get more of it.

More of her.

"I'm glad you made one. Last night was a lot of fun."

I was quick to agree, "Most fun I've had in a minute. Thanks to your ol' scary ass."

"You were screaming too, though!" she defended as the waiter came back with our drinks, setting two champagne flutes down in front of us.

At first glance, I was tempted to send that shit right back. But instead, I followed Savannah's food order with my own and then responded to our current conversation. "Damn right, I was screaming. That shit was wild. I swear they weren't like that back when I was growing up. They really changed the game with that R-rated shit," I told her before lifting my flute to my lips and trying a sip.

With her own flute near her lips, Savannah watched me intently for a reaction. And while I wanted to tease her about never taking her advice again, I had to admit, "Okay, you were right. This shit is kinda fire."

I was already on my second gulp, taking down half the glass

when she warned, "Don't drink it too fast. That champagne will sneak up on you."

"Are we really doing Vegas right if we pace ourselves?" I countered, the devilish little grin on her face in response telling me everything I needed to know about how the rest of this trip was going to go.

Lifting her flute, she met mine for a quick cheers as she replied, "Touché. Drink up, handsome."

Swallowing my sip, I teased, "Oh, I'm handsome now? You must be feelin' the champagne in that mimosa already."

She was quick to gush, "*Wow.* I can't even give you a compliment without you tryna blame it on the alcohol? You're too humble, Lincoln."

While it wasn't my first time hearing that, Savannah's résumé made it easy for me to fire back, "I just know the fine ass owner of an *award-winning* salon and the mother of an *award-winning* superstar athlete is not talking about someone being too humble..."

She blushed as she giggled, "Oh, you did some *real* research, I see. What else did you find during your cyberstalking?"

Leaning into the table, I wasn't ashamed to answer, "You were a beast on the track. *Like...* probably could've made it to the Olympics and shit if you would've stayed at it. So what happened?"

If Savannah was a balloon, that question would've been the needle that popped her considering the way she sank back into her side of the booth with a frown, glaring down at her lap before she peeked up with saddened eyes to reply, "*I...* got pregnant."

"*Oh,*" was all I could respond, feeling bad about bringing it up since it was clearly a sore spot for her.

She did her best to recover, sitting back up to agree, "Oh is right. I have no regrets, though. As you probably learned from your research, I am one *proud* mama."

"As you should be. For her to already have a college scholarship offer as a freshman is nothing to sneeze at. She must've gotten those good athletic genes from you," I complimented, hoping it would bring back her good mood.

Slowly but surely, a halfhearted smile grew to her lips as she admitted, "It was a joint production. Her father was an incredible high jumper back in the day. I guess you could say she gets her hops and height from him."

"And her speed and agility from you, right?" I asked, appreciating the way she smirked in response before taking a sip of her mimosa.

"Well look who's giving all the compliments now. Must be the champagne talkin'..." she teased with a little giggle.

Shaking my head, I told her, "Nah, it's not the champagne. I saw the way you dipped out on the chainsaw man last night. Your stride was impeccable, shorty."

"Oh, shut up!" she squealed, tossing a hand at me across the table before she added, "We all have our irrational fears. Mine just happens to be getting my glorious limbs cut off with a chainsaw."

Irrational seemed like an understatement, but I wasn't here to judge, instead doing my best to put her at ease about it when I insisted, "As long as you aren't in the cartel or cartel-affiliated, I think you're good, Vanny Marie."

"You *think* that. But you don't *know* that."

With how convinced she seemed to be about the concept, I gave it a second thought myself, nodding as I agreed, "*Touché*," just as the waiter showed up with our meals. And I wished I would've caught the candid picture of Savannah's face when she saw just how big her pancake really was cause shorty was thrilled.

Adorable ass.

After ordering another round of mimosas and requesting some hot sauce to go with my tower of chicken and waffles, we were ready to dig in; Savannah asking me to snap a picture of her holding the pancake by her face to post on *Instagram* before she took a bite.

She was a few bites in when she finally decided to post it, typing in a caption as she asked, "If I give you photo credit on this picture, I'm not gonna have some crazy ass girls in my inbox, am I?"

Shrugging, I stuffed my mouth before I answered, "Shit, you might. I can't make any guarantees."

Flashing her eyes back up to mine, I couldn't help but laugh when she replied, "On that note… *delete, delete, delete.*"

'I'm just messin' with you. Go ahead and give credit where credit is due. And let these niggas know who you're kickin' it with in the process."

While I wasn't even sure where that territorial shit had come from, I was surprised when Savannah's head snapped back once she repeated, "*These niggas*? Who are these niggas you speak of? Where are they hiding at? Cause Savannah has zero."

Brushing her off, I insisted, "I already know you bullshittin'. You're way too fine not to be."

I mean, it was either she was bullshittin' or the niggas from her hometown were bullshittin' by letting her stay single. But it sounded like a combination of both once she explained, "My time and attention are far too valuable to give them to just anyone, Lincoln."

"Yet, here you are… *with me.*"

"So glad you noticed," she replied with a smile before shoving a bite of her pancake into her mouth.

For whatever reason, watching her lips slowly swipe against the fork had me adjusting in my seat since… *damn, did she really have to make it look so sexy?*

"This must be that brunch drunk shit I've heard women talk about before…" I decided in my head, doing my best to shake off my apparent lack of sobriety along with all the lewd thoughts about what else she could do with her mouth when I asked, "Hey, what happened to us sharing?"

Giggling, she nodded towards my plate as she answered, "*Uhhh..* your hungry ass happened to those chicken and waffles."

"Baby, your pancake plate is half-empty. I wasn't the only one starving."

"*Baby*?" she repeated, her eyebrow piqued teasingly as I quickly tried to recover, "My bad. It slipped."

"Did it really, though?" she challenged with a smirk, bringing her fork to my plate to grab a piece of chicken and shoving it into her mouth.

Again, I caught myself adjusting in my seat, hiding it underneath a shrug when I replied, "I mean, I guess it depends on how much you were rockin' with it."

It would be just my luck to overstep, strike a nerve, do something to fuck up our damn near perfect vibe. But I was grateful to see Savannah's smirk remain as she said, "I wasn't *not* rockin' with it. It just surprised me… in a good way."

"Well you surprised me in a good way. Cause I definitely wasn't coming on this trip to drink... *mimosas* with a beautiful stranger." *Or for these mimosas to have me rambling at the mouth...*

The shit was honestly getting out of control, making me wonder just how much champagne they had put in these things. But it appeared I wasn't the only one feelin' it considering the extra glaze in Savannah's eyes when she asked, "Are we really still strangers, Lincoln?"

"We don't have to be, Vanny Marie," I answered smoothly, gnawing into the corner of my lip as I gave her a hard blink that made her lick her own lips in a way that had my heart pumping even harder.

Those damn lips.

I wanted them.

I wanted *her.*

But before we could pay the bill and make a move to make that happen, we were summoned by our intended company for a day at the pool.

SAVANNAH

IT WAS the picture that did it.

If I hadn't taken that picture - *shared that picture* - I probably wouldn't have had everyone and their mama in my business about my breakfast date with Lincoln. First, it was the bride-to-be and her crew teasing me about letting Lincoln beat my cakes - *my pancakes* - once I made it back to the hotel to get my stuff for the day party by the pool. Then, it was Lani texting me emoji eyes about who the man with the private *Instagram* was since she couldn't investigate on her own. And then, it was Russell joking with me about doing stuff in Vegas that won't stay here when I called to check-in about how Lani's tournament was going.

Honestly, everybody was getting on my nerves. And the only person who wasn't getting on my nerves was the person who had them all talking.

Lincoln.

If I was on a solo trip and Lincoln was just some man I met on-the-go, he probably would've already gotten the goodies by now. I mean, this was Vegas, so that would've been totally on-brand with the culture. But the fact that we really only had the rest of today and tomorrow morning to get acquainted with each other before we'd be going our separate ways had me pressed to capitalize on everything *him.*

It was now or never.

So when me and the girls finally made it to the poolside cabana, I wasted no time heading straight over to where he was lounging on one of the plush-white couches having another drink. He was already serving me a dimpled-smile by the time I asked, "You didn't learn your lesson at breakfast about drinking too fast, huh?"

He shrugged. "Vegas vibes, shorty. Have some."

Extending his glass to me, I thought about turning him down since I honestly hadn't learned my lesson at breakfast either and knew I was going to be paying for it tomorrow. But with his little tag about, *"Vegas vibes"* in mind, I accepted it, taking a quick swig before I started, "That is…"

"Better than those damn mimosas? *I know.* It's my signature drink," he replied with a smirk.

Glancing into the glass, I thought about stealing another sip, instead deciding not to be greedy when I asked him, "What's in it?"

Again, he shrugged. "If I tell you, I gotta kill you like that chainsaw cartel you're so afraid of."

"Oh, shut up!" I squealed with a giggle, stealing another sip after all since he wanted to be funny before finally handing him back his glass.

Instead of taking a sip of his own, he sat the glass to the side on a table nearby, standing to size me up as he said, "Yellow is definitely your color. Shit looks amazing on you."

While I wondered if it was really the color or the fact that my push-up bikini top had my titties looking worth a damn, I still couldn't help but smile when I gushed, "Thank you, Lincoln." And just like the first time I laid eyes on him in the hotel suite, I found us having one of those moments of taking each other in like we were the only ones around; a potent gaze that unfortunately only lasted until I heard a familiar voice behind us tease, *"Why don't y'all just go ahead and fuck already?!"*

Snapping out of my trance, I turned to find Ariel, Jasmine, and Jennifer all giggling at Jennifer's insistence; Lincoln laughing too until I turned back his way with a scowl. He quickly held his hands up to defend, "Don't look at me. I ain't the one who said it. Those are *your* friends."

He had a point.

It was my grown ass friends pestering me about my sex life, and it was my grown ass friends who were about to get a taste of their own medicine when I turned back their way to reply, "Maybe we would've already fucked by now if y'all would just mind your own business."

I was immediately pleased by the surprised look on all of their faces, Jasmine the first to respond with clear amusement in her tone. "Okay, sis. *Heard* you."

Ariel only chuckled as Jennifer agreed, "Consider my business *minded*, honey. Live your best life." Then the three of them got situated on the pool chairs in front of the cabana, giving them access to the sun as I finally turned back to Lincoln who was patiently waiting with a smirk.

Now that I had to face my words - *face him* - I honestly felt a little embarrassed, being quick to apologize, "I'm sorry. I shouldn't have put you, *or your dick*, on the spot like that."

Instead of just accepting my apology, he wrapped an arm around my waist to pull me closer, my chest pressed flush against the top of his thick abs when he asked, "You really think I'd trip off that? Shit, I'm actually glad you said it out loud so I can finally stop playin' nice about it."

"Playing nice about what?" I asked, though the way he licked his lips pretty much answered my question. And hell, my response to him licking his lips answered my question too.

Still, Lincoln had no problem making it plain as he gazed down at me to answer, "Playin' nice about how bad I want you, Savannah."

The way he said Vanny Marie typically came off in a playful manner. *But the way he said my full name?* I'd be damned if I wasn't ready to pull the drapes of the cabana shut and make it happen right then and there off that alone.

It was so sensual, so sexy. *He* was so sexy. And even if he didn't know it yet, I already knew how tonight would end when I asked, "Just how bad are we talkin', Lincoln?"

He moved to whisper a response in my ear, but his words unfortunately got cut off by Rod's annoying ass showing up. "*Wow.* A nigga tries to be a Good Samaritan by going to pee in the bathroom instead of peeing in the pool like I wanted to, and this is what I come back to? Loyalty is dead, on my mama."

Derek was only a few steps behind him, his fiancée already tucked under his arm when he looked between the two of us all hugged up and chuckled. "When the hell did this happen? We ain't even been here for twenty-four hours yet."

"You know the clock in Vegas moves a little differently, baby," Jennifer insisted with a grin, something I had to nod along with since it definitely felt like we had already been here for a few days; felt like I had already known Lincoln for a few days - *maybe longer.*

Regardless of the time frame, it wasn't enough to stop Rod from groaning, "Yeah, and niggas you thought were real ones apparently move differently too…"

Derek laughed even harder. "Bruh, leave Vanny alone. If cuzzo got her, he just do."

Turning to Lincoln with wide eyes, I teased, "Oh, so that's what this is? You *got* me?"

He shrugged, gnawing into his grin as he answered, "For the moment, yeah."

"And then what?" I challenged, wrapping my arms around his thick neck as his hands drifted lower towards the top of my ass.

I wanted him to keep going lower.

He didn't, though, keeping it audience-appropriate when he suggested, "We'll figure that out when we get there. If that's alright with you?"

Typically, it was the exact kind of thing I *wouldn't* have been okay with. I wasn't a fan of the unpredictable, wasn't a fan of spontaneity, and God forbid someone try to change what was already solidified in my head. But something about the circumstances, or maybe it was just the look in Lincoln's eyes that had me feeling giddy to reply, "*Actually*? It is."

Lincoln smiled wide in response, leaning in to press a kiss against my cheek that felt like punishment since he knew good and damn well I wanted more than that. But I suppose it was all a part of his plan to build anticipation for later since he called himself doing little things like that all afternoon.

Kisses against my shoulder blade as I stood between his legs in the pool, one of his palms gently squeezing my thigh to keep me close whenever I stood under the cabana and he sat, his eyes all over my body whenever I spent time with just the girls, referring to me as his "baby" instead of Vanny Marie. All things that had me wanting to skip out on the Halloween party Jennifer had finally decided on for tonight even though it was what she considered the main event.

For that reason and that reason only, I left the pool with them to go get dressed, the walk back to the hotel somehow turning into a *gas Savannah up* rally since they all couldn't wait to talk about Lincoln and I.

Jennifer had an arm tossed around my shoulder when she gushed, "If I didn't know any better, I'd think you were trying to turn my wedding into a collab event."

Glancing her way with a frown, I asked, "Girl, what? *Relax.* We're just having some fun. Enjoying each other's company. It's not a big deal."

It sounded good, but I knew better than to believe the butterflies I had in my stomach from just *thinking* about Lincoln weren't a big deal. Still, I had to play it cool, even when she insisted, "Maybe not to you, but Lincoln is *obviously* smitten. Don't you go hurting my future relative's feelings, Vanny."

"I'm not! Well, not on purpose. This shit has me in a vulnerable spot too, Jen," I defended, hoping that would help her understand my true perspective.

I mean, of course I had already agreed to be down for whatever would happen over the next day and change. But beyond that, when Lincoln and I were back into our own worlds, I wasn't sure how I would feel. I wasn't sure what would happen nor how open I really was to exploring the possibilities.

For now, though, I was staying in the moment. And Jasmine seemed to be on my side when she concluded, "Well whatever it is, it's super cute. *Y'all* are cute. Kind of reminds me of when Ariel and Jamison first met**."

"God, what a night," Ariel groaned as if the memories weren't as pleasant as Jasmine made them out to be.

"*Taxi Cab Confessions headass,*" Jasmine muttered with a giggle that had Ariel quick to push her in the shoulder and squeal, "Shut up, Jaz!"

Laughing even harder, Jasmine said, "*What?* No need to be embarrassed about it now. You certainly weren't embarrassed about showing up late to graduation because you were too busy throwin' ass the night before."

From the look on Ariel's face, I could already tell the details of that day struck a nerve. But it was nice having the attention off of my situation as Ariel whined, "Jasmine, that was literally top five embarrassing things that's ever happened to me. And you know I've been through *a lot* of shit."

Nodding as we stepped into the hotel lobby, Jasmine replied, "Well it worked out in your favor the same way shit is gonna work out for Vanny Van."

"I appreciate your vote of confidence, Jasmine," I told her with a halfhearted smile as we loaded the elevator to our floor and piled out just as quickly.

While the three of us were dragging after being out in the sun and drinking well beyond our normal limits, Jennifer was buzzing with energy when she made her way to a closet I hadn't noticed before and started singing, "*Okay, ladies. Now let's get in formation.*"

"*Should've known your ass would pull somethin' like this…*" Jasmine immediately sighed as Ariel took a step closer to the outfits hanging up and asked, "How much did you pay for this *Balmain* Beychella sweatshirt, Jen?"

"What's up with these bright yellow bodysuits and matching berets?" was my question since things weren't quite adding up for me. But Jasmine's original reaction made sense once Jennifer grinned to answer, "I'm gonna be *Coachella* Beyoncé, and you guys are gonna be my background dancers."

"*Jennifer…*" we groaned simultaneously, though she was quick to defend, "Oh, come on! It'll be fun!" She even added to her cause by insisting, "Lincoln already said he loves you in yellow,

Vanny. And Jasmine, the bodysuit will give you an excuse to show off that amazing ass of yours."

"What about me?" Ariel asked, as if not having a motive for her would somehow get us all out of this.

Jennifer struggled for a minute, but eventually came up with, "The beret will cover the part of your hair that Rod ruined at the pool when he decided to do a cannonball in the shallow end."

"*That motherfucker...*" Ariel groaned in response, pulling her slightly-damp hair out of the bun she had begrudgingly forced it into after Rod accidentally splashed her.

With a pat to her shoulder, I assured her, "Don't worry, Ariel. I'll hook you up. This will be fun. And if nothing else, it's Jen's night. So we're doing it."

Of course, Jennifer smiled wide at that as she started to do the infamous "Uh-oh" dance. And while that only made Jasmine roll her eyes, I couldn't have agreed with Ariel more when she muttered, "Girl, you are *so* lucky I like you."

LINCOLN

"THIS MIGHT BE inappropriate considering the occasion, but I highkey hate Jennifer for this corny ass shit."

Glancing at my bright yellow *Balmain* hoodie in the mirror that was identical to the one Rod had on, I couldn't help but laugh at his admission since I probably would've felt the same way if I wasn't already on one. It was really only a matter of time considering my ass had been drinking since way earlier this morning with Savannah. But after a quick power nap and a B12 shot, I was back like I'd never left, clinking my glass with Derek's as he replied, "Happy wife, happy life, bruh. You know how that shit goes."

I nodded to agree as Rod took a solo sip of his own drink before he insisted, "Well that shit sounds like a scam to me. Got you out here lookin' like the brokest Jay-Z I've ever seen. And got us out here on some *one-band-one-sound Drumline* bullshit with these matching yellow hoodies and white gloves on."

Laughing at his observation, I started playing my imaginary drum set as Derek fired back, "At least its designer, nigga. Be grateful."

"*Gonna take my grateful ass straight to Craigslist and sell it once tonight is over,*" he muttered like we wouldn't hear his naturally loud ass.

And while Derek simply ignored him, I was back in the mirror when I told him, "I think it's kinda fresh. I mean, for what it is. *But anyway*. I'm ready when y'all are."

I was still bobbing my head to the imaginary drum solo in my head as Rod insisted, "Man, you only sayin' that cause you're ready to get your ol' happy ass back to Savannah."

He might've been right, but I refused to give him the satisfaction since it was really none of his business. But of course, that didn't stop Derek from backing him up when he asked, "For real though, cuz. What's up with that? Y'all seemed *mad* cozy earlier."

Cozy honestly didn't seem like a strong enough word for what I felt when I was around Savannah. It was like we fit together perfectly at all times; were on the same wavelength at all times. I mean, even when we weren't in direct contact with each other, we still somehow felt connected which explained all the long glances we shared throughout the afternoon across the pool. *And when we were in direct contact with each other...*

"Damn. We can't enjoy the trip without y'all thinking it's something?" I defended, finishing off my glass under suspicious eyes.

Derek waited for me to set it to the side before he answered, "Nah, we just know it *is* something. I mean, you were all up on her at the pool, going on secret breakfast dates and shit this morning. I'm just tryna see what's really good."

Since I wasn't sure I could give an explanation for what was happening between Savannah and I without rambling myself into admitting I was damn near infatuated with her adorable ass, I gave him the simplest answer possible. "We're... *vibing*. That's it."

While Rod remained suspicious, Derek accepted my response for what it was and replied, "All I know is, you better not fuck that up. Savannah and Jennifer are really good friends. So if you end up in a bad spot with Vanny, that means you're in a bad spot with Jen which means you're also in a bad spot with me by default."

Holding my hands up, I defended, "Relax, D. We're good. I got this."

He gave me the, *"Aight, nigga"* nod as we finally headed out,

Rod and I walking down the strip behind Fake Jay-Z like some bootleg bodyguards and breaking a little sweat in the desert heat.

By the time we made it to the *MGM Grand*, the liquor had really hit me, a goofy smile on my lips when I noticed Savannah was missing and asked, "Uhh... aren't y'all short a background dancer?"

With a little toss of her hand, Jennifer replied, "She couldn't pick up the routine fast enough, so she got sent home. We'll send her luggage later."

I swear I sobered up a little in response until she added, "*Kidding*. Something happened with Lani, so she caught the first flight home."

"*Definitely sober now*," I thought, wanting to say fuck this little party and take my ass back to our hotel when she teased, "Kidding, again. She's right over there at the craps table talkin' to some baller nigga."

What the...

My fists tightened as I immediately started looked around for the nigga she was talking about and Jennifer started cracking up laughing. "Oh, shit. You got it just as bad as her. That was only a test, Lincoln. Relax."

"Damn, you really do got it bad," I realized, trying to shake it off as Derek wrapped his fiancée in a hug and asked, "Baby Beyoncé, will you quit playin' before you give my fam a heart attack?"

"*Fine, fine*," she agreed, tossing a hand towards the nearby gift shop when she shared, "She went to grab a bottle of water, but here she comes now."

This time, my search was simple since she really was headed our way looking fine as hell in her yellow long-sleeved bodysuit and shiny white boots while simultaneously giving an apology. "Sorry, y'all. This is the *only* way I'm gonna survive tonight." Then she gave me smile as she pinched at the front of my hoodie and said, "These are so cute."

"You are so cute," I countered, leaning in to brush a kiss against her cheek that made her giggle as she pressed her free hand into my chest to keep me at a distance.

"And *you are*… still drunk from earlier. I warned you about that."

Shrugging, I explained, "Nah, this is a new drunk. I slept that old one off."

She giggled again as we started heading towards where the party was located, Savannah taking a long swig of her water before she said, "A nap would've been smart. But I guess I was too busy doing hair anyway."

I tossed an arm around her shoulder to pull her closer - *or maybe because I needed the extra support as we continued the walk* - when I reminded her, "Shorty, you're supposed to be on vacation. You shouldn't have even brought your equipment with you."

Turning under my arm to find my eyes, she quickly countered, "And have Ariel out here lookin' like Buckwheat from the *Little Rascals* because of Rod's childish ass? Nah, I had to come to the rescue on that one."

I had to respect that, nodding along as I complimented, "Well you're wearing the hell out of this costume. If I ain't know any better, I'd think you were about to break it down on me right here in the casino."

"I might," she replied with a wink that went straight to my junk, making me pull her closer to plant a juicy kiss against her temple before we found our place in line.

It was going to be a good night.

"As long as they speed up this line," I thought, my mouth starting to water for whatever reason as I swallowed hard while Jasmine threatened, "Rod, I will *literally* strangle you with the strings of your hoodie if you don't back the hell up."

While we all started laughing at that, Rod only moved closer to her in the line, getting all up on her to insist, "Shit, we matching like a couple. Might as well act like one too. I promise I won't tell your husband if you promise not to tell my baby mama."

She tensed up in her stance, closing her eyes to groan, "*Ugh.* I can't wait to have Rich whoop your ass after the wedding in a few weeks."

The mention made him back up immediately, his hands in the

air when he said, "Aww hell nah. That nigga looks like he's been in the gym heavy lately. I'm *good.*"

Again, we all laughed. At least, I thought we all laughed, except… *did I laugh too? Or was that only in my head? And why the fuck is my mouth still watering like this?*

My internal confusion must've been more external than I realized since Savannah turned my way with a look of concern on her face and asked, "Lincoln, are you okay?"

I swallowed down the steady flow of saliva before I piped out, "I'm... *great.* Never been better."

She wasn't completely buying it. "Are you sure? Cause you look like you're gonna be sick."

"I told you, *I'm…*"

My words got cut off with a big ass burp that was a combination of pool snacks from earlier and my most recent dark liquor of choice.

I just know my grown ass isn't about to throw up...

As if she had read my thoughts, Savannah panicked. "*Oh, God.* A few more of those burps and your guts will be all over the casino carpet. Let's go."

She was already pulling me out of line by my arm as I chuckled and insisted, "Shorty, I'm good. Come on. We can't miss the main event."

While I felt pretty sure of myself, everyone else around us seemed anything but convinced, Jennifer skipping right over me to give her friend instructions. "Vanny, go ahead and take him upstairs to our suite. He's not gonna make it."

In my head, I felt like I could've made it. But my legs must not have agreed since they were already moving in the direction that Savannah was dragging me, the dinging of the elevator once we climbed on making my head throb as I told her, "I'm sorry. I feel like I'm ruining your night."

She quickly brushed me off with a smile. "Honestly, I'm still exhausted from earlier anyway. So you're good."

When we made it to their floor, I suggested, "You can just drop me off in the room and go back downstairs to the party. I'ma drink some water, get a little rest, and I'll rejoin y'all in a few."

Instead of taking my idea, she only laughed, using her keycard to unlock the door and guiding us inside. "Lincoln, you're crazy if you think I'm leaving you up here by yourself. You could throw up in your sleep, or choke on your tongue, *or…*"

This time, it was her words being cut off as I pulled her against me from behind and started kissing on her neck. Through her usual little giggles, she asked, "What are you doing, Lincoln?"

"We finally got some time to ourselves, Savannah," I replied as if I wasn't stating the obvious. But even if my words weren't making my intentions clear, I used my actions to do the talking as I slowly ran a hand against her abdomen towards the bottom of her little bodysuit.

Again, she giggled before she also stated the obvious. "And you're faded as hell."

"Trust me, baby. I know *exactly* what I'm doing," I assured her, running my hand back up towards her breast and palming it in a way that made her moan. She tilted her head back to give me better access to her neck, covering my hand with her own as she made me squeeze harder while I continued to kiss every inch of skin I had access to - *not enough thanks to these silly ass costumes.*

Still, that was all Savannah needed to believe I was well enough to make it happen since she turned around to face me with heated passion in her eyes and demanded, "Show me."

Those two words were something like a starter's gun for how quickly I could get Savannah out of her costume, suddenly thankful for Jennifer's silly pick since all it took was a long zipper and a few pulls to have shorty in her bra and panties. And I wasn't the only one on an urgent mission, Savannah making easy work of my hoodie and the t-shirt I had on underneath it, then moving onto the button of my jeans before coming to a screeching halt.

"What's the matter?" I asked, her change in demeanor lowkey helping to sober me up.

With a sigh, she groaned, "I *knew* I forgot to pack something," my look of confusion prompting her to continue, "Condoms."

Waving my hand, I finished what she had started with my jeans and told her, "Don't even trip. I got that on lock."

"*Oh, thank God,*" she sighed, relieved as that heated passion returned to her pupils the second my jeans dropped to the floor. And once we were both in next to nothing, it was game on, Savannah palming my face and delivering the kiss I'd been waiting on since I first laid eyes on her.

So sweet yet so sensual.

So pure and still fuckin' intoxicating.

Sexy ass Savannah.

Grabbing handfuls of her ass, I pulled her closer, lapping my tongue with hers in a perfectly-paced kiss as I found new focus to slowly guide us backwards to a nearby couch. And I could only hope no one else planned on ditching the party early to come up here since I already had Savannah's panties off in one quick pull before pushing her down onto the couch, the provocative look she was giving me as she waited for me to make my next move sending a rush of blood straight to my dick and making my mouth water for new reasons.

"Can I taste it, baby?" I asked, Savannah stretching her long, runner's legs to new lengths to answer my question and giving me the best damn pussy invitation I had ever received.

Shits pretty as hell too.

Without wasting any more time, I pressed into her thighs to open her even wider before dropping down in front and delivering a long swipe with the base of my tongue that had her arching away from the couch.

Oh, this is gonna be good.

Her eyes were already closed and her mouth was parted open as I continued my determined pursuit of making her go crazy, her hands buried in the short curls on the top of my head only encouraging me to lick with expert precision as she hummed my name. And I'd be damned if that shit plus the alcohol in my system didn't turn me into a full-fledged animal, my hands locking onto her thighs to keep her still as I took great pride in making a mess of her release and then cleaning it up - *only to do it all over again.*

I wasn't sure how much time had actually passed, but I felt like I was just getting started when I finally wiped my face with the back of my hand on my way to grab the condom from my jeans that had gotten left behind. And by the time I returned, Savannah had gotten rid of her bra and changed her position, her knees firmly planted on the edge of the couch cushions and her hands pressed into the back of it as she once again gave me an incredible invitation; this time with a seductive look over her shoulder and those three little words I was giddy to hear.

"Come fuck me."

It was in that moment that I realized I was completely enamored with everything Savannah. Her sweet, gentle, caring spirit, her boss mom vibes, and *especially* the energy she was putting out now as she waited for me to accept her arousing ass request as if I could be any more turned on.

Still, she had me hooked. And to show her just how much, I did exactly what she had asked, sliding the condom on and plunging into her from behind with a shared inhale.

"Oh yeah. I'm definitely hooked," I thought the second the warmth and wetness of her pussy surrounded me and she moaned, *"Dear God."*

The slapping of our skin immediately began to clash with the creaking of the couch underneath us as I continued to drive into her. And that only got louder when I increased the pace of my strokes, one hand at her waist and the other at her neck as I brought her close enough to whisper straight into her ear, "You like that shit?"

"*Y-yessss.*"

Her enthusiastic response only made me go harder, my fingers digging deeper into her gorgeous skin as I demanded, "Tell me how good it is, baby."

"*It's sooo good,*" she sang, literally screaming when I started going even harder. But I couldn't stop. I was on another level. We were on another planet. And if nothing else, regardless of what would happen between us after tonight, I was guaranteeing she'd never be able to forget this moment, forget this trip, forget... *me.*

I was in such a zone that it caught me by surprise when my dick gave me the tingly warning that shit was about to be over with. And thank God Savannah was on the same wave with her own orgasm, her throbbing pussy practically pulling my nut out of me as I growled through the sensation and then shuddered at our shared aftershocks.

"*Damn, Savannah,*" were the only words I could use to describe how I was feeling, every nerve ending in my body on high alert as I finally pulled out of her and collapsed onto the couch with my dick still on semi-hard.

Her giggles were back when she replied, "Damn, yourself. I mean, I was just sure you were gonna come up here and pass out. Now I feel like I'm the one who needs to take a nap."

With a smirk, I reminded her, "I told you I knew what I was doing. Shit, I honestly feel a lot better now. We can probably get dressed and head back to the party."

Maybe it was just the afterglow of my nut, but I swear I felt rejuvenated as hell until Savannah climbed on my lap with her lip pulled between her teeth and suggested, "Or we could… *not* get dressed and *not* head back to the party."

The party was officially a no-go, my heart content with whatever she was thinking as I placed my hands at her waist and asked, "Oh yeah? Well what you got in mind?"

Her hands were at my shoulders and her titties were right in my face, tempting me to pull one of her nipples between my teeth when she answered, "First, we need to get some water and BC Powder in your system so tomorrow's plane ride home isn't awful for you."

"Okay, Mom. And then what?" I challenged, the sexy little smirk on her face making me say *fuck it* and treat myself to a mouthful of her breast.

The way she immediately moaned in response told me it was just as much of a treat for her, my hand moving to palm the other one as she struggled to answer, "And *then*, I'm gonna show you how well I know what to do too. *In the bedroom*."

Pulling my mouth away, I teased, "Good thing you also know how to do hair, cause I'm really about to fuck your shit up now." I even gave it a little tug from the back to emphasize my point, the curls she had put in it to go under her beret from earlier already on the verge of looking like one of those bad wigs from a Madea stage play.

She's still fine, though.

Honestly, I wasn't sure how I expected her to react to that since it would be just my luck to fuck shit up by joking around too much. But in true *perfect-for-me* form, Savannah only smiled when she replied, "See. I knew I brought my equipment with me for a reason."

SAVANNAH

I NEVER MADE it back downstairs to the party.

In fact, I never even made it back out of the bedroom until the next morning when I found Rod asleep on the floor, Jasmine and Ariel sprawled out on the couch, and Derek and Jennifer cuddled in a chair; all of them still wearing their costumes from the night before.

Clearly Lincoln and I weren't the only ones who had had a good time.

With a pleased smile, I made my way back into the bedroom to find Lincoln stirring awake. Something about the morning sun peeking through the window and landing on his skin made him look especially handsome, particularly when he served me that dimpled-smile of his and asked, "Am I gonna have to do a walk of shame past your homegirls or what?"

While I didn't believe there was anything for him to be ashamed of, I couldn't help but grin even harder when I answered, "My homegirls, your cousin, *and* his friend. They're all out there knocked out."

He sat up a little straighter with a look of amusement. "No shit? That Halloween party must've been live as hell."

"Guess we'll never know," I replied with a smirk that wouldn't go away if I tried after last night.

Not that I wanted it to go away.

I mean, it truly felt amazing to just bask in the afterglow; especially since I wouldn't have that much longer to do so according to the clock. And it was almost as if Lincoln had read my mind, tossing his legs from under the comforter to the edge of the bed as he instructed, "Come here, shorty."

In my head, it felt like I was floating instead of just walking over to him, finding a spot to stand between his legs as he brought his hands to the back of my thighs and rested his chin in my chest. I could've stayed like this for the rest of my time in Vegas, with Lincoln wrapped all around me so I could absorb as much of him as possible. But the longer he stared at me, the quicker I felt pressed to ask, "What is it?"

"*Just...* thank you, Savannah Marie."

For whatever reason, that made me chuckle. "What are you thanking me for, Lincoln No-Middle-Name?"

Gripping my thighs a little tighter, he grinned when he answered, "For being dope. And making this trip one I'll never, *ever* forget for all the right reasons."

I couldn't have agreed more since I was already thinking of ways we could get this little group trip poppin' again in the near future - *sans the group.* Not that I didn't enjoy spending time with the girls and celebrating Jennifer, but meeting and spending time with Lincoln was most definitely the highlight.

Pressing my hands into his shoulders, I moved to climb on the bed and straddle his lap as I told him, "In that case, I should be thanking you too."

"How about we thank each other right quick?" he suggested, already kissing at my neck the same way he had done the night before. But the fact that I had accidentally left the door open behind me had me gently pushing him away.

"Our folks are right outside of that door. *And* I need to pack up my stuff. My flight is in a few hours."

Instead of backing up, he only squeezed me tighter when he whined, "*Noooo.* Don't leave me. Not yet. It's too soon."

While his reaction was flattering as hell, the truth was, "Unfortunately, it's time for me to get back to reality."

Between the shop and Lani, I was already dreading the pile of tasks I'd be going home to. But instead of letting me prematurely sulk about it, Lincoln nipped my chin with a kiss before he asked, "Well what do I have to do to become a part of your reality, Savannah? Since this weekend was obviously some sort of fairytale."

The question caught me a bit offguard since… "*I*… can't say I have an answer for that at the moment."

His disappointed reaction had me quick to recover, "I mean, not like that. I *want* you to be a part of my reality, Lincoln. But with us living in two different cities, I can't say that I know exactly how to do it."

He nodded in understanding, taking a moment before he looked me straight in my eyes and asked, "Are you willing to figure it out with me?"

The sincerity in his look, *the sincerity in his tone*, had me ready to agree to just about anything he had to say. But the fact that he seemed so serious about continuing whatever this was beyond our trip had me grinning hard as hell, even when I teased, "Depends on how thankful you are."

In one swift move, he had me on my back, his morning wood pressed into the seat of my panties as he insisted, "My sober dick is even better than my drunk one. You sure you want those problems?"

Gnawing into my lip, I countered, "Considering I'm not sure when I'll see you again? *Absolutely*." Then I maneuvered so that I was on top, straddling his lap again as he rested on his back and reminded me, "The wedding is only a few weeks away."

"Well, yeah. But I'll have my daughter with me, so that'll be different."

He wasn't too concerned about that, easily getting rid of the t-shirt I had slept in - *his t-shirt* - as he insisted, "She seems like a responsible young lady. I'm sure she won't mind me taking you to my crib for a little… refresher course."

"If I'm really about to go without this for a few weeks, I'm pretty sure I'm gonna need a lot more than just a little refresher course, Lincoln."

"Not if I give you something to hold onto," he said, pushing my panties to the side and dipping a finger inside of me, causing me to tip forward onto my palms.

He continued his in-and-out rhythm, using his thumb to play with my clit before adding a second finger. And while I would've taken any bit of Lincoln I could get - *finger fucks included* - I knew the only thing that would *really* hold me over was his dick that was practically begging me to ride it.

So I did.

I lifted just enough to free his dick from his boxers and sank down on top of it with a gratified moan, the pleased look on Lincoln's face as I adjusted to his girth only turning me on even more as I found my groove soon after. It didn't take long for his heavy hands to end up at my hips as he met me stroke for stroke, my head thrown back and my eyes tight as I gave and took everything I could while Lincoln did the same.

It was the perfect exchange of energy, truly symbolic of what the entire trip had been for us. And regardless of the fact that we hadn't figured out how things were going to work beyond this, I knew I had to get more of him.

I deserved more.

Falling forward, I kissed Lincoln *hard* as he stroked me harder from below, his arms wrapped around me in a hug as I felt weightless on top of him. And knowing this was the last of it until the weekend of the wedding, I never wanted him to stop; *never wanted this to end.*

But unfortunately, all good things had to come to an end. So instead of prolonging the inevitable, I let go; allowing the orgasm to rocket through me with a vengeance as Lincoln warned me about his own. And I moved just in time to catch his nut to my stomach, the sight making me lick my lips as I stroked him empty with my hand.

My touch made him shiver, his hands over his face as he stifled his moan before sighing my name. And after meeting his eyes with a faux-innocent look, he said, "Fuck waiting until the wedding weekend. I'm booking a flight to you ASAP."

I started to giggle until Lincoln panically yanked the comforter over me and shouted, "Rod, what the fuck?! How long have you been standing there?!"

Rod?

With just my eyes, I peeked from underneath to see him heading towards us as he replied, "Long enough to know I've been betrayed. After last night, I really thought I was over you, Vanny. But did you really have to go and twist the knife in my back like this?"

"*This nigga...*" Lincoln groaned, shaking his head as Jennifer busted in the room and yanked Rod by the arm while scolding, *"Rod, if you don't get the...* I'm sorry, y'all. He hasn't meditated yet. Proceed." Then she slammed the door behind them, Lincoln and I looking over to each other before bursting with laughter.

"So I'm sleeping with a certified heartbreaker, huh? Hopefully there's not a gang of other niggas out there just like him," Lincoln teased, pressing a simple kiss against my lips that told me he was far from concerned about the possibility.

Still, to put him at ease, I replied, "Trust me. You have nothing to worry about. Rod was a lone wolf. Truly disturbed as I'm sure you can tell."

He nodded. "Yeah, I can tell. But I can also tell why a nigga would be crazy about your pretty ass like that. I better be careful before I end up the same way."

Now I was the one teasing him, stealing a kiss before I asked, "It's a little too late for that, don't you think?"

"*I think...* I need one more round before we get you to the airport."

"And *I* think... I agree with you," I replied with a grin, doing just that before finally showing our faces to the rest of our company.

While Ariel and Jasmine argued over who called our "love connection" first, Derek and Jennifer were the ones taking the credit since it was their idea to do a joint bachelor-bachelorette party in the first place. And as for Rod... *well,* he eventually found some identical weirdo to spend the rest of his time in Vegas with, easily forgetting about little ol' me until he sent me off with a polite hug before I headed to the airport.

Since Lincoln acted like he couldn't stand to see me go just yet, he made the trip to the airport with me, our *Uber* ride quiet as he looked out of the window with me snuggled up under his arm in the backseat. And I suppose the drive to the airport wasn't long enough for him considering he decided to hang out with me inside the terminal until it was time for me to go through security.

He waited until the absolute last minute to ask, "Are you sure you gotta leave?"

With a sad smile, I nodded. "Yes, Lincoln. *TSA Pre-Check* gives me a little leg up, but yes. It's time."

Grabbing both of my hands, he pressed, "I mean like, leave the city. *Already*. You can't stay another day or two? With me?"

While his request initially shocked the hell out of me, I found myself giving it some thought; something I would've never done in the past since I absolutely *hated* changing plans. And it wasn't only the fact that I was really considering it that had me shook, but also… *is he serious?*

As if he could hear my thoughts, he continued, "I'll cover your flight change. Hotel too. *I'm just…* I'm not ready for this to end yet, Savannah."

In my head, I knew I should've been taking my ass to the security line so I wouldn't miss my flight. But in my heart - *and in Lincoln's eyes* - I had a feeling I would've been missing out on something truly special. Still, I wasn't the only one to consider here. So instead of making an impulsive decision, I found myself pulling my phone out of my pocket to make an important phone call.

Lincoln looked confused until he heard me say, "Hey Lani Bear. I saw you guys won the volleyball tournament. Congratulations."

I shouldn't have been surprised when, instead of responding to that topic, my inquisitive daughter asked, "Mommy, what's wrong? You haven't called me Lani Bear since I was like seven."

Peeking up at Lincoln who was waiting patiently, I flashed him a smile as I got to the real point of my call. "So… how would you feel about Mommy staying away a day, *or two*, longer?"

There was a long pause, and I almost told her never mind and that I'd be home soon until she asked, "Mom, you're changing plans at the last minute? On your own? *Willingly*? Are you being held hostage? Did you get into a gambling debt you have to pay back before you can leave? Did y'all lose Auntie Jen on a rooftop like that movie *Hangover*?"

"Lani, who let you watch that movie?"

Her little giggles in response reminded me of my own. "Daddy did. We watched it the same night you left for your trip because I asked him what Las Vegas was really like."

"And that's what he showed you?" I groaned with a hand to my forehead in disgust; though the mention of her father helped me make an executive decision when I continued, "*Anyway*. Tell your father I'll be back on *Mon*… Tuesday. I'll back on Tuesday, so he'll have to take you to school and stuff."

"But what about the salon?" she asked, something I should've considered before I even called her. And once again, I found myself getting ready to tell her never mind until I thought about my usual schedule of bookkeeping on Mondays and flexible morning appointments on Tuesdays; both things I could have the shop manager take care of until I got back.

With that, I felt even better about my decision, smiling as I told her, "The shop will be fine without me for a little while."

Again, she went quiet. And I started to ask her if she was still on the line when she gushed, "Wow, Mommy. He must be *really* cute."

"*Girl*… Goodbye. I love you. And I will see you on Tuesday."

Giggling again, she replied, "Have fun, Mommy! Love you too!" before ending the call. And now that things were mostly in motion, I couldn't help but smile, Lincoln's dimpled-one already matching mine when he asked, "So, it's a go? We're really doing this?"

"As long as you plan on making it worth my while. My time is *very* valuable, Lincoln," I reminded him with a grin as he grabbed my hand to pull me closer.

Wrapping me in an embrace, he did a little reminding of his

own when he countered, "And you're giving even more of it to me? Yeah, I definitely got your ass."

He started to laugh and I laughed too, thinking about how far we had come in just a few short days. And while the uncertainty of our future still lingered, right now, I was solely focused on making the most of my extra days in Sin City with a handsome stranger.

LINCOLN

Wedding Weekend.

I MISSED SHORTY LIKE CRAZY.

The extra days we had spent together in Las Vegas had only made things worse for me in that regard since it just gave me more reasons to want to be near her; from learning about her wild and adventurous side when she insisted on doing the SkyJump at the Stratosphere, to finding out how wickedly intelligent she was after watching her collect four-figures at the poker table, and then discovering her overall sports knowledge ran deep after watching her hit a huge bet on a spread in a *Lakers* game. Truth be told, staying in Las Vegas was Savannah's come up in more ways than one since not only had she won big currency-wise, but she had also won a solid place in my heart.

I thought our time apart would help that cool off a bit since I didn't want to come on too strong, but it really only had me showing up at the airport to pick her and Lani up even earlier than I needed to be since I was *that* damn anxious to see her again. And thankfully, I wasn't alone since Savannah called herself sprinting out of the airport the second I looped around the pickup area, her big ass smile making my heart swell as I found somewhere to park and got out to meet her.

The second we connected, she dropped her luggage and leaped into my arms, her long legs wrapped around my waist as she sprinkled kisses all over my face that I greedily accepted before groaning into her neck, "*Gotdamn. I missed you.*"

Dropping to her feet, she gushed, "I missed you too, handsome. Thanks for coming to get me."

"Wouldn't have had it any other way. *But, wait.* Where's Lani?" I asked, lowkey concerned about her parenting skills if she had really ran off without her, even if it was to get to me.

Thankfully, she put my concern to bed when she answered, "She stayed back. I wasn't quite ready to share you with anyone yet."

While I could honestly appreciate her being a little selfish about this - *about me* - I was still sure to remind her, "Well you know Derek's fam is my fam too, so you'll be sharing me a little bit this weekend."

She brushed me off, giving me her luggage to load into my truck as she replied, "That I can handle. As long as I get you all to myself too."

"You already know there will be plenty of where that came from," I assured her, pulling her in for another tight hug as I continued, "Gotta welcome you to my city the right way, baby."

Wrapping her arms around my neck, she replied, "It doesn't matter what city we're in, Lincoln. The only thing that matters is that I'm with you."

I had never heard truer words, the fact that we had conquered Las Vegas, were getting ready to conquer my hometown, and would soon conquer hers whenever I came to visit in the near future giving me a great lesson in how love worked. It didn't matter where you were in the world, that shit would still find you.

The End.

FEATURED TITLES

*Read all about Jasmine & Rich in,
An Unconventional Love.

Jasmine is on the not-it list when it comes to relationships.
A fling here and there?
Definitely.
But full blown commitment?
No way in hell.
Dealing with a man full-time is just not worth the trouble when you can get what you want and get away like it never happened.

That was the plan when she met Rich, a good and worthy fling, but exactly that...a fling.
Until the cravings start.
And Jasmine is forced into a whole new realm of life when she least expected it.

(Warning : This book contains a few spoilers for Getting The Edge)

**Read all about Ariel & Jamison in, Getting The Edge .

College graduation is only the beginning for Ariel as she lands her dream job working for a record label in The Big Apple. Not only is it the beginning of her professional career, but also the beginning of an unexpected romance with Jamison, a self-assured recent grad who is also getting his foot in the door of the music industry at a competing record label. The collision of business and pleasure is inevitable but when Ariel receives a personal assignment to help take down her label's top competition, she's forced to make a decision; her career or her newfound love? Just how far will she have to go to get the edge?

A TALE OF TWO CITIES

A THANKSGIVING NOVELLA

ORLANDO

IF I DIDN'T KNOW any better, I'd think he was dead.

Ol' man Clyde slept harder than anybody I had ever met before, and it didn't matter what was going on in the barbershop around him. There could be niggas arguing hoops, a baby crying over his first haircut, and a nigga getting cussed out by his baby mama all at once, but none of that mattered to the man *Clyde's Cutz* was named after.

If he was tired, he was getting his sleep.

Honestly, the shit made me a little jealous since I couldn't remember the last time I had gotten a decent night's rest. But it was a price I was willing to pay to have peace of mind when it came to my safety. Being an extremely light sleeper meant I was always ready for whatever, and that was exactly the kind of approach I had to take if I wanted to stay alive.

If I were to share that mindset with my boss, Tiana, she'd probably call me crazy; insist I had nothing to worry about now that I had uprooted my life and moved out here to cut hair in the shop she partially owned. But with the life I had lived, *the environment I had grown up in*, I knew better than to believe that bullshit since that was exactly how niggas got caught slippin'.

Shit was all too familiar.

Sweeping my booth, I heard the chime of the bell over the

door, peeking up to find Kelvin with his baby boy on his shoulders and his stepdaughter holding onto one of his legs wearing a frown that boss lady immediately picked up on as she abandoned her own booth to ask, "What happened to her?"

"Hello to you too, princess," Kelvin replied, puckering his lips for a kiss that Tiana got on her tippy-toes to deliver with an apology.

"I'm sorry. Hi, babe. Now what happened to Elliana?"

Instead of answering himself, Kelvin urged, "Tell her, Ellie."

From the big ass bandage on her knee, I could pretty much guess what had occurred. But since I didn't want to interject in what was really none of my business, I let little Ellie answer, "I fell."

"You fell?" Tiana asked, her eyes flashing back up to Kelvin's when she inquired, "Don't tell me it was that stupid swing at the park again. I'm about ready to ban y'all from going there in a minute."

Chuckling, Kelvin was quick to insist, "It was an accident, and we got her all cleaned up as you can see. She's just still in her little feelings about it." He even added a scrub to Ellie's curly mane that had her squeezing onto him even tighter.

Tiana only sighed in return, reaching up to pull baby Titan from Kelvin's shoulders as he finally acknowledged me. "What's good, O?"

Shrugging, I continued to straighten up my booth. "Same ol', same ol'. What's good with you?"

"Everything's good over this way. You see how big this dude is gettin'? I think I might've made a future Pro Bowler," he commented, pinching one of Titan's chunky legs as a frown immediately grew to Tiana's face.

"First of all, *you* didn't make anything. At least, not by yourself. Second of all, our son is *not* playing football. It's way too dangerous; especially if he's anything like his injury-prone big sister."

With Titan still in her arms, she bent down to take a better look at Elliana's leg, serving endless Super Mom vibes as Kelvin watched on with a smile that made his adoration clear. And when she finally stood back up, he couldn't wait to steal another kiss that had her smiling at him just as lovingly.

Shit was dope as hell to witness.

As Tiana returned to her booth with Titan, Elliana and Kelvin followed right behind her to share, "Princess, you might be on your own with the munchkins tonight. You remember my cousin Aspen?"

The question seemed like a silly one to me since I highly doubted there was a person in the shop - *baby Titan included* - who hadn't heard of Aspen Watson before. I mean, this wasn't even my neck of the woods, but it hadn't taken me long to learn she was something like the hometown superstar around here. And even though she hadn't been back to visit since I moved here, there wasn't a shortage of pride surrounding her acting career from the community.

Tiana pretty much echoed my sentiments when she replied, "How could I forget her, babe? She's only one of the biggest stars to come out of the city, she's your relative, and she pretty much lives on my TV screen these days."

Nodding along, Kelvin got to the real point of his announcement. "Well she's coming to town for the holiday, and Maxwell and I are gonna try to get her to host the Black Friday party at *The Max*."

While I hadn't been to *The Max* myself, preferring to stay lowkey while I figured this place out, I knew that it was easily the most popular spot to party in town. And being the avid businessmen Kelvin and his brother Maxwell were, I wasn't really surprised to hear they were trying to capitalize on their family ties. The family ties that had Tiana asking, "Considering she's family, how hard could it possibly be?"

With a sigh, Kelvin answered, "She may be family, but she can still be a damn diva sometimes. So we gotta come correct, starting tonight. Matter of fact…" Turning my way, he asked, "Orlando, what you got going on tonight?"

I didn't even need to check my schedule to answer, "Not shit. What's up?"

"You think you can do a little driving for us? I mean, we could hire somebody, but I'd rather use someone I know. Someone I trust."

I hadn't been in town long, but Kelvin and I had become fast friends in that time. We were close in age, had similar interests with far-from-similar upbringings that thankfully didn't stop Kelvin from being relatable, and he was married to the coolest boss I'd ever had which meant he was around often enough for me to know he was good peoples.

Good peoples to kick it with, *and* good peoples to work for.

Driving folks around had become something like my side hustle, giving me the chance to make a little extra money while also being able to learn my way around the area. And once Kelvin became hip to what I was on, he and Maxwell pretty much had me on speed dial to work for whatever celebrity they were bringing to town for *The Max*, a list that apparently included his pretty ass actress cousin.

"*Easy money*," I thought as I told Kelvin, "Count me in."

He seemed happy to hear it, planting another quick kiss to Tiana's cheek as he said, "Aight, princess. Let me get down to the lounge before Maxwell gets on my ass about doing this inventory check. I'll try to swing by the house for dinner. But if I don't make it…"

Tiana cut him off with a wave of her hand. "It'll be in the fridge, Kelvin. Now get going so I can get out of here too."

With a smile, he nodded before giving both of his kids kisses on the cheek and then telling me, "Orlando, I'll hit your line with the details as soon as I get to the lounge. Aspen's flight was a little delayed coming outta NYC because of the weather there, but she should be landing within the next few hours."

"I got you, bruh," I replied, the fact that my night was now going to be filled with activities making my exit from the shop a little more urgent. And I wasn't the only one, Kelvin dipping out just as fast as he had come in and somehow waking Mr. Clyde up in the process.

After a glance at the door, Mr. Clyde groaned, "I just know this little nigga didn't come in and out of my shop without speaking..."

Bouncing Titan on her hip, Tiana shook her head and reminded him, "Clyde, you were sleep."

Of course, Mr. Clyde was quick to defend, "I wasn't sleep! I was just resting my eyes for a minute! And even if I was sleep, he should've woke me up!"

"And get cussed out for doing so? Nah, he did the right thing," his son, Danny, commented with a chuckle, Mr. Clyde shooting him a fatherly scowl in response even though he knew it was the truth. But instead of admitting that, he stood up and changed the subject.

"Did I hear Aspen Watson is coming back to town for the holiday? I wonder if she'll come down to the shop and let me get a few pictures of her in my chair."

"Can't nobody sit in your chair if you're always sitting in it sleep, Mr. Clyde," I joked, Danny and Tiana chuckling right along with me.

Mr. Clyde wasn't fazed by my jab, shrugging when he insisted, "Then she can just sit on my lap like I'm her personal Santa. I'd make *all* her wishes come true. *Mmm*!"

Tiana was the first to groan, "*Gross…*" while Danny and I enthusiastically agreed since little mama was fine as hell on TV, and I was sure she was just as fine in person. With her butterscotch skin, and her blonde hair, and her stupid high cheekbones, and those dangerously-piercing hazel eyes, *and…*

"Tiana, you need anything else before I get up out of here?" I asked, purposely interrupting my mental black hole of everything Aspen Watson.

I expected her to send me on my way like usual. But to my surprise, she extended little Titan my way and asked, "Can you just… hold him for like two seconds? I just realized I haven't peed all day."

The baby was already in my arms before I could even answer. And while we just stood there staring at each other since we'd both been caught off-guard by the sudden handoff, Tiana grabbed her daughter's hand and urged, "Come on, Ellie. You need to come potty too before we make the drive home."

Using my observations of Tiana and Kelvin's parenting skills,

I put Titan against my hip, something he seemed to be satisfied with since he decided to rest his head on my shoulder. And honestly, the shit was heartwarming as hell until Mr. Clyde said, "If I was you, I'd be dropping that baby right on its head."

"*What?* Mr. Clyde, you wildin'," I told him with a laugh, peeking to make sure Titan was comfortable as he grabbed a handful of my shirt.

"*Oh, you* real *comfortable,*" I thought, smiling as Mr. Clyde replied, "One second, you're holding somebody else's baby. And the next second, you have one of your own. *Drop him.*"

That only made me laugh harder. "Come on, man. He's cute. Here, take him," I insisted, pretending to hand him off as Mr. Clyde shooed me away.

"Hell nah! I may be shooting dust and despair these days, but I'm still not taking any chances. If anybody's getting cursed with a baby, it's gonna be you."

"Or maybe it's gonna be your son. Here, Danny."

"Nigga, what? Watch out," he groaned, ducking and dodging my attempts to hand Titan off as he added, "Shawntel is on one of those long-term birth controls and I *still* wear condoms. Fuck that baby shit."

His resistance made me laugh, especially since, "Isn't Titan your Godson?"

"Who I love with all my heart… *from a distance*," he replied, Clyde giving an enthusiastic, *"That's right"* from the sidelines as Tiana and Elliana returned to the shop floor.

Pinching Titan's cheek, she commented, "Lookin' good, Uncle O. Keep this up and I'll be adding you to our babysitter list in a minute."

"This one I can do cause he's chill," I told her, glancing down at Titan once more before I directed my attention to Elliana. "*But that one?* She seems like she'd be a handful."

Elliana had the nerve to stick her tongue out at me from behind her mom, confirming my suspicions as Tiana brushed her curls back and said, "She's actually really good for other people. It's when her behind comes home that she starts acting up."

"*Sounds about right,*" I quietly agreed, finally handing Titan over to a willing acceptor as his mother added, "But anyway. Have fun with Aspen and the boys tonight at the lounge. And be sure to keep an eye on my husband for me. He has a history of showin' his ass."

I had no plans of actually stepping foot in *The Max* unless I absolutely had to. But from what I knew about her husband, I still felt confident telling her, "According to him, that life is *well* behind him."

From the stories I'd been told, Kelvin had done something like a one-eighty since getting with Tiana*, going from the irresponsible, playboy party animal to the guy I'd always known him as; the respected businessman, the father, the husband. He loved his family and he loved the lounge he co-owned with his big brother. And though it was clear to me that those two things had his total focus, that didn't stop Tiana from insisting, "It's still nice to have a set of eyes on the scene just in case it's not."

With a nod, I told her, "Got you, boss lady," before heading to the back to grab my things from my locker. And I was on my way to the door when Mr. Clyde caught me by the arm to say, "Snitches get stitches. Don't forget that when you're at *The Max* tonight," making me laugh as I headed out for the day.

ASPEN

THE LOCAL AIRPORT hadn't changed a bit, but its sameness was what I was looking forward to most since it signified one thing - I was home.

It had been months - *okay, maybe years* - since the last time I'd been home for a visit that lasted longer than a few hours. And even though my family was already acting funny about my homecoming thanks to my relatively-recent upgrade from D-list celebrity to high B-list, I was still excited about spending the next few days surrounded by familiar faces I didn't get to see nearly enough.

I mean, people were having babies, and getting married, and running successful businesses, and finding *love.* It was all so exciting yet so, so hard to keep up with which made this trip even more timely.

I needed *all* the updates and I needed to kiss on *all* the baby cheeks.

As if to kick things off right away, I ran into an old friend from high school when I was exiting the plane, completely breaking free of my incognito vibes to squeal, "Oh my God! Lincoln! I haven't seen you in person in… a *literal* decade."

Once he realized it was me, he cracked the biggest smile,

pulling me into a hug as he said, "Damn. That makes us sound old as hell, Ashy Aspen."

"I'm not so ashy anymore you know," I replied with a smirk, gnawing into my lip as if to show off just how *moisturized* I was these days.

Moisturized and fine.

Chuckling, Lincoln - *who was also moisturized and fine* - nodded to agree. "Oh, I know, superstar. What you doin' around here with us normal folks?"

While I was tempted to get on him about that whole 'normal folks' thing, I ignored it to give the obvious answer. "Tomorrow is Thanksgiving, fool. And I had some rare free time in my schedule, so I thought I'd come spend it with the family who's sending a driver to pick me up instead of coming to get me themselves. Ain't that somethin'?"

His eyebrow went up as he agreed, "That *is* something. But let me go get back in this line before I fuck around and miss my flight."

I should've been letting him go, but I couldn't help prying for my first update of the trip when I asked, "Going to spend Thanksgiving with your new Midwest bae, right? She's gorgeous, Linc. *Seriously*. Y'all are so cute on *Instagram*. Those pictures from Vegas were everything. And so were the pictures from Derek's wedding."

To be honest, I was a little jealous of Savannah - *yes, I even knew her name* - for getting at Lincoln** before I could. I mean, it would've been straight out of *Hallmark* holiday movie heaven for me to come home and reunite with my high school crush who was even cuter now than he'd been back in the day. But unfortunately, that idea was just going to have to stay a fictional storyline in my head, especially once Lincoln lowkey embarrassed me by replying, "Haven't seen me in a decade, but you still know my moves. The internet is *crazy*."

Blushing, I was quick to defend, "You say that like you don't follow me too, though!"

Thankfully, he chuckled and agreed, "You right. Tell that nigga LeBron I said what's up next time y'all end up at the same party again."

"Mmhmm, I'll think about it," I teased, the fact that more eyes were now looking my way making me feel a bit uneasy since I'd made the bold decision of going without security.

But this was home.

I could do this by myself.

At least, I thought I could do this by myself until I saw that first not-so-sneaky picture get taken of me by a stranger and realized it was only a matter of time before there were more. Lincoln must've realized it too since he knew to end our interaction with a simple, "It was good seeing you, Ashy."

"Good seeing you too, Sausage Linc," I joked, using the nickname he had acquired as a rumor about his dick.

Before I could get too far, he replied, "I'm more of a footlong frank now. Just ask my woman."

"Well Happy Thanksgiving to *her,*" I gushed with a smile that he matched as I gave another wave then finally made my way to baggage claim. And again, I was grateful for the local airport that had everything in close proximity, making my getaway easy once I made it past the security point.

I was waiting for my bag to come around the luggage carousel when I received a text.

Cousin Kelvin: "Orlando should be pulling up now. He's in a black Cadillac XTS with tinted windows."

"Orlando," I repeated out loud with a grunt, shaking my head at the fact that my cousin was really sending the help instead of letting the poor man be with his family for the holiday like I'd done with my staff. In fact, I considered giving the guy a break myself and just getting a rental car instead… *until I saw him standing outside of that Cadillac.*

He was leaning against the hood with one hand in the pocket of his black denim jeans, lifting the other to check his watch before he started looking around - *looking for me.* And while I was tempted to announce myself so he wouldn't be antsy, I was a little more interested in just checking him out from afar since he was so damn fine.

Too damn fine.

From the peanut-butter skin coating his thick, manly frame, to his perfectly-wide nose with full lips to match, to his shapely beard that I *definitely* wanted to make my seat at the Thanksgiving table, he was looking like the only meal I needed during my visit. In fact, I was already daydreaming about it when he finally noticed me, and I smiled like a lunatic as if I hadn't just been thinking about putting my pussy all over this stranger man's face.

"Let me get that for you, Miss. Watson," was what he said when he saw me heading his way. But all I heard was, "*Come ride my face, Miss. Watson*," forced to shake it off so I could tell him, "Aspen is fine."

"Aspen *is* fine," he repeated with a look over his shoulder that made me blush. But it wasn't in the same way that Lincoln had made me blush with embarrassment earlier. Nah, this was the kind of blushing that came with an increase in heart rate and a suddenly-sensitive clitoris.

Whew, this dude is a whole problem.

I mean, it had been a while since a man really got me riled up off the rip. But here I was, clocking his every move; particularly the way his arms and back flexed under his black long-sleeve thermal when he lifted my suitcase to put it in the trunk. And then how strong his hands looked once he slammed the trunk door shut.

The little things.

Since I was still all in his business instead of minding my own, he offered me a smirk before he said, "I hope you don't take this the wrong way, but you're a lot smaller in person than you look on TV."

Typically when someone acknowledged my size, I got annoyed since it was often used in a way to try and undermine me; undermine my power. But with him, all I could think about was how easy it would be for me to sit my little ass right on his broad shoulders, the thought alone making me grin mischievously when I replied, "Glad you noticed, Orlando."

His eyebrow went up in surprise, and I didn't know why until I thought back on what I had said, quick to give a little wave of my phone and explain, "Kelvin just texted me your name."

With a nod, he replied, "Oh, right," moving towards the car door as he continued, "Well let's get you outta here before someone recognizes you."

Even with earlier's close call, I still managed to shrug. "Pretty hard to do without all that blonde weave hanging down my back."

It was something like my signature look, what bloggers and strangers alike loved to comment on the most which was exactly why I had ditched it for my trip home. The inches upon inches of blonde turned me into Aspen Watson the actress. But my pixie cut of the same color made me Aspen who was just coming to see her family for Thanksgiving with plans of eating all the good food that came with it.

Because that's the important part, right?

Once again I caught myself daydreaming, this time the culprit being Aunt Marie's macaroni and cheese until Orlando caught my gaze to say, "Nah, it's all in your eyes. One look at those, *and*… you ready?"

"Absolutely," was my immediate answer until I saw Orlando continuing on his way towards the door and realized he *wasn't* asking if I was ready to ride his face, and that the ending of the statement he had cut off *wasn't*, "*One look at those and I wanna rip your clothes off the same way you obviously wanna rip mine.*"

"*Maybe you are still ashy*," I thought to myself with a groan, taking my time to follow him since, "I don't even know where they have me going since apparently they think I'm too good to stay with family for a couple days like normal people do."

I don't know why it bothered me so much that my family insisted on making expensive accommodations for me instead of just setting me up with a sheet, a comforter, and a pillow on somebody's living room couch. But considering I didn't want to sound ungrateful, I let it fly, not really surprised to hear Orlando answer, "According to Kelvin, some five-star downtown. But if that's not where you wanna go right now, I can take you wherever. As long as we make it to *The Max* by eleven. That was his only request."

With a quick glance at my phone for the time, I realized we still had a few hours until then and that it had been more than a few hours since my last real meal, prompting me to ask, "Is that one sandwich shop by Jackie Robinson Park still open?"

"Yeah, I just ate there for lunch," Orlando answered, the fact that he even knew about one of my favorite places in the city already making him good in my book.

"That's where I wanna go. I'm starving."

Nodding, he moved to finally open the door for me. But I quickly bypassed him in a move towards where I really wanted to sit; a move that surprised him according to the way his eyebrow piqued when he asked, "You're… sitting in the front seat?"

"Is that a problem?" I asked with a smile, opening the door and getting ready to climb in when he answered my question.

"Nah, not a problem. Just… unusual."

Since I'd already gotten my way once, he couldn't help trying to, at least, close the door behind me. But not before I could explain, "I'm in my city. I'm *home.* I should be able to ride wherever I want to, right?"

"Fa sho," he agreed. Then he slammed the door in my face like he didn't really agree but just wanted me to shut up, his annoyance making me giggle by the time he finally joined me from the driver's side.

He didn't say any more, he didn't even play any music; he just took off towards the sandwich shop with his eyes on the road and my eyes on him as I tried to figure out why the hell he intrigued me so much outside of his good looks and the big dick energy he wore like a second skin. But after staring at him in search of familiarity, I realized my interest lied in the fact that I couldn't place him with anyone else I knew from the city, making me ask, "Who are your people?"

"*My people*?"

Nodding, I turned in my seat and continued, "Yeah, you don't look familiar to me. Who's your family? What high school did you go to? What year did you graduate?"

He chuckled at my interrogation, somehow answering all of my questions without technically answering any of them when he said, "I'm not from around here."

"Ahh, that explains it. Explains… *you.*"

Since I'd come up in the industry, people from the city usually loved to act like we had been friends since the very beginning even if I didn't know them at all. But the fact that Orlando hadn't even pretended to have any connections with me told me more than he realized, the confusion on his face giving way for me to explain, "Your demeanor. Your vibe. It's not like the people from around here. Not that everybody from around here is the same, *obviously.* But… I could tell you were different. An outsider."

He chuckled again. "I mean, guilty but damn. Way to make a nigga feel warmly welcomed around here."

"I can do a lot more than make your welcome warm," was what the sexy devil on my shoulder told me to say. But the emo-version came out instead when I replied, "I'm the one who has a driver picking her up from the airport like her family members don't own *multiple* cars. If there's anyone who should feel less than welcomed, it's me."

Orlando didn't let me sulk in what was really just a matter of me being a brat, peeking over at me with a smirk when he offered, "Welcome home, Aspen."

"From the outsider. Thank you so, *so* much," I replied sarcastically, Orlando giving another rumbling chuckle in response - *and reminding me how much I liked the sound of it.*

It had the perfect balance of jubilance and strong bass, showing off just a hint of his perfectly-straight top row of teeth that wouldn't otherwise be shown since he seemed to prefer keeping conversation to a minimum in the little bit of time we'd been together. But maybe that was just his personality; less into talking and more into action.

My kind of… I mean, *what?*

As if I needed any more reason to find out what kind of action Orlando was into, he complimented, "You're funnier than you are on TV, too. And prettier. You are *really* fuckin' pretty, Aspen."

With a flattered grin, I teasingly replied, "If you're trying to make me feel better about my own family treating me like a celebrity instead of as their relative, it's working."

"Good. Now let's get you that sandwich since that's guaranteed to make you feel better too," he offered like he didn't know good and damn well the item at the top of that list of things that could make me feel better was sitting right between his thighs.

Then again, did the quietly-confident fine niggas ever act like they knew they were downright fuckable?

Nope.

They just moseyed through life, being attractive as hell and making thirsty women like me sweat over the simple things; like the way Orlando put his arm across the back of my seat so he could parallel park into a spot outside of the sandwich shop.

Yes, that *little.*

After putting the car in park, he asked, "What's your order? I'll go in and grab it so you don't have to. I mean, since you're not traveling with security or whatever."

Shrugging, I explained, "It's the holiday. They deserve to be with their families too."

Once the words left my mouth, I felt a little bad about Orlando not being able to do the same, giving me a spur of the moment idea that may or may not have been influenced by the smell of his cologne still lingering around me. "I want to go in and order myself. And then I want to eat at a table like a normal person, *with you.*"

"With me?"

My nod might've been overly enthusiastic when I answered, "Yes, outsider Orlando. I mean, I guess you don't have to eat since you already ate this same thing earlier, but…"

He cut me off. "I can always eat, Aspen."

Again, the sexy devil on my shoulder started acting out when she asked, *"You can always eat this pussy, or…?"* But the low rumble in my stomach put her right back in her place, a friendly smile coming to my lips once I urged, "Then come on, Orlando."

For whatever reason he didn't seem super enthused; maybe because he was worried about my safety and didn't think it was the best idea for me to be running around the city all willy-nilly, or maybe because he really wasn't checking for me like that and didn't appreciate me forcing the interaction. But by the time we made it inside, right before closing which meant the place was mostly empty, he finally relaxed some, dapping up the employee who was obviously familiar enough with him to know his order without him even needing to say it.

When the employee turned to me, I could tell when it hit him that I was... *who I was.* But after the initial shock, he thankfully didn't make a big deal of it, getting ready to ask me for my order until I cut him off after seeing what he was putting together for Orlando. "I'll have the exact same thing he's getting."

"*Wow.* Copying sandwich orders from the outsider, huh?" Orlando teased, moving towards the cashier as I followed right behind him with a frown.

"Excuse me? That's been my order since like, the fifth grade. They should've named that sandwich after me by now if we're being honest."

"I'll start the petition," he insisted with a smirk before telling the cashier that our orders were together which somehow ended with them being on the house.

Still, it was the thought that counted. And that applied to his first idea too, even when I told him, "You don't look like the petition type. More like the strong arm, *'give me what I want or I'm beatin' somebody's ass'* type."

He shrugged. "Eh, maybe in my past life."

"*Your past life?* But you're not even that old," I countered like I'd known him forever when the truth was I hadn't even known him for an hour.

From the same wavelength as my thoughts, Orlando asked, "Yo, why do you think you know so much about me already?"

This time, it was me shrugging. "I don't. I'm just really good at reading people."

Grabbing the tray with our food and drinks, he asked, "Oh yeah? Then tell me more about me. Since you're so good at reading people."

I shouldn't have been surprised when the first thing that came to mind was, *"You have a big dick. It's in your energy."* But thankfully, the walk to the table gave me a chance to think of something with more substance beyond what the sexy devil was telling me to say when I threw out my first guess. "You're… in a new phase of life."

"How you figure?" he asked, taking his sandwich and drink from the tray before pushing the entire thing to me.

Just the smell of the melted pepper jack cheese had my mouth watering and my stomach rumbling again with anticipation. But I held off on digging in so that I could answer, "Tomorrow is the holiday and you're here, *in a new city*, being a driver for my cousins instead of spending time with your own family; instead of visiting wherever home is. Because you're so focused on moving forward from whatever your *alleged* past life was."

His short chuckle in response was filled with more disbelief than anything as he peeled the wrapper of his sandwich back and replied, "Nothin' alleged about it, little mama. That shit was very, *very* real. But it was all I knew."

While he was first to mention my eyes, it was the troubled look in his as they drifted off that told me so much about him without me needing any details. Maybe one day I'd get the details, but not right now. Right now was about letting his very real past be the past and fostering whatever positive changes his new phase was bringing about.

Obviously, I was already *way* more invested than I should've been. But him even being willing to share that little bit with me only encouraged me to reach across the table and give his hand a supportive squeeze, his eyes shooting up to mine in surprise when I told him, "Welcome home, Orlando."

When he only returned a look of confusion, I continued, "Here. *This city*. It's your home too now, right?"

With a nod and a smile, he answered, "It is."

"So… welcome home," I repeated with a smile of my own, giving his hand another squeeze before I dropped it. And while I wasn't looking for a response, I couldn't help but smile to myself when I heard him mutter, "Back at you, little mama."

ORLANDO

HER CURIOSITY CONFUSED ME.

I mean, I didn't see myself as some lame ass nigga or anything like that. But I couldn't help wondering what it was that could possibly have someone like Aspen Watson this interested in learning more about very regular me; sharing sandwiches and asking a million questions like any of it actually mattered to her.

She was a famous actress with a box-office hit under her belt, and I… cut hair with a side hustle as a chauffeur - *was currently her chauffeur.* She did everything she could to make it seem like that wasn't the case - *sitting in the front seat, opening her own door, inviting me up to her hotel suite when she went to do a quick change of clothes for The Max instead of letting me stay put in the car like I insisted* - but the facts were still the facts. I was spending time with her as a part of my job.

A blessing of a job it was, though, since it somehow had Aspen walking out of the bedroom of her suite towards me in only her bra and panties with two dresses in her hands.

"I've never actually been to *The Max*. Which one of these is more appropriate for the vibe there?"

I was supposed to be looking at the dresses, but I struggled to pull my eyes away from her bangin' ass body. The wardrobe team for the movies she'd been a part of must've worked overtime to mask it since I would've never guessed she was workin' with so much of everything.

Tits, and hips, and ass, and...

"I'm sorry. I guess I'm so used to being in front of strangers in next to nothing that I forgot how uncomfortable it could make you. I'll go cover up."

She was already headed back to the bedroom when I quickly stood up to tell her, "Nah, you're good." And that was enough for her to turn back around, holding the dresses in front of her as I scrubbed a hand against the back of my neck and decided, "Uh... the red one looks nice."

With a smirk, she challenged, "You mean, the red one that's so *obviously* burgundy?"

I shrugged. "Still red."

She was sure to emphasize, "*Burgundy* dress it is then," before she headed back into the bedroom. And not even a few minutes later, she was calling out to me from there. "Hey, Orlando. Can you come here right quick?"

The possibility of her still being in her bra and panties had me quick to respond, only slightly disappointed when I got to the room and discovered she'd already gotten the dress on. Well, *most* of the dress on, the back of it hanging open which explained her request for me to come to her.

Standing in the mirror, she clutched the front of it to her chest that was now braless as she asked, "Can you zip this up for me, please?"

"Do I look like a wardrobe assistant to you?" I teased, moving behind her to take care of her zipper as she did a little teasing of her own.

"Nah, they're never as good lookin' as you, Orlando."

Her compliment made me chuckle. "If gassing me up is your way of making me feel better about being your lackey, that shit is *not* working."

"Oh my God. It is *just* a zipper!" she whined, making me even chuckle harder since I was only joking around.

Letting that be known, I told her, "I'm messin' with you, little mama," catching the smirk on her face through the mirror as I took another glance at her dress and asked, "You mind if I smooth you out back here?"

The back of her dress wasn't exactly wrinkled, but the way it was designed had the fabric sitting weird in certain places I wasn't sure she could reach on her own. And I suppose it was nothing for Aspen to have someone fix her clothes for her - *touch her* - since she was quick to answer, "Please do."

Once she gave me the green light, I was careful about adjusting it against her frame without leaving a stain since the whole thing had my palms sweating. And after I was finished, Aspen gave me another appreciative smirk through the mirror, turning around to face me when she gushed, "Thank you, Orlando."

"I got you."

I was already stepping away, mainly so I wouldn't get lost in those pretty ass eyes of hers, until she said, "Okay, one more thing. Then I'm done getting on your nerves, for real."

I couldn't help but laugh at that, turning back around as I told her, "It's not a problem, Aspen. I told you before, I was just messin' with you."

She was quick to agree, "I know, I know. But you signed up to drive me around; not... *do all of this*."

Ignoring her reasoning, I asked, "What you need, little mama?"

Sifting through her box of jewelry, she answered, "This necklace always gives me trouble when I try to put it on myself. But from your vantage point, it should be easy peasy."

Before she could even hand it to me, I insisted, "Lemme wipe my hands off first," knowing there was no way I could mess around with a necklace latch with sweaty hands. But instead of letting me go by myself, she followed me inside the bathroom, standing next to me at the counter as she explained, "So this part right here hooks onto this part right here. And then this part hooks onto this part, but you have to do this part first."

"Why'd they make this shit so complicated in the first place?" I asked, squeezing the towel against my hands as hard as I could to get rid of any excess before accepting the jewelry I could already tell had cost her a pretty penny.

Aspen only doubled down on that thought when she gave me her back and replied, "Because that's what these overpriced brands do. We call it complicated, they call it exclusive."

"You right," I agreed, doing my best to follow her *exclusive* ass instructions. And with a little maneuvering plus getting all up in her personal space to see better, I got it taken care of, taking a step back with plans of checking out my job well done in the mirror. But that quickly got turned into checking *her* out in the mirror, the dress and necklace in combination with the touches she'd put on her hair and makeup damn near making my mouth water as I finally pushed out, "Looks good on you."

Instead of responding to me with words, she turned around towards me with her burgundy-painted lip pulled between her teeth, her hazel eyes doing a dangerous number on me as she got closer… *and closer*. And in no time at all, her hand was wrapped around the back of my neck as she pulled my face down to meet her lips for the sweetest kiss; a kiss that hardly registered in my head as real before she was already pulling away to say, "We should probably get going."

Again, I found myself struggling to push out, "Yeah… we should." And just like that, she went back into the bedroom to get her shoes on, leaving me in the bathroom to figure out what the hell had just happened.

Did I really just… kiss Aspen Watson?

Nah, nigga. She definitely kissed you, though.

With a hand to my lips, I checked for any tell-all signs in the mirror, the teeny bit of burgundy lipstick on the corner of my mouth giving me the answer I was looking for as I gently wiped at it before heading back to the bedroom to find Aspen checking out her full assemble one last time. Then she grabbed her purse and started to head out of the room as she asked, "You ready?"

Before she could escape, I caught her by the wrist to answer, "Yeah. Ready for you to explain what that little stunt you just pulled in the bathroom was all about."

She had already confused me enough with her interest

alone. Letting something like a kiss go unexplained wasn't even an option. But of course, she tried to make it sound simple, brushing a gentle hand against my chest when she said, "It was just a kiss, Orlando. Consider it a... thank you for your services."

"In that case…"

Catching her off-guard the same way she had caught me, I brought my hand to her chin, tilting her head back before I crashed my lips against hers. Then I took things a step further than she had when I slipped my tongue between her red lips and devoured her mouth, eliciting a moan from deep down in her throat before I pulled away and told her, "Consider that a you're welcome."

For a second, she looked stunned. But then that stunned expression turned into a sexy smirk that had me wanting to do it again until I felt my phone vibrate in my pocket. Aspen stayed nearby as I pulled it out to see what it was, neither of us being surprised that it was a text from Kelvin.

Kelvin: "Y'all on the way?"

Aspen didn't make things any easier on me, running a hand down my beard as she sweetly asked, "Are we… on the way, Orlando?"

Her touch in combination with the look in her eyes and the kisses from a few moments earlier had me ready to answer no and take her pretty ass straight to the bed. But I wasn't about to embarrass myself by believing any of this was real just to find out she was only fucking with me. I mean, she *literally* did this shit for a living, went into character at the drop of a hat, teased and taunted with no real plans of acting on it before the scene was cut. And even if she was the one asking the question - *had been the one to deliver the first kiss* - I wasn't convinced of her motives enough to not pull away with an excuse.

"I'm a man of my word, Aspen. And I told my boss for the moment I'd have you there at eleven, so..."

She let off a chuckle that almost seemed filled with disbelief. "How *respectable* of you."

"I do what I can," I replied with a shrug, releasing a breath I hadn't even realized I was holding once she started walking towards the door.

Damn.

Little mama really has you shook.

Of course, my first inhale was filled with the scent of her perfume, teasing me in the same way her touch had when she peeked over her shoulder to say, "Somehow, I never doubted that." And while I wondered why she felt so confident, I figured this was just another example of her displaying her talent for being able to read people - *read me.*

The elevator ride down to the lobby was quiet. But once we were there, I was reminded of who Aspen really was when a gang of teenage girls immediately recognized her then swarmed her for pictures and autographs that she happily delivered; even going as far as asking me to take a few pictures of her and the group on her own phone.

It was cool to see her in action, dope to see how adored she was by the community. And honestly, I felt silly for skipping out on what might've really been my chance with her since I wasn't sure she'd ever make the offer again.

It seemed as if that was the case once we finally made it to my car and Aspen chose to sit in the backseat instead of the front, spending the entire ride on her phone instead of playing twenty-one questions the way she'd been doing since I picked her up from the airport. And by the time we pulled up to the club, I was more annoyed with myself than anything when I told her, "Here's your stop."

Peeking up from her phone for the first time, she asked, "Wait. You're not joining us?"

I shook my head. "Nah, the club scene ain't really my thing. I'll be here to pick you up and take you back to the hotel when y'all are done, though."

While it was obvious she wasn't too happy about my response, she still managed to save face, gnawing into her lip before she pushed out, "*Oh.* Well, alright. I guess I'll see you then."

With a nod, I climbed out of the car to go open her door, surprised that she actually waited for me to do it. But the saddened look in her eyes once she made it out had me feeling a way, struggling to speak myself when I simply told her, "Have fun, Aspen."

ASPEN

DISAPPOINTMENT.

That was the only word I could use to describe how I felt leaving my hotel suite without screwing Orlando, leaving the car without talking to Orlando, leaving Orlando's presence, *period.* I mean, first the man didn't want to fuck me, and now he didn't even want to be around me?

Was I really *that* bad? Or was he really just that… *aloof?*

But he also kissed you, though.

Honestly, the shit was confusing which meant my arrival at the lounge was right on time since I needed a distraction and I *really* needed a damn drink. The security guard must've been alerted by Kelvin and Maxwell to be prepared for my arrival since he swooped right in to escort me inside the second Orlando dropped me off. Then he led me to a section that Kelvin, his wife Tiana, and his sister-in-law Nori were already occupying, just the sight of them making me smile knowing it had been far too long since the last time I'd seen them all at once.

Nori was the first to notice me and she smiled just as wide as I already was, quickly pulling me into a hug as I teased, "Well if it isn't Mrs. *Pleasures-R-Us* herself."

My acknowledgment of the family-owned high-end sex toy company she worked for made her chuckle - *probably because of the special orders I'd put in on several occasions since learning about it* - when she replied, "Girl, don't let my mama hear that. You know she's the real queen around those parts and will wave a vibrator with her signature on it in your face if you don't believe her."

It sounded so aggressive. But in the single time I had met Nina Davis at Nori and Maxwell's wedding, I knew it was true which was why I only nodded to agree before turning to hug the other recent addition to our family. "Tiana! It's so good to see you, mama. I didn't even know you'd be here."

Returning the hug, she replied, "Me neither. But Granny Marie volunteered to watch the kids tonight so mama could come out and shake her ass a little bit."

The little dance she did with it had Kelvin quick to smack her on the butt before he smirkingly teased, "Watch yourself, princess." And the lusty look she gave him in response told me they'd definitely be putting in work towards child number three tonight if she kept at it.

It also gave me hope for my own love life because if Kelvin of all people could find love, anybody could. Not that my cousin was total trash. With the Watson name, he didn't have it in him to be. But he'd done a hell of a lot of growing up since meeting Tiana, his transformation honestly admirable in a way that had me grinning hard when I told him, "Boy, leave her alone and come give me a hug."

With a grin of his own, he pulled me into a hug, squeezing hard enough to crack my back as he said, "Happy you made it to town, cuz."

"So happy you sent a driver to pick me up instead of coming to get me yourself?" I challenged with a side eye that might've been even stronger than he deserved since his appointed driver was currently giving me mixed signals.

But considering that part of the game wasn't his fault, I couldn't really hold it against him, even when he teased, "I know you like to roll exclusive now, Box Office Bae."

"Oh, whatever," I squealed with a smack to his arm and a giggle, looking around the area before I asked, "Where's Maxwell?"

As if my question had triggered him, Kelvin left us to go get his brother while Nori tossed a hand in the same direction and answered, "He's up in his office being a loser and actually getting work done like he doesn't have a special guest in the building."

I was quick to brush her off with another giggle. "Oh, stop it. I'm no one's special guest."

Of course, Nori only upped the ante. "Girl, what? Wearing the hell out of that dress like you are right now? You *gotta* be special."

Her mention of my dress made me blush a little bit, reminded of how cute Orlando was when he tried not to touch me in it even though he very well could have; very well *should* have.

But… respectability and all that, right?

Still, there was no ignoring the butterflies I felt in my belly from him just admiring me from behind through the mirror. And that giddy feeling came out through my words when I sighed, "*Actually*… this was Orlando's pick."

Tiana's eyes went wide as she repeated, "Orlando? My Orlando? My *barber*, Orlando?"

"He's a barber? I thought he was just the driver?" I asked, realizing that I must not have gotten as deep into his business as I thought I had.

Shaking her head, Tiana explained, "Nah, driving is just something he does on the side. He cuts hair in my shop full-time."

"So, wait. He works for both of y'all? This nigga is practically family, and I just…"

Nori's burst of laughter stopped me from curling into a ball of shame. But it didn't take me long to realize it was only so she could roll me into that ball herself once she said, "Girl, you've been in town for like, two seconds. And you *know* I'm the last person to judge you, but I'm also the first person to be curious about how y'all got down that fast!"

"We didn't!" I defended, quieting down to continue, "*I mean*, it was just a kiss, but… I was ready. I'm *still* ready."

It annoyed me to no end how badly I wanted Orlando considering he had pretty much hit me with his own special version of Future's, "*I'm good, luv. Enjoy.*" But the potency of his big dick energy in combination with the kiss he gave me after I'd only *playfully* kissed him first left me craving so much more.

Thankfully, Tiana was on my side when she handed me a drink and insisted, "As you should be, cause he's definitely fine and he's *definitely* not family."

Now that I knew she agreed, I felt comfortable doubling down on my attraction to him, taking a sip before I spilled, "He's so fuckin' fine, y'all. The *worst* kind of fine. Like, mysterious, total gentleman but also lowkey thug fine."

Tiana was quick to correct, "*Uhhh*... not lowkey at all. I pulled that man straight from the hood, and probably saved his life in the process."

Again, I realized I hadn't probed enough into Orlando's *very* real past life when I asked her, "It was that bad, huh?"

"He was just... involved. *Connected.* It's what he was born into, you know. But when I saw his haircuts on *Instagram*, I knew I had to have him in the shop. He's wicked talented with a pair of clippers."

"And probably just as wicked with the d-i-ickkkk," Nori sang, giving me a much-needed laugh as Tiana squealed, "*Nori!*"

Unsurprisingly unfazed, Nori replied, "What? Sis, you know he looks like the type who will call you pretty as fuck or some thug shit like that, and the next thing you know you have a whole dick down your throat. *Thug dick*."

Tiana didn't disagree, only groaned when she quietly defended, "He's not a thug, Nori."

While I could appreciate her trying to stick up for her employee, Nori was quick to call Tiana's bluff. "You *literally* just said you pulled him straight from the hood and saved his life, though. So if he's not a thug, that means your math ain't mathin', princess."

With a roll of her eyes, Tiana redirected the conversation. "*Anyway*. What's your move, Aspen? I mean, you're only here for a few days, right?"

Nodding, I answered, "I have a red-eye to Atlanta on Saturday night."

That was all Nori needed to hear, giving a toss of her hand as she said, "Oh, girl. That's plenty of time to let Orlando thug you down."

I couldn't help but laugh again, though Tiana wasn't nearly as entertained when she asked Nori, "Will you shut up? This is a serious matter! We need to help her."

"*We* need to mind our own Watson boys-branded pussies and let Aspen do the same with Thuggy O," Nori insisted, making me giggle against my glass when I took another sip of my drink as Kelvin rejoined us with Maxwell in tow.

Maxwell greeted me with a quick hug then made a beeline for his wife, wrapping an arm around her shoulder and planting a kiss against her temple before he asked, "Baby, what you down here telling my cousin?"

Peeking up at him with a grin, she answered, "Fuck or be fucked. Very on-brand of me, huh?"

"And why I love you," he gushed, this time going for a kiss on the lips that Nori chuckled against before he gave his attention back to me; notably in business mode by the way his voice changed a little when he asked, "Aspen, did Kelvin tell you anything about what we're trying to do here?"

"I mean, he got me here tonight, but that's about it."

With a nod, he invited me to sit down with him and Kelvin in a nearby booth which was another tell-all sign that Maxwell was going into business mode; something I didn't really understand since... *what did business have to do with Thanksgiving?*

Clasping his hands together, he answered the question I hadn't spoken out loud. "Aight, so... basically we want you to host this little party for us on Friday. Here. At the lounge."

"*Wow.* My first semi-extended trip home in forever and y'all are tryna put me to work?" I asked, legitimately annoyed since I wasn't supposed to be doing anything work-related for the next few days; had come home for that *exact* reason.

Of course, Kelvin tried to play good cop when he reasoned, "Come on, cuz. We'll pay you a more than fair rate for your time. *And* you'll be getting paid for something you'd probably be doing regardless."

He had a point. Considering a huge part of coming home was

to be spending time with family and these two were more like brothers than cousins to me, the chances of me ending up at *The Max* on Friday night were pretty high. Still, the fact that they were not only propositioning me but propositioning me at the last minute had me doing a quick brainstorm of ways to make this truly worth my time, deciding on the only thing that made sense.

"I want a cut of bar sales too."

"*What?*" they asked in unison.

Serving them the smile that got me cast on a consistent basis, I replied, "Bar sales. If I'm here, *if my name is attached to this*, that means the lounge will be poppin' which also means the drinks will be flowing. I want a percentage *on top* of my hourly hosting fee."

I hadn't even noticed that Nori and Tiana had joined us until Nori said, "*Whoa.* Sis is really about her coin. I think I might actually be a little turned on right now."

With a roll of his eyes, Maxwell insisted, "I talk numbers to you all the time, babe."

While Nori gave her husband an, "*Eh*" look in response as if his version didn't give her the same high she got from listening to us go back and forth, Kelvin was quick to clown, "All I remember is her talking you into some bullshit ass rental fee back when y'all first met***."

Shaking both of them off, Maxwell groaned, "*Anyway.* I'm willing to negotiate a *small* percentage of bar sales in addition to your hourly rate."

Now that all eyes were on me with the girls silently rooting me on from the sidelines, I was really in my bag, glancing at my fingernails when I told him, "I can work with small. But if it's really as small as you just emphasized, you can save it, Maxwell. I'm not going any lower than fifteen percent."

Maxwell was obviously peeved by my number, letting off a grunt as Kelvin urged, "Just give her the cut she wants, bro. Ain't like we won't be able to afford it with the crowd her name will draw."

"But we're already paying for her accommodations at the hotel *and* to have Orlando on call," Maxwell reasoned, a fact I took great joy in responding to when I chimed in, "Neither of which I asked for. Oops. *Y'all bad.*"

While Nori and Tiana giggled in the background, Kelvin and Maxwell did a quick little huddle, whispering back and forth between each other before Maxwell finally agreed, "Alright, fine. You got a deal."

"Nice doing business with you, cousin," I told him with a slick smirk, shaking his hand as his wife turned into my personal hypewoman.

Grabbing my shoulders, she cheered, "That's what the fuck I'm talking about! Get that money, Aspen. Run his pockets. Shake them empty. Know your worth."

I couldn't help but laugh in response, especially once I saw the annoyed look on Maxwell's face as he poured himself a stiff drink. And while his attitude only had Nori getting ready to offer drinks all around on her husband's behalf, I faked a yawn before I told her, "Actually, it's been a pretty long day. I think I'm ready to go back to the hotel now."

"You mean, ready to go get *thugged down* by Orlando?" Tiana asked, giving Nori a wink and a shoulder bump as Kelvin repeated, "Thugged down? *Orlando*? What's that all about?"

"Nothing," they sang in unison, their little giggles that followed telling him it was definitely something as he pulled out his phone.

"Mmhm. Y'all ain't slick. I'll shoot him a text and let him know you're ready to get picked up. Or to get… *thugged down.*"

Nori and Tiana bursted with laughter as I downed the last of my drink and groaned, "Don't you start, Kelvin..."

I sat my glass to the side as he sent the text while sharing, "Nah, Orlando is cool peoples. Quiet, but chill. A real nigga, no doubt. If he's your type, he's a good look, cuz."

While I fully believed everything he had said, I could only sigh when I replied, "Well thanks for your vote of confidence on something that's not even happening."

Nori frowned, sipping from her own glass before she asked, "Why not, Aspen? Ja Rule said it best. Every thug needs a lady.

And I know there's gotta be, at least, a few down ass bitch bones in that little body of yours."

"Down ass bitch bones," Tiana repeated, her and Kelvin sharing in a hearty laugh at my expense as I rolled my eyes in a pout.

"I am *so* glad y'all think this is funny. It's the perfect reminder for why I don't come home often."

I was only playing with them since my crazy schedule was the real reason behind that fact. Still, Kelvin had no problem challenging, "Nah, it's exactly why you came home. Where else can you experience a premium roast session like this, Ashy Aspen? Nowhere but here. *With family*."

He pulled me into a shoulder hug that I pretended to fight against but eventually sank into, knowing he was right. And as we waited for Orlando to show up, I got a chance to get a little roasting in myself, reminding Tiana of her cougar status and jabbing Kelvin for marrying a grandma, then catching Maxwell with something like a stray bullet of a joke when I asked Nori what it was like getting used to his little size compared to her mother's toys.

By the time Orlando showed up, I had forgotten he was even on the way. But regardless of how much I thought I wanted to stick around the lounge a little while longer, the real ass yawn that came out told me it was best to save my energy for the rest of my time here, giving everyone a hug before the security guard escorted me outside to Orlando's *Cadillac*.

To my surprise, he was already standing on the sidewalk with the passenger door open; something I was sure to comment on when I approached him and asked, "How do you know I wanna sit in the front seat?"

"I'm not exactly asking you, Aspen," he replied with an arrogant smirk that was too damn sexy for me to even fight him on as he shut the door behind me.

Ugh.

I managed to not look at him once he climbed in on his side even though his presence dominated the car - *dominated me*. His clothes were the same, but his enticing masculine scent seemed more potent than before. Or maybe me and my womanly parts were just more aware. Either way, it was a struggle to stay fake mad at him with him smelling so delicious and having the looks to match.

But I wasn't going to look at him.

Nope, my attention was completely on the window which was the only reason I realized we weren't going in the right direction. And after going a few more streets that only took us further away from our intended destination, I decided to speak up.

"Umm… I know you aren't from here, but I'm pretty sure the hotel is back that way."

"I know," he replied shortly, continuing on the route as if I hadn't just identified a problem.

In fact, his nonchalant reaction made me panic a bit, turning his way to ask, "Where the hell are you taking me, Orlando?"

Instead of answering my question, he chuckled, settling deeper into his seat as he insisted, "Just relax."

Maybe if we were on different terms, I'd be able to relax. But the fact that he'd gone cold on me had me crossing my arms with a scowl to challenge, "How do I know you aren't kidnapping me? And that I won't call the cops?"

Chuckling again, he confidently replied, "You won't. So just relax, little mama." He even added a little pat to my bare knee that may or may not have made my kitty tingle once he let his hand stay there for the rest of the ride to… *Jackie Robinson Park*?

He pulled into the darker side of the parking lot - *the side that used to be unofficially reserved for hotboxing and makeout sessions* - and I felt myself having flashbacks of my high school days when Ashy Aspen would dream of some fine upperclassmen bringing her here for some hot and heavy… *petting*. But just like back then, I was stuck lusting over a guy who wasn't even checking for me, even when the entire *world* was checking for me.

Ain't that a bitch?

We sat in silence once Orlando turned off the car. And I was tempted to pull my phone out and request an *Uber* until he started, "After I dropped you off at *The Max* earlier, I came here to do some thinking about… why you might've kissed me, why I kissed you the way I did, why I was... psyching myself out of being worthy of your attention. And honestly, the shit feels stupid now; it felt stupid then. But I thought it was too late to change my mind and that I'd already missed my opportunity with you, so I was just… annoyed with myself, which came off as feeling a way towards you and I don't want that shit to be confused. I…"

Before he could say anything more, I reached to pull his face towards mine over the center console, meeting him in the middle with a kiss against his perfectly-full lips that had me closing my eyes as he returned it with just the right amount of pressure. Then he unbuckled my seatbelt for me to get even closer, practically on my knees by the time I broke our kiss to whisper against his lips, "I understand."

The air from his sigh of relief tickled my nose and the smile that came with it had me crawling across the center console to straddle his lap, a move that he was pleased with as his hands landed against my hips and mine wrapped around the back of his neck.

Staring into his eyes, I gave an important spiel of my own. "Believe it or not, I know how that feels. To wonder if you're really good enough for someone, to not *feel* good enough. And honestly, that's what this place reminds me of, even though not getting fucked in the backseat of somebody mama's car probably worked out for me in the long run."

The way his eyebrow piqued had me rushing to continue, "*But...* to make things clear, my attraction to you isn't some fluke, Orlando. Your fine ass is more than worthy of my attention."

"*More than* worthy, huh?" he asked, nipping my chin with a kiss that made me shudder in his lap. And when he went for another against my neck, I could only groan, "*Mmhm…*" as he nipped and sucked and kissed it with the expertise of a nigga who'd definitely been on the right side of the high school hot and heavy petting spectrum.

"*How lucky*," I thought as I turned my head to find his lips with my own, my hands pressed against his cheeks as I wrestled my late-blooming tongue with his in a dance that already had the windows fogging up around us. But the extra heat only added to the moment, looking exactly how I always imagined it in my past. Except now, I was a grown ass woman with the sex drive to match which meant this little kissing shit wasn't nearly enough.

I needed more.

I needed… *him*; inside of me as soon as I could get him there.

Sitting back against the steering wheel, I reached between us for the button of his jeans, getting it unfastened just as Orlando gushed, "Little mama, you wildin'." But instead of responding with unnecessary words, I only doubled down on his claims when I yanked at his zipper and gave him a look to encourage his participation since that was honestly the most I could do from my position.

Thankfully, he had no problem finishing the job, lifting enough to get his jeans down towards his knees. Then he pushed the fabric of my dress into a bunch against my waist, taking a moment to appreciate the fact that I wasn't wearing any panties as I did the honors of pulling his dick free from his boxers.

Big dick energy never lies.

It was so full and weighty in my hand, matching everything else about him as I teasingly asked, "This is all you have? Did you leave your real one at home?"

Chuckling, he lifted the center console, blindly sifting around for what I realized was a condom when he said, "You funny." Then he handed it my way and instructed, "Take care of that for me."

"My pleasure," I gushed with a smirk, ripping the gold package with my teeth then sliding the condom onto his dick that I swear had gotten even harder in the few seconds it was out of my hand. But it only had me more eager to follow right behind the condom, lifting just enough to align us and sliding down on top of him with a long, throaty moan.

"Not enough for you?" he asked arrogantly, pumping into me with a single stroke that almost sent me through the roof with how quickly I tried to run away. But I suppose that was exactly what my ass deserved for playing around; receiving the best kind of punishment as I found my rhythm in the confines of his front seat with my hands pressed into his shoulders and his hands guiding my hips.

The windows grew foggier as I moaned with each descent, fighting against the burn in my thighs to take every inch of him I could. And when I caught myself getting lazy, Orlando greedily picked up the slack, driving into me from below with strokes that had me begging him not to stop as he groaned a strong, "*Fuck, Aspen*" right against my neck.

Yes.

Fuck Aspen.

The car had to be shaking under our weight with how hard we started going at each other, fucking away every bit of *unworthiness* as if we couldn't get caught. But getting caught was the last thing on either of our minds; the first thing being fucking each other senseless and the second, riding the wave that had me biting into his thermal-covered shoulder so I wouldn't scream as I came undone and had him exploding into the condom a few minutes after.

Resting in his lap with his dick still inside of me, my forehead was against his shoulder as I tried to catch my breath, giggling when he grunted through an aftershock that I might've encouraged with my own. And when I finally sat back, the ridiculously-sexy satisfied look on Orlando's face under the bit of moonlight peeking through the fogged-up windows had me itching for a round two that deserved better than a car.

So before I could think myself out of it, I blurted, "Stay with me tonight."

His eyebrow piqued, urging me to continue, "At the hotel. I want you to stay with me tonight, Orlando."

For a second, he went quiet. And I worried that meant he was about to go cold again too. But then a very warm grin grew to his lips when he licked them and replied, "I almost missed out on you once by second-guessing myself. I'll be damned if I let that shit happen again."

ORLANDO

I HADN'T SLEPT this well in years.

Honestly, the last time I'd slept this well - *and without interruption* - was probably when I was still in my mama's stomach; *God rest her soul.* But there was something about having Aspen's naked body draped across mine as she slept off the rounds of sex from the night before that allowed me to sleep like a baby and wake up feeling like one too.

A happy ass baby.

How I'd gone from strangers to lovers with a woman like Aspen Watson in the matter of a few hours wasn't something I could dwell on, feeling more thankful than anything that the universe thought I was deserving. But I suppose that's what this particular season was all about; being grateful and giving thanks. And I was more than excited to show every bit of my appreciation when I started landing little kisses against Aspen's forehead, sitting up to deliver those same kisses to her shoulder blade as she woke up giggling in response.

Her voice was groggy when she said, "Good morning to you too," running a hand down my beard before she used it to tug me towards her for a kiss.

A morning kiss with morning breath that I greedily accepted, stealing one myself before I asked, "How you feelin', little mama?"

Gnawing into her lip as if she was reliving the night before in her mind, she answered, "I feel amazing, actually. How are *you* feeling, Orlando?"

With a content sigh, I told her, "Better than I have in years if we're being real."

It wasn't that I'd lived a completely unhappy life, and the last few months had definitely been filled with plenty of highlights. But there was something about making myself a little vulnerable, *being understood*, and then the sex plus the good sleep that followed that had me waking up on cloud nine; Aspen only making that even more potent as she rubbed a gentle hand against my cheek and replied, "That's what I like about you. *Your realness*."

When she moved to climb from the bed, I thought about pulling her back but was glad I hadn't since there was nothing like seeing Aspen's naked body from behind under the morning sun beaming through the window, her skin legit glowing as she headed towards the closet and asked, "Does all that feeling better than you have in years have anything to do with me?"

"It has everything to do with you. Last night felt like a dream," I admitted, not even caring about sounding like a fuckin' simp.

It was what it was. *The whole truth*. And Aspen seemed happy to hear it, pulling on one of the hotel's robes as she questioned, "If last night felt like a dream, what's this morning feel like?"

I shrugged. "Shit, this gotta be heaven or somethin'. *I don't know*."

Her sweet little giggle in response made my dick flex under the cover, though it went right back flaccid when she teased, "You're so cute."

Frowning, I repeated, "*Cute*? Nah, Aspen. I'll be a lot of things for you, but cute ain't one of 'em."

"Well stop being so cute then," she challenged with a smirk, grabbing the menu from the nightstand as she crawled back onto the bed. "Should we order room service?"

"You mean, you ain't ready to get rid of me yet?" I asked as she moved even closer to me, practically straddling my lap by the time she made herself comfortable and answered my question.

"Oh, hell no. *Unless*… you're ready for me to get rid of you?"

With my hands at her waist, I reminded her, "Like I told you last night, I'm not letting that shit happen again. I'm here for as long as you'll have me."

How long that was, I wasn't sure. But again, I wasn't letting myself worry about that, right now my focus being on Aspen's pretty ass smirk as she dropped the menu to plant her hands against my shoulders and asked, "So that means you'll be joining me and the fam for Thanksgiving dinner at Nori and Maxwell's too, right?"

"Should've known all this sexy ass shit was a set-up," I thought, avoiding her eyes as I stammered, "Ahh… *I mean*… I didn't say all that, but…"

"Oh, come on! It'll be fun. I mean, it's not like these people are total strangers to you. *And* my auntie Marie makes the best macaroni and cheese you'll ever taste."

Considering it had been a good minute since the last time I had some auntie-certified mac and cheese and I didn't really have any other plans for the day outside of watching football, I was already sold on her invitation. But having Aspen still pantyless in my lap put my mind in a different space, just the thought of having her for my Thanksgiving meal making my mouth water when I asked, "Who can think about tasting macaroni and cheese with your fire ass pussy this close to me?"

She grinned at that, only encouraging me to, *at least*, have a piece of her for breakfast as I told her, "Come 'ere, Aspen."

She started to only lift her hips, but I lifted her completely to a standing position on the mattress, moving so her pussy straddled my face before I pulled her down onto my mouth. The front of her robe was smashed against my eyes, but I didn't care, not needing to see a thing to devour her like my final meal request on death row. And when Aspen *did* remove the tie of her robe, it only made things all the better, the look of pleasure on her face and the bounce in her titties as she rode my mouth only making me go harder, imprinting the tip of my tongue on her clit until she damn near stopped breathing before she collapsed against me with an orgasm.

She must've thought her tapping out equated to me being done. But that wasn't the case at all as I gripped into the back of her thighs to keep her steady as I continued to taste her, her juices coating my beard like a moisturizer by the time I finally let up after licking her through a second orgasm. And it was the second one that made her too weak to move, relying on my help to get back down into a sitting position on the mattress as she groaned, "God, I wish I could pack you up in my luggage and take you everywhere with me."

With a chuckle, I moved from the bed to head to the bathroom, grabbing my boxers on the way and tossing over my shoulder, "I don't think my clients down at the shop would be very happy about that."

"I'm still mad at you for not telling me you were a barber, though," she shouted back, making me chuckle again since it was literally the only thing she hadn't asked me about.

After taking a long piss, I moved to wash my hands, shaking my head at myself in the mirror since my face looked crazy as hell. *"Well worth it, though,"* I thought as I grabbed a washcloth to clean up just as Aspen joined me in the bathroom after finally making that call for room service.

She made herself comfortable sitting on the counter, the trail of wetness running from her thigh to her ankle making me smirk until she asked, "How'd you get into cutting hair?"

It wasn't exactly the most heartwarming story which was why I mostly kept it to myself. But something about Aspen had me comfortable enough to give her the full truth, scrubbing my face clean as I answered, "My uncle's influence. My mother passed when I was young, and my father was in and out of jail all my life. So whenever he was in, I'd be with my uncle down at the shop learning the craft."

"And when your father was out?"

"*When he was out…* I'd be on the same shit that landed him in jail over and over again."

It sounded ridiculous now, but it was the truth, my father's connection to the game the only reason I was ever a part of it. I didn't necessarily want to be like him, but I also couldn't help my desire for his approval which came off as me doing whatever he wanted for me to get it – *being like him.*

Without pressing for details, Aspen asked, "The very, *very* real past life, right?"

Nodding, I rinsed my cloth, giving it a squeeze to wring it out before I ran it over my face again and answered, "Yeah, which is crazy to think about cause we're talking about my *real* dad, my blood. He was supposed to have my back, steer me in the right direction and all that. But I got in the most trouble with him; behind *his* shit, tryna live *his* lifestyle."

Again, ridiculous as fuck. But Aspen wasn't judging, only nodding along before she followed up, "So what made you decide enough was enough?"

"I got shot."

The look of surprise on her face in response was expected. And knowing Aspen, I figured another question for details was coming so I continued, "Thankfully, it went right through the flesh and didn't cause any nerve damage or anything like that. But a bullet to the ass cheek will have you rethinking that lifestyle *real* quick."

I said it with a laugh, but it really wasn't all that funny since a few centimeters to the left could've made a world of difference. But it wasn't just the bullet with my father's name on it that made my decision, more so his reaction to me taking it; something I felt compelled to share since that part was what really answered Aspen's question.

She was completely tuned in as I explained, "Of course my father was on some retaliation shit off the rip. I'm talking, in the hospital with me calling his niggas from the block before I even knew if I was gonna be alright or not. But it was in that same hospital bed that I got a DM on *Instagram* from Tiana asking if I'd be interested in taking a booth at her shop, wanting to add someone who specialized in more artistic haircut designs and shit. I took her offer and I never looked back."

Now that we'd made it to something like the happy-for-now of my little story, a sneaky grin grew to Aspen's lips when she asked, "So you know I gotta see your booty cheek wound now, right?"

My eyebrow piqued with amusement. "You playin', right?"

To answer my question, she grabbed my hand to pull me between her legs, pinching at the waistband of my boxers as she teased, "Drop those drawers, Orlando. Lemme see."

Shaking my head with a chuckle, I turned around and pulled them down just enough for her to see. But I wished I hadn't once I heard her suggest, "It kinda looks like a butterfly. Or maybe a Bat signal..."

"*Aight, aight.* You got the picture," I told her as I yanked them up, getting ready to leave the bathroom until she caught me by the wrist with a, "*Hey.*"

She pulled me back between her legs, wrapping her arms around my neck when she said, "Thank you for showing me that. And for sharing all of that with me."

It had come so easy that I honestly hadn't even considered the magnitude until she was thanking me for being open. But the truth was, "You should feel special, little mama. Not a lot of people get that much out of me. Not exactly the easiest thing to talk about."

"I can only imagine," she agreed with an empathetic nod.

Still, her empathy didn't stop me from insisting, "Aight, now you gotta tell me about you so I'm not the only sucka in the room."

With one of her little giggles, she replied, "You're not a sucka, Orlando. You've just… lived a life. We all have."

"Then tell me something about you that I can't find on *Google*," I challenged, not surprised to see the way she immediately averted her eyes before she dropped her hands onto the counter.

She was uncomfortable.

But considering I'd just been in the same position, I didn't back down, giving her all the time she needed to contemplate, and sigh, and close her eyes to gather herself before she eventually opened them and shared, "I… was *also* mostly raised by my father before he passed a few years ago because, *like you*, my mother passed away when I was young. I've always known I wanted to be on the big screen, but I didn't necessarily have the look for it growing up, so people never really believed in my dreams; *believed in me*. Because of that, I was *extremely* insecure, and honestly still battle with that even now. But I'm happy to be doing what I love and proving people wrong in the process."

Without going into lots of details, she had managed to package her response in a way that told me she was trying; something I could appreciate when I complimented, "I gotta hand it to you. You're damn good at what you do, Aspen."

While I admittedly hadn't seen everything she'd be featured in, I'd seen enough to know she was talented as hell. And even if she still battled with her insecurities like she claimed to, she owned her talent in a way that had her smirking once she replied, "And this is only the beginning."

I wholeheartedly believed her. And now that I felt like I knew her on a more intimate level, I'd be rooting for her success even harder than I had been as a bystander. But before I could dive any deeper into her business, there was a knock on the door from room service, prompting Aspen to hop off the counter so she could answer it.

Since I wasn't exactly dressed, I stayed in the bedroom while she went to handle it, waiting until I heard the suite door close before I showed my face. And by the time I made it out, Aspen already had a piece of bacon in her mouth, groaning until she noticed me watching and said, "Don't tell anybody about this."

Even though I didn't think it was that big of a deal, I still replied, "Shit, I ain't gotta choice but to keep your secret now. I caught you bashin' the swine and you saw my... butterfly Bat signal ass wound. We're practically even."

The reminder made her snort a chuckle as I continued, "You breaking code eating breakfast on Thanksgiving, though. You know you're supposed to starve all day until the real meal."

Let my folks back home tell it, starving all day made the food taste better. But Aspen didn't care either way, smirking against the crunch of her bacon before she fired back, "Shouldn't have worked up my appetite if you expected me to be able to starve myself."

Now I was the one smirking. "I'd work it up even more right now, but I don't want your food to get cold."

Her eyebrows furrowed. "You think all of this is for me? Boy, you better come eat," she insisted, reaching under the cart as she said, "Here, let me make you a plate." I realized that was what she was reaching for once she pulled it out and started plating a little bit of everything before inviting me to take the space next to her.

"First, you put that pussy on my face. And now you makin' plates for me? You bouta have a nigga spoiled in a minute, Aspen."

With a playful shrug, she handed me the plate followed by a set of silverware. "I'm so used to people doing stuff for me. It feels good to be able to do a little something for someone else. And besides, I can't eat all of this food by myself and I definitely can't eat my own pussy, so..."

"You sure? You lowkey kinda flexible. Might be able to swing it with a little maneuv… *aye*!"

The grape she'd thrown at the side of my head to cut me off was already rolling across the floor when she threatened, "Shut up and eat before your pussy-eating privileges get revoked already."

I couldn't help but laugh knowing good and well if her moans from earlier were any indication, that would never happen. But for the sake of not ruining the vibe with a petty argument, I dug into my plate and replied, "Ain't gotta tell me twice."

ASPEN

HAVING Orlando drop me off at Nori and Maxwell's wasn't my first choice, but I knew it was the smart one once he reminded me that he'd kept me away from my family for long enough and promised he would be back right after he went home to shower and get dressed. Still, waiting for him to show up had me on edge, anxious to be in his presence again as I kept myself busy organizing and reorganizing the silverware on the dinner table and stirring shit that didn't really even need to be stirred on the stove.

Nori was the first to notice my antics once she joined me in the kitchen after changing out of her cooking clothes into something fancier, pulling the spoon from my hand as she sighed, "*Whew.* You got thugged down in the worst way, didn't you?"

"What?" I asked, snapping out of my daydream of exactly what she was talking about.

She knew it too, clarifying with a simple, "Orlando. He *did* that, didn't it?"

With a sigh of my own, I replied, "He definitely, *definitely* did."

It gave me goosebumps just to think about the night - *and morning* - we had shared, learning about each other, and loving up on each other, and just… being strangers with hearts that already felt so, so familiar.

But of course, while that sounded all sweet and adorable in

my head, Nori was only concerned about one thing when she asked, "So… what happened? Spill the tea. I've been waiting for this recap all day and you better not leave out *any* of the super sexy details."

Instead of indulging her, I simply replied, "Jackie Robinson Park."

"*Oh, wow,*" Tiana gushed once she returned from checking on baby Titan who had been down for a nap since I'd shown up, catching just enough of the conversation to know the context as Nori repeated, "Jackie Robinson… *girl.* Y'all grown asses fucked in the park like some little heathens?"

She was already laughing by the time I whined, "I know, I know. But we were talking, and he shared some things, and *I* shared some things, and we kinda got caught up in the moment, *so…* we had to do what we had to do. And honestly, it was perfect."

"Yeah, perfectly-amateurish. I mean, what's the point of having a five-star hotel suite if you're just gonna fuck in the backseat of a *Cadillac*?"

Nori's question was fair. But instead of feeling any shame about it, I gave her the facts. "Actually, we were in the front seat. And I mean, we fucked a bunch at the hotel too, so…"

"You used a condom, right? Niggas like that will have your ass pregnant if you're not careful," Nori warned, Tiana shaking her head with a giggle as I averted eyes because...

"We did. *Mostly,*" I admitted, Tiana inhaling a sharp gasp as I continued, "I mean, we did the first time in the car. And the second time in the hotel. The third time, he pulled out. And the fourth time, he came in my mouth. *Or was that the fifth time*?"

"Oh, so y'all were *fuckin'* fuckin'? I'm so proud," Nori complimented, getting ready to give me a high-five until Tiana loudly cleared her throat. In fact, Nori's hand was still lingering in the air as she asked, "What now, Supermom?"

Crossing her arms, Tiana scolded, "Don't high-five her over this! I mean, don't get me wrong, Orlando is a great guy. But she just met him! She should've been using protection every time."

Slowly dropping her hand, Nori groaned, "Girl, how many

times do I have to tell you to mind your own pussy? This is the most romantic story I've heard in years."

With a roll of her eyes, Tiana clapped back, "Says the girl who was anti-love until it bit her on the ass; *literally*."

"Which is coming from the girl who almost missed out on love with her youngin' being a scaredy cat. You ain't low, Tiana," Nori replied, earning a quick side eye as someone behind us came in singing, "*The macaroni and cheese has arrived.*"

I turned around and found Nori's parents walking in, the ever-so-fashionable Nina Davis carrying a foil pan in her hands and wearing a sinister grin on her face that made total sense once her daughter whined, "Mama, I know for a fact that I told you Marie was making the macaroni and cheese."

"But Nori, I make macaroni and cheese every Thanksgiving. I was supposed to stop my personal tradition to satisfy *her*?"

The undertones in regard to my aunt spoke volumes, especially once Nori scolded, "Don't start, mama."

With a huff, Nina moved to set the pan on the kitchen island with the rest of the food, wiping her hands off before she stuck them out to me for a hug. "Oh, Aspen. It's so good to see you again. If I would've known you were coming, I would've hand-delivered your quarterly re-up instead of shipping it."

Returning her hug, I told her, "It's okay. I'll get it when I get back. But it's good to see you again too, Mrs. Davis. *Mr. Davis*."

Once Nina let me go, he pulled me into a quick hug as he said, "From the big screen to my son-in-law's condo. Welcome back, superstar."

"Thank you so much," I replied with a smile that only grew wider once Tiana returned from the back room with a very-alert Titan in her arms. I couldn't help but abandon the Davis's to coo, "Oh my goodness, look at those chubby cheeks! Baby fever overload."

When she handed him to me, that feeling only grew stronger, even when Nori teased, "Girl, don't say that too loud. You aren't in the clear yet, Little. Miss Mostly."

"Shut up, Nori," I snapped, bouncing little Titan in my arms as I sang, "Him just so handsome."

Titan was already reaching for my hoop earring when his father joined us from the couch, pinching his son's cheek on his way to the kitchen where he asked, "I thought Ma was bringing the macaroni and cheese?"

"*She is…*" Nori muttered just loud enough for Kelvin to react.

"Aww, damn. That means World War III is about to pop off when she gets here and sees this. Let me snag a bowl to-go first, though."

Peeling the foil back, he caught a pop to the hand from an already-irritated Nori. "*Aht*! We're not eating until everybody gets here. Now call your mother and get her ETA before I have to gut you with the electric knife."

"*Electric knife*? Better put that shit away before she gets here, or she'll be using it as a weapon in the fight with your mom over that rival macaroni and cheese," he joked, Nori's scowl only egging him on when he added, "Matter of fact, lemme go ahead and get my kids outta here before the first bomb drops. Princess, it's time for us to jet."

The smack Nori gave him on the arm had Tiana and me both giggling just as another guest arrived.

My guest.

Once again, he was dressed in all black with a simple gold watch and matching chain. But somehow he looked even better than he had the night before, maybe because of all the good sleep he had gotten thanks to me.

While I was stuck admiring his fine ass, Tiana was the first to say, "Hey, Orlando," followed by Kelvin's "What's up, O". And after addressing them, he directed his attention to the host who was grinning like a fool when he told her, "Appreciate you for lettin' me crash, Nori."

"*Crash Thanksgiving, or crash Aspen's…* I mean! We're more than happy to have you joining us, Orlando," she told him, peeking over at me just as I rolled my eyes while she gave him a hug.

Finally, it was my turn. And while I fully expected him to downplay things in front of our nosy audience, I was pleasantly surprised when he leaned in to press a gentle kiss against the corner of my lips, serving me a knowing smile before he asked, "They got you holding the baby too, huh?"

"They sure do," I sang more to Titan than Orlando, his little baby gurgles in response doing a number on my heart as Orlando smiled down at the both of us. But of course, the fact that we weren't alone meant Orlando's eyes weren't the only ones on me, the rest of the group watching the three of us intently until I looked up from Titan and asked, "*What?*"

My question was never answered since my aunt Marie and uncle Roger were walking in, Marie looking like she'd stopped at the mall for a makeover as she strutted further into the condo with her head held high and Roger followed behind her carrying what I now knew would be the second pan of macaroni and cheese.

It was a whisper to his wife, but somehow still loud enough for me to hear Kelvin say, "This shit is about to get ugly." And right on cue, Nina showed back up in the room with a look in her eyes that told me her shade gun was fully loaded which meant somebody needed to intervene.

That somebody ended up being me as I approached them with an obnoxious, "Auntie Marie! Uncle Roger! I missed you guys!"

Pulling me into a hug as best as she could with Titan still in my arms, she replied, "And we missed you too! Look at you holding this baby boy like he's not almost bigger than you."

With that baby being her grandson, I wasn't at all surprised when she stole him from me, even when his father - *her son* - said, "Aye! Leave my boy out of this, Ma."

She only chuckled in response, uncle Roger stopping by to give me a quick kiss on the cheek on his way to the kitchen. And I thought all would be well until he asked, "Where should I put this?"

"Nori, I thought you said you were saving a space for it?" Marie asked, a question we all knew the real answer too.

But thankfully, Nori was the only one tasked with giving a response, struggling as she explained, "I was… and now it's filled. But we can keep it in the oven until the first pan runs out."

Of course, that only confused aunt Marie even more. "The first pan?"

"My pan," Nina answered with a smirk, giving my aunt a snooty onceover before she said, "Interesting choice of ensemble, Marie."

"*Okay, what is this all about?*" I wondered, Orlando giving me a look that pretty much asked the same question as Nori cleared the air with a strong, "Nope! We're not doing this. I'm not letting y'all do this. Not today. Not in my place. If y'all wanna hash out this old ass beef, take it to somebody else's house, or take it outside, or take it to the church. *I don't care*. But in here, we are going to eat, and be thankful, and enjoy each other's company as a family. Understood?"

Everybody went quiet, even the damn baby as Maxwell showed up carrying a laughing Elliana on his back, one look at his distressed wife being enough for him to ask, "Damn. What did I miss?"

Instead of answering his question, Nori sighed, "Get in here and cut this turkey before I have to cancel Thanksgiving altogether." Then she moved towards the kitchen as the tension in the room kept the rest of us cemented in place, glancing between each other before Kelvin finally broke the silence.

"*So*… anybody want a drink?"

There was a collective exhale that pretty much equated to, *"Hell yes"*, the little bit of laughter that followed being enough to neutralize the air. And once the turkey was cut and a group prayer was said, it felt like a real family Thanksgiving again with pots and pans clinking in the background and plates being overloaded with the foods that truly didn't get enough love year-round.

They were getting *all* the love today, though.

Well, except for the honey ham that Orlando and I shared a silent joke about as I skipped it to put turkey and dressing on my plate, then did the same for the plate he was holding before asking him, "Is that enough for you?"

"Coming from your lips, that's a trick question," he teased with a wink that made my stomach flutter - *or maybe I was just hungry*.

I decided it must've been a combination of both since, once we made it to the table, I couldn't stop grinning and I couldn't stop eating. In fact, I started to unbutton my pants to give my food baby more room to grow while I finished off the last of the macaroni and cheese that I'd taken from aunt Marie's pan to show solidarity. It was the least I could do for the woman who might've been married into the family but was the closest thing to a motherly figure for me after I'd lost my own.

She was as good as blood in my book.

Slumping back into my chair with a satisfied groan, I placed a hand on my rounded stomach that was hard as a rock now that I had stuffed myself. But I had no regrets, even when Orlando joked, "First you all on Titan. Now you holding your stomach? You got somethin' you need to tell me, Aspen?"

While my first instinct was to shoot him a playful side eye, I couldn't help doing a little teasing of my own as I rubbed my belly and told him, "Congratulations, baby daddy. We're having a TV dinner."

He started cracking up laughing at that, making me laugh too as Nori sang, "Awww! Y'all are so cute," from across the table. And though it might've embarrassed me a little to be put on the spot, the adoring look Orlando gave me in response to her claim made it easy to agree with her; and made me feel more than happy to be home.

ORLANDO

I SHOULD'VE TAKEN the day off.

Aspen only had one more full day in town before she'd be leaving tomorrow night to head to Atlanta for the filming of her next feature, and I was stuck in the shop cutting hair instead of spending more time with her; many of my clients squeezing in emergency appointments for a quick line-up after getting word of the Black Friday party she was hosting down at *The Max* tonight.

It was sure to be a hit, which was the exact reason I wasn't trying to be in the building. Me and big crowds just didn't get along. But I imagined telling Aspen I wasn't coming being similar to telling a child Santa Claus wasn't real, and honestly, I didn't even have it in me to break her heart like that.

I'd just have to take one for the team.

As if I had thought her up, the chime of the bell over the barbershop door cued me in on her surprise arrival, the entire shop quietly staring at her in awe the second she walked in and gushed, "Oh, wow. This place looks nothing like I remembered it."

Abandoning my booth along with the customer in my chair, I approached her and asked, "Aspen, what you doin' here?"

She was all smiles, bouncing on the toes of her *Balenciaga* sock shoes when she started, "*Well…* after I snuck in some cuddle time with Titan and some diva time with Elliana at aunt Marie's and uncle Roger's house, I went down to the lounge to run through plans for tonight with Maxwell and Kelvin. But that got boring once they started talking numbers I didn't care about, so I thought I'd drop by here and say hey."

"Well hey to you too," I told her, scrubbing a hand down the back of my neck and taking a quick glance around the shop. Since I'd been working here, I swear I'd never heard the floor so quiet which meant every ear must've been tuned in to our conversation.

The last thing I needed was a bunch of big mouth niggas in my business, and *especially* not in hers. So without letting things go any further, I suggested, "Uh… how about we take this conversation to the back."

Aspen was happy to do so, waving to a few of her admirers on the way as I told my client I'd be right back. And once we were there, she asked, "Where's Tiana?"

With a shrug, I locked the door behind us. "I think she's out taking advantage of the Black Friday sales with her mom and sister. She didn't even come in today."

Now that we were alone, Aspen wasted no time snuggling up to me, giving my beard a tug as she said, "You should've taken a page out of her book. I need some company."

Wrapping her in a low hug, I agreed, "Was legit thinking the same shit before your pretty ass showed up. But now I got a day full of heads thanks to that little party y'all having tonight."

With a giggle, she pressed her hands into my chest and asked, "Oh, niggas are actually gettin' fresh for this? It's about to be a *movie*."

"Yeah, I bet," I groaned, already feeling antsy about the prospect. And apparently, I hadn't done a very good job of masking that anxiety since Aspen immediately frowned once she picked up on it.

"What's the matter, Orlando?"

Shaking my head, I sighed, "Nothin'. It's just… the butterfly Bat signal. It happened in the club, at an event just like this. Thought shit was real sweet and then… *bam*. Got snuck from behind."

I couldn't forget that night if I wanted to; when what was supposed to be a fun time out with my niggas to celebrate one of their birthdays turned into the worst night of my life thanks to my dad's dealings. Of course his old ass wasn't in the club, but I guess I was something like collateral since the people after him came for me the second they saw I was out. And from there, it was nothing but shattered bottles, screaming women, and so, *so* much blood.

A damn nightmare.

As if she could see me slipping back into that dark moment, Aspen put a gentle hand against my cheek and said, "*Hey.* You created a better memory of Jackie Robinson Park for me. Now let me create a better memory of the club for you. You're safe here, Orlando. I promise you."

While I wanted to believe her, the truth was, "Little mama, you been back in the city for all of two days and will be skipping back out just as quick. You don't know that for sure."

"These are still my people!" she defended, her enthusiasm making me smirk as she continued, "This area is… it just isn't like that. It's never been like that. But I understand if you're still a little paranoid about it. And I *completely* understand if you don't wanna come tonight because of that."

As crazy as it sounded, her being so understanding only made me want to show up for her even more, scraping my bottom lip with my teeth before I assured her, "Nah, I'ma come. Can't have some lame ass niggas tryna come at you crazy; security guards, be damned."

With a smirk, she groaned, "*Mmmhmm.* Sounds like you're concerned about a little more than just my safety, Orlando."

"Shit, what you expect? You ain't no ordinary woman, Aspen Watson. Walked in here and turned heads in a damn... oversized sweatshirt and biker shorts. And I already know you about to be on another level tonight."

Honestly, that part of it was probably what excited me most. Seeing Aspen dressed down in her own special way like she was today was a vibe in itself. But seeing Aspen all dressed up already had me anxious to get her back to her hotel room for the night, especially when she gnawed into her lip to add, "With you on my side only making me look even better."

"*Eh*. I'll see what I can do," I told her with a shrug that made her give a playful roll of her eyes as she pulled herself out of my hold.

"Anyway! Let me get out of here before your clients start a riot. You're still picking me up tonight, right?"

"As long as Kelvin still has me on the payroll. Otherwise, you gotta call a jitney," I teased, her sharp inhale in response making me laugh as I moved towards the door and admitted, "I'm playin'. I'll be there. I'd *be there* regardless; *for you*."

"*How cute*," she sang, giving me an adorable look to match that had a nigga feelin' goofy when I told her, "Aight, aight. Enough of that sweet sucka shit. I'll see you later, little mama."

She waited until we were back on the shop floor to reply, "You better." And while I thought that was end of her visit, I was completely caught off-guard when she turned back around and lifted to her tippy-toes for a kiss in front of everybody, sealing it with a little pat to my cheek when she finally said, "Bye, Orlando."

My, "*Bye, Aspen*," came out as more of a whisper as I watched her every step out of the shop, then continued watching until she safely disappeared into the car she must've used to get here since I wasn't driving her today. And the second I finally shook out of the trance she'd left me in to get back to my booth, I heard Mr. Clyde shout, "Gotdamn, boy! She's got you buttercream frosting whipped!"

The whole shop roared with a laugh that had me shaking my head as I told him, "Man, go back to sleep."

"I already slept through one fine woman walking in here. Now I gotta stay up just in case Thelma from *Good Times* shows up. You know she's still just as fine now as she was back on the show," Mr. Clyde said, on some old school shit that had most of the youngins in the shop confused and all the oldheads agreeing since they were the ones who knew who he was talking about.

Meanwhile, I was solely focused on getting back to my client, peeping to see where I had left off in his cut until Danny said, "I ain't gon' lie. I ain't think you had that in you, chief. Good shit, bruh. For real."

While my first instinct was to be offended and respond as such, I only offered him a nod, hoping that would dead all the conversation surrounding me and Aspen. And though it did from Danny, it didn't from the client in his chair who chimed in, "Gotta be tough, though. Knowing you don't really stand a chance with her long-term, but still playing it like you do."

My clippers were already in my hand when I told him, "I don't really think it's your business either way."

From my peripheral, I caught the shrug of his protective cape as he continued, "I'm just sayin'. Your regular ass is competing with actors, ball players, niggas who just got long money in general. Why would she want you when she's got access to all that?"

Considering this nigga was a nobody to me, I wasn't sweating his commentary enough to even respond. But for some reason, it bugged me to hear Mr. Clyde agree, "You know, he's got a point in there somewhere. Better protect yourself, youngblood. Don't get too attached."

The thought of him being right was already manifesting in my head, even when Danny advised, "Man, don't listen to these dudes, Orlando. They don't know what it's like to have a shorty really rock with you for who you are."

"Who you are might get you the panties once or twice, but it damn sure ain't enough to keep a girl like *that* interested. She's the type who wants to be treated to the finer things. Shit that's way outta your pay grade," his client added with a laugh that really got my blood boiling since his ass obviously didn't know when to shut the fuck up.

Dropping my clippers onto the booth, I snapped, "First of all, nigga you don't know my pockets. Second of all, you don't know Aspen like I do, so don't even speak on her like that."

Instead of taking me seriously, he only laughed some more. "Nigga been Driving Miss. Daisy for two days and now he think he knows somebody. Aight, bruh. You got it."

I honestly don't even know how it happened. But one second,

I was standing at my booth and the next I had my hands around the dude's neck as Danny and my client both tried - *and failed* - to pull me off of him. It wasn't until I heard Tiana squeal, "*What the hell is going on in here?!*" that I actually let go, already feeling guilty about disrespecting her spot over his bum ass.

With my hands up, I told her, "I'm sorry, Tiana. I..."

She cut me off with a look of concern. "Orlando, are you okay?"

The dude must not have gotten enough since he still found it in himself to ask, "Is *he* okay?! This nigga just tried to kill me with his bare hands, and you're asking about him?!"

"Yes! Because I know you must've said something ignorant like you always do," Tiana replied with a scowl before turning back to me with that same concerned expression. "Orlando?"

To cool off, I started pacing back and forth as I told her, "I'm good, I'm good. *My bad.* I'm better than that. That's my fault."

It might've sounded like enough to me, but Tiana wasn't impressed, grabbing my arm to drag me to the back room where she snapped, "Don't scare me like that, man! *I...* I've never seen you get like that before; never seen that dark look in your eyes before. And I wasn't even planning on coming in today, but I'm glad I showed up when I did, or his ass might've really been dead."

Shaking my head, I assured her, "Nah, I wasn't gonna kill him. I know just when to stop."

That only made her sigh. "Look, I know it's in your blood or whatever, but you gotta leave all that hood shit outside of the shop, Orlando. This is my business, *my livelihood*, which means I have to protect it. I can't have it turning into a damn crime scene over some petty nonsense between you and a customer."

Though I knew she was right, I was still quick to remind her, "I told you I wasn't gonna kill him, Tiana. And that wasn't even on no hood shit. He came for me as a man, so he had to deal with the consequences."

"Well you still have too much to lose now to be dishing out consequences that could ultimately land you in jail; *especially* over him."

Nodding, I agreed, "You right. I was buggin'. It won't happen again, Boss Lady."

"It better not. Now stay in here until Danny sends him on his way. I'm not taking any chances of him saying something else slick to set you off."

Since I really didn't have time to be waiting for Danny if I wanted to get out of here on time, I, *once again*, insisted, "I'm good, Tiana. For real. And my client has been here since before Aspen even showed up, so I need to finish him up before I get too behind schedule."

Stopping in her tracks, she turned back to ask, "*Wait.* Aspen was here?"

"Yeah, she just stopped by to say what's up," I explained, trying to sound as nonchalant as possible so Tiana wouldn't even think to put two and two together.

Of course she did anyway, a knowing smirk on her face when she crossed her arms and questioned, "Did that little... *situation* have anything to do with her?"

Brushing a hand against the back of my neck, I told her, "Nah. I mean, not really. It kinda started off about her, but then he made it personal."

It sounded good in my head until Tiana responded with an unconvinced groan. "*Mmmhmm.* Sounds like somebody's been bitten by the lovebug. First she's inviting you to Thanksgiving dinner, sitting in your lap eating dessert and shit. And now she's surprising you here at the shop? That girl is *in-to* you, dude."

When she mentioned someone being bitten by the lovebug, I assumed she was talking about me. But the fact that she'd noticed the ways in which Aspen had reciprocated that feeling had me questioning why I had let ol' boy and Mr. Clyde get to me in the first place; something she left me to think about as she went back out to the shop floor and I got myself together to finish out the day.

ASPEN

ASHY ASPEN WAS OFFICIALLY DEAD.

At least, that's what the fine ass girl looking back at me in the mirror said as I fluffed my short curls around with my fingers just as there was a knock at the door. Knowing who was on the other side, I smiled with anticipation of what his reaction to me would be. But I'd be damned if he didn't hijack the moment when I opened the door to find him in a fly ass all-black suit that hugged his thick frame in all the right places, making him look downright delicious. In fact, I couldn't even give him a proper greeting, stuck standing there with wide eyes as I whispered, "Oh… *my God.*"

The smirk he responded with only made him that much more attractive when he said, "What's up, Aspen?"

"Uh… let's start with you, sir? I mean, *damn.* I thought I was looking good and then you showed up looking like a *whole* snack. The snack cabinet. Zaddy really showed up as an entire vending machine full of snacks."

The rumbling chuckle he let out sent a tremor through me that made my knees weak, grateful I hadn't put my shoes on yet since I definitely would've stumbled on my heels. "Yo, you gon' let me in or just keep throwing jokes?"

I moved to the side making space for him to enter, but not without telling him, "Oh, these aren't jokes at all. These are the facts. You got *Hostess* beat, baby. A whole company of delicious snacks, and you won. I stan a snack legend."

"You silly, for real," he laughed, gnawing into his lip as he gave me onceover before he asked, "But I mean, if I'm a vending machine, what the hell does that make you? A fuckin' concession stand? *Fine ass.*"

While I was glad he had noticed, his compliment wasn't enough for me to steal the spotlight as I told him, "I might be a baby snack too, but you're definitely the king of snackdom right now, Orlando."

"What's a king without his queen, Aspen?" he asked teasingly, pulling me into a hug that included his cologne's assault on my nostrils that easily made me moan after the first inhale.

In fact, I stole a second greedy whiff before I answered, "In your case, a fine ass nigga who better keep his hands to himself before I miss out on a bag tonight fuckin' around with his handsome behind."

Smirking, he insisted, "Nah, I wouldn't do you like that. I'm a gentleman, meaning I'd fuck you good and still get you to the lounge on time so you don't miss out on no money."

"See what I mean? A legend," I teased, earning myself a kiss to the neck that only made me moan even louder than the cologne had as I pushed him away with a giggle. "Let me go grab my shoes so we can get going before I'm forced to test how much of a gentleman you really are."

Catching a smack to my ass on my way to the bedroom, I could already tell tonight was going to be one for the ages. My family would be in the building, old friends were sure to show up too. There would be good drinks flowing, better music bumping, and of course, Orlando would be by my side the entire time.

Oh, and let's not forget the easy check I was about to make.

It was a win all-around, making the grin on my face come naturally until I walked back into the living room and found Orlando glaring out of the window, appearing to be in deep thought about something. Placing a hand against his bicep to get his attention, I simply asked, "You good?"

It was clear he had to shake out of whatever he was thinking about when he sighed, "*Yeah.* Yeah, I'm good."

"You sure?"

He sighed again. "Yeah, I was just… aight, so earlier at the shop today, I got into a little altercation."

"A little altercation?!"

"Just keep listening," he requested with a halfhearted smile that only partially calmed me down since… *a little altercation?!*

It was a struggle, but I managed to stay quiet as he pulled me to the couch for the both of us to sit down, only worrying me even more by the time he started, "So after you left, this random nigga in the shop was talking shit about how you couldn't possibly wanna fuck with a nigga like me for real, how you got access to niggas with more status and all that. And I… I choked him. Not because of that specifically, but… I guess I'm sharing all of this because that whole situation just made me realize that I *for real* fucks with you, Aspen. Like, I fucks with you on a level I ain't never even experienced with anyone else before. And that shit is scary cause I know there's some truth about me maybe not having it all and there's always the possibility of you wanting that, but…"

Grabbing his hand, I cut him off. "I'm with you, Orlando. I may not know what our future holds right now this second, and it honestly scares me shitless that it only took me a couple days to like you this damn much because you could very well decide you want something different too. But make no mistakes, you are not *at all* alone in how you feel."

The boyish smirk he gave me in response made my heart flutter when I added, "And by the way, whoever said that deserved to be choked for not minding his business. And his mama's a ho."

With a laugh, he leaned in and pressed his forehead to mine as he whispered, "Glad you feel me, baby." Then he gave me a sweet little kiss to the corner of my lips to show his appreciation, staring into my eyes and communicating the things he'd just shared with a look that told me he'd meant every word.

Returning his look with a sexy one of my own, I admitted, "I know you hate me calling you cute, but that spiel was like… top two and not two cute shit."

He immediately pulled away with a chuckle, standing up and straightening out his suit as he said, "Yeah, aight. Sucka time is officially over. Let's get outta here before I gotta remind you who I really am."

Leading us to the door, I tossed over my shoulder, "Is that a threat or a promise? Either way, I'm already wet for it."

He chuckled again. "You crazy, little mama. But I like that shit."

"Top five reason why you fuck with me, right?" I teased as we loaded the elevator, Orlando standing behind me and keeping a gentle hand at my waist the entire ride down to the lobby. And in the car, he kept a hand latched onto my thigh as he drove to the point that - *even though I loved it* - I joked, "I promise I'm not gonna jump out while the cars rolling if you let me go."

It was almost like he hadn't even realized he was doing it the way he snatched his hand away in a quickness. "My bad. I guess I just like touching you."

Grabbing his hand, I put it right back where it was. "Say less. Do more. *Please.* Cause I'm probably gonna be whining about how much I miss you and your touch come next week. Matter of fact..." Using my free hand to push the hem of my dress up, I leaned back in the seat and put his hand right between my thighs. Then I moved his fingers to exactly where I wanted them against the seat of my panties, making him smirk.

"You playin' with fire, Aspen."

"No, *you're* playing with fire, Orlando," I told him, the feel of his fingertips bypassing the fabric to rub lazy circles against my swollen clit making me close my eyes in ecstasy as we passed street after street. Then he pulled his hand away from me and slipped the same finger into his mouth before he agreed, "Definitely fire."

As expected, I wanted much, *much* more. But unfortunately, we were already pulling up to the lounge so I'd have to wait until later since now, it was game time. After a quick check of my face in the mirror, I waited for Orlando to help me out of the car, a little surprised to see just how many people were waiting outside in line. And once they realized it was me who had arrived, the crowd went nuts with cheers and requests for pictures, a few that I granted before I gave a wave and let Orlando lead us past security.

With the line that was outside, I was shocked to see how packed the inside of *The Max* was too, the music loud and the bartenders busy which meant business was already doing well. And while I mentally patted myself on the back for negotiating a little extra coin, I was also happy to be using my influence to help my favorite cousins get their money too.

Speaking of my favorite cousins...

After giving Orlando a quick dap, Kelvin announced, "The woman of the hour. Your section awaits, Miss. Watson."

He said it with some fake regal tone that had me cracking up laughing as I followed him towards the short set of stairs that led to VIP. But as we started to ascend them, Orlando put a hand against the small of my back and whispered in my ear, "I'ma run to the bathroom right quick. I'll be back."

I only got a chance to respond with a nod before I was distracted by a familiar voice saying, "There goes my twin blonde babe. I am *living* for this short do on you, Aspen!"

Turning around to see the face that matched the voice, Orlando quickly became forgotten as I squealed, "Jules! Oh my God! It's so good to see you! I didn't know you were coming!"

I already had her hemmed up in a hug when she said, "Now, sis. You know I couldn't miss your homecoming celebration, *especially* not at the spot I used to work at."

"You worked here?" I asked, surprised to hear it since the Jules I knew had always been a television star.

But it made sense once she explained, "I was a bartender here before I started acting. In fact, I was here working the day I got the call for my first audition. My *only* audition."

"And you've been killing it ever since. How's Levi?" I asked, the mention of her basketball player boo making her visibly light up even in the darkness of the club.

With a proud grin, she answered, "He's good! He would've came with me tonight, but they have a string of away games so he couldn't make it."

"Well he still came *through* you. Pregnancy slay on a thousand, mama," I complimented, the fact that her heels were higher than mine even with her baby bump serving all sorts of mommy goals.

Rubbing her bump, she groaned, "Girl, if you say so. Cause I definitely feel closer to my cattle sistren than anything."

Laughing, I brushed her off. "Oh, stop it. You fit in just fine around here."

"It's actually funny being back in here considering this is where Levi and I first met before we even became roommates****. And now I'm carrying our baby. I really let him turn me into the pregnant bitch in the club. I gotta fight him for that shit."

How she got to that particular conclusion, I wasn't sure. But that didn't stop me from laughing even harder when I told her, "I see you haven't lost a bit of crazy."

Instead of responding to me, she looked past me with a grin on her face and said, "Well hello to you, fine sir."

Turning to see who had stolen her attention, I shouldn't have been surprised to find the finest man in the building, grinning my damn self when I introduced the two. "Jules, this is Orlando. Orlando, this is Jules. One of my *favorite* sitcom stars."

"Coming from the baddest bitch to hit the big screen. You giving out *premium* gas tonight, I see," she teased, sticking her hand out for a shake as she continued, "But it's nice to meet you, Orlando. If you're connected to this woman in any way, you are *so* blessed. She's a literal angel."

While he returned her handshake, I started dabbing at my invisible tears. "Okay, now who's giving out premium gas? *Jesus.* About to have me crying in the club."

"Which will only make me cry too, and this baby makes me do the *ugliest* of boohoos. So just take the compliment and save the tears, babe," she insisted with a wink. "I'm gonna go say what's up to some of my old bartender boos, but I'll be sure to swing by before I get out of here."

"You better!" I called after her just as two of her bartender friends delivered a few bottles to our section. And now that Orlando was back, I got a chance to really process what he had even said, turning his way to tease, "Had to go take a boo-boo, huh?"

His eyebrow piqued with amusement. "*What?* Nah. I was just… having a little moment. The crowd, *all these people*, had me trippin' for a second. I'm good now, though."

Now that I knew he'd had a bad reaction to the environment, I felt bad for joking, placing a hand against his bicep to ask, "Are you sure? I'm sure Maxwell won't mind you crashing in his office if you need a break. Come on. I'll go with you."

I was already pulling him towards the secret office door when he pulled me back with a smile. "I'm *good*, Aspen. *Swear.* Now put that ass on me so I can remember what I came here for in the first place."

The way he said it had me ready to take him up to Maxwell's office for different reasons, wrapping my arms around his neck to tease, "Oh, so you didn't actually come to support me? Only to feel on my ass?"

As if to answer my question, he grabbed an attractively-arrogant handful of my left cheek, giving it a squeeze that made me moan as he answered, "*Literally* the only reason. So what's up?"

Averting my eyes and popping my lips, I playfully replied, "I mean, I *guess* I can throw a little somethin' your way."

"*Mmhm.* That's what I thought."

With perfect timing, the DJ started playing a mix of Cardi B songs that was really all it took for me to be in turn up mode, Orlando tickled as hell to see me rapping along and twerking to one of my favorites as the DJ gave me a shoutout.

"We got our hometown girl, Aspen Watson, in the building! I see you, baby!"

"Yeah. We see you, baby," Nori mocked with a teasing grin as her and Tiana finally joined us in the section, Kelvin and Maxwell not too far behind and sending even more bottles of liquor which got emptied *real* quick amongst the six of us. But with as much money as they were making tonight, they were more than happy to supply whatever we needed to keep us live and keep the party going.

And man, was it going.

While I was only joking back at the shop when I told Orlando the party was going to be a movie, it seemed like a serious claim now with how good of a time everyone seemed to be having. Even he was on his feet with a drink in his hand and a content tipsy grin on his face, turning my way to say, "Thanks for this, little mama."

"How about you thank me later with that *mouf*?" I asked teasingly even though he and I both knew I wasn't playing at all which was why he only shook his head and muttered, "*Silly ass...*" in response. But after the party was over and we finally made it back to the hotel, he showed me a lot more than just what his mouth could do, the liquor turning him a whole different breed of nasty that I was excited to match with a little liquor-induced nastiness of my own.

Not that either of us really needed it.

Still, that didn't stop me from trying to suck the skin off of his dick. And it didn't stop him from *almost* making me tap out when he lifted me onto his shoulders to eat my pussy in the air until I came all over his beard. And it didn't stop *us* from gladly submitting to whatever sex positions the other person had in mind; my reverse cowgirl being the one that earned a guttural, "*Fuck. You bouta make me cum, baby*."

I'd heard him loud and clearly, but I was too close to my own release to actually stop riding him, cumming hard and sliding forward just in time for him to nut right against my ass. And while I was honestly impressed by my quick reflexes in such a hazy state as I worked to catch my breath, Orlando wasted no time issuing me a firm warning. "You better quit playin' like that, little mama. Cause if you lettin' me shoot the club up, I'm not shootin' to miss."

I was honestly a little disgusted with myself for getting so turned on by his fine ass already being ready to get me pregnant. But considering we were nowhere near the family planning stage, I wiped his nut off of my ass with my fingertip and teased, "*Uhh… Alexa*, play *Rain* by SWV at ignorant levels."

Orlando's eyebrow immediately piqued as he brought a hand to his chin and said, "Hold up. *That's* what they were singing about?"

Returning his inquisitive look with one of my own, I asked, "Is it not and I've been thinking it was this whole time?"

If it wasn't, it sure matched up with the concept well. But instead of agreeing with me, Orlando only laughed. "*Yeahhhh.* I think you might just be a little too into cumshots, Aspen."

With a shrug, I crawled up the bed and snuggled up against his chest, wishing I could see his face when I joked, "Well those will be the only kinda shots I'm taking to the ass; unlike you."

The rumble in his chest when he laughed vibrated right against my temple. "*Wow.* So you going for the jugular now, huh? Gimme ten minutes and I'ma make you pay for that shit."

"Can't wait," was what I told him. But it soon became clear that neither one of us had truly taken into account how long of a day it had been since both of our asses were knocked out in no time at all.

In fact, the only reason we woke up was because of Orlando's phone incessantly vibrating against the nightstand, his quick glance to see who was calling making him hop up from the bed as he hissed, "*Shit.* I gotta get down to the shop. I already got a client waiting on me."

Seeing him leave the bed had me pouting like a baby, quick to suggest, "Just tell him to grow his hair out, or put a hat on, or… let Mr. Clyde do it."

"If I let Mr. Clyde fuck his head up, he'd probably never come back to the shop," he replied with a chuckle, putting his clothes on from the night before when he added, "But what I *can* do… is clear my schedule for the afternoon so we can spend it together before you get up outta here on me."

Clutching the comforter to my chest, I told him, "When you say it like that, it sounds like I'm dying. I'm just going back to work."

"Yeah, in a different city for who knows how long. But don't get it twisted, your grind is much respected."

"And yours is *not*," I countered, quickly correcting, "Well, it *is*. But not right now cause I don't want you to leave."

According to the smirk on his face, my whining had him flattered. But it wasn't enough for him to stop getting dressed, instead insisting, "Go spend some time with your family. Ain't that what you came here for?"

When he sat down on the bed to put his shoes on, I draped myself over his broad shoulders, my breasts pressed into his back when I admitted, "They might've been the reason I came, but you're the reason I wish I could stay a little while longer."

Peeking over his shoulder at me with a smile, he confessed, "Aight, now I know what you mean with that cute shit."

"Oh, whatever!" I squealed with a laugh, falling back onto the bed as he stood up to grab his wallet and keys. Then with a simple kiss to the forehead, he bid me a, "*See you later*" leaving me to figure out how to spend the rest of my day until he got off of work.

ORLANDO

MY LAST CLIENT of the day might've gotten the quickest haircut in barbershop history. That's how anxious I was to get back to Aspen; being sure not to compromise the quality of my work while also going as fast as possible so I could get out of the shop at a reasonable hour since my time left with Aspen was extremely limited.

Her flight wasn't until later tonight, and it didn't take long to get through security at the little airport in the city, so it wasn't like she had to be there stupid early. But time wasn't slowing down no matter how much either of us wished it could, which is how we found ourselves back at a surprisingly-empty Jackie Robinson Park.

This time, instead of boning like teenagers in my *Cadillac*, we were chillin' at one of the picnic tables eating sandwiches since Aspen claimed she couldn't leave the city without having one more. And with the sunset serving as our background, the shit was honestly a little romantic until Aspen randomly asked, "Are you gonna break my heart?"

"*What*?"

Peeking up from her food, she repeated, "Are you? Let me know now before I get more invested in this than I already am."

While I could appreciate her speaking her mind, the truth

was, "Shit, if that's the case, I should've been asking you the same question after that first night we spent together."

She only gave a halfhearted smirk in response, picking at her food like the thought was starting to make her lose her appetite. But since I wasn't about to let her waste a good sandwich, I stood up and moved to her side of the table, grabbing her hand to remind her, "You told me I wasn't alone in how I felt, so that means you already know I'm just as invested as you are. You got me, little mama. Real shit."

Her smirk turned into more of a teasing grin when she looked directly into my eyes with her pretty ass hazels and asked, "Real shit?"

Doubling down, I repeated, "Real. *Shit.*"

Gnawing into her lip, she pulled herself onto my lap, keeping an arm wrapped around my shoulder when she said, "Guess that means I'll be coming home a little more often now, huh?"

Snapping my head back, I asked, "*A little*? More like, whenever you can. Even if I gotta fuck you in my car in the back of the airport garage and put your pretty ass right back on the plane."

She started laughing even though I was deadass. Little mama had turned me into something like an addict for that pussy. She knew it too, her adorable little grin full-blown when she asked, "You gonna come see me too, right?"

With a nod, I answered, "If that's what you want, I'll be wherever you at. The city don't even matter."

"Even if it's international?" she challenged, her eyebrow piqued as she started to stroke my facial hair.

"I mean, *shit.* Let me cut a few more heads and get my bread up first, but then I got you."

She laughed again, adjusting in my lap to wrap both arms around me. "Once I build my empire, you can be the Stedman to my Oprah."

"Yeah, aight. I'ma hold you to that," I told her with a chuckle of my own. "But in the meantime, I'ma be busy building my own shit."

While cutting hair in Tiana's shop might've been what got me here and I was more than grateful for the opportunity she'd given me, I still had aspirations of possibly owning a little something of my own one day. Or maybe even taking my skills mobile and working for a clientele of a different caliber. Either way, Aspen seemed confident when she said, "This city is definitely the perfect place for that. It's a great place to live, period."

"I mean, I found you here. So you might be onto something," I replied, catching the goofy look on Aspen's face that told me she was about to call me out for saying some cute shit. But honestly, I didn't even care, willing to do that and more if it meant making her happy.

Damn, she really got you good.

Now that we'd settled things, Aspen felt more comfortable finishing her food and I did the same. Then we took a little trip to the swings since Aspen claimed she needed to redeem herself from the last time she was here as a kid and got clowned for being too afraid to jump off mid-air.

Her little ass was flying today, though.

She even made me capture a video of her doing it a second time to share with her followers on social media that turned into us having to hurry up and leave since her local fans immediately started showing up to the park in response to it.

Real celebrity shit.

Since we still had a little bit of time, I started to head to my crib in hopes of squeezing in one last fuck until she said, "I'd like to make one more stop before we head to the airport, if you don't mind. Actually, two more stops."

"Where to?"

It took her a moment to respond. But when she did, her hesitation made sense. "My parents' gravesite. I need to leave them some flowers. Well I need to go *get* some flowers, and then take them to their gravesite. *If we can.*"

With a nod, I simply replied, "I got you." Then I made the short drive to the local grocery store, Aspen starting to get out of the car with me until I told her, "Nah, you stay here. You've caused enough hysteria today."

Thankfully she agreed without much fuss, making my trip to grab some flowers a quick one before we took the GPS-guided trip to the cemetery. And once we were on the grounds, Aspen did the rest of the guiding to her parents' companion burial plot that included a joint headstone with their names on each side and their wedding date in the middle; something I found interesting since the two of them had died more than a decade apart.

As if she had read my mind, Aspen said, "I remember visiting my mother here as a kid and seeing my dad's name already engraved on the headstone. But he'd always be standing right next to me, so it was strange to even imagine him ever being here. Now they're together again."

The sadness in her voice ate at me, though I was still sure to mention, "I bet they're real proud of you up there."

"Yeah. *Probably*," she quietly replied with a shrug before asking, "Can you just… give me a minute? *Alone*?"

"Absolutely. Take your time. I'll be at the car," I told her, stopping to give her a kiss on the forehead before I left her to it. But once I was there, I couldn't help watching her every move as she bent to place the flowers, ran her hand against each name on the headstone, then looked to be saying a quick prayer before giving them each a finger kiss.

Her head was down the entire walk back to the car so I couldn't see her face until she climbed in, my first question being, "You good?"

"Yeah, I'm good," was her answer, though the obvious tears in her eyes contradicted it. But since I knew it wouldn't really be helpful to press her about it, I simply reached over and grabbed her hand, giving it a supportive squeeze that only made the tears start falling as she turned towards the window and shared, "Another reason I haven't come home often as of late is because of that. Because *that* never gets any easier. It's like the more successful I become, *the more I accomplish*, the more it hurts because they're not here to share in it with me, you know? When something good happens, my father is always the first person I wanna tell. But I can't because he's... *here*."

Rubbing my thumb against the back of her hand, I honestly struggled with what to say knowing there was nothing that could make that type of hurt go away. Still, I tried my best to at least soothe her for the moment when I offered, "I may not go to church every week, but I do believe in it all. And I know he's watching over you. The both of them are. The same way my mama watched over me that night at the club. Hell, she's probably the one who sent your pretty ass my way. Like some type of heaven hook-up or some shit."

Her little giggle in response was a good sign, her lip pulled between her teeth when she turned back my way to suggest, "I think my silly might be rubbing off on you, Orlando."

Shaking my head, I agreed, "*Damn.* I think you might be right."

She giggled some more, pulling her hand away to wipe her face with an exaggerated sigh. "Thank you for that. And thank you for… coming with me."

"Glad to. Now let's get outta here before you try to blame me for making you miss your flight."

It didn't take long for her to get right back into teasing mode, slugging me in the arm when she said, "Come on, gentleman. Don't fuck up your perfect streak at the last second." Then we laughed together as we made the drive to the airport that truly wasn't long enough considering it was the last time I'd be seeing Aspen for who knew how long.

"*Hopefully not too long,*" I thought as I went to pull her luggage from the trunk before making my way to open her door for the final time. And I suppose I wasn't the only one trying to prolong our last few moments together since Aspen was slow to get out, stopping on the sidewalk to say, "*Well…* this is it."

"Yeah, I guess it is."

Instead of wasting time exchanging pleasantries, she threw herself into my arms, pulling my face down to hers for a kiss that was as sweet as the first one she'd ever given me back in her hotel bathroom. And considering how deeply we'd fallen for each other since then, it also felt like a guarantee that it wouldn't be our last; something for me to hold onto when she finally pulled away to whisper against my lips, "Until next time, outsider Orlando."

"Until next time, little mama."

Again, she was slow to move, this time with her walk inside the airport. But after one final peek back and a wave goodbye, she disappeared into the sliding doors, taking a piece of my heart with her.

She'd be back, though.

I trusted that she'd meant everything she said, trusted that she was serious about figuring out how to make this whole thing work. And since I knew I was too, I was fine with missing her while she continued after her dreams, the whole thing only inspiring me to focus even harder on my own. In fact, my drive home had turned into something like a brainstorming session for all the moves I wanted to make in the near future, putting an extra pep in my step by the time I pulled up and could actually get to my phone to jot some of it down. But before I did that, I checked the text I had gotten from my little superstar.

Little Mama: "Welcome to my world." {1 attachment}

Clicking to open the attachment, I was surprised to see it was a screenshot from *Instagram* with a picture of us at *The Max* from the night before that neither me nor Aspen had taken. But it made sense once I saw it had been posted by a gossip blog and then read the caption.

"Actress Aspen Watson caught canoodling around her hometown with new mystery man."

For a second, I was a little annoyed since it wasn't like I had given anyone permission to take a picture of me, let alone share the shit with some trash ass blog site. But my annoyance went away instantly once I saw the top comment included in the screenshot.

"@aspenwatson: He's cute, right? ;)"

She was making a statement, letting the world know that I was the one who had her attention while also managing to tease me from afar with that cute shit. And though there very well could've been a bunch of negative comments about us from strangers with nothing else to do on the post, none of that shit even mattered when I finally sent her a reply.

Outsider Orlando: "More than happy to be here. Have a safe flight, baby."

ASPEN

Three Days Until Christmas

WITH CHRISTMAS RIGHT around the corner, my holiday fate was only becoming more and more real - I wasn't going to make it home.

I knew it was always a possibility with how off the film schedule had been for the last few days, but that didn't stop me from holding out hope. The same hope that only dwindled with each scene we filmed, *and refilmed,* because people not named Aspen kept fuckin' up.

By the time we were finally called for a walkaway lunch, I was beyond annoyed, opting to go straight to my trailer to decompress instead of actually finding something to eat. But once I was there, I only became even sadder after I checked my phone and saw a text from Orlando asking the same question he'd been asking me for the last couple of days.

Outsider Orlando: "Think you gonna make it for Christmas?"

Little Mama: "It's not looking good, babe. :/"

Outsider Orlando: "You are, though. ;)"

While I appreciated the compliment, the fact that we hadn't seen each other in person since my Thanksgiving visit had me quick to dispute his claims.

Little Mama: "You don't know that. You haven't seen me. I could've turned butt ugly in a month."

Outsider Orlando: "Aspen, you always look good. And I just saw how fine you were lookin' a couple minutes ago on set before your mad ass stormed off."

"A couple minutes ago on set…?" I read out loud, confused until I saw the door of my trailer being opened *and*… "Oh my God! Orlando! What are you doing here?!"

My arms were already wrapped around him in the tightest hug I could give as he chuckled and answered, "When you said you didn't think you were gonna be able to make it home for the holiday, I figured why not just come to you."

"But how did you… get all the way here? *On set?*"

With a shrug, he simply replied, "I have my ways." But from the side eye I gave him in response, he knew damn well that explanation wasn't good enough, prompting him to continue, "Nah, I actually wasn't sure how I was going to pull off this part of it. But when I showed up, one of the assistants outside recognized me from all those pictures of us on *Instagram* and plugged me in once I told her I was here to surprise you."

Whoever it was deserved a damn raise for helping my man get to me with perfect timing since the day had been all-around shitty before he showed up, urging me to ask, "Do you remember her name? I've gotta grant her a Christmas wish or something for this."

Shaking his head, Orlando said, "Nah, little mama. It's already handled. She was *well* compensated for her assistance. But for the record, her name was Madison."

"Well shoutout to Madison," I tossed out, squeezing him even tighter as I sighed, "God, I can't believe you're really here."

It almost seemed like a dream, even when he teased, "You acting like you really missed me or somethin'."

Snapping my head back with a frown, I repeated, "*Acting like*? Nah, I left that acting shit out there on set. This is very, *very* real."

The lingering kiss he gave me to my forehead in response was exactly what I needed, my shoulders sinking as he said, "Good. Cause I missed your pretty ass too. A nigga ain't been sleepin' too well without you all over me at night, so I needs that as soon as I can get it."

Considering it was still the middle of the day, I had a feeling sleep wasn't what he was really talking about, making it easy for me to tease, "You mean, you just need some good pussy as soon as you can get it?"

Again, he shrugged. "Shit, I need both. I need… *you*, Aspen Watson. *All of you*. However I can get you."

Little did he know, I'd pretty much felt the same way about him since that time he picked me up from the airport, before I even knew the magnitude of what I'd actually be getting. But instead of indulging him with a bunch of cute shit I could save for later, I went and made sure the door of my trailer was locked before I started unbuttoning my pants and told him, "In that case, come on home, Orlando."

THE END.

FEATURED TITLES

*Read all about Kelvin & Tiana in, In Spite of it All

Love is not on the drink menu.

At least not for Tiana St. Patrick as she nurses the broken heart caused by her ex after their sudden, unexpected, yet incredibly necessary break-up. But when a generous stranger offers to jumpstart her healing process, and doubles down with a chance encounter at her business, she can't help but wonder if his presence is worth something more than just a helping hand even though he seems to be exactly the type of guy she should be avoiding at all costs.

Kelvin Watson is a man on a mission. Between the lounge he co-owns with his big brother, and the ladies that frequent it, it's no secret that he has plenty to keep himself busy.

Still, when a particular patron catches his eye and then manages to ease her way into his heart with her easygoing vibe and natural charm, he can't help himself in pushing for something more. And when more turns into a discovery of past indiscretions, present reservations, and future obstacles, Tiana and Kelvin find themselves attempting to navigate their budding romance, in spite of it all.

(Note: This book is a spin-off of, Love at First Spite. While it can be read as a standalone, it does contain major spoilers for that title.)

**Read all about Lincoln & Savannah in,
A Tale of Two Cities: A Halloween Novella

When people think of a holiday for love, they automatically come up with Valentine's Day.
But who's to say that's the only one?

A trip to sin city for a Halloween-themed joint bachelor-bachelorette party is all it takes for Savannah and Lincoln to learn this the... not so hard way. ;)

A Tale of Two Cities Collection:
Cute & Sweet Millennial Meets Over a Holiday,
All With One Thing In Common; Cities.

Note: This is a short novella with a happy-for-now ending.
If you prefer your stories longer, I'd recommend checking out another Alexandra Warren project. :)

***Read all about Nori & Maxwell in, Love at First Spite

Love is not on the drink menu.

At least not for Nori Davis as she basks in the single life which includes frequent happy hour visits, lots of alone time in bed with her "favorite things", and of course being sought after by guys she's not interested in.

But when she's caught off-guard by a man who's a little different than usual - on a mission a little different than usual - she can't help but to get lost in his seemingly impossible potential no matter how hard she tries to fight it.

Maxwell Watson doesn't have time for a serious relationship. Between opening a lounge, being the owner of a lounge and… the lounge, there's just no room for anything beyond it.

Still, when he notices one particular patron who is palpably dissatisfied with his business, going after her for more information isn't even a question. And when more turns into a whirlwind of energy neither can deny - turns into an encounter that can't be forgotten - Nori and Maxwell find themselves attempting to navigate what can only be identified as love at first… spite.

****Read all about Jules & Levi in, Accidental Arrangements

Not all arrangements are truly by design. Some happen by chance, by fate, by… accident.

Jules Tyler is in desperate need of a roommate. Levi Graham is in desperate need of a room. And while it may seem like the perfect match from the outside, it doesn't take long for egos, expectations, and experiences to say otherwise.

But what happens when the proximity builds a chemistry between them that neither is prepared to handle? Will living as roommates become too much to bear? Or will it be the perfect jumpstart to a happily ever after?

(Note: While it can be read as a standalone, this book does contain major spoilers for the Spite Series.)

A TALE OF TWO CITIES

A CHRISTMAS NOVELLA

MADISON

THIS MUST BE what Santa feels like all the time.

That was all I kept thinking as I made my way from Studio Lot A where I'd just dropped off a *ridiculously* fine man to surprise one of my favorite actresses, Aspen Watson, to the smaller Studio Lot B where I should've been twenty minutes ago.

So maybe more like, Santa on CP Time.

Still, if Aspen's excited squeal was any indication, it was worth being late - *according to industry standards* - for. Well, that and the fact that her man had stuffed my pockets with more than enough cash to give me a happy holiday even after my co-worker, Danielle, stormed over to me and shouted, "Madison, where have you been?! I've been looking all over for you!"

Completely ignoring her question, I asked one of my own. "Why were you looking for me?"

"Because you will not *believe* who just showed up to set!" she shouted excitedly, her eyes twinkling as she struggled to hold in the secret for even a second longer.

Thinking back on what was left of today's call sheet, it was easy to brush her off since I was pretty sure I knew exactly who she was talking about. In fact, I could only sigh when I replied, "My crush on G. Griffey is long gone, Dani. He's been happily married for a minute now, and it's past time for me to accept that.

I've already stopped leaving heart eye emojis on all of his *Instagram* pictures and everything. Well, *mostly...*"

There was that one picture of him recently rapping his latest hit at a charity event with his lip all curled up that just… *whew*.

Shaking her head, Dani replied, "Not him, Maddie. Dallas Bryant."

"*Dallas Bryant*?" I repeated, my face scrunching with confusion before my heart took off in a panic. "Dallas Bryant is on *our* set, and you let me show up to work today looking like this?! My hair is barely brushed, these jeans are from high school, my makeup is on hour fourteen of twelve-hour coverage, and I didn't even bother putting my contacts in this morning! Dani, I'm literally serving four-eyed hobo chic!"

Instead of offering me any assistance, Danielle only smirked as she insisted, "Well you better get over it quick cause him and Alexis are headed our way right now."

I couldn't help turning around to see if she was playing with me, only to discover she was being honest in the most satisfying way possible *since*… Dallas was just as fine in person as he looked in every picture I'd ever seen of him. With golden brown skin coating his face, including his chiseled jawline that was covered in a fresh, thick coat of facial hair, his bushy eyebrows that were just as dark as his eyes, and a fade with perfectly-sponged short curls on the top of his head that I already wanted to run my fingers through, I found myself cemented in place as I watched each confident step he took in our direction.

Thankfully, there was still enough distance between us for me to admire him without being a total creep. And the longer I stared, the more I realized that while Aspen's boyfriend from earlier had this mysterious attractiveness to him, Dallas Bryant wore his more overtly, stealing the attention of everyone in the room - *me included* - even when he was in the presence of some of the finest celebrities on the planet. In fact, his handsome in combination with how charismatic he was in every interview I'd watched of him almost made me wonder why he'd ever chosen to be behind the camera instead of in front of it. But apparently all my wondering had me teetering the line of being creepy now since my boss, Alexis, gave me a look to shake me out of it the second they finally made it over to us, the fact that she was already married to her fine ass college sweetheart making it easy for her to warn me with her eyes about my *hopefully-not-that-obvious* crush.

At least, I think that's what she's doing.

I was already squinting through my smudged-up glasses to check when she started to introduce us. "Danielle. Madison. This is Dallas Bryant. He's here to help me see the end of this Christmas special through since Jessaline decided she just *had* to go into labor last night."

"*I'm pretty sure it was the baby who actually decided, but…*" Dani muttered, earning a stiff side eye from our boss as she extended her hand. "It's nice to meet you, Mr. Bryant. Danielle Smith. Huge fan of your work."

Returning her handshake, his thick eyebrow piqued when he asked, "Oh yeah? What's your favorite project?"

"*Oh, God. I hope he doesn't ask me the same question,*" I thought, knowing I'd probably have to name his entire filmography since there was no way I could leave out any of the works by one of my favorite directors. I mean, he was the one whose film style I had studied, from his box office hits to his indie projects only available online, the one whose interviews I had used for inspiration during those long, *long* nights in film school when nothing I did seemed right, and the one who had me confident I'd be able to use my current job as a production assistant to break into the industry because he'd taken the same path.

Basically, he was something like my idol which meant I was literally mesmerized by his presence, especially once I saw the amused smirk on his face after Danielle finally replied, "Umm… all of them?"

"Good answer," he agreed with a chuckle, turning my way as he continued, "So if she's Danielle, that makes you Madison, right?"

Through my daze, I somehow managed to push my hand forward. "Madison Walker. Pleasure to meet you, Mr. Bryant."

We'd already met the quota as far as professional handshake

length went, but he kept ahold of my hand anyway to say, "Dallas is fine, Madison. Unless you prefer I call you Ms. Walker."

"Only when I'm nasty," was what immediately came to mind for obvious reasons. But after seeing the reactions on Dallas, Alexis, and even Dani's face, I realized that response hadn't only been in my head and…

"Oh my God, did I really just say that out loud..." I groaned, snatching my hand away to cover my mouth. And in an attempt to save me from my own demise, Alexis chimed in, "Madison and Danielle are two of my best production assistants. They'll be a great resource for you if there's anything you need while you're here over these next couple of days."

Dallas was already nodding along when Danielle emphasized, "Literally anything. I mean, *literally*. You name it, we got you. We're your girls."

With another chuckle, Dallas replied, "I'll keep that in mind. It was very nice to meet you, ladies. I'm sure I'll see y'all around."

"Most definitely," Danielle stated calmly, her cool demeanor making me a little jealous since it was clear I couldn't keep it together to save my life.

Once Alexis and Dallas continued on their way, my shoulders sank with disappointment, embarrassed that I hadn't been able to hold my own when dealing with an industry titan. They didn't stay down for long though, tensing upwards in reaction to Danielle smacking me on the arm when she whispered, "*Bitch.* Dallas Bryant must be into four-eyed hobo chic cause that man could not stop looking at your raggedy ass."

Pulling my glasses off my face, I used the bottom of my shirt to clean the lenses as best as I could while I replied, "He was *not,* Dani. He was just being polite."

She shook her head in disagreement. "No lie, Maddie. *Like…* he was lowkey giving you bedroom eyes. I mean, if I was into niggas, I'd definitely be jealous. Shit, I'm not into niggas and I'm *still* kinda jealous. So that should tell you just how serious I am."

While someone like Dallas Bryant showing even an inkling of interest in me would've been a Christmas wish come true - *a damn miracle, really* - I could only roll my eyes. "Whatever, Dani. I know you're messin' with me. You're just tellin' me this to set me up to make a bigger fool of myself later on."

Instead of confirming, she only giggled when she insisted, "Does it crack me up when you make a fool of yourself saying stupid awkward shit like *'only when I'm nasty'*? Absolutely. But I don't have to bait you, Maddie. You're already goofy as hell on your own."

"Damn. Good point," I thought, putting my glasses back on as I told her, "*Anyway*. I might not be as far as I wanna be, but I've still worked too hard to get to where I am in this industry, and I'm not about to blow it for anyone; not even the love of my film life Dallas Bryant."

It sounded good, but Danielle was quick to call me out. "I said he *lowkey* gave you bedroom eyes and you're already proclaiming you're not gonna risk it all, which means you're *definitely* gonna risk it all if given the opportunity and possibly end up ruining your industry reputation in the process. Damn, Maddie. It was nice working with you, girl."

This time, it was me smacking her on the arm, making her laugh even harder as both of our walkies went off. "Madison. Danielle. G. Griffey and his family are on the premises. Please standby."

"Copy that. M & D standing by," I replied for the both of us in my walkie, releasing the button as I told Dani, "*Welp*. Sounds like we have work to do which means it's officially time for you to get off my neck about this."

She didn't completely agree, the both of us walking towards Lot B's entrance as she asked, "Get off your neck about Dallas? *Sure*. But I already know this G. Griffey shit is about to be funny as hell."

Shaking my head, I told her, "It is no… *oh my God*."

Just like that, all of my words got caught in my throat as G. Griffey strolled into the building with his baby boy slung against his hip and his wife a few steps behind him carrying a diaper bag.

While she was a beauty in her own right, I couldn't take my eyes off the man whose early mixtapes were still in heavy rotation in my car as I gushed, "He's *beautiful*, Dani. And the baby! *I can't*."

This time, she actually agreed. "Their little matching outfits really are cute as hell."

Honestly, they were cuter than cute, and I knew they would look perfect on screen for the segment on their family's holiday traditions which was probably why they had dressed alike. But just as I started imagining myself in Mrs. G. Griffey's *So Kate Louboutins* that matched her husband's sneakers, I felt a tap on my shoulder.

"Excuse me. Madison?"

Without even turning around, I held a finger up to say, "Hold on just two sec… *wait.*"

Spinning on the heels of my overworn sneakers, I was quick to apologize to who had essentially become another one of my bosses. "I am *so* sorry. Can I help you find something, Mr. Bryant?"

He wasn't offended by my initial response, instead smirking as he said, "Actually, I was looking for you. I need your help with somethin'."

Doing my best to keep my internal panic to a minimum, I replied, "*Oh.* Of course." And I was already taking off behind him when I gave a quick peek back over my shoulder to Dani who immediately mouthed, "*Told you.*"

"*She can't be right,*" I decided in my head as I turned back around, almost bumping into Dallas's back when he came to a sudden stop in front of where they'd be filming to say, "Since we're gonna have a child on set during quite a bit of the interview but we want to keep the vibe as natural as possible, I need you to babyproof the area for me."

I was sure he was expecting a, "*Yes, sir*" or something equivalent in response. But as I looked at all the cords, and lights, and miscellaneous shit Baby G. Griffey could get his hands on knowing babies got their hands on everything, a frown grew to my face.

"*Babyproof the area*? Like… the entire thing?"

Nodding, he turned my way and put a hand to my shoulder to reply, "As much as you can, as best as you can, as quickly as you can. I just don't want his parents being worried the entire time since that energy will translate onto the screen."

I was already making a list in my head of mandatory things to do, like making sure certain cords were taped down properly as I gave Dallas a nod, his hand dropping from my shoulder when I whispered more to myself than him, "I knew we should've just filmed this at their house..."

Even though the comment wasn't directed at him, he still responded, "You're right. That would've been smart of us. *Well...* smart of *them*, since I wasn't exactly here to be a part of the pre-production plans. But hey, make sure you speak up next time you have a good idea like that, aight?"

Again, I nodded since I would've been a fool not to take what was solid professional advice. But the fact that he was giving me professional advice - *giving me directives, period* - was also a great reminder to stay in my lane, completely wiping away the tiny bit of hope I might've gotten from Dani's claims until Dallas brushed a quick and gentle thumb against my chin and said, "Thank you, Ms. Walker."

He even added a wink that told me I hadn't imagined his flirtatious move - *nor his use of Ms. Walker* - the whole thing putting a little extra pep in my step as I got to work on making the set as safe as possible.

It was the least I could do for my new... *boss.*

DALLAS

IT WAS USUALLY nothing for me to lock-in the second I stepped behind the camera. But admittedly, I was distracted as hell. And while it would've been easy for me to blame it on the fact that I'd been thrust into a directorial position at the ninth hour of this particular project, I knew the actual job really had nothing to do with it.

It was her.

The brown-skinned, curly-haired cutie with the glasses who was busting her ass to make sure things went off without a hitch the second production resumed. Her work ethic was admirable honestly, even when it came to the shit I could tell she didn't really want to do like making sure the set was safe for the baby. But it was her attention to detail that made even that seem like an easy task, pleasing both G. Griffey and his wife Reagan* in a way that made capturing their family dynamic a breeze for me.

Still, while I was grateful for her help - *her efficiency* - I was also a little annoyed by the fact that it was a struggle for me to keep my eyes off of her cute ass. Even now, as Alexis and I made small talk with the couple of the hour, I was peeking around to see if I could find her, hoping I'd catch her doing something that made her less attractive. But when I didn't spot her at all, I figured it was a sign for me to chill, turning my attention back to Reagan as she said,

"I can't wait to see how it all comes together, you guys. Thank you so much for the opportunity."

Extending her arms for a hug, Alexis replied, "Of course! Thank you guys for coming in. It was an honor to include you two. Well, you *three*."

With the ladies showing each other love, me and G did the same, Gavin pulling me in for a brohug as best as he could with his son his arms. "Good lookin' out, bruh. 'Preciate you."

"No doubt. You know it's always a pleasure workin' with you, G."

And that was true.

From the few music videos I'd shot for him for his sophomore album to the docuseries we'd put together following his most recent tour, Gavin had honestly become one of my favorite clients, a call I'd always answer if he needed some directorial work done. And it was almost as if he had read my mind when he replied, "Keep that same energy when I start working on this next album. Might need you for some behind the scenes promo shit."

"Whatever you need, you know I'm there if my schedule allows it. Just let me know," I assured him, giving Reagan a quick hug before Alexis and I sent them both on their way.

The second security safely escorted them out of the building, Alexis turned to me with her arms crossed and a smirk on her face. "*See.* That wasn't so bad, was it?"

Shaking my head, I answered, "Nah, it wasn't. But it's still the last time I'm doing your ass a favor. Got me out here slaving for the holiday when you know I was supposed to be on the beach already."

It was something like a ritual of mine to treat myself to a vacation for Christmas since it was often the only real break I got during the year. But when my former classmate turned industry confidant, Alexis Martin-Ross, called with an emergency after her first director went into labor, I quickly found myself doing Santa's work by coming through in the clutch; though Alexis tried to play that down a little when she insisted, "The beach will still be there when we're done, Dallas. And besides, you know we always make magic when we link up. This is just like old times."

I would've been lying if I didn't agree since my early work with Alexis when we first got out of school was the same stuff that eventually got me promoted from production assistant to the hybrid director/producer/writer I was now. And even when our careers started to go in different directions, she never shied away from putting me on whenever she had the chance while I did the same for her, solidifying a real friendship that had a genuine smile on my face when I told her, "You're right. It's been a minute, Lex."

"Too damn long," she countered before she continued, "And since you're in town, that means you better have your ass at me and Jaden's Christmas Eve party on Monday too."

The mention of a party made me chuckle. "*Damn.* I don't think I've been to one of y'all parties since college. Remember that Back to School shit Jaden and his brother used to throw every year?"

Between those and Jaden's elaborate birthday parties, I was surprised he was even still into partying at all considering how live those always were. And according to the content smile on Alexis's face, the memory was just as fresh for her as it was in my head when she sighed, "*Man.* What a time."

She left it at that, but I could pretty much fill in the blanks considering the two of them had just recently shared their crazy love story** in a magazine interview. And it was that same interview that had turned them into the latest #relationshipgoals couple, even for someone like me who wasn't looking for a relationship at all.

Not that I wasn't into the idea of having someone to call my own, or even having a family one day. I honestly just didn't have the time for it right now and wasn't about to spend time trying to make the demands of my career make sense to someone who didn't care to understand. I mean, between the long hours on a daily, the long weeks of filming and editing, and then the panels and promotional tours, it honestly didn't even seem fair for me to pretend I had time to devote to anything serious.

Still, that didn't stop me from having my fun, a particular woman coming to mind when I told Alexis, "If I come to the party, I'ma need you to do me a favor and invite that production assistant of yours too, though."

Instead of agreeing, she only laughed. "Sorry, bro. Danielle isn't into your kind."

"Nah, not her. The other one," I urged, watching as Alexis's face went from confused to completely amused.

"*Madison*? You want me to hook you up with Madison?" she asked with another laugh as if she couldn't believe it.

In fact, her reaction had me quick to ask, "Why you say it like that? Something wrong with her?"

She shook her head with a frown. "Oh, not at all. But she's like… sweet, and hardworking, and unproblematic. Pretty much exactly opposite of any girl I've ever seen you with."

"*Wow*. So now I only date mean, lazy, troublemaking women?" I asked, Alexis immediately bursting with laughter before she gave a better explanation.

"I'm saying you have a type, Dallas. And Madison Walker doesn't exactly align with that which is probably a good thing. So if you want me to put you on…"

Gnawing into my lip, I cut her off. "*I mean*… you ain't gotta hook me up *directly*. Just put me in a better position to get at her, and I'll do the rest."

Saying it out loud lowkey made me feel ridiculous since pursuing a woman had never been a complicated thing for me. My looks alone were usually enough to, *at least*, get my foot in the door. But something about Madison, particularly the fact that we were working together and I was considered her superior, told me I had to be a little more delicate in how I handled the situation.

That conclusion was only further solidified when Alexis replied, "If that's the case, I've already done that by including you on this project. Cause if you really wanna get at Madison, it's gonna happen here at work; not at the party. I don't think she's really the party type. Then again, I guess I've only ever seen her here, so I wouldn't know. I'll invite her."

With a nod, I told her, "Bet. I appreciate you," knowing that was the most I could ask of her. And after giving a nod of her own, Alexis jumped back into boss mode.

"So call time for our last segment with Zalayah, her mother Erin, her boo Gabriel, his brother Gray, and their mother Constella is at nine tomorrow morning. I have editors working around the clock since we're on such a tight deadline, but they should have something for you to review and put your final touches on by tomorrow afternoon. Then I'll take a last look tomorrow night, though I'm sure you'll make it perfect. That work for you?"

Again, I nodded. "You got it, boss. I'm about to go take a peek at the footage they've already worked through right now."

I was already taking off in the direction of the editing suite when Alexis caught me by the arm to suggest, "Take Madison with you. She loves stuff like that, to be a sponge for free game, and maybe another type of game if you play your cards right."

Using my free hand, I pointed a finger at her when I replied, "*See.* That's why I rock with you, Lex. You always looking out; always thinking with that big ass head of yours."

Though she knew I was only teasing her, she was still quick to squeal, "Hey! This big ass head also gets me paid the big bucks. Thank you very much."

This time, instead of pointing I stuck my hand out. "Lemme borrow a dollar," I asked, Alexis giggling as she knocked my hand away.

"Boy, what? Let *me* borrow a dollar. You're the one doing everything from Box Office smashes to the most-viewed music videos on *YouTube.* I'm so proud of you."

"Yeah, well I'm proud of you too. You been making big moves with that sitcom, and still finding time to do the important work like this project; putting on for black families and black love. Keep shinin', for real."

"Always," she replied with a smile before sending me on my way with a, "Good luck". And it quickly became clear that I was going to need more than just luck when I couldn't spot Madison anywhere on set for the life of me.

I thought about getting on my walkie to call for her but quickly decided that was doing too much; especially considering I had plenty of work to do anyway. So with that, I took my ass to the editing suite, expecting to find the editing team screen deep into the Christmas special. But almost immediately, I realized I must've been in the wrong room when instead of finding a team of people working on said project, I only found one person working on something totally different; the one person I had been looking for all along.

She had headphones on, so I was sure she hadn't even heard me come in. But her not hearing my intrusion gave me a chance to watch her work from behind as she appeared to be editing some old family home video footage.

I had already been impressed with her work ethic earlier on set. But seeing her work her way around all the professional editing software with ease told me she was destined for something much bigger than just being a production assistant. Well, that and the fact that whatever she was working on instantly had me captivated even without sound, a video of toddler Madison being upset after opening one of her Christmas presents making me laugh loud enough to draw her attention.

Spinning around in her chair, she squealed, "Oh my God!" snatching the headphones from her ears as she stood up and asked, "*What are you*… I mean, did you need something?"

"I was actually looking for the editing team," I explained, hoping that would be enough to cover up the fact that I'd been lowkey creeping on her.

With a toss of her hand, she replied, "They're next door." Then she crossed her arms over her chest, standing in a way that guarded the screen as she waited for me to leave.

Now that I'd seen a glimpse of what she was working on, it only made me want to see the project in its entirety. Or maybe I just wanted an excuse to stick around a little longer so I could figure out what it was about her that had me so damn intrigued.

Either way, instead of leaving right away, I asked, "You mind if I see what you're working on?"

For whatever reason, that made her tense up, tapping her foot and chewing on her lip before she challenged, "It depends. Are you gonna tell on me for using company equipment to work on a personal project?"

Since it was a little late for her to be asking that question considering she was already in trouble if that was the case, I was half-amused, half-offended when I asked an important question of my own. "Do I look like a snitch to you, Madison?"

"You look like you have the power to get me fired, Dallas."

Since it was a fair point, I nodded as I told her, "Trust me, I used to do the same shit when I was coming up. Your secret is safe with me. Now let me see what this is hittin' for. Toddler Madison seems like a bit of a diva."

She smirked at that, slowly uncrossing her arms and then using them to direct me to take the chair she had just been occupying. And after pulling the cord for the headphones, she adjusted the volume and started the video from the very beginning.

Just like before, I was completely enthralled, the sound only enhancing that feeling as I watched Christmas after Christmas of Madison and her parents doing everything from singing and dancing to all the classic R&B Christmas songs, to baking cookies for Santa, and of course opening gifts. But it wasn't just all the amazing old school footage that had me captivated, but also the way Madison had pieced it together to tell the story of a loving family and their Christmas traditions.

Pretty much everything Alexis was trying to do with this Christmas special.

So why is she only using Madison as a production assistant?

Since I knew I wouldn't be able to get that question answered right this second, I directed my attention back to the ending of Madison's short film as the creator stood nearby with her lips pursed together, anxiously waiting for me to offer her some sort of critique on what I had learned would be a Christmas gift to her parents according to the file's title.

I must've been taking too long to give feedback since Madison urged, "Well… what do you think?"

Spinning around in the chair to face her, I answered, "Those transitions were fire. You picked the perfect mood music. *And that footage?* Pure gold."

With a proud smirk, she replied, "Shoutout to Pops for always keeping a camera in our faces long before it was considered the thing to do."

"Forward thinker. A true creative. Must be where you get it from," I complimented, Madison immediately averting her eyes as she tried to hide the fact that she was flattered. But instead of letting her hide anything, I only upped the ante, standing up and grabbing her hand to get her full attention when I told her, "Thanks for sharing that with me. Your parents are gonna love it."

She struggled to look me in my eyes as she pushed out, "I'm… glad you think so."

No lie, it was adorable as hell to see her get all flustered under my gaze, again making me up the ante as I took a step closer and brushed my thumb against the back of her hand while quietly asking, "What is it?"

There was a flicker of panic in her eyes that she tried to play off when she swallowed hard and sighed, "*Nothing*. It's just… your Dallas Bryant, sharing an editing suite with me, giving a positive critique of my work. Excuse me for having a bit of a fangirl moment right now."

Chuckling, I finally dropped her hand. "Well I think I might officially be a fan of you too, Ms. Walker. I can't wait to see more of your work."

"And now I'm just gonna assume you're trying to kill me via cardiac arrest because… *what*?!" she gushed, putting a dramatic hand to her chest.

That made me laugh even harder. "Quit being so humble, love. Your talent is evident, and you clearly don't shy away from puttin' in the work. You're gonna go far in this industry. I'm calling it now."

"Okay, seriously. Can I like… get that on video, or in a voice memo, or somethin'? So when I'm having an awful day on set, I can use it as a reminder to not give up on my hopes and dreams of doing what you do one day?"

Why does she have to be so damn cute, though?

I mean, at this point, I probably would've done whatever she needed me to do; career-related or not. But instead of agreeing to one of her ideas, I offered up one of my own, giving her a onceover and scraping my bottom lip with my teeth before I suggested, "Or I could… remind you myself. Whenever you need to hear it. Just give me a call, and..."

"My pork rinds are ready for the preview of Walker Family Christm… oh! I am… *so* sorry."

The shock of Danielle's surprise entrance was written all over Madison's wide eyes that were only partially shielded by her glasses, and then in the way she scrambled to get as far away from me as possible like we had gotten caught doing something inappropriate. And even though we hadn't - *Thank God* - her reaction was still enough for me to see I had a long way to go in convincing her that I was interested in more than just her work, even when I told her friend, "Danielle, you're in for a real treat. The film is great."

She offered a polite nod in response before I turned back to Madison to say, "Keep up the good work, Ms. Walker."

With a nod similar to Danielle's, she paired it with a half-hearted smile as I saw myself out. And once I shut the door behind me, I could only shake my head after hearing Danielle yell, *"Whew, girl! You've got some explaining to do!"*

MADISON

"WE WISH YOU A MERRY DICK-MAS. We wish you a Merry Dick-mas. We wish you a Merry Dick-mas. And a Happy Pap Smear."

While I wanted to be mad at Dani for remixing a damn Christmas carol at my expense first thing in the morning, I could only laugh as we made our way onto set, triple-checking to make sure everything was in order for today's shoot with one of my favorite singers ever. In fact, I was already trying to prepare myself to not freak out on sight when Danielle started singing, "And this Dick-mas... *will be*... a very special Dick-mas... for Mad-dieeeee."

"I swear I hate you, Dani," I groaned with another chuckle, knowing all of her teasing was just a result of her walking in on Dallas and I last night when were... *doing absolutely nothing.*

We weren't doing anything.

Still, for whatever reason, I couldn't get the interaction out of my head. And apparently Danielle couldn't either, even when she tried to play it off by asking, "Why do you hate me? I'm just spreading a little Christmas cheer on the eve of Christmas Eve!"

"You mean, spreading a little Dick-mas cheer?" I challenged with a roll of my eyes that only made Danielle laugh.

"Nah, that's for Mr. Bryant to do," she replied, immediately catching a stiff side-eye that didn't stop her from continuing,

"*What?* You know you wanna have a Merry Dick-mas with Dallas, boo. Shit, you probably would've gotten an early Merry Dick-mas if I wouldn't have come in the editing suite when I did last night."

Even if she was partially right since… *who wouldn't want to have a Merry Dick-mas with fine ass Dallas Bryant?…* I could only sigh before I reminded her, "I already told you, it wasn't like that at all. We were just talking shop. He liked the film I put together for my parents."

It sounded good, but Danielle wasn't buying it, grabbing me by both shoulders to say, "Let me make something clear, Madison. It *is* a super cute Christmas gift, and he probably *did* really like it. But that man was *not* coming in there for that. He came in there for you."

"He was looking for the editing team."

"But he stayed for you."

"But he went there right after he left," I countered, lowkey whining as I tried to talk her out of being right. But my whining quickly proved itself useless once I saw the smirk on Dani's face.

"Still stayed for you, boo."

"He held my hand," I blurted, needing to get that part of things off my chest since it had stuck with me the most; his touch and what its simplicity had stirred up inside of me. Well, that and other things that I felt inclined to share after seeing the look of, "*What?*" in Dani's eyes.

With another sigh, I explained, "Dallas. He held my hand, and called me "love", and pretty much offered up his phone number to me…"

"Because the nigga wants to give you a Merry Dick-mas! I told you. I know bedroom eyes when I see them, and that man wants you bad," Danielle concluded the same way she had a day ago. Except this time, she actually had some evidence to back up her claims.

Still, it didn't make sense to me; something I tried to talk my way through when I replied, "But like… how is that even possible, though? I mean, don't get me wrong, I look *bomb* today. But yesterday, I was… not exactly first impression worthy, and *definitely* not sexy enough to pull somebody like Dallas Bryant off the rip."

Considering how closely I followed Dallas's career, it was inevitable that I ended up following his personal life too. And the type of girls Dallas seemed into were very much… *not like me*. Not that anything was wrong with them, or wrong with me for that matter. It just hardly seemed possible for him to genuinely be into me if he was also into them.

Then again, guys weren't really all that complicated. And I thought Danielle was getting ready to agree with that thought when she shrugged to reply, "Nigga must've saw right on through those worn threads, I guess. On some ghetto Cinderella shit."

"And now you see exactly why I hate you," I told her, wishing I could've held back the laugh that came with it but unable to as Alexis approached us.

With a quick glance at my outfit, she announced, "Well don't you look extra cute today. But I sure hope you brought another pair of shoes with you cause those six-inch heels are gonna do you in if you didn't."

"*Thot rookie mistake,*" Danielle muttered, earning another stiff side-eye from me as Alexis continued, "I may have some sneakers in my office. We look about the same size. They're yours if you want them, but you only have about… twenty minutes to decide."

I barely let her finish her sentence before I was already taking off towards the offices that were in a separate building between the two studio lots. But with a push out of the door came a sharp gasp as Dallas just barely balanced the tray of coffees in his hand on the other side of it.

"Damn. That was close, huh?" he asked with a smirk, glancing at the tops before pulling one of the coffees out to hand my way. "I believe *this one*... is for you."

While I appreciated the gesture since getting for real dressed this morning had cut into my drive-thru coffee time, I was a little confused considering directors were *never* on coffee duty. In fact, I couldn't help but ask, "What are you doing bringing *me* coffee? This is supposed to be the other way around."

His smirk remained as he replied, "Nah, I'm taking a step back… *well*, more like to the side and sharing the director's chair with you today. I see you're already dressed up for the occasion. Nice shoes, by the way."

Now that he had complimented me on them, wearing them all day didn't seem like such a daunting task. In fact, I was already smiling to tell him, "Thank you," before the rest of what he had said actually registered in my head and...

"Wait a minute... sharing the director's chair?"

My heart immediately took off in a sprint of nerves, even when he assured, "Don't worry. I'll be there with you every step of the way. But it's time to show the people what you're made of, Madison. Time to get some real experience doing what I do like you said you wanted to. No more watching from the sidelines. No more keeping your talent a secret for family projects. *No more...*"

I cut him off with a whined, "Dallas, I can't do this. I mean, I appreciate you trying to give me an opportunity to showcase my skills, *but...* this isn't my project to take control of."

Instead of agreeing, he fired back, "Uhh, it wasn't mine either, but I'm here anyway."

It was true, but that still didn't make me feel any better considering he was an experienced director who had been there, done that and I was just a... production assistant with very limited professional experience. But of course, none of that stopped Dallas from reasoning, "Look, Madison. It's one last segment with the little singer girl and her folks. I'm pretty sure you can handle that."

For a brief moment, my nerves were able to go to the backburner as I held up my free hand to say, "Hold up. *The little singer girl?* Don't disrespect Zalayah like that! That RoseGold album got me through a lot."

"Oh yeah? Well how about you tell me all about it over dinner tonight?" he offered so smoothly that I almost stumbled back on my heels since... *is this real life?*

Did Dallas Bryant really just ask me out?

"*Maybe I need to get those sneakers after all...*" I thought, crossing my arms over my chest to strengthen my stance when I asked, "Is that why you're promoting me? So I'll let you take me to dinner?"

With a laugh, he took a step closer and answered, "No. I'm

promoting you because I believe in your talent and I know we all need somebody to give us a break in this industry. Dinner is its own thing that I'm pretty sure I could've gotten without promoting you, love."

"Don't get cocky, Mr. Bryant," I warned even though I knew he wasn't lying.

I mean… not even a little bit.

And honestly, his arrogance about it only made him that much more attractive; especially when he licked his lips to ask, "What you gonna do about it, Ms. Walker?"

Instead of responding with words, I offered a smirk that he matched when he pressed, "So, dinner tonight…"

"Okay."

"Okay?"

Nodding, I clarified, "Yeah. *Okay*, I'll go. If that's really what you wanna subject yourself to."

For whatever reason, that made him chuckle. "*Subject myself to*? Because taking you out to dinner is, what? Some kind of punishment?"

Shrugging, I replied, "Maybe not a punishment, but you definitely might end up getting your feelings hurt by the end of the night."

With an astonished look on his face, he gushed, "*Oh, wow*. So Madison Walker is a player? Is that what you're tellin' me?"

I shook my head with a grin knowing that was the furthest thing from the truth. But considering he didn't need to know all that, I gave him the more important reason why he might get his feelings hurt when I replied, "Madison Walker is telling you she doesn't have time for anything more than just dinner at this current stage of life. Take that how you will."

"Not anything?" he challenged, his eyebrow piqued teasingly as he tried to get me to go back on my word already. But like I had told Danielle from the very beginning, I had worked way too hard to get to where I was, and I wasn't about to blow it for Dallas no matter how charming and fine he was.

But damn, does he look especially fine today.

He was being especially charming too, making it a struggle for me to answer, "Nope." And thankfully, that was enough for him to fall back for the moment, giving me a chance to gather myself as he left me with, "*Hmph.* We'll see about that."

With my coffee cup near my lips, I watched his every step as he finally made his way onto set to deliver the other two coffees, keeping one for himself that he sipped from as he ran through today's call sheet with Alexis. And I was clocking him so hard that I totally missed Danielle coming my way until I heard her singing, "*I'm… dreaming of a brown dick-mas…*"

Smirking, I teased, "Oh, are you now? I'm telling Tracey."

The mention of her on-again, off-again girlfriend who she was currently off with made her frown as she replied, "Nah, I hid all the brown ones a long time ago. She was starting to do too much. Walking around the house with it strapped on and shit like it was real just because it matched her skin tone. *But anyway…* how much closer are you to a Merry Dick-mas with Dallas?"

Even though I had no real plans of making it a Merry Dick-mas like she continued to insist, I couldn't help bragging, "He's making me co-director for the day and taking me to dinner tonight."

Snapping her head back, she gushed, "Wow. So he's really pulling out all stops, huh? If I would've known I could build my resume and get a free meal, I might've faked straight. Heyyyyy, Mr. Bryant. I am delivert!"

"Oh my God, Dani. Shut up!" I squealed with a laugh, taking another sip of my coffee and almost choking when Zalayah and her team walked through the doors unexpectedly.

Dani and I were both in awe of her ethereal beauty, staring hard enough to cut through glass as I sighed, "*Dude.* She looks like a goddess. How are we almost the same age? More importantly, where did I go wrong in life to not be just as goddess-like?"

Putting things in perspective, Dani didn't take her eyes off the international superstar singer to explain, "She's been swimming in money since her teenage years. I'd be more concerned if she didn't look like a goddess."

Nodding to agree, I watched as Zalayah was immediately greeted by Alexis with a hug, Alexis appearing to give her all the compliments that were also in my head before she turned and waved me over. Placing a hand to my chest to confirm the request was actually for me, I was a little taken aback when Alexis gave an enthusiastic nod in response, Danielle all but pushing me in their direction when I found my feet cemented to the ground. But if I was really going to be bossin' up today like Dallas insisted, I knew I had to walk the walk, attempting to channel all of that energy as I took a deep breath and finally headed their way.

Alexis wasted no time introducing us. "Zalayah, this is Madison. She and Dallas, *who should be back shortly*, are going to be doing all of the directing today."

With a pleasant smile of acknowledgment, she stuck her hand out for me to shake as she glanced down at my feet and sang, "*Ooh*! Cute shoes, Madison."

"Wearing these every day for the rest of my life," I decided, returning a smile that was equally pleasant when I told her, "Thank you. It's so nice to meet you. I was just telling someone a little bit ago about how that RoseGold album got me through some things."

Giggling like we were old friends, she replied, "Me and you both, girl. *Seriously*," just as her boyfriend approached us. And after snuggling up under his arm, she rested a hand against his chest to share, "Babe, this is Madison. One of the directors."

"Gabriel," he said, giving me a handshake that was notably more stern than friendly before he introduced the rest of the gang who had followed him over. "This is my mother Constella, my brother Grayson, and my… soon-to-be mother-in-law, Erin."

Zalayah grinned harder than ever at that, something I found adorable even before I put two-and-two together the way Alexis had when she asked, "Wait a minute… am I hearing what I think I'm hearing?"

To answer the question, Zalayah pulled herself from under Gabriel's arm so she could wiggle her left hand our way, damn near blinding us all as she showed off her engagement ring that looked like it was worth more than my organs on the black market.

"Talk about goals," I thought as Alexis squealed, "Oh my God! Congratulations, you guys! That's so exciting!"

"Thank you so much. My baby did good, didn't he?" Zalayah asked, peeking up at her fiancé with a smile that was enough to break right on through his seemingly-tough demeanor as he pressed a kiss against her forehead that she relished in. And while the sight was seriously the cutest thing ever, I couldn't help but feel a little jealous since I couldn't remember the last time I'd gotten a forehead kiss.

And I didn't want to remember the last time I'd been in a man's arms.

And I wasn't sure if I had ever been looked at the way Gabriel was looking at Zalayah*** right now.

And… they were making me want all of that and more even though I'd sworn off of it for the sake of putting everything into my career.

Then again, if someone as busy as Zalayah could have it all while still being able to maintain her career, why couldn't I? Was it really that impossible to find someone who supported my quest for greatness, someone who understood the demands of my career and wouldn't hold it against me, *someone who…*

"Dallas Bryant. It's a pleasure to have you guys joining us today."

I really didn't even need to hear him to know he was near, his presence alone dominating the scene right away. But I'd be damned if the extra bass in his voice didn't make my skin tingle as I became enthralled watching him interact so effortlessly, watching him be so comfortable amongst the stars, watching him just… *work.*

Damn, girl.

You got it bad.

After Zalayah shook his hand then let Gabriel do the same, she squinted her eyes at him before asking, "*Wait.* You're the one who directed G. Griffey's docuseries, right?"

"I am," he answered proudly, making me jealous for different reasons since I couldn't *wait* to be known for my work like that.

I also couldn't wait to hear things like, "Mommy, get his card for me, please. I'd love to run an idea for something similar past you. Maybe set up a meeting for first thing in the new year?"

"Sounds like a plan," he answered, digging in his pocket for his wallet then extending a card to Erin who looked a little too excited to accept it on her daughter's behalf. But before I could read too much into it - *or read into it at all* - Alexis escorted the group to get mic'd up just as Dallas put a hand against the small of my back and leaned in to whisper near my ear, "You ready to do this, Madison?"

It took me a second to gather myself since I swear there was something sacred in his touch, sending a surge through my body that forced me to straighten up so I could answer, "I absolutely am."

Instead of removing his hand, he used it to gently guide me towards set, walking next to me with a smirk when he complimented, "I like that confidence."

Even if my confidence was rooted in more *"fake it 'til I make it"* energy than anything, it felt good to hear it was actually working, an easy smile on my lips as I shared, "Alexis introduced me as a director, and then Zalayah did the same, and I'm *just*… grateful. *Excited.* Thank you."

Since none of this would've been possible without him backing it, it was only right for me to show my appreciation. But I was tempted to show that same appreciation in another way after watching the way he sexily licked his lips to reply, "My pleasure."

All sorts of freaky thoughts started running through my head until he reeled me back in with a simple request. "Now let's kill this shit, bet?"

"Bet," I agreed with a nod, trying to snap back into professional mode since… this was my big chance after all; the first of many if I was lucky. And even if my panties were soaked, I still had to perform if I didn't want this to be the last.

So that was exactly what I did - talking through expectations and ideas with Zalayah and her family, making sure the production crew was where they needed to be, watching Dallas go into command and taking mental notes of his efficient directorial style while also admiring how incredibly fine he was in go-mode.

Not that I didn't already know that.

Still, it was all so thrilling, and challenging in a good way, and exactly what I wanted to do for the rest of my life.

In that moment, it was confirmed.

And I could only thank Dallas for pushing me to do it.

After getting the very last footage of Zalayah and her family cheesily wishing everyone a Happy Holiday, I was grinning from ear-to-ear, turning to Dallas who was sitting in the director's chair next to mine to ask, "Can I say it? Please let me say it."

With a smile of his own, he urged, "Go ahead, love."

"And that's a wrap!" I shouted, the production crew giving our last group and themselves a round of applause before moving to get the group un-mic'd.

Removing his own equipment while I did the same, Dallas insisted, "It may be early to call, but I think we make a pretty decent team, Ms. Walker."

"I'm the pretty. You're the decent," I teased, clearly riding the high of the moment.

But it was worth it once I saw the look on Dallas's face as he gave me a onceover before agreeing, "You are *definitely* the pretty."

I honestly couldn't have stopped smiling if I wanted to, so I didn't even try; especially after hearing Zalayah give praises on how much fun she had and how she was looking forward to working with us again in the future.

Us.

The both of us.

What is life?

It was the single greatest day of my life thus far, and it only got better when Dallas urged, "Come on, Madison. We still have a lot of work to do if we're really trying to make it to dinner tonight."

That's right.

Dinner with my dream guy is still on the agenda.

He wasted no time getting us over to post-production, the editing team already reviewing the footage from the shoot on multiple screens as I teased, "Glad you know where the correct editing suite is today, Mr. Bryant."

Shooting me a playful side eye, he commented, "You just got all the jokes today, I see. Must be in a good ass mood."

"I'm always in a good mood. But yeah, today was special," I admitted, once again feeling the urge to show my appreciation in more ways than one even though one of those ways was a little risky.

More than a little risky.

I didn't want him to get the wrong impression, didn't want him to think I was trying to… exchange favors. But damnit, I wanted to celebrate this major accomplishment with a Merry Dick-mas, and this felt like a "go big or go home" moment with Dallas Bryant of all people at my fingertips.

"Danielle tried to warn your dumb ass," I thought, annoyed with myself for already being so caught up. But it really shouldn't have come as a surprise, especially after the way he glanced at me over his shoulder to remind me, "It's not over yet, Ms. Walker," adding a wink that sent a thick chill down my spine which meant he knew exactly what effect he had on me.

But he wasn't alone in that regard since, *for whatever reason*, I had his eye as well. Now I just had to figure out what to do with it.

DALLAS

DINNER NEVER HAPPENED.

Well… not in the way I had in mind.

Madison and I ate, but it ended up being Chinese takeout in the editing suite since final edits were taking a lot longer than either of us expected them to once it was discovered that there was a noticeable difference between the footage captured with Jessaline at the helm and the footage I'd gotten.

How we'd made the mistake with so many other eyes familiar with the project around, I wasn't sure. But regardless, it was my job to figure out how to smooth things out as much as possible. And honestly, I was grateful to be working with Madison on the task since it was her calming spirit that had me confident we would figure it out eventually.

"Eventually" was taking forever though, a yawn escaping my lips before I told her, "My eyes need a break. You wanna takeover?"

"*Like I haven't been staring at the same screen you have all this time…*" she groaned, getting ready to exchange chairs with me until I agreed, "Good point. How about we both take a break?"

That seemed to satisfy her as she plopped right back down into her original seat, pulling her phone out as if going from the big monitor screen to the small screen of her phone would somehow help her eyes relax. But her being occupied gave me a chance to watch her, particularly the way she read something on her phone and then busted out laughing; the whole thing making me wonder about something that hadn't exactly been clarified.

Instead of asking right out, I started, "I appreciate you sticking around to help me out with this."

"We're a team now, right?" she asked, peeking up from her phone just long enough to serve me the most adorable grin.

I couldn't help but match it when I agreed, "Yeah, we are. But hopefully I'm not getting in the way of any *personal* teams by keeping you here this late."

There.

I'd said it.

And of course, she made me sweat about it, taking her time to sit up a little straighter and give a non-answer when she countered, "A little late to be asking that, don't you think?"

Shrugging, I moved towards the edge of my chair - *closer to her* - and replied, "I mean, you agreed to dinner, so I assumed you must be single. But you never know these days."

It was much better to find out directly from the source instead of finding out via some disgruntled nigga who thought he was a boyfriend and wasn't. But I was glad to see the slightly amused smirk on Madison's face when she said, "I'm single, Dallas. That clear enough for you?"

"Yes and no," I answered, watching her eyebrow pique before I explained, "Yes, I heard you. But no, it's not clear because I'm curious to know why someone hasn't cuffed your pretty ass yet."

Again, she smirked, her eyes - *notably without the glasses today* - squinted as she cocked her head to the side and challenged, "Well I'm curious to know why you assume my pretty ass wants to be cuffed."

"Touché," I agreed with a nod, falling back in my seat as I told her, "Shits for the birds, honestly."

"Now you're speaking my language," she replied with a giggle that told me she'd definitely dealt with some lames in her past.

Unfortunately, that was something I could relate to, releasing a heavy sigh before I shared, "Dating is difficult, period. But it's *espe-*

cially difficult in this industry. I mean, unless someone's been down with you since the beginning and they already know what's up. But introducing someone to this hectic filming life is…"

"*Impossible*," she finished for me, doubling down when she added, "It feels impossible. Which is why I'd rather not even pretend to try, especially when I could be putting that energy towards perfecting my craft."

Now I was the one chuckling, shaking my head as I replied, "Definitely learned that shit the hard way. Tried to balance my first big-budget film with dating someone new, and… *yeah*. You can assume how that ended."

"*Like all the others according to the blogs…*" she quietly replied like I wouldn't hear her shady ass, teasingly averting her eyes in a way that made me roll my own and made her quick to defend, "*What*? It's not my fault your personal business is the news."

"Nah, you're right. And for that exact reason, my next situation will be hella lowkey. I don't even think I want a full-blown relationship, honestly. Just somebody I can kick it with when our timing aligns, but not super pressed about it cause she's got her own shit going on. Someone I can share good news with and who can share good news with me. An ambitious girl who I can just… root for, be excited about, you know?"

She was nodding along, but her face remained confused for reasons I didn't understand until she asked, "So you want a… *friend*?"

Thinking back on the description I had given her, that simple title definitely made sense. But considering I hadn't exactly covered all the bases of what I was looking for, I made a small amendment when I answered, "Well, yeah. A real good friend… *who I can fuck*. A nigga got needs out here, Madison."

The way she immediately licked her lips in response told me that might've struck a nerve, though she covered it up well by crossing her legs to ask, "So you want a friend with benefits?"

This time, I shrugged. "I mean, I guess. If I have to put a name to it, that would be the closest thing. But really, I just want what I want; want someone who wants the same thing as me."

"Which is to be your good friend, *who you can have sex with*, and also do other random stuff with when y'all both have time in your *oh-so-busy* schedules?"

The fact that she was steady searching for an explanation had me quick to agree, "*Exactly*," just so I could follow-up by asking, "Know anybody who might be interested in something like that?"

Since she claimed she didn't have time for anything more than dinner in her current stage of life, I honestly wasn't sure what her answer would be. But I felt hopeful after seeing the way she immediately started gnawing on her grin before she sang, "*Maaaybe*. I don't know if she's your type, though. I mean, she's not like *any* of those girls you've dated before."

Sitting up to put a gentle hand against her knee, I told her, "I'm not looking for them, Madison. I'm looking for… *her*."

That made her grin even harder. "Well how about we talk about the *her* I have in mind after we solve our little problem with this footage?" she suggested with a wink, rolling her chair towards the computer desk before I could even respond. But the fact that she was putting the project first only proved how much she already fit the bill, watching her work both making me proud and making me want her all at once.

The latter almost ruled out the former until I peeked up at the monitor screen and… "*Hold up*. I think you might've fixed it. Play back that last minute for me."

Clicking the mouse a few times, she did exactly what I asked, the both of us watching as the segment that was giving us the most trouble transitioned perfectly into the next.

"Fuckin' seamless. What'd you do? Better question, why didn't you do it earlier?"

Since I was standing behind her, I couldn't see her face. But I could clearly hear the amusement in her tone when she giggled and replied, "I can't let you know all my secrets, Dallas. Gotta use those to get me hired later on."

"Well I can guarantee you'll never have a problem with that, Madison. Too damn talented," I complimented, pressing my hands into the back of her chair then bending to whisper straight into her ear, "And too damn pretty."

Punctuating my sentence with a little kiss to her temple, I

admired the way she played off her reaction with a quick deep breath before asking, "One last viewing?"

Instead of answering with words, I gave a nod she couldn't see, moving to turn off the lights then taking the seat next to hers so we could watch the Christmas special from the top.

At least, that was the plan. But I quickly found myself distracted watching her instead, the glow of the screen against her skin as she closely examined each frame only making her that much more attractive to me. And by the time she noticed me staring, turning towards me with the look of, *"What?"* in her eyes, I had already built up the courage to just… go for it, reaching over to grab her by the chin then moving forward to press a gentle kiss against her lips that had her immediately closing her eyes as she sweetly moaned into my mouth.

It was her moan that only made me want more, pressing a hand against the back of her curls to bring her closer as I slipped my tongue between the threshold of her lips and found hers for a sensual tussle. And the project quickly became an afterthought, only serving as background noise when I pulled Madison from her seat to mine without breaking our kiss, already rock hard by the time she straddled my lap and brought her hands to the back of my head when I moved my lips to her neck.

When she groaned my name while subconsciously rolling her hips against my lap, I knew I had to have her for real, only stopping long enough to confirm, "You were the "her", right?"

Even if she wasn't, she was going to be. But it was the extra millisecond she took to answer that saved us from getting caught in the act, the rattle of the door handle behind us making Madison hop out of my lap in a quickness and find her chair just as the light was turned on by Alexis who asked, "Are y'all finished, or are y'all done?"

Madison was too busy fixing her clothes on the low to respond, so I did the talking for the both of us when I answered, "Just about," peeking behind her to say, "What's good, Jaden?"

According to their dressy attire, they must've been out on a date or something before they showed up here. And really, I shouldn't have been surprised by the late-night pop-up since

Alexis had that same super ambitious blood running through her that Madison did, going above and beyond to get whatever job that lied ahead of her done.

Jaden didn't seem bothered by the extra stop, extending his hand my way for some dap as he said, "My nigga Dallas. It's been way too long. Lexi told me you're coming through the party tomorrow."

Before I could respond, Alexis exclaimed, "*Oh!*" directing her attention to Madison to say,

"I forgot to tell you, you're invited to the party too."

Madison seemed surprised, snapping her head back to ask, "*I am?*"

"Yeah, you and Danielle. And a plus one, because we want you to have a *really* good time. You deserve it after the way you killed it today. I mean, Jessaline who?" she asked teasingly with a laugh before continuing, "*Anyway*. I'll email you the details. Now show me what y'all came up with to fix that problem y'all were having."

She was already moving towards the screen as Madison said, "*Actually*, I need to… run to the bathroom first. *Excuse me*."

I watched as she took off without even a glance back my way. And thankfully, Alexis and Jaden were completely oblivious to what was going on before they came; though it was all I could think about even when I told Alexis, "I can't take any credit for this, by the way. It was all Madison."

"Of course it was. She's brilliant," she replied, scrolling through the footage to the part that we'd already told her about and pressing play as I watched on and agreed.

"Brilliant ain't even a strong enough word for that one."

In the same way I had been just a few minutes earlier, Alexis was immediately impressed, giving an enthusiastic, "Damn. That *was* good. Definitely keeping her on my crew."

"As more than just a production assistant, right?" I asked, nodding at the conversation we'd had just last night that led to her being promoted to director in the first place.

With a sigh, she playfully groaned, "Yes, Dallas. I'll put your girl on. *Relax*."

"Oh, that's you, DB?" Jaden asked, his eyebrow piqued as thoughts of her cute ass in my lap flashed through my head and… *damn.*

Being as honest as possible, I replied, "Working on it, even though your wife just *had* to extend that wack ass plus one."

Of course she was quick to defend, "It's a polite gesture! I'm not sure who she knows that will be in attendance, and I would hate for her to be uncomfortable around a bunch of unfamiliar faces."

"I was supposed to be the familiar face," I reminded her, rolling my eyes as Alexis smacked me on the arm.

"Boy, if you don't find some game and leave me alone. I've done my job here. Now it's your turn to close the deal; *if* you really got it like that."

She had a point, but that didn't stop her husband from shaking his head as he warned, "Man, if she plays as hard to get as this one did, you're in for a wild ride. Good luck with that shit, for real."

Alexis was already shooting him a scowl that made me chuckle as Madison returned to the room, locking eyes with me for just a split second before making her way back to her chair. And while I could only wonder what she was thinking since I knew she wasn't about to speak on it in front of present company, I was already looking forward to getting answers and continuing what we'd started at the party tomorrow.

MADISON

"DO you think some famous people are gonna be at this party? Or is it just gonna be a bunch of work people? Today was my first full day away from those niggas, and I am *not* in a rush to have them back on my nerves already."

It was a struggle for me to maintain a straight face in response to Danielle's inquiry as she put the finishing touches on my makeup, only giving a shrug to answer her question since I didn't want to mess anything up by trying to speak.

Considering the circles Alexis and her husband ran in, I certainly wouldn't have been surprised to see a few stars amongst the crowd at their holiday party. But Danielle made it seem like my answer was more of a cop-out once she teased, "I bet you don't know since you're only worried about one person in particular being there. You givin' up the pussy tonight or nah?"

"What the fuck, Dani?" Tracey asked as she stepped into the bathroom with us, serving Danielle a sharp scowl through the mirror that lowkey had me nervous. I mean, Tracey and I might've been the same height and probably even weighed the same number of pounds. But where mine came in as chub in random places, hers was all muscle.

Basically, I was confident she could beat my ass and I wasn't about to chance it getting involved with their drama.

Holding up her hands - *makeup brush and all* - Dani was quick to explain, "That was *not* what it sounded like, babe. Her wannabe boo is gonna be at the party we're going to. She's one step closer to a Merry Dick-mas."

Instead of finding humor in it the way Dani was trying to sell it, Tracey only transformed her scowl into a straight line as she replied, "Y'all weird," before exiting the bathroom just as quickly as she had come in.

It wasn't until Danielle shut the bathroom door that I felt comfortable asking, *in a whisper*, "So… you two are back together for good now?"

Dani shrugged. "*Eh.* I really just wanted a Christmas present from her. We'll see what happens after that. *But back to you…* what's the move? Are you going with the flow, or are you gonna be a scary little bitch like you were last night?"

"First of all, I wasn't being scary last night. Alexis and her husband just showed up," I reminded her, more than grateful that the door had been closed which gave me a chance to escape the… compromising position.

I mean, I could only imagine how bad of a look it would've been on my behalf for my boss to walk in on me screwing around with a co-worker; especially considering the issues we were having with the footage and the tight deadline we were on at the time. Even if she wasn't quick to judge me, it wasn't exactly the kind of thing someone would easily forget about, and with the level of clout she had in the industry, I needed to keep her on my side.

Danielle wasn't thinking about it anywhere near as deeply as I was, serving me a skeptical eye when she asked, "So you're tellin' me you would've had sex with Dallas in the editing suite if they didn't show up?"

"Oh, absolutely not," I rushed out without thinking twice, knowing no matter how far I planned on letting things go with Dallas last night, sex at the workplace wasn't going to be one of them.

Sure, it was cool to read about in books and hot to watch on TV when I wasn't busy dissecting the scene. But honestly, I didn't trust my luck for it to go anywhere near as smoothly for me. Though of course, that didn't stop Danielle from insisting, "See what I mean. *Scary*."

With a roll of my eyes, I groaned, "*Anyway*. To answer your question, I'm going with the flow. Because I deserve."

It was a decision I had made after reflecting on the entire day during my drive home late last night; all the new experiences, all the excitement, all the *him*. With the project being over with, it wasn't a guarantee I'd even see Dallas again beyond tonight's party. And after the way he had kissed me - *the way we had kissed each other* - I wanted more.

I *deserved* more.

Snapping her fingers, Dani sang, "Okayyy! Listen to you. A bitch gets the director's chair for a day and now she's feelin' herself. That's what I'm talkin' about. Now let's get going before you change your silly ass mind."

I wanted to dispute her claims, but I knew she was right. It would be just like me to chicken out, find an excuse to fall back, find an excuse to wipe this makeup right off and not show up to the party at all. But considering that wasn't an option if I didn't want to have regrets about it later, I finished getting myself dressed in a very festive hunter green dress Dani had let me borrow, complemented with jewelry she had also let me borrow, and stilettos I had brought myself.

The same stilettos from a day ago that both Dallas and Zalayah had complimented me on.

My lucky shoes.

With Tracey volunteering to drive, we made our way over to Alexis and Jaden's Atlanta home that was allegedly half the size of their home out in California. But I had a hard time believing that considering how huge the place was, Jaden's app and Alexis's film work clearly treating them well as we pulled around the circle drive to a valet station.

A valet station.

For a house party.

This was crazy.

We were making our way up the short set of stairs when the front door was pulled open by Alexis. "Madison! Danielle! I'm so happy y'all made it."

"We're happy to be here, Boss. Thanks for the invite," Danielle replied for the both of us, accepting the hug extended her way and waiting for me to do the same before introducing our plus one. "This is my girlfriend, Tracey."

Giving her a quick handshake, Alexis said, "Tracey, it's so nice to meet you. Now come on in, y'all. The music is already bumping, and the fully-stocked bar is already flowing with whatever your heart desires."

Following her deeper into the house, Danielle insisted, "My type of party, indeed. Come on, babe." Then she grabbed Tracey's hand and pulled her towards where the bar was set up in a side room, making me realize my third wheel status on what was very much a two-wheeled bike.

"*This is some BS,*" I thought, glancing around the crowd and getting ready to follow them until Alexis put a hand to my arm to share, "Dallas isn't here yet, but he will be. I mean, if that's who you were looking for. Not that it's any of my business. Have fun tonight, Maddie! You look amazing."

Before I could respond, she had already taken off to do more mixing and mingling, the fact that she even knew Dallas's presence mattered to me making me wonder what else she knew about our… involvement.

Or lack thereof.

Since allowing myself to read into it too much would be just the thing to have me calling an *Uber* to take me home, I did my best to shake it off, finally making my way towards the bar just as Danielle turned around with two drinks in her hand.

Shoving one into my hand, she said, "Here you go, boo. Drink up."

"Boo?" Tracey asked with a frown, her own glass of brown liquor near her lips as Danielle immediately rolled her eyes.

"*Oh my God.* Will you chill, Tracey? Nobody wants Madison's prude ass."

"Hey!" I screeched with a frown of my own that only made Danielle laugh. And after a quick sip of her drink, she defended, "I'm just sayin'. You're cute and all, but nah."

"Whatever," I replied, finally sipping from the glass she'd handed me, happy to discover it was only juice.

At least, I think it's only juice.

Instead of wondering, I asked flat out, "This is non-alcoholic, isn't it?"

Clearly annoyed by my question, Danielle groaned, "*Yes, Madison.* I know you don't drink like that, so I got you a kiddie cup. You're welcome."

Surprisingly enough, it was that that cracked Tracey's scowl, making her give a huff of a laugh as she repeated, "Kiddie cup," before she took another sip of her drink. And while I wanted to give her a side eye in response, I really didn't want any smoke with her strong ass. So I kept it to myself, directing my attention towards the crowd in the main room instead as Jaden and two other guys gave an impromptu performance of, "*Let It Snow*" by Boyz II Men - one of my favorite Christmas songs.

Their rendition was entertaining as hell, everyone joining in to sing by the time the chorus rolled around for a second time. And while it was dope to hear how well the harmony actually came together, I was more impressed to see everyone in the moment instead of trying to record it all for the internet to see, following the stern yet polite request for no phones from the emailed invitation.

When the song transitioned into, *"Sleigh Ride"* by TLC, I couldn't help but catch the vibe, Danielle and I singing along at the top of our lungs as Tracey watched on with a content smirk. And when Destiny's Child, *"8 Days of Christmas"* came on, you couldn't tell us we weren't in the music video, Alexis becoming our third member as we sang, and danced, and laughed our way through the entire song.

I was having such a good time that I'd forgotten all about Dallas until Danielle tapped me on the shoulder to point out that he'd shown up. But I wished she hadn't since the only thing I got when I turned around was an eyeful of him giving some woman an *incredibly* enthusiastic hug; the type of hug that spoke volumes as far as their history was concerned. In fact, I caught myself feeling a little jealous until a man - *one of the Boyz II Men members from earlier* - walked up and gave Dallas a handshake and hug that was just as enthusiastic before encouraging the woman to show off her left hand.

So she's married?

As if she could read my mind, Alexis shared, "My brother-in-law Jordan *finally* stopped playing and proposed to his longtime girlfriend, Ashley, earlier today. It was seriously the cutest thing. I mean, from the set-up, to the surprise, to…"

The rest of her words fell on deaf ears once Dallas peeked my way, locking eyes with me and immediately licking his lips before excusing himself from the newly-engaged couple to head our way. At least, that's what he tried to do, getting stopped for greetings, hugs, and handshakes from just about everyone he passed, reminding me just how well-known he was around these parts.

I wasn't bothered by the delay, though. In fact, it only made me more excited to be his final destination. And it was like Danielle and Alexis both knew to ditch me since they were nowhere to be found by the time Dallas finally made it over to me, not even letting me say hello before he held up his hand to say, "Hold on. Gimme a second to just look at you."

I couldn't help but smirk as he gave me a slow onceover, his hand at his chin as he groaned, "*Gotdamn, girl.*" Then he shook it off, running a hand over his face like that refreshed everything and putting a little extra swagger in his tone when he said, "Aight. What's up wit' it, Ms. Walker?"

Giggling, I replied, "Hello to you too, Mr. Bryant. Out here lookin' all dapper and what not."

Brushing a hand down the sleeves of his Christmas red blazer, he joked, "You know I had to do a little somethin' somethin' for the people."

"Yeah, I saw exactly how you do it for the people. You're pretty popular around here."

With a shrug, he explained, "I'm not usually in town for this particular gathering, so it was good to see some old faces."

"Where are you usually?" I asked, knowing that even though he had attended school out on the West Coast, Atlanta was where he called home.

Honestly, I knew an embarrassing amount of random facts about him that I planned to keep to myself so I wouldn't come off like a stalker, though I only became even more curious when he answered, "*Usually*, I'm on the beach. That's been my thing for like the last three or four Christmases."

While the beach sounded like a dream right now with how up and down the temperature had been around the city lately, I couldn't help asking, "Does your family not celebrate?"

I suppose his family's traditions weren't really any of my business, especially since it wasn't like my family did a traditional Christmas anymore either. And after seeing the way the question visibly made him uncomfortable, I wished I wouldn't have pressed, getting ready to tell him he didn't have to answer until he started, "My mother was something like the black sheep of the family when she was alive, so it wasn't like we ever spent time with her side for the holidays. And I was my father's "break baby", so his wife never really liked me coming around even when he insisted I did. Eventually, I just stopped bothering with it and started doing my own thing."

My immediate reaction was, "I'm so sorry." Though he quickly brushed that off.

"Nah, it's all good. I honestly didn't even think about it until you asked."

"Too busy thinking about your next box office hit, huh?" I asked playfully, hoping to lighten the mood that I had so blatantly messed up by getting personal.

"*Way to go, Maddie,*" I scolded in my head as Dallas smiled, taking a step closer to me to reply, "Or maybe just too busy thinking about you. You look so damn beautiful, Madison."

With the way he professed it, I couldn't help but smile hard enough for my little dimples to show up, getting ready to compliment him right back until I heard Alexis sing, "*Well, well, well.*

Looks like someone found the mistletoe! Y'all know what that means."

In a flash, I peeked up to see we were indeed standing in the threshold between the two rooms that lent itself to a mistletoe being hung right above our heads. And though I knew it wouldn't be my first time kissing Dallas, it would be the first time we did it in front of other people - *his people* - the thought making me panic as I replied, "I uh…"

Before I could say anything more, Dallas wrapped an arm low around my waist to pull me against him, tucking his other hand under the curls at the nape of my neck and leaning forward to press a fervent kiss on my lips that left me… *breathless.*

I literally couldn't breathe.

I mean, here I was, on Christmas Eve, practically making out with Dallas Bryant in a room full of mostly-strangers.

Perfect place to stop breathing and die, right?

"I see you, DB!" someone shouted loud enough to get Dallas's attention, making him pull away with a warm chuckle as he whispered right against my lips, "Merry Christmas, Madison Walker."

"Merry Dick-mas, Dallas Bryant," I replied, the way his eyebrow immediately piqued in response making me rethink what I'd said and… *"Oh my God, I really said that out loud, didn't I?"*

My embarrassment only made him laugh harder. "Nah, don't get all shy now. *Merry Dick-mas*? What's that all about?"

"Just something silly Danielle made up," I explained as plainly as possible, knowing the origin lied a little deeper than that since the whole thing had started with him.

I shouldn't have been surprised when he saw right through my hollow response, quick to press, "Are you sure that's all it is?"

Instead of answering his question with what would've surely been a lie, I deflected by asking one of my own. "Shouldn't you be enjoying the party instead of questioning me?"

"You're at the party. I'm enjoying you. That means I'm enjoying the party, right?" he challenged, licking his lips in a way that only encouraged me to agree.

And I did… *partially*, though I also couldn't help toying with him a little bit when I replied, "*Wrong.* But I'll let it slide because I just so happen to be enjoying the party too."

He smirked at that, amusement in his eyes as he said, "Yeah, aight. Let me get you a drink or somethin'." Then he grabbed me by the hand to guide us towards the bar, ordering up an Old Fashioned for himself before turning to me to ask what I wanted with a look.

While I was tempted to press my luck by ordering a "real" drink, I had a feeling that would be just the thing to mess up the vibe since alcohol had a way of turning me into an annoying, overly-talkative mess. And considering I'd already had a close call earlier by bringing up his family, I decided not to chance it.

"Uh… I just want some juice."

"Like, a cranberry and vodka?" he asked, getting ready to put the order in with the bartender until I told him, "Minus the vodka."

For a second, he froze. And I assumed he was getting ready to tease me the same way Danielle had until he looked me dead in the eyes to ask, "*Wait.* You *are* old enough to drink, right?"

Since it wasn't the first time my age had gotten questioned - *shoutout to good genes and melanin* -, I could only laugh when I replied, "*What?* Of course! I have an entire quarter-century under my belt. I just… don't want to."

"I got you," he replied with a nod and a very lowkey sigh of relief that made me chuckle. And in no time at all, he was handing me a glass as he announced, "One cranberry juice over ice, with a light garnish for some swag."

Giggling again, I gave him a nod of thanks before taking a short sip from the straw while watching him take one straight from the glass, the lazy yet ridiculously sexy grin on his lips as he stared me down afterwards making my nipples rock hard in a way I knew could probably be seen right through my dress. And Dallas wasn't even ashamed to let it be known how much he appreciated them, his gaze settling right on my chest when he took another sip before asking, "You drive yourself here tonight?"

Shaking my head, I tossed my free hand towards where I

assumed my friends were and answered, "No. I rode with Danielle and her girlfriend."

"Good. Cause you're leaving with me," he stated so confidently, *so calmly*, that I almost missed what he'd actually said. But after repeating his declaration to myself in my head, I realized why he had said it the way he did, leaving no room for uncertainty since.... *yes. I was more than happy to leave with him.*

Even though the decision was already made in my head - *had already been made before I even got here* - I couldn't help asking, "Is that so?"

"Merry Dick-mas, right?" he asked with a teasing grin that had me shooting him a playful scowl as I shoved him in the arm, only making him chuckle as he insisted, "You're the one who said it."

There was no room for me to deny it, so I didn't even bother, no longer feeling as embarrassed about it now that I knew he was game to bring it to life. In fact, I didn't feel embarrassed about it at all, more giddy than anything as I gnawed on my lip and asked, "Can I tell you a secret?"

The inquisitive look he gave in response was enough for me to admit, "You're the reason I came out tonight. I mean, I *might've* came off the strength of wanting to see how my boss was living, but you're the reason I *had* to be here."

"So, wait... you got *this* fuckin' fine and came out to the party, just for little ol' me?" he asked as if he really couldn't believe it.

Either that, or he was just trying to gas me up.

Regardless, I couldn't but giggle when I repeated, "*Little ol' you*? Literally everyone in here showed you love when you walked in. There's nothing little about you, Dallas."

"That goes for a lot of things, love," he insisted with a wink over the rim of his glass, finishing his drink off with a long swig that had me ready to fast-forward through the party now that I knew for sure how the night would be ending. But instead of being impatient, I decided to take it all in, grabbing Dallas by the hand and pulling him towards the dance floor once, *"Give Love On Christmas Day"* by Johnny Gill started to play.

"About to be giving love on Christmas day, alright..." I thought with a

devilish grin, Dallas wrapping his arms around my waist from behind as he started singing the chorus loud as hell in my ear, making me crack up laughing, especially once Jaden cosigned, "Sing that shit, DB!"

And that was how the rest of the party went, filled with laughs, and off-key singing, and so much fun that I honestly didn't want it to end. But since the ending of the party meant the beginning of my Merry Dick-mas, I could only smile once Dallas finally asked, "You ready to go?"

DALLAS

I SHOULDN'T HAVE BEEN SURPRISED that Madison wanted to see the Christmas lights. There had been buses of people rolling through to check out my neighborhood for the same reason, costing me a pretty penny since I definitely wasn't going to be the only one on the block without my shit shining. But apparently I hadn't spent enough since Madison wasn't nearly as impressed with my display as she had been with some of the others, giving a nonchalant, *"Oh, that's cute,"* in response instead of the, "*Oh my God, that's gorgeous!*" everyone else had gotten.

Some bullshit, honestly.

I wasn't going to sweat it though since none of those houses had pretty ass Madison Walker walking inside of them, the sight of her calves in the stilettos she had on making my mouth water the same way it had when I saw them on her at work. Except this time, I could actually do something about it. And I didn't plan on wasting a second to do just that until she asked, "So you know I need the grand tour, right?"

"You really want me to give you a tour, or would you rather mosey around and be nosy by yourself while I go change out of these clothes into something more comfortable?" I suggested, watching a sneaky grin grow to her lips that answered my question long before she even spoke.

"Ummmm…. you can go change."

With a chuckle, I replied, "I figured you'd say that. I'll be right back." Then I headed up the stairs as Madison took off down the hall, surely getting ready to examine every picture hanging on the walls that led to my home office. There, I had a feeling she'd want to look at my collection of awards, things that were certainly in her future if she kept at it. And from there, I wasn't quite sure where she would go which meant I was rushing to get out of my party clothes into a t-shirt and sweats so that I could jog back downstairs as I asked, "*Madison?* Madison, where you at?"

"Down here!" she yelled from the basement, forcing me to jog down another set of stairs to find her.

Well… find the glowing light from the home theater that told me her exact location; though I wasn't at all expecting the sight I walked in on.

"Oh, shit…" was the only thing I could say in response to Madison occupying one of the oversized theater chairs with nothing but her lingerie and those damn stilettos on, taunting me with a smirk when she asked, "This *is* where the magic happens, isn't it?"

"Shit, it is now," I told her, snatching off the shirt I had just put on and tossing it to the side as Madison stood up from the chair, pushing me down into it the second I made it her way and then straddling my lap the same way she had done in the editing suite.

Since this time I knew for sure no one would be interrupting us, I held nothing back, grabbing greedy handfuls of her ass as she pressed her hands into my shoulders and professed, "I wanna be your friend, Dallas."

"We are definitely that, Madison," I told her, moving to take a few nibbles of her collarbone and give her all the proof she needed of just how well acquainted we were now.

Through her moans, she replied, "No. I wanna be *that* friend. The one you talked about in the editing suite yesterday. *Her.*"

"I thought you didn't have time for any of that?" I asked, pulling back to find her eyes along with the grin on her lips as she licked them before giving me an answer that was something like the perfect score to my ears.

"I didn't… until you put words to exactly what I *do* have time for. A friend; who I can be excited for and will be excited for me, and who will do stuff with me when we have the time, and who will… fuck me. Because I also have needs."

"Say that shit again," I groaned, riled the fuck up now that I knew she was really on-board.

Though I shouldn't have been surprised when she made me sweat again, taking her time to playfully ask, "Say what?"

"That last past."

"I also have needs?" she asked with a grin that told me she knew the real answer.

If she didn't, I had no problem making my request clear when I told her, "Nah, the part right before that."

Pretending like she had to think about it, she brought a finger to her chin as she said, "Hmm… *the part right before that, the part right before that…* What did I say? *Oh.* Fuck me?"

"Got you," I told her as if she was really asking me to do it and not confirming that's what I was talking about. But she didn't seem to care either way, accepting my onslaught of kisses and nibbles against her neck that trailed across her throat to the other side once she tilted her head back to give me access.

Since I had her wide open, I figured it was the perfect opportunity to get rid of her bra, anxious to see the nipples underneath since those mothafuckas had been asking for me all night. And when I finally had them free, I was more than happy to introduce myself, swirling my tongue around the right one before nipping it with my teeth in a way that made Madison shudder as I soothed it with a kiss. Then I paid the same attention to the left one, Madison grinding against my lap as she moaned, "*Fuck. That feels so good.*"

I don't know what it was about the way she said the word, "Fuck", but I swear that shit turned me on in the worst way, this stage of foreplay no longer being enough as I wrapped an arm around her waist to keep her close. Then I stood up with her still in my lap, laying her down where I was just sitting and dropping to my knees so I could get her panties out of the way and taste her.

"Gotdamn, I shouldn't have done that," I realized after my first swipe of her pearl, her sweet flavor instantly addictive as I went in for more. And Madison only egged me on, her hands buried in the curls on top of my head as I delivered a combination of slow and fast licks with the tip of my tongue that had her bridging up from the edge of the seat until she descended with an orgasm that left my beard-coated.

I loved that shit.

She was still panting as I stood up and dug in the pocket of my sweats for the condom I was glad I had grabbed on a whim, wanting to be prepared just in case we never actually made it upstairs. But the second I ripped the package open, Madison sat up to say, "*Nu uh.* Christmas is about giving *and* receiving." Then she yanked my sweats down and grabbed my dick like it was never not hers, stroking it in her hand as she asked, "May I?"

"Just like her sweet ass to ask for permission," I thought with a smirk as I told her, "Shit, be my guest."

Matching my smirk, she started teasing me with little licks against the tip as she continued to stroke me, finding pleasure in swiping at the pre-cum before she took me into her mouth. And I'd be damned if I didn't shudder the same way she had earlier, burying my hand in the back of her curls for leverage as I watched her go crazy with it.

Just like with the art of filmmaking, she took great pride in putting in the work, driving me out of my damn mind as she sucked, and stroked, and massaged my balls, and then deepthroated me to the point that my toes were curling up in my damn socks. And before I knew it, I had both of my hands buried in her hair, practically fucking her face as she held onto my thighs for leverage of her own. But she wasn't backing down, taking it like a pro even with a mess of saliva running down her chin and tears forming in her eyes.

The shit was sexy as hell. And honestly, it was surprising as hell too.

Not that I was complaining.

In fact, it only made me more excited to learn all the other secrets she was keeping about herself, getting ready to tackle one more when I finally pulled out of her mouth so I could put the condom on while she worked to catch her breath.

"Second time you've tried to kill me in just a few days," Madison groaned, wiping her chin with a devilish grin like she actually enjoyed coming close to death a little bit.

I couldn't help but smile as I grabbed her chin to tell her, "Nah, I'd never hurt you, baby. I mean, I *am* about to fuck the shit outta you, *but...*"

She didn't even let me finish before she was turning around in her seat, propping her ass up with an invitation for me to take her from behind. And once I got the condom secured, I did just that, the warmth of her pussy alone when I slid in making me hiss, "*Shit,*" just as Madison grabbed onto the back of the seat.

Without waiting for me to make a move, she started throwing it back on me, damn near making me stumble since it had caught me offguard. But it wasn't long before she was letting me take over, completely consumed by the pleasure she was receiving as I kept one hand at her waist and wrapped the other around her throat.

"You like that shit, don't you, Ms. Walker?"

She could only moan and nod in response, damn near about to rip the fabric off the seat cushion as I killed her shit from the back. And the sight of her coming undone only made me go harder, moving my hand from her neck to her hair and giving it a stiff yank that earned me an, "*Oh, God...*"

"Ms. Walker if you nasty, right?" I groaned, leaning forward to bite into her shoulder as she begged, "*Dallas, please...*" And well, now that it was officially Christmas, I was in a *real* giving mood, digging her out with deep strokes that had her holding her breath until she came with a beautifully loud scream that had me busting only a few seconds later.

"Merry Dick-mas, baby," I teased with a hard smack on her ass once I pulled out, her laughs muffled against the seat as I told her, "Let me grab you a towel."

The basement bathroom made the task an easy one, taking a second to get rid of the condom and clean myself up before grabbing a warm towel to take her. But apparently I had taken too long since, by the time I made it back, Madison's naked ass was already curled up in the chair knocked the hell out.

"Don't need no cover or nothin', huh?" I asked out loud with a chuckle, doing my best to clean her up a little bit without waking her. Then I put my clothes back on and went to grab a few blankets from the closet to cover her up with, hoping they'd be enough since the basement tended to get a little chilly at night.

"*Guess one more won't hurt,*" I thought, adding another blanket to the bunch that already looked like a mountain on top of her and using the other half of it to cover myself in the seat next to her before reaching for the remote. And apparently Madison wasn't the only one tired since I didn't even make it past the home screen of *Netflix* according to the sight I woke up to - that and a still very much asleep Madison who had shedded two out of three blankets over the course of the night.

Shaking my head, I pulled myself out of the chair to find my phone, not all that surprised to see a text from Alexis.

"Merry Christmas, bro! The mistletoe was a sweet touch last night, huh?" - Alexis

"Definitely was. Merry Christmas. From me and Madison. ;)" - Dallas

"Wowwwww! You better be good to her! And get her something nice!" - Alexis

"*Shit,*" I whispered, knowing I hadn't even thought about getting her a Christmas present since I had no idea we'd end up like this.

But with a quick glance at the clock and another glance at Madison who hadn't budged since I'd been awake, I realized I still had time to make it a true Merry Christmas for her.

MADISON

I WOKE up with my hair a matted mess, a crick in my neck, dry ass contacts that I hadn't gotten a chance to take out before I fell asleep, and a hint of soreness between my thighs. But I could only smile to myself because of what it all represented.

Dallas Bryant was mine.

I mean, he was my friend. But like... not in a normal friendly kind of way, or even a strictly professional way. It was more than that, deeper than that. And if last night was any indication, it had the potential to be something really special in the future; already felt like something special to me.

Clutching one of the covers Dallas must've brought me to my chest, I gnawed on my lip as I replayed the night in my head.

The party.

The mistletoe.

The singing.

The sex.

The sex.

It was like something I'd never experienced before, bringing out a side of myself that I hardly recognized but was already so, so in love with.

Yeah, I wanted to be *that* Madison from here on out. And not because Dallas appreciated it so much, but because it felt so good to *me* to finally let that side free.

"As long as she doesn't get your ass in any trouble," I thought with a chuckle, tensing up a tiny bit from the surprise of Dallas rounding the corner with a red box in his hand and a big ol' grin on his face.

"Merry Christmas, Ms. Walker. This is for you."

The box was already in my hands as I squealed, "Awww, Dallas! But I didn't get you anything!"

Taking the seat next to mine, he asked, "You mean, last night wasn't the gift? I thought I was behind in the game and was tryna play catch up. Shit, in that case, I'm taking this stuff back."

Just like that, my grin was replaced with a faux pout until he started laughing. "I'm playin', I'm playin'. Go ahead and open it, love."

Gnawing on my lip, I was more than anxious to see what was inside, giving the box a little shake first before I pulled off the top to find… "A new hard drive; *always clutch.* A three-day stay at the Golden Door Spa; *will definitely be making some time for that.* And a… diamond bracelet? Dallas, this is way too much!"

Don't get me wrong, the bracelet was absolutely gorgeous. But it felt way too early for a gift of such luxury; especially in combination with the other two amazing gifts he'd included in the box. In fact, it only made me feel worse about not getting him anything, even though I had no idea I'd even be coming in contact with Dallas Bryant just a few days ago.

And what a difference a few days can make...

Grabbing my hand, he insisted, "Let me explain. The hard drive I had actually bought for myself a while back, but I figured you could make better use of it. And the spa stay and bracelet were both in one of the gift bags from an awards show I went to last year."

Now that I knew he, *at least*, hadn't spent a ridiculous amount of money, I felt a little better about accepting them, putting my free hand to my blanketed chest as I teased, "Your awards show leftovers. I'm touched."

"Hey, at least their nice leftovers!" he defended with a chuckle that made me chuckle too as I gave his hand a squeeze.

"Seriously, though. I really *am* touched. This is definitely the nicest thing anyone has ever gotten for me."

Even if it was just a collection of his expensive junk, they were all things that would be put to good use on my end, making it perfect. And even if it hadn't been perfect, it would've still been perfect because it was coming from him, an almost boyish smile on his lips when he asked, "So I did a good job, huh?"

"You did a *great* job. Thank you, *friend*," I sang as I pulled him closer to give him an appreciative kiss on the cheek while he gave a sarcastic, "*Yeah, yeah, yeah, you're welcome,*" in response. And I was just getting ready to call him out on it when my phone started to buzz in the middle of the floor with an incoming *FaceTime* call from my mother.

"*Oh, shoot…*" I groaned, scrambling to make something of my hair, and then to make sure I was completely covered before reaching to grab the phone just in time to answer with an obnoxious, "Hi Mom! Merry Christmas! How's London?"

I was careful about keeping Dallas out of my background, though he still watched both me and the screen from the sideline as my mother gushed, "Merry Christmas, Maddie! London is beautiful! I so wish you could've joined us."

Turning down my parents' offer for a Christmas family vacation because of work had lowkey crushed me in the moment, especially when they decided to go to freakin' London of all places. But in the end, it had all worked out since not only had I gotten the opportunity of a lifetime to get in some experience as a director alongside one of the best to ever do it, I'd also… *well*, you know the rest.

With a sigh that was more to cool the warmth that rushed over me just thinking about Dallas's face between my thighs than anything, I told her, "I know, but… *work*. Did you get my video?"

Since my parents weren't exactly the most technologically-savvy people, preferring to stick to the old school gadgets they grew up with, I was worried they'd have trouble figuring out how to view it. But it made me proud to hear my mother answer, "*Did we*? Girl, that video had your father boo-hoo crying all over my English breakfast this morning."

Suddenly, my dad appeared in the background of the screen to say, "No, I wasn't! There was just something in my eye! Merry Christmas, baby girl."

"Merry Christmas, Dad. I'm glad you liked the gift."

Dominating the screen, my mother replied, "It was truly beautiful, Maddie. I can't wait to watch it again later tonight. We're both so proud of you, honey. And make sure you tape that Christmas special you worked on for us to watch when we get back. You know how much I love me some G. Griffey."

While I was already chuckling at her asking me to "tape" it as if that concept hadn't been replaced with DVR, I started for real laughing when my dad showed back up in the screen to say, "Relax, woman. His high yella ass ain't even all that, and neither are his lyrics. I mean, who can't rhyme a couple words together?"

Pulling her head back to face him, she defended, "You can't, negro! And that boy is as handsome as he can be! If you die first, I'm going after him. And don't you even *think* about haunting us from the grave with your hatin' behind."

"These two," I thought, shaking my head with another giggle as I broke up their bickering to say, "Y'all enjoy the rest of your vacation, and I'll see you when you get back, okay?"

"*Wait.* Did you get our gift? I paid extra for it to be delivered last night."

Out of my peripheral, I saw Dallas take his eyes elsewhere with a guilty grin, knowing he was part of the reason I had no idea about the gift they'd apparently sent me last night. And without giving too much away, I told my mother, "I uh… I haven't been home yet to check."

"Oh. *Oh!* Well then. Merry Christmas to you, hot stuff," she practically purred, my cheeks flooding with heat as I decided it was officially time to rush her off the phone.

"Bye, Mom! Bye, Dad! Love you both!"

"Love you more, Maddie! Bye!"

The three little beeps signaling the call had been ended made my shoulders sink with relief, still staring at the empty screen with a grin when Dallas said, “Your parents are a trip, hot stuff.”

Giggling at his use of my mother’s impromptu nickname, I replied, “They definitely are. Gotta love ‘em though.”

“As you should,” he agreed. “They seem like really good people. And they raised a really good you.”

Turning his way with a smirk, I asked, “A really good me, huh?”

“Really, *really* good,” he emphasized, glancing at my blanketed chest and licking his lips before he asked, “You’re probably ready to get on home though, huh? Got some big plans with family and all that?”

“Uh… you just saw my family who is clearly an international flight away,” I answered as I started to address the notifications on my phone from the night before and this morning; not at all surprised to see a message from Danielle teasing me as usual.

"Merry Christmas, Mistletoe Maddie. I hope Dallas had the stamina of thirty-two hoodlum elves last night ;)" - Danielle

With a quiet chuckle, I typed out a response that rivaled hers with jokes about Tracey’s unlimited stamina just as Dallas asked, “What about your cousins, and aunties, and play cousins?”

“Both of my parents were solo kids like me, so no aunties, no cousins. And all of my play cousins are out in Savannah where I was raised which means I’ll be responding in this group chat and calling it a day,” I answered, hopping over to the thread of texts they’d already started to do so before I could forget.

“So you’re spending Christmas by yourself?”

My fingers froze on the screen at his question, the idea not sounding nearly as exciting as it had in my head when it was first decided. I mean, I was still very much looking forward to having the day off and doing as close to nothing as possible. But something about the way he’d asked gave me a spur of the moment idea, gnawing on my grin as I pushed out, "Or maaaaybe... spending it with you."

"*With me*?"

"Unless you have other plans," I rushed to follow with so I wouldn't sound too pressed.

Because I wasn't pressed.

"Okay, maybe I am a little bit pressed," I thought, knowing it was hard not to be after last night. But I was grateful to see the excited grin on Dallas's face when he finally replied, "Nah, I'm game. What we doin', Mistletoe Maddie?"

"Oh my God, you saw that?!" I squealed, making Dallas laugh as he explained, "Your font size is like the E at the top of the eye chart, love. I could've read that shit from upstairs."

"Shut up!" I screeched with a smack to his arm that only made him laugh harder as I finally got back to the topic at hand. "But anyway… what *I* was going to do, was hang out on the couch in my Christmas pajamas watching cheesy *Hallmark* movies all day with my filmmaker eyes off until the Christmas special airs later on. But now that you're involved…"

"*We'll* be watching cheesy *Hallmark* movies with our filmmaker eyes off, doing all the fuckin' they can't do on the *Hallmark* channel until the Christmas special airs later on," he suggested, scraping his bottom lip with his teeth as he served me that sexy, heated stare again, letting me know exactly which part of his version of our plans was on his mind.

I certainly wasn't complaining, though I also couldn't help toying with him a little bit when I asked, "Why do you assume I wanna fuck you, Dallas Bryant?"

Instead of answering my question, he groaned, "*Mm.* Say that shit again, Ms. Walker."

"Say what?"

"Just the last half," he urged, his eyes already sitting low as he waited for me to fulfill his request.

Since it was clear I had him on edge, I took my dear sweet time, licking my lips before I sat up on my knees with the cover still wrapped around me and asked, "I wanna fuck you, Dallas Bryant?"

"*Bingo*. Time to go. Merry Dick-mas round two. It's happenin'. *Ho, ho, ho...*" he rattled off as he popped up from his chair then swooped me up in his arms, making me giggle as he took us up both sets of stairs with the strength of thirty-two hoodlum elves. And once we made it to his bedroom, he kept that same energy, making it a Christmas morning - *a Christmas day* - I'd never forget.

DALLAS

January 2nd.

ZALAYAH WASN'T PLAYING about setting up that meeting for first thing in the new year.

It was only day two of three-sixty-five and I was already on a plane headed out to meet with her and her team to discuss the project she had in mind to go with the release of her next album, something I was excited about since I wouldn't be doing it alone.

Glancing over at Madison who was knocked out in the window seat, I could only smile to myself as I thought about how much had happened in the last week and a half; how we'd gone from strangers to… something special.

Something really damn special.

But it wasn't just about what was going on between the two of us on a personal level that had me hyped, I was genuinely excited that her work on the Christmas special had paved the way for this opportunity, knowing this would only propel her to something even greater. And from there, the sky was truly the limit, forcing me to step my game up so her talented ass wouldn't be taking my job.

"*Talented and adorable,*" I thought as I brushed my thumb against the drool at the corner of her lip before it could slip down onto her shirt, that little touch enough to pull her from her slumber as she sat up to stretch her arms over her head. Then she reached for her glasses that she'd left in the seat back pocket for her nap, the fact that she was a little more aware now giving me room to tease, "Must've been dreaming about me doing all that drooling over there."

Her voice was groggy as hell when she responded, "I feel like I'm still recovering from New Year's Eve. Is it possible to be drunk for days straight after one long night?"

The mention of New Year's Eve made me chuckle since drunk Madison was a whole new beast; one who had barely made it to midnight trying to keep up with me on the alcohol tip knowing her ass was a lightweight. But we'd had a good time - *I always did with her* - sharing a Happy New Year's kiss that rivaled our one under the mistletoe but didn't have shit on what she did to me later that night.

The next morning was an entirely different story, though. In fact, I was a little worried she wouldn't be able to make the meeting with me today since her ass couldn't seem to stay off the toilet one way or the other. But like the soldier she was, she managed to pull it together enough to catch the flight after sleeping the entire first day of the new year away. Though apparently, she still wasn't at full strength.

Grabbing her hand, I finally replied, "You aren't drunk, but you probably still are recovering; especially since you didn't really eat anything yesterday. We'll take care of that when we touch down."

With a nod, she adjusted so she could lay her head on my shoulder, the whole thing feeling comfortable as hell as I turned to press a quick kiss against her forehead before settling deeper into my seat. And I hadn't even realized I had dozed off until I felt the jolt of the plane landing, Madison's hand still in mine when I woke up even though she was wide awake staring out of the window.

Again, comfortable as hell. But I didn't feel guilty about it, especially once I saw the smile on Madison's face as she turned my way to tease, "Must've been dreaming about me with all that drool running into your beard."

Pulling my hand away, I used it to check how much there really was, happy to find it was only a little damp even when I told her, "You ain't real for lettin' it get that far, though."

"Maybe if you would've let my hand go, I could've gotten it," she defended with a laugh, wiping at what I had apparently left behind before she added, "But for the record, I'm very much into your sweet, cuddly side, Mr. Bryant."

"Mmmhmm, I bet you are..." I groaned with another quick kiss to her forehead that made her smirk just as we got the green light to deboard the plane.

I was happy to see the improvement in her condition, bringing an easy smile to my lips by the time we made it to baggage claim. Well… that and the fact that she was wearing those damn stilettos I loved, giving me plenty of ideas for after our meeting with Zalayah. But for now, the meeting was the focus, Madison and I patiently waiting on the curb of the rideshare pick-up area for our *Uber* driver, Boston, when I asked her, "You ready to do this, Ms. Walker?"

Glancing up at me with a halfhearted smile, I worried the nerves of the moment were finally beginning to settle in. Either that, or she wasn't feeling as good as I thought she was. But I quickly learned neither of those were true when Madison rushed to throw her arms around my neck, giving me a kiss that completed the trifecta before pulling away to say, "Now I'm ready."

THE END.

FEATURED TITLES

*Read all about Reagan & Gavin in, The Real Deal.

Reagan is living the dream.
She has a wonderful, fulfilling job working at the local community center. She has her own place and a comfortable lifestyle. The only thing she's missing is someone to share it all with. Unfortunately, the second she thought she may have found the one was only a few short months before she found his fiancé. And now, the only way she can prove that she has really moved on from him is by showing off her new man. But there's only one problem. The new man doesn't actually exist.
Insert Gavin.
An innocent bystander and up-and-coming rapper caught in the chess match of Reagan's game on his first day of community service. When she desperately needs him to fulfill the role as her boyfriend to save face, Gavin quickly finds ways to also benefit from their arrangement.
But what happens when the line between fulfilling a role and real companionship begins to blend? Can something that starts off as a deal between two strangers actually turn into something real?

**Read all about Alexis & Jaden in the Attractions & Distractions series.

Attractions & Distractions: Freshman Year

Alexis + men = disaster. At least, that's how it's always been. Still, she's easily tempted by her new surroundings at the University of California to put a foot forward into the dating pool; just not her best one. Relationships and situation-ships quickly become a balancing act as she tries to survive her freshman year.

Jaden is something like an "it guy", but not by choice. He would much rather live a quiet, normal life exactly opposite of the one the media portrays. So when he meets Alexis by chance, he instantly falls for her beauty, charm, and… normalcy. But he learns very quickly that dealing with her is anything but normal.

Tyree isn't a man of many words; he prefers action. When, sweet, sexy, naive Alexis Martin becomes a resident in his dorm, he can't help trying his hand at getting with her, even if she is a freshman.

Attractions and Distractions will take you on a bumpy ride through the struggles and triumphs of finding love on the college scene.

***Read all about Zalayah & Gabriel in, Heated Harmonies.

The music industry has always been her world, but it almost crushed his…

International superstar Zalayah is desperate to break out of her popstar box with a completely new image, a new look, and most importantly, a new sound. But after years of working with some of the biggest producers in the land, she knows she must go beyond the usual to get exactly what she's looking for.

Gabriel has sworn off being in the music industry regardless of how talented he is as a musician. But when one of the biggest popstars in the world comes knocking at his door with a proposition he can't refuse, his initial disdain quickly becomes a battle of the head and the heart as he finds himself not only falling under the guise of the industry but also falling for her.

Creating the perfect harmony in the studio is an easy feat. But when outside influences find their way inside, it's only a matter of time before things become too hot to handle...

A TALE OF TWO CITIES

A NEW YEAR NOVELLA

CHEYENNE

I COULDN'T WAIT to see him.

It was New Year's Eve, and I hadn't seen my *almost*-boyfriend since the very first time we met well over a month ago while he was on a business trip in my city which meant this reunion was long overdue. I mean, we might've texted every day, and shared pics, and slid into each other's *Instagram* DMs to be funny, and even snuck in the occasional *FaceTime* call when he wasn't too busy with work. But there was nothing like a real face-to-face interaction which was why I called myself surprising him for the holiday even though he claimed he'd be out to visit me the following week.

Obviously, I wasn't interested in waiting. In fact, I'd just barely touched down in the city before I was already changed out of my travel gear into something slinky, shiny, and short that I knew he would love, putting in a request for the *Uber* that would get me to the building he owned as I made my way back down to the hotel's lobby.

Honestly, I probably shouldn't have even booked a night at the hotel since it was pretty much a guarantee I'd be staying at his place. Then again, maybe he'd want to come back to my hotel room and reenact our very first night together; just the thought giving me chills as my phone alerted me my *Uber* driver was already pulling up.

Glancing at the screen, I first made note of the car type and color, then the name of the driver, and finally the first few letters of the license plate before looking up to find a license plate that matched the one listed.

"Boston?" I asked after I opened the door, leaning in to find a thick and muscular khaki-brown man with the most beautiful hazel-green eyes I'd ever seen; eyes that lowkey reminded me of my own.

Just like people seemed to do when they looked at me, I quickly found myself lost in his eyes until he asked, "Cheyenne, right?"

Answering with a nod, I climbed into the backseat of his SUV, my super tight dress and sky-high heels making the task a lot more difficult than it needed to be. But it was also enough to hold Boston's attention, the hem of my dress riding up my thigh in a way that had him watching me intently before eventually turning around to start our trip.

"I know Drew's ass better look at me the same exact way," I thought as Boston started the GPS while commenting, "Damn. I've dropped like three people off at this same place already tonight. Must be a really special event going on."

"My… boyfriend is throwing a New Year's Eve party," I responded a little too proudly since Drew and I had yet to actually make things official. But I assumed that's what tonight would be, especially since he'd already been hinting at how badly he wanted me to be his.

Just the thought had me giddy until I heard the driver mutter, "*That's what the last girl said too...*"

"What?"

Shaking his head, he kept his eyes on the road as he replied, "Nothin'. I mean, it's none of my business. I'm sure you'll have a great time with your boyfriend."

He was trying to play it off, but I wasn't buying it, sitting up towards the edge of the seat to see his face when I urged, "No, tell me. The last girl? What last girl?"

Instead of answering my question, he peeked over his shoulder to warn, "Ma, you look pretty as hell tonight. But if you wanna stay pretty, I suggest you sit back and put your damn seatbelt on."

His compliment might've had me blushing, mainly because his voice was sexy as hell. But I still didn't budge, putting on my prettiest face to bargain, "I will... once you tell me what the last girl said."

For all I knew, he could've easily been fuckin' with me on the strength of never having to see me again. I mean, I could only imagine how bored he got driving people around, so he was probably just teasing me for entertainment. At least, that's what I wanted to believe since I better not have traveled all this way and gotten this fine just for Drew to be on some bullshit.

I was already starting to become upset at the possibility when, *instead of submitting to my request*, Boston replied, "Admittedly, I didn't read the *Uber* driver handbook. But I'm pretty sure that goes against rider confidentiality or somethin', ma."

"I don't need to know who she was. I just need to know what she said," I begged, bordering the line of pathetic.

It was all in my demeanor, all in my tone, fuckin' up all the baddie vibes I'd gotten into his truck with. And unfortunately, that feeling remained when Boston groaned, "I already told you that."

With a heavy sigh, I finally sat back, my excited energy from before almost fully replaced with anxiety as I tried to talk myself through it. "Her boyfriend is throwing a New Year's Eve party. At the same place my boyfriend is throwing his. Because it's not impossible for there to be two parties going on at the same place."

"Sure. That's probably it," Boston chimed in with a lick of sarcasm in his tone that had me hot.

In fact, I was so annoyed that I used the only weapon I had when I spewed, "Four stars."

Through his rearview mirror, he peeked back at me with a frown. "*What?* Come on now. It's not that deep. For all I know, I could've heard her wrong."

His sudden alibi only made me go lower. "Three stars."

This time instead of defending himself, he only shrugged. "Fuck it. I'ma give you three stars too then. Shit, maybe even two stars since you wanna fuck up a nigga's rating over some he said-she said nonsense."

The way he said it, you would've thought he wasn't the "he" of that phrase; though I could only focus on the first part of his threat when I sat back up to ask, "Wait. You'd really do that?"

"You'd really give me three stars for tryna help you out with a little intel when I didn't have to?" he challenged, giving me another quick peek over his shoulder since apparently I'd gotten a little too far into his personal space. Then again, it wasn't my fault his ass was so… husky.

Husky and handsome.

Still, regardless of how handsome he was, this was a total stranger who had quite a bit of control over my life with him being in the driver's seat. So I created a bit of room when I released another sigh before asking, "*Just*… did she say a name?"

He immediately shook his head. "Nah. And I didn't ask. Because it was none of my business. Now put your seatbelt on before I really have to downgrade you, ma."

Even though the entire interaction had me pouting, I still did what he'd asked since I wasn't trying to be out here with a shitty rider rating. But I only became more annoyed when, by the time I finally settled in, we were already pulling up to our destination.

Without even looking at me, Boston offered a plain ass, "Enjoy yourself, ma," knowing good and well he'd thrown a wrench in my plans to do just that. But after reminding myself it was highly unlikely he really knew what the hell he was talking about, it was easy for me to reply with an even more plain, "You too," before I climbed out of his truck to head inside with my shoulders pulled back and my head held high.

This was my moment.

The exact location of the party was made obvious by the steady flow of people going in and out of one area of the building in particular, everyone dressed fancily with a champagne flute in hand as a jazz band quietly played on in the background. But the deeper I got into the crowd, the more out of place I felt since it all seemed so… stiff, and cold, and… *sophisticated.*

Yeah, it was *that* kind of party because Drew ran in *that* kind of circle. But he wasn't like them which was what had attracted me to him the most. Sure, he could hold his own around these people, but he wasn't a cornball. At least, he wasn't a cornball when he was with me.

Now, I was starting to think differently since, when I finally spotted him, I could tell he was letting off one of those overly-nasally laughs without even hearing him, my eyes squinted as I watched him toss his arm around some woman's shoulder.

"*Who the hell is she?*" I thought as I snatched a flute of champagne from one of the servers' trays, downing it in a few gulps before continuing my observation. But apparently, I wasn't the only one interested in what Drew had going on, a second woman approaching him with a scowl that had Drew immediately dropping his arm from the woman's shoulder to address her.

The previously-shouldered woman wasn't at all happy about that, matching ol' girl's scowl as Drew looked to be struggling to explain what was so obvious to me from afar.

His slick ass had gotten caught up.

And I was about to put the cherry on top.

Slowly making my way through the crowd, I got close enough to be noticed without having to acknowledge him first. But I could tell the exact moment he realized who I was, even going as far as ditching the other two women to make his way over to me.

"Is that shit supposed to make me feel better?" I wondered as he approached me with a sighed, "*Baby*. What are you doing here?"

"*Baby*? Who the fuck is this, Andy?" the original shit starter asked, clearly the angriest out of the three of us for reasons I was slightly curious to hear.

Well, slightly curious to hear after I figured out… "Andy? Who the hell is Andy?"

"*Andrew* clearly has a lot of explaining to do," the once-shouldered woman chimed in, the ring on her left hand giving away her role in all of this even though she'd been the one to help me put two-and-two together.

"*Oh, right. Nicknames and shit…*" I realized, crossing my arms over my chest as I agreed, "He *does* have some explaining to do. *To y'all.* Cause my eyes have already told me everything I need to know."

It was honestly a shame that all that good dick was being wasted on a man who thought he was somehow doing us a favor by sharing it with the community. But I suppose it was better for me to find out now before I got too caught up, planning to leave every memory of his triflin' behind at the doors of this wack ass party until Drew reached out for my arm and begged, "Cheyenne, wait."

"Andrew, are you serious right now?" his wife asked in a harsh whisper, seemingly more concerned about not making a scene than what the hell her shitty ass husband had been up to. And while their business was really none of mine beyond this moment, I couldn't help putting a hand to her arm to tell her, "Honey, you can do *so* much better."

Snatching her arm away, she spewed, "Screw you, you whore. If it wasn't for *disgusting* women like you, *and her*, my husband and I wouldn't be in this mess."

"Disgusting women?" I repeated, my face scrunched at the audacity before I went in. "Now I see exactly why you're in this mess. This nigga is obviously a dog. But instead of saying to yourself, "*Hey, maybe I should hold my husband accountable for his actions*", you choose to take that anger out on me; the one who didn't even know his trash ass was married because he damn sure didn't have a ring on when we met. Otherwise I wouldn't have fucked him."

"I knew he was married when I fucked him. I just didn't care," the mad woman chimed in with a proud smirk, making me shake my head since…

"*Girl*, you're kinda fuckin' up my argument here," I whispered her way, her lips pulled into an immediate frown until Drew grabbed my hand and confessed the unthinkable.

"Cheyenne, I only want you. *I just…* I didn't know how to tell her."

My eyes were already wide at his statement, but they only grew wider at the sight of his wife slapping the shit out of him, making the entire crowd gasp including the jazz band who had stopped playing their instruments to see what was going on. And once I realized that meant I had somehow become the center of attention, I knew I had to get out fast, yanking my hand away and taking off as best as I could through the crowd towards the exit with Drew's crazy ass right on my heels.

"Baby, wait! Just hear me out!" he shouted after me as I started going even faster, grateful for all of my professional dance training that made running in heels a breeze. But the closer I got to outside, the more I realized I didn't really have an exit strategy since I hadn't driven here myself, beginning to panic until I saw a familiar truck sitting in the drop-off area.

BOSTON

"APPRECIATE THE RIDE, MY G."

Giving my last passenger of the night some dap, I unlocked the door for him as I replied, "Keep that same energy on a five-star rating for me, bet?"

With the pretty ass passenger before him still on my mind, I knew I needed all the five-star ratings I could get to balance out the possibility of her fuckin' me over. And I was glad to hear him say, "I got you," before he closed the door behind him, his exit prompting me to grab my phone to not only mark his ride as completed but also end my night as an *Uber* driver since I wasn't about to have a bunch of drunk ass mothafuckas throwing up in my backseat.

That shit wasn't even worth the extra money.

After doing both tasks, I scrolled over to my messages to confirm the plans for tonight with my homeboy, Khalid. Typically, I would bring in the New Year with my girl and her family, so I didn't even get a chance to kick it with him like that for this particular occasion. But for the first time in a few years, I was going into the new year a single man while he was the one in a whole ass relationship.

"*Lucky him,*" I thought as I finally shot him a text.

"Party at the Miller's still a go?" - Boston

"You already know. Make sure you grab a liquor contribution on the way though. Mama Annie don't play that showing up empty-handed shit." - Khalid

"I got you. Send me the address." - Boston

I was waiting for the text with the location when my passenger door was suddenly yanked open by the fine ass girl from earlier, her climbing into my truck catching me completely offguard as I started, "*What the…*"

"Drive! Please, just drive!" she begged as she slammed and locked the door behind her, the sight of some random nigga running out of the building in a suit making me do just that since it was obvious she had gotten herself into some shit she needed me to get her out of. But I also didn't know her, so I wasted no time getting answers the second we were in the clear.

"Care to explain what's going on, ma? Or you just expect me to be kindhearted and give you a free ride back to the hotel I just picked you up from?" I asked, her heavy breathing telling me she must've really been getting chased for a minute before she jumped into my whip and whatever it was must've been hella messy since she felt more comfortable with a stranger than with the suited and booted nigga.

Instead of answering my question, she simply replied, "You were right," my piqued eyebrow making her explain between breaths, "About the girlfriend. The guy had a girlfriend. And a wife."

"*Definitely messy as hell,*" I thought as I inquired, "The nigga who was chasing you? Your boyfriend?"

Now that she had caught her breath, her sentence was a lot

more cohesive when she answered, "Well, he wasn't technically my boyfriend yet. We were just talking."

"You called him your boyfriend earlier. Said you were going to your boyfriend's party," I challenged, the way she immediately rolled her eyes in response telling me she didn't appreciate my attention to detail. But it was that same attention to detail that even had me comfortable "just driving" like she'd insisted since I had immediately recognized her.

Not that I could forget a face like that.

Or those eyes.

They were more hazel now than the green they appeared to be earlier, but still beautiful as hell in combination with her golden-brown skin and long ass hair that was straightened to perfection. But the fact that she had a nigga literally chasing after her told me to stay in my lane, even when she quietly answered, "Well, he's not anything to me now."

Something about the sadness in her tone made me feel a way; not that it should've even mattered to me. But it was obvious the reality of the situation was beginning to settle in; mainly the fact that the plans she thought she had for the holiday no longer existed and the person she thought she'd be bringing in the New Year with wasn't making it out of this year after all.

If anybody felt that shit, it was me.

So instead of letting her slip into the hole I was still digging myself out of, I offered, "You should come to this little party with me, ma."

"*What?*"

Speaking on the party reminded me I needed to stop and pick something up to bring, pulling into the first gas station parking lot I saw as I explained, "A friend of a friend's mom is throwing a New Year's Eve party. You should come with me. Shits gonna be live."

I shouldn't have been surprised when she turned my way and asked, "Are you crazy? *Come to a party with you?* I don't even know you. I don't even… know your name."

"Well that sure didn't stop you from getting in the car with Boston Reed, did it?" I asked teasingly, the amused smirk she gave me in response letting me know she had caught my drift as she stuck her hand out to reply, "Cheyenne Foster."

It was only supposed to be a handshake, but I swear I felt a little tremor shoot between our palms when they connected. But when I didn't see a reaction on her face, I shook it off to tell her, "Pleasure to meet you, Cheyenne. Now you rollin' to this party with me or not?"

Gnawing on her lip, she answered, "*I mean…* I'm already in your truck, so do I really have a choice?"

"You always got a choice. I just know you might need a distraction right now. Unless you'd rather go back to your hotel room and cry yourself into the new year…" I trailed, giving her the only other option I envisioned.

But with another roll of her eyes, she groaned, "I am *not* gonna cry over his wack ass. Not even a tear."

"Okay, Cheyenne J. Blige. *Heard you,*" I joked as I climbed out of the truck and watched her do the same on the other side, getting a better look at her dress the second she rounded the front.

Even though her hair was mostly covering it, I could now see that the entire back was out, giving off sexy ass vibes that explained exactly why ol' boy had been chasing after her. Well, either that or her sculpted legs and ass that lowkey had me wondering if she was one of those *Instagram* fitness models. But regardless of what she did for a living, one thing was for certain.

Baby girl was bad as hell.

Again, I found myself shaking it off since I didn't want to freak her out, letting her lead the way and then opening the door for us to enter the gas station. But instead of following me straight to the counter, she headed to the aisles to pick out a snack, returning with a bag of white cheddar popcorn as the store clerk moved to grab the bottle of *Ciroc* from the shelf behind him.

Tossing her popcorn onto the counter, she offered, "I'll pay you for the ride. Just let me know how much it'll be." But I quickly brushed her off.

"Don't even worry about it, ma."

"At least let me pay for the alcohol then," she pressed as the clerk finally turned back around and damn near dropped the bottle after laying eyes on Cheyenne.

Honestly, I couldn't even blame him.

Still, after he pulled it together and rung us up, I couldn't let her do that either, paying for both the liquor and her popcorn as I told her, "I got it."

Thankfully, she didn't continue to push, reaching past me to grab her popcorn in a way that had her titties brushing up against me before she said, "Thank you, Boston." And after giving her a short nod in return, I couldn't help but chuckle when the store clerk gave me the, *"I see you"* look on our way out, clearly under the impression that Cheyenne and I were together even though we were strangers in the most literal way possible.

Things didn't have to stay that way, though. And I suppose I was taking the first step to break that ice when I pulled off towards the Miller residence and asked, "So where you from, ma?"

Instead of answering my question, she fired back one of her own. "Where am I from, or where do I live? Cause those are two different things."

"Both then," I replied over the sound of her ripping into her bag of popcorn.

She stuck a handful into her mouth before she answered, "I'm *from* Kansas City, but I live in Los Angeles now. I work out there, as a professional dancer."

"That explains your legs," I commented more to myself than her. But it was clear she had heard me when she turned my way to ask, "*What*?"

In an attempt to not cause any controversy, I didn't even look her way to answer, "Nothin', ma."

But of course she wasn't buying it, her face pulled into a slight scowl when she pressed, "No, what did you say? What about my legs?"

Since she didn't exactly strike me as the type to just let shit go, I released a heavy sigh before I answered, "They're just… *strong*. In a good way. But if you dance for a living, that makes sense. Dancers need strong legs, right?"

Agreeing with me was too much like right, so she avoided doing so by asking, "What do you do? Or is *Uber* your full-time thing?"

Shaking my head, I shared, "Nah, it's just something I'm doing to keep busy during the off-season. I actually just got back to the states not too long ago."

"Back to the states from where?"

"Canada. I play in the CFL," I told her, lowkey still feeling the effects of the season on my body from the work I had put in at tight end.

While it might not have earned me the same NFL money I'd gotten in the past, it was still enough to keep my bills paid as I earned a little extra on the side whenever I felt like it with this *Uber* shit. But Cheyenne hadn't made it that far yet, still stuck on the main part of my occupation when she asked, "And the CFL is…?"

"The Canadian Football League."

"Ohhh, well that explains your size," she commented with a smirk before tossing another handful of popcorn into her mouth just as I asked, "*My size?*"

Nodding enthusiastically, she answered, "Yeah, man. You're like… *huge*. In a good way. I mean, you gotta be huge to play in the KFC, right?"

With a laugh, I corrected, "CFL, Cheyenne."

"Yeah, that too," she replied with a wave of her hand as we made our way past where the party was happening to find a parking spot on the street that it took us two extra blocks to locate and made Cheyenne worry. "Damn. There's a lot of cars here. You sure it's okay for me to just be showing up? Will there even be any room?"

"The more, the merrier around these parts. Miss. Annie lives for a good time. Or so I've been told…" I trailed, only able to go off the word of my homie and whatever he shared on social media about it every year since I usually missed out.

Cheyenne picked up on that immediately, her eyes filled with a hint of concern when she repeated, "So you've been told? You've never been here?"

I couldn't focus on her question as I maneuvered into a parallel parking spot. But according to the look on her face once I finished, she still needed answers. "Uhhh… not exactly. I've heard enough about it to know what to expect, though."

Instead of responding to me, she only sighed, "*God, what am I getting myself into*?" And honestly, the same question was on my mind as we started the walk towards the party, the drop in temperature doing Cheyenne and her dress no favors as she wrapped her arms around her body to keep warm.

The gentleman in me wasn't having that.

Stopping her with an arm in her path, I told her, "Yo, hold up. I think I got an extra jacket back in my truck you can wear."

"A jacket that will hide the dress I spent a pretty penny on just for this night? I think not," she replied as she moved past me to pick up the pace in her walk, the sight of her already a few feet in front of me making me shake my head as I jogged to catch up before shooting Khalid a text to let him know I was outside. And by the time we made it to the door, he was already pulling it open with some goofy ass New Year glasses over his eyes.

"The Bos! What's good, bruh? It's been too long," he announced as he let us inside and immediately pulled me in for some dap and a hug.

When I pulled away, I couldn't help but agree, "Man, tell me about it. It's good to be back, for real."

It wasn't that I didn't enjoy my time in Canada. And obviously, I was grateful for any opportunity that paid me for playing a sport I knew like the back of my hand. But there was nothing like home, nothing like being around familiar faces, even if one of the most familiar faces of all no longer wanted anything to do with me.

Damn.

Before I could fade, Khalid turned back towards a woman I hadn't even noticed standing behind him to say, "Baby, this is my boy, Boston. He plays football up in Canada. Bos, this is my woman, Jayla."

"*Oh, right. Whole ass relationship*," I thought, trying not to be salty about it as Jayla served me a polite smile to say, "It's nice to meet you, Boston. *And…*"

The way she trailed off had me confused for a split second until I remembered I hadn't shown up alone. "Oh, my bad. This is Cheyenne," I told them, turning towards her to say, "Cheyenne, this is Khalid and Jayla*."

Her feistiness from earlier was replaced with some syrupy sweet shit I hardly recognized when she said, "Pleasure to meet you both. You two make a beautiful couple."

"And so do…" Jayla started before Cheyenne jumped in to cut her off.

"*We're not…* a couple. Just friends."

Friends was honestly a stretch since I'd really only known her for all of two car rides. But that didn't stop Khalid from quietly teasing, "Yeah, we used to say the same thing," before putting a hand against Jayla's back to say, "Baby, go ahead and take Cheyenne to get a drink. I need to rap with Bos right quick."

To my surprise, Cheyenne went right along with it, clearly already comfortable with the new surroundings as her and Jayla made their way through the crowd. And the second Khalid knew for sure they were out of earshot, he gave me a little punch to the arm when he asked, "Bro, what the fuck? You keepin' *those* kinda secrets now?"

Even though it was obvious he was talking about Cheyenne, the fact that she was far from some secret I'd been keeping had me asking, "What you mean?"

That reaction only riled him up even more. "My nigga out here rebounding better than Dennis Rodman talkin' 'bout some *'what you mean'…*"

Shaking my head, I tried to explain, "Nah, it's not like that. It's a long story, really."

Long story felt like an understatement since I still didn't have all the details from Cheyenne about what exactly had led to her getting chased out of the party. But that wasn't enough to stop Khalid from insisting, "Tell it to the judge, my nigga. Cause I already know what's up."

Outside of us showing up together and her being fine as hell, I wasn't sure what it was that had him so convinced. Then again, maybe his unspoken reasons weren't all that far off; though I still tried to play it off when I admitted, "So she's bad. But to be real, I don't even know her like that."

With a hand to my shoulder and a goofy grin to go with his stupid ass glasses, he replied, "Well New Year's Eve is the perfect time to do just that, even though your ex might be hatin' from a distance."

My face immediately scrunched. "*My ex*? Amber is here?"

The annoyed look on his face in response told me everything I needed to know, but I still listened intently as he explained, "Yeah, you know she started messin' around with Londyn's big brother, Eric, after y'all fell out. And it's his mama's party so…"

"Amber is here as his date," I finished for him, releasing a deep breath to shake it off as best as I could before I told him, "It's all good. Nothin' I can't handle."

It sounded good, but I had a feeling it would be a struggle until Khalid added, "Yeah, I bet ol' Cheyenne is gonna make that real easy for you."

Cheyenne.

I might not have thought of her in that way from the jump, but something about his words had me reconsidering as I found her in the crowd talking to Londyn and Jayla. And the longer I stared at her, the more I realized there really wasn't a good reason for me not to, *at least*, enjoy the night with her.

So that was exactly what I planned to do. And of course, Khalid was excited as hell to hear me agree, "She sure is."

CHEYENNE

"GIRL, I am *so* glad you're here. Cause I thought for sure Boston was gonna come in here and knock my brother into next year an hour early for fuckin' around with his ex."

There was so much to take in from Londyn's statement, so much to take in from the environment period. I mean, sure I might've been in a room full of strangers, but it didn't exactly give me that same uncomfortable feeling like Drew's party from earlier; the vibe much more my speed with a playlist to match as I struggled to stay still instead of dance like I wanted to. But considering I was around people I didn't know, *including the person who had invited me here*, I kept my groove to a minimum as I played Londyn's words back in my head and asked, "*Wait.* Boston's ex? Boston has an… *I mean*… who's Boston's ex?"

It really shouldn't have mattered to me who she was since it wasn't like I was after her man - *or her ex-man* - regardless of how fine and kind he was. I suppose I was just curious to see what kind of girls he was into, following Londyn's line of sight when she answered, "See the girl over there against the wall? In the gold dress like yours, except you look way better in it?"

The way she said it told me she obviously wasn't a fan. Still, I couldn't help acknowledging the truth once I gushed, "Oh, wow. She's… *pretty*."

"Yeah, pretty and petty," Londyn replied with a roll of her eyes. "Boston sure knows how to pick 'em. *No offense.*"

"None taken. We're just friends," I reminded her, though the way Jayla immediately averted her eyes and sipped from her drink nearby told me she didn't believe me the same way her man hadn't believed me earlier.

Apparently, Londyn was on that same wave when she asked, "But like… why though? I mean, don't get me wrong, my fiancé is the finest nigga in the room no question. But Boston's big, burly ass is *easily* number two."

"Number three. With a two-way tie for number one," Jayla chimed in, making Londyn roll her eyes again before she begrudgingly agreed.

"Fine, number three. But my point still remains. He's definitely not the type of guy you should be playing off as a friend unless you have a damn good reason to."

Naturally, I wondered why she was so Team Boston and why she felt so comfortable pressing me - *someone she'd just met* - about it. But there was also the other side of my brain that had me interested in finding an answer to that first why on my own, something I tried to ignore so I could tell her, "We just met tonight. He… rescued me; from a little situation. And I'm flying back home in two days. Those are my damn good reasons."

To me, they were valid. But instead of agreeing with my explanation, Londyn only shrugged. "Sounds like two days to get thoroughly fucked by your hero to me. I mean, do you see how that man walks? You *know* he's gotta be carrying something heavy between his thighs."

She was right.

I had definitely noticed during our walk to the party which was why I had done my best to stay in front of him; so I wouldn't stare too hard. But before I could comment on my appreciation for his third leg to someone who already understood, Jayla chimed in again to say, "Londyn, I don't think your future hubby would appreciate you speaking on that man's dick like that."

With a wave of her hand, Londyn defended, "Chance knows I'm not blind. And he knows I only want his dick for the rest of my life as proven by the head I gave him in the car on the drive into town, so…"

My eyes went wide at her effortless admission. But according to Jayla's calm reaction, it must not have been out of the norm for her, Jayla only shaking her head as she groaned, "TMI, sis."

"He's a happy man. That's all I'm sayin'," Londyn replied with a proud smirk that I respected since… a little head in the car never hurt anybody. But since my opinion on it wasn't really any of their business, I stayed quiet as I looked out into the crowd and found Boston standing alone, sipping from a drink while giving laser eyes across the room in the direction of… *his ex and her new guy?*

"*Aww hell,*" I muttered as I excused myself from the girls and made a beeline his way, getting right in his face to ask, "You havin' a good time?"

I could tell he had to shake off whatever crazy shit he was thinking in regards to them to answer, "Yeah, yeah. I'm good. You good?"

"I'm great. But I'd be better if you'd come dance with me. I mean, you look like you could use the distraction. Unless you'd rather cry yourself into the new year in the car…"

"Cry myself into the new year? Why would I do that?" he asked, obviously trying to play off what I'd already seen for myself.

Even if he didn't realize it, I had no problem making it plain for him when I answered, "I know your ex is here with another guy, Boston. And I know you… feel a way about that."

Now that he knew he'd been caught, his eyes dropped to the ground. But I didn't let them stay there, brushing my hand against the light brown hair on his chin to get his attention as I continued, "Look, I don't need the details. But after what you did for me, I can't let you go into the new year with a frown on your face over the pretty, petty chick."

It was only fair that I pay him back in some way for being my hero as Londyn had put it. And I was glad to see my words alone make his eyes a little brighter when he asked, "Londyn said that, didn't she?"

"She did. And considering she seems to be very open and honest about… lots of things, I don't think she's telling a lie."

With a half-hearted smile and a nod to agree, he straightened up to change the subject. "What you drinkin', ma?"

Glancing at my emptied glass, I tried to recall which option I'd picked from the customized drink list. "I think it was called Annie's Amaretto Sour. Or maybe it was Ellen's El Presidente. One of the two."

"Well I need another. Let's get you one too," he insisted, already taking off towards the kitchen where a bartender was staffed as I followed closely behind him and finding a line of people trying to do the same thing once we made it there.

"Oh, so this is what we're doing? We're gonna drink it away like Solange in *Cranes in the Sky*?" I teased as we waited in line.

Instead of directly agreeing, he turned towards me and asked, "You down? I mean, I still ain't forget about that nigga chasing you outta the building, and I'm sure the story behind it ain't exactly somethin' you're tryna remember."

"You're right. Let's drink," I agreed, not even wanting to speak on the situation with Drew. "But wait. How am I gonna get back to the hotel if my favorite *Uber* driver is drunk?"

His half-hearted smile turned into a full-blown smirk once he gushed, "*Wow*. Now I'm your favorite? Cause I could've sworn I was only worth three-stars earlier, ma."

I couldn't help but laugh at the mention of our little argument over ratings, knowing good and well he deserved a gazillion stars for getting me away from Drew. But it only made me wonder if Londyn was right about Boston being into pretty and petty, even when I teased, "Damn. Do you remember everything? I thought all football players had bad memory because of too many concussions or somethin'?"

"All the football players in the KFC, right?" he asked in an equally-teasing tone that told me his mood was really on the up-and-up. And honestly, I felt proud of myself for being a part of the movement by the time we finally got our drinks, lifting my glass to his in a toast.

"To new, unexpected friendships with an unlimited amount of useless facts."

His smirk remained as he clinked his glass with mine before taking a drink while I did the same; though my sip almost got caught in my throat when I noticed… "Hey, isn't that the woman who went viral for twerking in a snow bunny pajama onesie awhile back?

It was a video I knew like the back of my hand since me and some of the other dancers I was working with at the time had created our own little version of the twerking pajama animals. But I was completely blown away to hear Boston explain, "Yeah, you know that Annie Amaretto shit you drinkin'? It's named after her. This is her party. That's Londyn and Eric's mom."

Finding out that she threw bomb parties like this one made her dancing abilities make a lot of sense. But the fact that the woman looked like she could be Londyn's sister instead of the mother of two grown ass children was also impressive; though I couldn't help asking, "Eric is the dude whose ass you wanna beat for being with your ex, right?"

Boston shrugged, glancing down at me with the corner of his lip pulled between his teeth before he answered, "Nah, it is what it is. I'm happily distracted."

The way he was looking at me in combination with how ridiculously sexy his voice was when he said it had me taking another thick swallow from my drink to calm down even though it really didn't help since he was still looking at me the same way when I finished. And instead of acting like I wasn't at all interested, I playfully asked, "Are you flirting with me, Mr. Uber Driver?"

Again, he shrugged. "I clocked out a long time ago, ma. You know my name now."

"Yeah, I do. *The Bos.* That's what Jayla's man called you, wasn't it?" I asked, for whatever reason finding the nickname a turn-on.

Or maybe I just found him to be a turn-on, a fact that only became clearer after watching the way his Adam's apple bobbed when he swallowed a sip from his drink and answered, "Yeah, that's what they call me on the field."

"Sounds... *dominate*. You must be good."

"I'd like to think so," he agreed before he continued, "Wasn't good enough for the NFL to keep me around, but the CFL shows love so I can't complain."

"Okay, now that one I've actually heard of. But I don't watch it out of support for Kaepernick."

For whatever reason, that made him chuckle. And I was getting ready to ask what could possibly be funny about Kaepernick's very serious cause until he inquired, "Do you even like football, Cheyenne?"

"Well, no. But it's the thought that counts!" I defended, knowing I would've at least been tuned in for the Super Bowl commercials and halftime performance otherwise. But nope, they weren't getting my viewership; especially since I could just watch it all on the internet later.

For now though, my focus was completely on Boston, a semi-tipsy smile on his lips when he said, "You're funny, ma."

"Well I'm glad you find me good for a laugh. I mean, since you wouldn't let me contribute in any other ways," I teased with a little jab at the fact that he wouldn't let me pay for anything.

Not that I was complaining.

His grin remained as he gave me a slow onceover before insisting, "From here on out, you can contribute in any way you want to."

There was a sensual undertone to his words that gave me goosebumps, forcing me to swallow hard to respond, "I'll keep that in mind. Now come on. I've held off on dancing long enough."

He didn't fight me on it when I used my free hand to grab his and pulled him towards the makeshift dance floor, finding my place in front of him as we caught an easy groove to, *I Like That* by Janelle Monáe; something like my theme song as far as the new year was concerned. And apparently I wasn't the only one familiar with it since Boston called himself belting a loud ass, "*Ayeeee*" over the music, making me laugh as Jayla and Khalid joined us with Londyn and her fiancé** in tow. But then the song changed to something a lot slower, a lot sexier. And while the transition was natural for the couples around us, things became a little awkward between Boston and I until he asked right against my ear, "You said you wanted to dance, right?" wrapping an arm low around my waist as I sank into his thick frame.

It felt like heaven, especially once he buried his face in the crook of my neck and inhaled me as H.E.R. sang about leaving the lights on. And in that moment, I knew I'd be following his lead for the rest of the night, fully embracing everything he was putting out as we went song for song that included one of my favorites by H.E.R. and Daniel Caesar.

My eyes were practically closed as Boston hummed the melody of *Best Part* in my ear, soothing me into a lazy smile that unfortunately got ripped from my lips once I heard someone ask, "Excuse me. May I… cut in? This song is just…"

All the easygoing air around Boston immediately turned tense as he snarled, "This song doesn't mean shit anymore, Amber. So no, you can't cut in. I'm good."

The fact that she had so blatantly fucked up our perfect vibe was enough for me to cosign, "He said what he said, sis. Sorry not sorry."

Looking past me, she begged, "Boston, come on. We're better than this."

"I thought so too. But you being here with ol' boy says otherwise," he replied like that was the only reason he wasn't interested in rekindling things with her. And because of that, I planned to stay quiet until she said, "Like you aren't here with…"

"Watch yourself, Amber," I warned, cutting her off before she could get too ahead of herself.

Their business may not have been any of mine, but any words spoken about me certainly came with consequences; especially after mostly-sparing Drew's wife earlier.

Thankfully, she knew not to try me, releasing a heavy sigh to say, "*Look.* Can we just go talk, Boston? In private?"

Since her request had come out calmly, I thought Boston might go through with it just to hear what it was she had to say.

But to my surprise, he didn't budge, his tone laced with annoyance when he answered, "There's nothing to talk about, Amber. We're here with other people for a reason. Go be happy with yours cause I'm damn sure happy with mine."

"Hold up, what?" I thought, trying to mask my immediate reaction to Boston's claims since it was obvious he was trying to stick it to his ex. But when she finally gave up and moved to leave the party with a petty, "*I was always too good for you anyway,*" I couldn't wait to release the breath I was holding.

"Whew, shit. I almost cracked under pressure. You could've warned me about being used as a pawn," I scolded, though I totally understood why he had done it. And honestly, I probably would've done the same thing because… *pretty and petty*.

With a heavy breath of his own, he turned back towards me to say, "I'm sorry. I didn't know she'd be here. And I… wasn't completely lying. I mean, you obviously aren't mine, but I *am* happy to be here with you, ma."

I don't know if it was the genuine look in his eyes, the Annie's Amaretto Sour running its course, or the fact that I just felt a little sorry for his fine ass. But regardless of my reasons for accepting his apology, I had no problem admitting, "I'm happy to be here with you too, Boston."

BOSTON

I HAD TO HAVE HER.

Khalid was the one to put it in my head, and now it was all I could think about as I watched her shake her ass on the dance floor with Miss. Annie and Londyn, having the time of her life like we both hadn't been through some shit tonight.

But that was the thing about it. We'd both been faced with some wildly difficult situations, and she was still smiling, still excited, still… so damn beautiful; making it easy for me to find some of that same energy to recover myself.

And that's why I had to have her.

Even if it didn't go beyond tonight - *didn't really have much of a chance of going beyond tonight* - I had to fully experience Cheyenne Foster who had turned my world upside down in the matter of a few hours.

"What a fuckin' troublemaker," I thought, shaking my head with a grin just as she looked back at me over her shoulder like I could really focus on her face with the way she was throwing that ass. But I did my best to anyway until she started isolating her ass cheeks like a damn professional.

Because she was a damn professional.

Not even Miss. Annie could keep up; though she did her best and impressed the hell out of her ol' man in the process. And he certainly wasn't the only one mesmerized, my teeth damn near jammed into my bottom lip as Cheyenne started whining her hips to the change in music - *looking at* me *as she whined her hips to the rhythm.*

Yeah, she knew exactly what she was doing. But before I could make my way to the dance floor to act on it, the music was cut by Londyn who announced, "It's almost time! Everybody get a glass!"

Grabbing two of the already-prepared flutes of champagne, I brought one to Cheyenne who snuck a little sip before it was actually time to do so. "All that dancing got me thirsty as hell."

"I bet it did," I replied with a quick glance back at her ass that made her smirk just as Londyn shouted, "Fifteen seconds!"

Everybody got in position of at least looking in the same direction as Londyn started the final ten-second countdown for us to join in on. And after excitedly shouting Happy New Year, I was getting ready to take a celebratory sip from my glass until Cheyenne grabbed me by the chin and pulled my face down to hers for a midnight kiss.

It was… unexpected, but immediately appreciated; an appreciation that I was sure to show as I kissed her like it was the only time I'd be able to do so. But just like with chips, I already knew one wasn't going to be enough, even when she pulled away to say, "Happy New Year, *The Bos.*"

"Happy New Year, ma," I replied, sneaking another nip of her lips that made her moan before she finally downed her champagne flute. And after doing the same, I pulled her back in for another kiss flavored with sparkling wine, adding some tongue to let her know I wasn't bullshittin' about having her.

Thankfully, the message was well received. And thankfully the situation from earlier with Amber had been enough to sober me up, making getting us the hell out of there an easy task once the party started to wind down.

This time, Cheyenne didn't fight me on it when I offered her my jacket. And she was all smiles as we made it back to my truck hand-in-hand, grinning even harder once I pressed her back up against the backseat passenger door for another kiss.

Shit was addictive.

She knew it too, her smirk telling it all when she pulled away to say, "You know I'm about to fuck up your life, right?"

"You mean, you haven't already?" I challenged, pecking her lips before she slickly replied, "Nah. Not at all."

Even though she had yet to give me a full explanation, now that I had gotten a small taste of her, it suddenly seemed easy to put two-and-two together to ask, "So that's why that nigga was running out of that building like that, huh? Cause you fucked up his life?"

Averting her eyes, she gnawed into her lip as she pushed out, "*I mean…* that might've had a little something to do with it."

"Is that how you gon' have me too? Ruining dress shoes and sweating out good suits to chase after your pretty ass?"

It was crazy that the idea didn't bother me as much as it probably should've, especially after being a witness to just how sprung out she had niggas. But it did put me a little at ease to hear her reply, "If you do right, you won't have to chase me. Hell, you see I'm already here. I might just be the one chasing you."

"How about we just meet in the middle, ma?" I suggested with a lick of my lips that had her hazel-green eyes darkening under the moonlight.

But even with all the passionate energy surrounding us, she couldn't help teasing, "I gotta see what the dick is like before I agree to terms like that."

With a laugh, I stepped back to finally open her door as I urged, "Let's go, silly. Since you're so pressed to see what the dick is like..."

"As if you aren't equally pressed to find out what has the boys out here trippin' so hard..." she fired back with an arrogant smirk that only had me more anxious as I rushed to close her door so I could make it over to my own. But by the time I climbed into the driver's seat, Cheyenne's entire demeanor had changed, her face pulled into a scowl as she stared at her phone and groaned, "*No fuckin' way...*"

"What's the matter?" I asked as I pulled out of the parking

spot, trying to pay attention to both the road in front of me and Cheyenne out of my peripheral.

Her frustration was all in her posture and tone when she answered, "I'd left my phone in here because I had a feeling Drew's ass would be blowing me up and I wasn't trying to deal with that. But according to this text message from his wife, he never came back into the party after our… fall out, so she thinks he left with me. Threatening me and shit because her husband is missing like I have anything to do with that."

Hearing that someone was threatening Cheyenne already had me on edge. But somehow, I found a little bit of chill to ask, "Do you think he's alright?"

Even if she no longer planned to have any type of relationship with the guy, he had obviously been important enough to her at some point for her to have traveled all this way to see him meaning the situation could still take a toll on her. And I could only imagine what was going through her head until she finally sighed, "*I…* I don't know. And I really don't care. I mean, of course I *hope* he's alright, but… that's their problem. I don't even know how she got my number."

With a nod, I continued the rest of the drive to her hotel in silence as she fired off text messages back and forth with who I assumed was the wife, only growing more frustrated the longer she went. And the more frustrated she got, the less interested I became in trying to make something shake when we got back to her hotel.

Not that I didn't want to fuck her. But I could tell there was a lot on her mind, especially when she totally missed the fact that we had arrived until I cleared my throat.

First peeking up to see where we were, she turned my way with a frown to ask, "*Wait.* Why are you pulling up here instead of into the parking lot? You're not coming inside?"

Shaking my head, I explained, "You seem like you might have a little too much going on right now, and I ain't tryna take advantage of that."

"But I want you to come inside, Boston," she whined, dropping her phone into her lap to grab my hand.

Her soft touch alone was enough for me to reconsider, though I still found it in me to ask, "Are you sure?"

"I'm positive. So go park," she insisted, ignoring the buzz of her phone until she knew for certain I was going to join her. And with the change in her demeanor, I decided to take her for her word, happy to find someone near the entrance pulling out which made my park job a breeze and made our entrance into the hotel swift.

Well… swift until we spotted the suited and booted nigga from the party sitting in the lobby. And then everything slowed down for a second, Cheyenne taking a moment to gather herself before she stalked over to him and asked, "Drew, what the hell are you doing here? How did you even know where I was staying?"

Popping up from his seat, I could see the stress in his face when he grabbed her hands to reply, "I had to see you, baby. *I*… I need you."

With a roll of her eyes, Cheyenne snatched her hands away. "Drew, please. You have a wife *and* a side chick. Take your ass home to one of them cause I'm beyond through with this."

Of course that didn't stop him from grabbing them again when he begged, "Baby, just hear me out. I promise I'm done with them. I only want you. You know we're meant to be together."

While it really wasn't my place to get in their business, the fact that he kept touching her when she obviously wasn't feeling that shit had me quick to step in. "My guy, she said she's good. Now get the fuck outta here."

"Who the hell are you?" he growled, trying to puff his chest out like his skinny ass measured up to me in any way.

Even if he thought he did, I had no problem putting him in his place about it, getting right in his face to reply, "I'm the nigga who will beat your prim and proper ass into a pulp if you don't leave Cheyenne alone. Try me if you want to."

Bro started breathing all extra hard like he was thinking about charging up. But all it took was one look for him to fall back, instead looking past me to give a whined, "*Cheyenne…*"

"Goodbye, Drew," she stated plainly, her arms crossed and her stance firm as she stared him down and waited for him to leave.

It took him a minute, but he eventually gave up, looking sad as hell on his way out of the lobby like Cheyenne was the one who had gotten away when in reality she had just started claiming his ass on a whim. But if this was any indication of what she meant about "fuckin' my life up", I was starting to wonder if I was really as strong-minded as I thought I was, leading the way towards the elevators as I asked, "What floor you on, ma?"

"Three," she answered quietly as we climbed on, going straight to the back wall as I stayed in the front and pressed the button. And she stayed quiet until we made it to her floor, climbing off and directing me to the right when she said, "The room is this way."

Her steps were slow and steady as if the whole situation was hitting her in the worst way, making it a lot less of a surprise when we made it to her door and she turned back towards me to say, "Boston, you were right. I do have a lot going on now, *and…*"

Cutting her off with a hand cupped against her cheek and chin, I told her, "You ain't gotta explain nothin', ma. We had a… *crazy*, yet great time tonight and I'm sure you're exhausted. Maybe we can do lunch or somethin' tomorrow."

"I'd like that," she replied with a half-hearted smile, unlocking her phone to hand to me so I could program my number in. And when I handed it back, there was a hint of sadness in her eyes as she said, "So I guess this is good night."

"Sleep well, baby girl," I offered, leaning forward to press a lingering kiss against her forehead before turning to leave with no plans of looking back since I knew that would only make leaving her a little harder. But when I didn't hear the door open until I made it all the way back to the elevators, something in me clicked.

And I turned back around.

CHEYENNE

WHAT A FUCKIN' *night.*

My back was pressed against the door as I released a heavy sigh, finding everything that had happened between the time I first left this hotel room and now almost unbelievable since there was so, so much. I mean, when I left I was just sure I'd be bringing in the new year with Drew, but somehow I ended up tonguing down a stranger at midnight.

A fine ass, CFL-playing stranger named Boston Reed.

Yeah, I remembered everything now because he'd embedded himself in my mind - *on my body* - even without us going all the way. But the fact that he hadn't pressed me about any of it only made him that much more attractive even though I still wanted him so, *so* bad.

We had plans for tomorrow, but that did nothing to cure my desire for him now, part of what had made watching him walk away so hard. But when he didn't even turn around for one last look at me, I figured that was a sign for me to take some time to reflect on it all, getting ready to do just that until I realized I still had his jacket on.

"He needs his jacket," I said out loud, pulling the door back open with plans of chasing him down to give it to him until I realized he was already right in front of me.

He didn't say anything in response to my gasp of surprise, just took a step towards me and grabbed both sides of my face so he could kiss me *hard.* There was none of the playfulness like the kisses outside of his truck, none of the gentleness like the forehead kiss he'd given me a few moments earlier. Just all heat, and aggression, and passion that had me stumbling back into the nearest wall for leverage as I dropped everything I was holding to wrap my arms around his neck which he took as an invitation to lift me from the ground so my legs were wrapped around his waist.

With his lips a mere inch away from mine, he asked, "You still want me to leave, ma?"

I shook my head no.

"What you want me to do then?" he pressed, using his thick fingertips to grip into my bare ass that was no longer hidden under my dress.

Licking my lips - *and a little bit of his too because of how close we were* - I answered, "I want you to... be my distraction."

"As long as you'll be mine too," he countered, the look in his dark green eyes letting me know he was very serious about this; very serious about his need for me. And since I felt the exact same way, it was easy for me to agree with one simple word.

"Deal."

My response made him smirk as he pressed another kiss against my lips; a kiss that quickly turned intense as he carried me from the wall towards the nearby desk to deposit me on top of it so that he could get out of his shirt. And when he tossed it to the side, my hands immediately went to his abdomen, slowly running them from top to bottom where I landed at the button of his jeans.

"Feeling distracted yet?" I asked teasingly as I undid the button, Boston watching me intently as I pushed his jeans down his legs as far as I could before reaching into his boxers for his dick that matched everything else about him - thick, and weighty, and mouthwateringly full in a way that had me anxious to get him inside of me.

I was already stroking him in my hand when he finally answered, "Only a little bit cause you still too dressed up."

"So do something about it," I demanded with a smirk that he matched as I turned up the intensity of my handjob in a way that had him gripping into the edge of the desk to stay upright.

"*And I'm just getting started,*" I thought as he replied, "Nah, cause I can't guarantee I won't straight up rip that dress off of you and you said you paid a pretty penny for it. But you know what? Keep it on. That shit is fire on you, ma."

My, "I'm glad you think so," was barely off my lips when he pulled me back down onto my feet so he could turn me around, making quick work of the condom I didn't even realize but was grateful he had grabbed before plunging into me from behind.

"Bet you're the one feelin' distracted now, huh?" he growled, grabbing handfuls of the fabric bunched against my waist as he drove into me over and over again without even giving me room to answer. But in my head, the answer was a strong, *"Hell yes"*, my eyes closed and my lips parted as he seemingly slipped deeper with every stroke.

It was magical.

Pure magic that had me struggling to stand on my heels as he fucked me like no one else had ever done before, hit spots that no one else had ever hit before, and lowkey had me trying to run away even though there was nowhere for me to go.

I couldn't go out like that.

So I didn't, throwing my ass back against him as he growled, "*Oh shittt.*" And that only boosted my ego, even as I continued to breathlessly beg, "Distract me, Boston."

My wish was something like his command as he wrapped my hair around his hand to pull my head back, the slight change in position giving him new ground to explore as he asked, "You distracted yet? Huh? Who was that nigga from earlier, ma?"

"Nobody!" I shouted, earning another tug of my hair that felt disgustingly satisfying as Boston pulled out of me and agreed with a hard smack to my ass.

"Damn right, he was nobody. Now come ride this dick."

He was already sitting on the edge of the bed by the time I found the strength to move. But the fact that he had proved his point had me eager to do the same as I made my way over to join him, crawling onto his lap and sliding down onto his dick with ease before I asked, "Who was that girl at the party, Bos?"

Smirking, he quickly grunted, "*Shit.* I don't know who you're talkin' about, ma."

"Oh, you don't?" I challenged, wrapping an arm around the back of his neck to keep him close as I found the rhythm in my hips and asked, "She couldn't do you like this, could she?"

"Never," he groaned, pushing one strap of my disheveled dress to the side so he could reach my nipple and beyond excited to discover it was pierced.

I was excited too, appreciating how especially careful he was in using it to his advantage as I continued to ride him. But when he started meeting me stroke for stroke from below, everything became a blur as more words got exchanged at tones I was sure the rest of the hotel could hear, more distracting was successfully completed, and more raw passion was expressed until I collapsed against him as we both came undone.

Falling back onto the mattress and pulling me down with him, he waited for me to find a comfortable spot against his chest before he asked, "You happy I came back?"

"*Obviously*," I answered with a giggle. "But for the record, I was already coming after you because you forgot your jacket."

Attempting to find my eyes, he adjusted so he could at least see my face when he asked, "Oh, so that's the only reason why you were coming after me? To give me my damn jacket like you couldn't have just given it to me tomorrow?"

Peeking up at him with a guilty smile, I insisted, "It's cold out."

That made him laugh. "Ma, I've played in single-number temperatures up north. That shit out there don't faze me."

"Okay, so maybe I just wasn't ready for you to go yet," I admitted, getting ready to drop my chin until he grabbed it to tell me, "Thanks for the honesty."

"And thanks for the dick that I hope you brought more condoms for," I replied with a hint of amusement in my tone even though I really wasn't playing. And to let him know I wasn't, I moved out of his hold to first remove my shoes and then the rest of my dress, leaving me in absolutely nothing but the jewelry on my nipples.

Licking his lips, he sat up on his elbows and asked, "Damn. It's like that?"

"Yeah. It's like that. I mean, unless you're the one-and-done type…" I trailed, hoping that wasn't the case since my body was already ready for round two. But when I saw the heated expression in Boston's eyes, I knew I was in for more magic as he climbed from the bed to exchange the used condom for a new one then returned with a simple request that I was happy to oblige.

"Let's distract each other."

BOSTON

DAY one of three-sixty-five was off to a great start as I watched Cheyenne put in work through groggy eyes, effortlessly riding me reverse cowgirl style first thing in the morning like we hadn't spent the majority of the night doing the same shit. But I certainly wasn't complaining, greedily accepting every bit of her I could get as she tipped forward onto the mattress with her tremor of an orgasm then gave a muffled, "Good morning, Bos."

Chuckling, I smacked her on the ass. "Good morning to you too, ma. Couldn't wait for a nigga to wake all the way up, huh?"

It was honestly a miracle that I'd even been conscious enough to put a condom on, though it ended up only being for Cheyenne to get hers. But it was just as satisfying to watch her pretty ass under the morning sun, especially once she peeked back to ask, "I'm screwed, aren't I?"

Shrugging, I climbed from the bed to head to the bathroom as I answered, "For now, you're good. But you might be outta luck tomorrow night when you're back home and my dick is still here."

She immediately groaned. "Ugh, don't remind me. I still need to figure out where I'm gonna stay tonight."

"What you mean?" I asked loud enough for her to be able to hear in the room.

Though I quickly realized she was a lot closer than I thought once she joined me in the bathroom with her robe on to explain, "Well I didn't think I'd need another night at the hotel because I planned on staying with Drew, *but...*"

I cut her off. "Nah, we ain't speakin' on that nigga no more. If you need somewhere to stay for the night, I got you."

It sounded like a no-brainer to me. But instead of accepting my offer, she only giggled. "Boston, you've done enough for me. I'll just see if the hotel has anything available for me to extend my stay."

Her plan sounded solid. But for reasons I wasn't quite ready to accept, I found myself arguing, "Cheyenne, I have plenty of room at the crib. Why spend money when you can stay with me for free?"

Licking her lips, she wrapped her arms around me as best as she could from behind to answer, "Because I clearly have a problem keeping my hands to myself when I'm around you, and I've already been enough of a burden; especially when you consider I just met you yesterday."

Covering her hands with my own, I asked through the mirror, "You don't hear me complaining, do you?"

"Well no, *but…*"

Again, I cut her off. "So stay with me. It's only a night. And I'll take you to the airport tomorrow."

It took her a moment, but eventually she smiled to agree. "Okay, fine. But you have to at least let me pay for gas."

"*Or...* I could not, and we can pretend you did if that makes you feel better," I suggested, making her groan with annoyance before she turned to leave the bathroom with me right on her heels.

"You know what would really make me feel better?" she asked over her shoulder. "A plate of black eyed peas, greens, and cornbread. I need all the luck I can get this year. Or a fatter ass. Whichever comes first."

Shaking my head since we both knew her ass was already perfect, I started to gather my clothes from the night before to put back on as I offered, "I'll buy the groceries if you cook."

"*Or...* I'll buy the groceries if you cook since I'd hate to burn your place down," she counter-offered with an exaggerated grin that made me chuckle as she took the clothes from my hand to set them aside, then used that same hand to drag me back towards the bathroom.

I wasn't exactly sure what she was up to, but I was down for whatever, grinning when I told her, "You lucky my mama taught me a thing or two in the kitchen, but I still ain't lettin' you pay."

"We'll see about that, after we see about this..." she slickly replied as she turned on the water in the shower then dropped her robe, giving me a seductive look over her shoulder before she stepped inside. And while I was content just watching the soapy water drip in and out of every crevice of her naked body, I had a feeling she didn't bring me in here for that alone; though I didn't make a move until she asked, "You comin' in?"

My response came in the action of stepping in to join her, the satisfaction in her eyes as she lathered her hands with soap then used them to wash my chest and abdomen damn near making me float as the steam rose around us. And when she made her way down to wash my dick, I thought for sure I was on my way to hell since there was no way I could actually be getting clean via a method so dirty.

I *was* getting clean, though. Cheyenne made sure of it, eventually turning me around to wash my back while also landing kisses in random places against my skin that felt so damn intimate. But it was her intimacy that encouraged my own as I turned around to press a slow, sensual kiss against her lips before pulling back to whisper against them, "Thank you, ma."

She might've thought I was only thanking her for the scrub, but really I was thanking her for everything. Thanking her for lighting up my world, thanking her for bringing some excitement to my New Year's Eve and Day, thanking her for just… being her, even in the face of some adversity. I mean, neither of us really knew what we were getting ourselves into when we crossed paths, but it had somehow worked out in our favor. And part of it working out in our favor was her willingness to participate, something I was especially grateful for as she whispered back, "You're welcome."

It was a struggle, but somehow we made it out of the shower without having each other for second breakfast, getting dressed and getting her checked out of the hotel so we could head to the store to get everything we needed for our New Year's meal. And even though I'd already told her I wasn't letting her pay for anything, she managed to pull a fast one on me by sliding her card into the slot of the self-checkout register before I could stop her.

"You're lucky you're cute," I told her, earning myself a smirk as I reached to grab the grocery bags before she could do that too. But when we finally made it to my place, Cheyenne had no problem being as hands-off as she could, even sneaking in a little nap as I put together everything she had asked for plus some macaroni and cheese and fried fish that she claimed didn't align with her Beyoncé-inspired New Year's Resolution of a plant-based diet but still devoured anyway.

In fact, she was devouring everything like her nap had worked up her appetite, practically moaning when she complimented, "Okay, your mama taught you more than a thing or two in the kitchen. This is *so* good, Boston."

Considering I was smashing too, I couldn't have agreed more even when I replied, "I'ma tell her you said that too, cause she loves to believe I'm still on the same *McDonald's* dollar menu diet I used to be on back in school."

Over our clinking forks and plates, she asked, "Does she live around here?"

"Yeah, but she's been staying in the city for the last few weeks helping my big sister and her husband with the twins."

"*Awww. Uncle Boston,*" Cheyenne cooed, making me laugh since it was the same thing big sis had been calling me ever since she gave birth. And my smile was prouder than ever as I agreed, "Yeah, that shit is dope. Almost makes me wanna have some kids of my own one day. *Almost.*"

Considering I was still back and forth between countries and honestly didn't know how much longer that football shit was going to last, I figured it wasn't in my best interest to be bringing a shorty or two into the world before I got my situation more stable.

Not to mention, I no longer had anybody to make that happen with anyway.

I was already feeling a little somber about it when Cheyenne asked, "You and whatsherface never talked about it?"

Shrugging, I answered, "Not really. I mean, we did early on. But shit started to get too toxic towards the end, so all we really did was argue."

Between the distance, her lack of support for what she viewed as a demotion after being in the NFL, and then the rumors of her fuckin' around on me while I was away, I was honestly surprised we had made it as long as we did. But it all made sense once Cheyenne asked, "Do you still love her?"

I *did* love her, and I believed she loved me too which had to be the only reason I had tried so hard to make it work. But now that a little time had passed since our break-up and I had survived our first run-in, I realized I deserved better, making it easy for me to answer, "I'll probably always have love for her, but that ship has sailed. I'm ready to move on."

Nodding over her plate, Cheyenne replied, "Well that's good to hear. Cause if you keep fuckin' and feedin' me like this, I'll happily give you all the little CFL-playing babies you want."

Just like that, a smile was back on my face when I chuckled and challenged, "You mean, when you're not too busy dancing your way around the world?"

"Oh no, I'll make time! Good sex and good food are *that* important to me," she insisted, leaving her plate with nothing but food residue on it as proof that she wasn't playing. And judging from the last twenty-four hours, I knew she wasn't playing about the good sex part either; both things I could appreciate as we let the itis send us to the couch to watch all the college football games Cheyenne did her best to make sense of.

"Why are they kicking the ball if they still have another down left? You get four downs, right?"

"Yeah, but if they don't make it to the first-down marker, the team gets to take it from that spot instead of having to start way back there."

"Wait. Why do they get two points for that?"

"It's called a safety."

"Why is that a penalty? Aren't they supposed to tackle the quarterback?"

"They are. But not that hard after he's already thrown the ball."

"These kids really aren't getting paid for this?"

"Maybe under the table. But most only get a scholarship."

"Did you get paid under the table when you were in college?"

"The answer to that question depends on if you're an undercover FBI agent with a case open against my university or not."

That one made her smirk as she watched the rest of the game mostly in silence until the last twenty seconds that turned into a nail-biter as the offense drove the ball into the red zone.

"Now I see why I don't watch this shit. I'm stressed, and I don't even know these people!" she squealed from the edge of her seat, making me laugh as I told her, "That's the fun part, ma."

She wasn't convinced, letting out a loud grunt when the quarterback overthrew a pass into the end zone then popping up from the couch to shout, "What are you doing?! He was wide open!"

"I see I've created a monster," I teased from my seat as she turned back my way with her hands on her hips and a smirk before returning her attention towards the game for what would be the final play.

Instead of watching the television, my eyes were on Cheyenne as she held her breath then started jumping up and down to cheer, "*Run! Run! Yessssss!*" Then she hopped into my lap to say, "Okay, I get it now. Cause my adrenaline is definitely pumping like crazy, but I'd hate to ever be on the losing side of this."

"That's why you see so many babies being made no matter the outcome of big games. You either fuck to celebrate the win, or you fuck to forget about the loss. But either way, you're fuckin'," I explained, watching her give a slow nod of understanding.

"*That*… makes a lot of sense. Being a football fan sounds right up my alley."

"I bet it does, *witcho little freaky ass*…" I teased, leaning forward for a kiss that she dodged to fire back, "You sure didn't seem to mind this little freaky ass when it was riding you this morning, though."

I was quick to agree, "Damn right, I didn't. And I'm not gonna mind it later tonight when it's riding me either."

"If you're lucky," she joked, finally letting me get that kiss before we settled in for the next game. And that's how we spent the rest of the night; cuddled up with me watching football as she continued to learn everything she could about it, joking around and sneaking kisses, going back to the kitchen for a plate of left-overs to snack on, and of course, Cheyenne reminding me just how lucky I was to have her in my bed even if it was only for a night.

A night that went too damn fast as far as I was concerned since the next day, I had to take her to the airport with no plans of when I'd actually be seeing her again. And honestly, that shit sucked since I'd already gotten used to having her around just that quickly.

"She wasn't playin' about fuckin' up your life, bruh," I realized as I pulled into the drop-off area, releasing a heavy sigh before I turned towards her to say, "*Well.* I guess this is it."

"Yeah. *It is*," she replied quietly, turning my way with a half-hearted smile and grabbing my hands to tell me, "Thank you for… saving my trip; making it worthwhile."

"It's nothin', ma," I insisted, though she was quick to disagree.

"Nah, it's definitely somethin'. Cause you really didn't have to do any of it, but I'm so glad you did."

"Well I'm glad I did too," I replied with a squeeze of her hands, accepting the kiss on the cheek she leaned across the center console to give me before she got out of my truck and I did the same. And after grabbing her suitcase from the trunk to set at her feet on the sidewalk, I told her, "Until next time, Cheyenne Foster."

"See you in the middle, Boston Reed," she offered with a wink, speaking hope into the possibility of an actual future together as she brushed her hand against my cheek then pressed up onto her tippytoes for one last kiss.

Those addictive ass kisses.

Before I could overdose, I set her free, leaning against my truck to watch her until she disappeared into the airport. And after another beat, I finally got back inside, letting off a bigger sigh once I realized I now needed a new distraction - *from thoughts of her.*

"A little Ubering should do the trick," I decided, logging into the app and almost immediately getting an assignment for someone to be picked up from the airport. And while I lowkey wished it was Cheyenne putting in the request, it was cool to pull up on what looked to be a happy black couple who was finishing off their kiss the same way baby girl and I had just done a few minutes before.

After confirming they were the right people, I hopped out to help them with their luggage, closing the trunk just as the woman leaned out of the backseat and said, "Umm… it looks like someone left a note back here for you. The outside says, *"To my favorite Uber Driver"*."

At first, my face scrunched with confusion. But after reading who it was addressed to a second time, I knew exactly who it was from, smiling hard as hell as I unfolded it to find a handwritten message on hotel notepad paper.

Boston "The Bos" Reed,

I don't know when you'll actually find this, but thank you for being the best New Year's distraction a girl could ask for. ;)

With love,

Your Number One CFL/KFC Fan, Cheyenne <3

CHEYENNE

Super Bowl Sunday.

I COULDN'T WAIT to see him.

It was February 3rd, and I hadn't seen my *almost*-boyfriend since the very first time we met about a month ago when I visited his city - *for someone else* - which meant this reunion was long overdue. I mean, we might've texted every day, and shared pictures, and slid into each other's *Instagram* DMs to be funny, and even snuck in the occasional *FaceTime* call when I wasn't busy with dance. But there was nothing like a real face-to-face interaction which was why I called myself surprising him even though he claimed he'd be out to see one of my shows in a few weeks.

Obviously, I wasn't interested in waiting. In fact, I'd just barely touched down in the city before I was already changed out of my travel gear into something slinky, shiny, and short that I knew he would love, putting in a request for the *Uber* that would get me to him the fastest - *because he was the Uber and I'd already checked with his friend, Khalid, to make sure he was working in the area* - as I made my way back down to the hotel's lobby.

Honestly, I probably shouldn't have even booked a night at the hotel since it was pretty much a guarantee I'd be staying at his place. Then again, maybe he'd want to come back to my hotel room and reenact our very first night together; just the thought giving me chills as my phone alerted me he was pulling up.

By the time I made it out front, he was already standing on the outside of his truck, an excited smile on his face when he asked, "You really think you're slick, huh?"

Stalking over to him, I felt alive once he pulled me into the tightest hug, giving me a kiss filled with the same amount of excitement before I told him, "I *am* slick. If anyone knows that, it's you."

With a smirk, he replied, "Yeah, your slick ass had me circling the block for the last hour waiting for this request to come in after the homie accidentally tipped me off about your little plans."

"*Wait.* So you knew I was coming?" I asked, already knocking Khalid off the list of people I could trust in my head.

Of course Boston had to rub it in, damn near lifting me off of my feet when he squeezed me tighter and peppered kisses against my face as he gushed, "Sure did. And I'm fuckin' ecstatic about it, ma. I missed you."

Even though the surprise had gotten ruined, I couldn't stop smiling when I admitted, "I missed you too, Boston. *Like…* you seriously have no idea."

"Yeah? Well how about we go up to your room right quick, and you can show me just how much before we head over to Miss. Annie's Anti-Super Bowl party?" he suggested, dropping me back down to my feet but keeping me near in a hug as I snorted at the party's title.

While I was already excited about attending another one of Miss. Annie's parties, I still couldn't help but ask, "You're really not gonna watch the game?"

Knowing how much Boston loved football - *and had somehow got me loving football too* - it hardly seemed possible for him to skip out on watching the biggest game of the year until he answered, "Nah, I'd much rather watch you shake your ass on the dance floor."

"You know it doesn't take a dance floor for me to shake my ass, right?" I reminded him as he led us into the hotel.

We made it all the way to the elevators before he replied,

"Why you think we comin' in here, ma? Your cute face and charming personality ain't the only things I missed about you."

That made me blush, remembering how around this time last month he was taking me up this same elevator after dealing with Drew's triflin' ass in the lobby. But as I stared at Boston while we waited for it to arrive, I felt warm inside knowing they were nothing alike, *knowing that we were building something real*, putting a hand to his thick bicep to suggest, "In that case… let's take the stairs."

THE END.

FEATURED TITLES

*Read all about Khalid & Jayla in, *The Lessons We Learn (FWB Book 2)*

Jayla Anthony had it all.
At least, that's what it looked like from the outside. But from the inside looking out, she knew there was much more to life than her current situation. And when she decides to press the reset button on everything she thought she knew with her newly divorced status, her new occupation, and her move to a brand new town, she hardly expects that to somehow end up including the young, handsome security guard from her company's building.

Khalid Irving is a man on the come-up now that he's found a steady, good-paying job, a better living situation, and most importantly, a better outlook on life after a few years of no real direction. And now that he feels like he's on the right track, he's ready to pursue the woman who stole his attention the second she stepped into his building, even if that means he has to become her client first.

Jayla knows the risk of mixing business and pleasure. Khalid knows how bad he wants her. And when the two finally get together, the chemistry is electric.

But just because the fire is there, that doesn't mean there won't be a few tough lessons to learn along the way...

(Note: While this book can be read as a standalone, it's HIGHLY recommended that you read, The Games We Play: FWB Book 1, first!)

**Read all about Londyn & Chance in, *The Games We Play (FWB Book 1)*

Chance Washington only has a few things on his mind when he embarks on a trip back to his hometown. Completing the assignment for work that's sending him there in the first place, helping his mom make progress on her fixer-upper home, and catching up with some of his best friends who he doesn't get to see often enough. What is not a part of those plans is hooking up with one of his best friend's little sister. But it doesn't take long for him to realize that just because you walk into a game with a strategy, doesn't always mean things are going to go as planned.

Londyn Miller isn't looking for a relationship; a casual fling more her thing after blowing through the limited dating options in her hometown. But when a handsome – familiar - face returns to town for an extended stay, the decision to pursue him for a little fun is an easy one; as long as she's sure not to let that fun turn into real feelings while also managing to keep it all from her overprotective big brother.

Just like Chance, Londyn quickly learns that plans and strategy can only get you so far before you're forced to make in-game adjustments. And when those in-game adjustments evolve into something neither expected, it becomes a race for the finish line that Chance nor Londyn saw coming…

A TALE OF TWO CITIES

A VALENTINE'S NOVELLA

AUTHOR'S NOTE

Stories rarely make it out of the, "Leave this sh*t alone" folder on my computer since... *well*... I'm supposed to be leaving them alone lol. But somehow, this novella I started around Valentine's Day last year stuck with me, turning itself into a collection of holiday novellas that I absolutely adore.

I figured it was only right that I share the couple that truly started it all.
So please enjoy the final *(but somehow also the first)* A Tale of Two Cities Novella - Valentine's.

With love,
alexandra

BROOKLYN

"*GIRL*... I'd drink his bath water like a freshly brewed coffee from *Starbucks*."

I sat on my bed, cackling at my roommate Raina as she scrolled through her *Instagram* feed and I scrolled through mine right next to her. It was practically our Saturday night ritual to eat ourselves into a food coma, drink ourselves silly, and then look at pictures of fine ass men we'd never get to meet in real life. They were the type of guys who showed up on every girl's radar, as every girl's *"Man Crush Monday"*, and on every girl's list of, *"Who I'd Risk It All For"*. And while I wasn't exactly ready to take the ultimate plunge for any internet crush, lurking and creeping was way too much fun to stop any time soon.

"Ooh, look at him, Ray! He's gorgeous!" I squealed as I clicked on the page of another tall, dark and handsome.

His closed-mouth smirk made him especially sexy, giving a hint of mystery that intrigued me enough to click on his profile. But when Raina leaned in to look with me, her face scrunched.

"Ew. He looks a little *too* gorgeous."

"Raina!" I shouted, smacking her in the shoulder and taking up for him in his absence when I defended, "Look. He works out. He eats healthy. He has a nice smile. *And*..."

"He has a boyfriend. *Next*."

While they were indeed a cute couple, the fact that a boyfriend existed definitely killed my vibe. So I backed out of his page to continue my search while Raina went back to doing the same.

"Now this right here is worth risking it all for."

I leaned over Raina's shoulder and..., "*Damn*, he *is* fine. And look at those biceps. I bet he gives the best hugs."

"*The best hugs*? Girl, look at those shoulders. You could sit comfortably in the air while he devours you whole. Just hold onto his big ass head like a life preserver," she said with a laugh.

A laugh I couldn't help but join in on when I added, "He *does* have a big ass head." Then I went back to my own search, scrolling through a bunch of guys I could easily find something wrong with.

Why does he take so many selfies in the car? Must be self-absorbed and/or homeless.

Why is there a different girl in every picture? Must be a manwhore.

Why is he so ripped? Must be on steroids and his dick is dealing with the consequences.

The longer I searched, the more annoyed I got, meaning the more I drank. And *that*... was not necessarily a bad thing.

"Oh, Brooklynnnn. I think I found your future baby daddyyy," Raina sang as I cut my eyes to her phone to see who she was talking about.

When I finally got a good glimpse, I quickly agreed, "He could *definitely* get it. What do his stats look like?"

Her smile seemed optimistic when she answered, "So far, so good. He looks single, he looks responsible, and he looks like a father of one… two… three… *four*…"

"You're kidding," I cut in, though that didn't exactly cut the list.

"Five… six… *wait*, those were twins. So six, and seven. *Eight*…"

"Maybe he's a teacher? Runs his own daycare?" I tossed out, hoping that would give us the answers we needed.

But Raina quickly shut that down when she replied, "Girl, no. He couldn't deny these kids if he wanted to. I mean, they all look *just* like him. Same eyes, same noses. Just a matter of hair or no hair."

Her little spiel reminded me of an episode of *Maury* which meant it was definitely time to move on from his page. Still, I couldn't help acknowledging, "*Well...* at least we know he makes pretty babies."

Even though there were a shit ton of them, there was no denying how cute they all were; in an assortment of sizes, shapes, and skin tones while still all managing to look like him. But what I saw as a positive, Raina only scrunched her face at when she replied, "And at least we know from afar instead of getting invested just to get let down. Or worse; *pregnant.*"

"You can say that again," I told her, taking a sip of the vodka and... *other shit* concoction that Raina had put together for us before I continued my scrolling. And after a few minutes with no prospects, I started to grow bored, tempted to hop offline and get back to reality until a new profile caught my eye.

From the selfie alone - hickory brown skin, a perfect white smile, a fresh haircut instead of that mophead bullshit guys my age preferred, and a pair of sexy ass dimples - he was a shoo-in for the top spot on my personal *Risk-it-All* list. But before I shared him with Raina, I jumped to his profile, my silent stalking leading me to discover the dude was lowkey a celebrity.

"*Or not lowkey at all...*" I thought, quickly realizing that while I may not have been familiar with him as a professional basketball player, there were thousands of people who were. And they weren't all just regular fans complimenting him on his game, but women who were deep in his comments with everything from heart-eyed emojis, to eggplant emojis, to... *pizza emojis*?

What the hell are those for?

Girls were throwing panties and proposals left and right, almost making me want to back out until I heard Raina say, "*Brooklyn*. Oh my goodness."

"*What*? What's wrong?" I asked, extra panicky thanks to the buzz that had now fully consumed my body.

Raina damn near crawled on my shoulder to respond, "Him. He's... *perfect*. Too perfect. Please tell me you found some dirt."

"Besides the hundreds of girls who feel exactly how we do? Can't say that I have," I answered as I kept on scrolling through his pictures, finding them especially normal for someone who supposedly lived a life of stardom. I mean, if his team name and number thirty-two weren't in his bio, I probably wouldn't have even known he played ball since his profile was filled with typical guy stuff.

Occasional gym equipment pictures.

Occasional stuck-in-traffic selfies.

Occasional vacation pictures.

Occasional food pictures.

He seemed so… *regular*. Well, except for the fact that he was way finer than any dude I had ever come across on the street. And Raina enthusiastically agreed with my thoughts when she said, "He's fine as fuck. *Like*... multiple fucks. Like, I don't usually give a fuck, but this chocolatey mothafucka *deserves* my fucks. I'd gift him my fucks for his birthday. I'd feed him fucks like strawberries dipped in his skin. *I…*"

"I… kinda wish I could ride his face right now," I blurted, my tipsy state making me laugh while also turning me horny the longer I stared at his pictures.

Apparently, I wasn't the only one since Raina asked, "Well can we take turns? Cause *oh my God*, look at those dimples! I mean, he's almost *slide-in-the-DMs* worthy."

My face scrunched as I repeated, "*Slide-in-the-DMs worthy*? Raina, please. I'm not *that* damn desperate. I don't even know this dude."

Not that I wouldn't have tried to get to know him if I were to have seen him live and in person. But approaching someone - *a celebrity* - on social media via direct message to say nothing more than, "*Hey, you're cute and I'd consider screwing you if I could even though I can't,*" just felt too ridiculous.

Of course, that didn't stop Raina from trying to normalize my feelings about the situation when she explained, "Girl, people do it all the time. Hell, Yo Gotti made a whole song about it for a reason. Starts with a DM and ends with a Happily Ever After, or at least a good story to brag about to your future grandchildren the same way my grandma still brags about her one-night stand with James Brown in between his second and third wife."

The glow in her eyes had me wishing there was actually some truth to her words - *the happily ever after; not her grandma hooking up with James Brown, God rest his soul.* But considering we had already spent most of the night fantasizing about guys we couldn't have, I knew better than to get my hopes up, quick to reply, "Well I can guarantee his inbox is full of girls who had that same exact thought process, only to get denied or no reply at all."

With a poke to my shoulder, she insisted, "Those girls aren't you though, B. And besides, what the worst that could happen?"

"*Uh...* did you hear what I just said?" I asked, knowing good and well rejection and vodka didn't mix no matter who the person doing the rejecting was.

But instead of letting it go, Raina pushed the envelope a little more when she said, "Brooklyn, quit being a scaredy cat and just hit him up. Matter of fact, I double-dog dare you to send him a message."

"*Raina...*" I whined, knowing I had never been one to turn down a good dare no matter how damning.

She only upped the ante when she challenged, "You either send him a message or finish off the rest of this liquor. Your choice."

My first thought was, "*I'm already drunk*" which meant the rest of the liquor probably wouldn't have made that much of a difference anyway. But for whatever reason, Raina's dare enticed me much more, especially when my eyes went back to his *Instagram.*

It only took a few more scrolls for me to decide to go through with it. And while I really wasn't expecting anything to come from it, I relied on the courage in my roommate's words - *what's the worst that could happen?* - to press send.

AUSTIN

"YO, all these chicks in your DMs are crazy. Fine as hell. But crazy as fuck."

I paused my video game, dropping the controller on the couch before I snatched my phone out of my cousin Calvin's hand so that I could see what he was talking about. It wasn't unusual for him to be going through my messages since I had put him in charge of keeping up with all my social media accounts so that I wouldn't miss anything important. But naturally, I was curious to see what had prompted him to point out whatever "crazy" thing he had come across, scrolling through the recent collection of messages that all looked pretty normal to me.

"I usually don't do this, but…"

"Do you have a girlfriend? And if so, is it me?"

"My God, you are so fine."

"Is that a cucumber in your basketball shorts, or have you just been scrolling through my pics? ;P"

Okay, maybe that one was a little crazy. But everything else looked completely… *wait.*

@B_AdamsFinest: ***"I don't really know you. And of course, you don't know me. But I couldn't scroll by without saying anything. So... here it is."***

For whatever reason that one had me intrigued as I looked for a follow-up message, only to realize the first one had been sent late last night. And while I considered replying right away to see what she was talking about, I decided to click over to her profile first to see if a response was even worth the trouble.

"Damn. Definitely worth it," I thought based on her little profile picture alone, her black hair cut into a bob just long enough to frame her face that was maybe a hue or two darker than mine. And though I couldn't tell for sure if it was a good filter, good selfie lighting, or just her natural glow, there was no denying how radiant her skin was along with the smile she wore; a smile I couldn't help but match once I stopped to read her bio that simply said, *"Where Brooklyn at?"*

Her profile almost seemed professionally curated considering how clean and organized it was as a whole. And once I began to look at the pictures individually, I quickly got lost in the story she was telling without too many words, using intimate close-ups, classic filters, and snippets of song lyrics – *mostly R&B* - as her captions to create a vibe that had me weeks deep in her *Instagram* in no time at all.

"Damn, bro. You better slide in her DMs before I do."

I peeked over my shoulder at Calvin who was way deeper in my phone than I was, more than likely because of the black and white picture I was stuck on of the girl from behind with the caption, "*All on Instagram, cake by the pound…*"

Whoever she was definitely had some impressive cakes, though I tried to play it off when I told my cousin, "Chill out, man. I'm just peepin' game. Seeing what she's about and shit."

It sounded good, but I knew I was already a lot more invested than I should've been. I mean, I didn't even know the girl, didn't know her name, didn't even know where she lived. But I was way too far into her profile to turn back now, being careful not to "like" any pictures on accident as Calvin insisted, "That body tells me everything I need to know. What's her username so I can follow her too?"

"Man, take yo' thirsty ass on somewhere," I told him with a laugh, hitting a quick "Follow" on her page before going back to my inbox to accept her message. And without thinking twice, I replied with a set of emoji eyes that said I was definitely interested in whatever she had to say.

To my surprise, a response came quick - *two, in fact* – reeking with sarcasm I couldn't help but chuckle at.

@B_AdamsFinest: "Oh wow. You actually responded. What'd I do to make the cut?"

@B_AdamsFinest: "I'm Brooklyn, by the way."

"*So it was her first name that sparked her Instagram bio,*" I thought, finding it clever while also typing out a response.

@ABTreyTwo: "I'm an honest man, so keep that in mind when I tell you it was the ass that got me. But it's nice to meet you, Brooklyn. You from NYC?"

I was really only teasing her since I knew firsthand the whole *being named after where you're from* thing wasn't always the case. But to my surprise, she really did have some ties according to her reply.

@B_AdamsFinest: "No, but my parents are. I was actually born and raised in Dallas."

@ABTreyTwo: "No shit? I live in Miami now, obviously. But I'm from Houston. You know, the better city of the two. Lol."

Even if I didn't get back to my hometown often, I still repped it heavy everywhere I went, wanting to be a good example for the little homies coming up after me. But Brooklyn managed to turn the whole thing into a joke when she responded, **"Austin from Houston, and Brooklyn from Dallas. How fucked up are we? ;)"**

@ABTreyTwo: "Happy to share in the struggle with you, baby. Guess we gotta be friends for real now."

I wasn't even sure where that had come from, especially since I rarely ever entertained unfamiliar women hopping in my DMs. But something about Brooklyn was just… *interesting*, keeping me tuned into the conversation instead of going back to the video game that Calvin had taken over when I wasn't paying attention.

@B_AdamsFinest: "If you're curious to know, the dimples were what got me."

Naturally, they flared in response to her words as if they were taking a bow, my smile full as hell when I replied, **"They're my secret weapon. Glad to know they still work their magic, even if it's via the internet."**

@B_AdamsFinest: "They certainly do. Last night, I told my roommate I wanted to cover them with my inner thighs. But that's a lot to tell a complete stranger, so I'm gonna chill."

"Well damn," I said out loud, garnering Calvin's attention as he paused the game to ask, "*What?*" But I quickly shook him off, leaning forward on the couch with my phone in my hand as I tried to decide how I wanted to play this.

Not responding would've been the easy thing to do since Brooklyn was starting to feel like the exact kind of trouble I should've been avoiding. But on the other hand, I was far too intrigued to turn back now, quickly typing out, **"Yo, you're really just gonna drop a bomb like that and pretend it's nothin'?"**

It was bold as hell, but I didn't mind her taking it there, appreciating the honesty that seemed to match my own. To be real, the shit was refreshing, especially after dealing with some of the local South Beach women who almost all seemed to be on that fake shit one way or another. But unfortunately, it was my locale that had Brooklyn attempting to dead our conversation according to her next reply.

@B_AdamsFinest: "You're in Miami. I'm in Dallas. Which mean it's definitely nothin'."

@B_AdamsFinest: "This was fun though. Have a good day, Mr. Basketball Player Dude. <3"

Somehow, her lowkey curving me still came off as sweet and sarcastic, making me smirk as I sent another response anyway.

@ABTreyTwo: "Wow. So your fine ass is really just gonna slide in my DMs, get my full attention, then bounce out on me before I even get to respond to your desire to ride my face by tellin' you I'd definitely let you ride my face?"

I could see when she read the message, and I worried I might've said too much when she didn't respond right away. But no more than a minute had passed when she finally replied.

@B_AdamsFinest: "Well played. ;)"

Now that it seemed as if I had her attention the same way she had mine, I felt confident enough to really shoot my shot, not holding anything back when I went for the kill.

@ABTreyTwo: "So what's up? You want me to fly you out, or what?"

@B_AdamsFinest: "Is that what you do? A pretty girl slides in your DMs, and you immediately flex by offering her a plane ticket?"

Ironically enough, this was my first time putting a plane ticket on the table. In fact, I had made fun of some of my teammates for doing the same shit in the past, especially since there was plenty of local pussy to go around. But it wasn't even just about the pussy with Brooklyn, her whole energy - *even through messages* - enough to have me wanting to know more about her, wanting to experience her in person. So I kept it all the way real when I replied, **"Nah, I've never done this before. But I get a certain vibe from you, Brooklyn. And I want more."**

"Damn, nigga. You still messaging back and forth with ol' girl?"

I didn't bother answering Calvin with anything more than a head nod, my eyes focused on the screen as I read her response that was actually another question.

@B_AdamsFinest: "What if I turn out to be a Catfish?"

For whatever reason, that made me crack up laughing until I considered the possibility, scrolling back to her profile as if I could somehow check its authenticity. But once I clicked her profile picture to watch the story of videos she had shared from the night before of her and a friend drunk as hell singing offkey to Beyoncé, I realized this was just her being silly again, allowing me to respond, **"It'll be one hell of a lesson learned. But considering the recent videos on your *Instagram* story, I think I'm good there."**

@B_AdamsFinest: "What if I forward a screenshot of these messages to one of those gossip pages?"

Once again I laughed, knowing that was just another reason I usually didn't entertain women in my DMs. But with Brooklyn, I felt secure enough to challenge, **"Screenshots of me**

offering a fine ass woman the opportunity to ride my face? Honestly, I'd probably gain some new fans."

@B_AdamsFinest: "Wow. You're good."

@ABTreyTwo: "I know. ;)"

With a real grin on my face that matched the one I had sent, I sat back against the couch, watching Calvin get his ass kicked in the game as I waited to see what Brooklyn would come up with next. But I became a little worried when I read, **"Okay, one more honest thing."**

Naturally, my mind went to some worst-case scenarios, trying to evaluate which things I would or wouldn't be willing to tolerate.

She's a stripper or somethin'… no biggie.

Kids… eh.

Crazy baby daddy… hell nah.

@B_AdamsFinest: "Sliding in your DMs was a vodka-induced dare."

"*That's it?*" I asked in my head while typing out, **"So you're sayin' you wouldn't have been checkin' for me otherwise?"**

I could pretty much assume that wasn't the case since our conversation had gotten this far. But I was glad to see her confirm that in her latest message.

@B_AdamsFinest: "Nah, you're fine as hell. I'm just saying our... virtual paths might not have

crossed otherwise. Hopping into a stranger's DMs isn't exactly my style."

While it stroked my ego to know I had her doing new shit the same way she had me - *even if hers had come off a dare* - it was that honesty that really had me feelin' her when I replied, **"Well I'll be sure to thank Diddy for making *Ciroc* next time I see him. Now are we gonna link up, or are you chickening out on me? I wanna meet you, for real."**

After I sent the message, I realized how desperate it probably made me sound; shit that definitely wouldn't go over as smoothly in the comments of the gossip pages if she really did go through with screenshotting. But I was surprised to see her take a different angle, bringing up my career instead when she asked, **"Don't you have basketball games and stuff to be worried about?"**

Being that it was mid-season, I probably should've been more worried about basketball than a chick I didn't even know in my DMs. But it was just my luck that the only real break we got during the season was steadily approaching, allowing me to reply, **"All-Star Break is coming up, so I'll have some rare downtime to spend with you."**

Spending the extended weekend with a girl like Brooklyn seemed like a great plan, giving me enough time to get to know her a little better, have a little fun if she was really down, and send her off with pleasant memories for the both of us. But I hadn't even realized what I was accidentally setting up until I read, **"That's Lovers' weekend, Mr. Basketball Player Dude. Reserved for real couples. Not fly-outs with rand-os."**

She had a point, the commercialized holiday of flowers and chocolates surely on the radar for most people. But just because the "rules" said one thing didn't mean we couldn't do our own, something I expressed when I typed out, **"Well nothing says Happy Valentine's Day to me like having a beau-**

tiful woman ride my face. Especially one who looks like she tastes like *Hershey Kisses*."

Once again, I knew I was running the risk of doing too much and getting my ass embarrassed if she decided to switch up on me. But I was happy to see Brooklyn on that same witty shit she had been on from the very beginning, correcting me with her reply.

@B_AdamsFinest: "*Godiva*. I'm more of a gourmet type of bitch. ;)"

I bust out laughing, catching a side eye from Calvin who was obviously in his feelings about the major L he was now taking in the game. But I wasn't about to let him ruin my vibe, feeling too good as I typed, **"Yo, you're really cute as hell. Can I get your number?"**

It felt a little silly to just now be asking for her number considering how deep our conversation had already gone. But I knew it was best for me to get off of Al Sharpton's internet before I really started talking some nasty shit that someone could hack into and put me on blast about; not that I was at all ashamed of my game.

I suppose I just preferred my privacy as much as the next person, which also meant I'd definitely be deleting these messages before I gave Calvin back control of my social media. And I was only reminded to do so when I read, **"I mean, you already gave me permission to ride your face. Asking for my number kind of feels like taking a step backward at this point."**

I smirked as another message came in, this time with a phone number that included a very familiar Dallas area code and a kiss emoji. And while I was tempted to hit her up right away, hear her voice, or maybe even see her face on a video call, I decided to play it cool instead, replying with a simple, **"I'll be in touch, baby."**

BROOKLYN

"SO YOU'RE REALLY DOING this? You're really going to fly to Miami and spend the weekend with some stranger you met on Al B Sure's internet?"

As I sat perched on a stool in the shop watching Raina give herself yet another tattoo to pass the time, the same question sat heavy on my brain, the concept sounding a little crazy now that I wasn't wrapped up in the original conversation Austin and I had had about it. I mean, I suppose it wasn't *completely* crazy since men with the ability to pull the kind of strings Austin had talked about did and did often. But the details of it all were still too foggy for me to answer with anything more than, "I haven't told him yes, but I haven't told him no either. And he really hasn't brought it up again so… *I don't know.*"

Since Austin and I had only exchanged a few texts back and forth outside of our conversation on *Instagram* less than a week ago, I wasn't exactly sure where his head was at, wasn't sure if he was even still interested in "linkin' up" as he had called it. But I also understood that he was a busy guy, and me still technically being a stranger didn't exactly scream "priority" which meant I was going to try my best not to get too invested either way.

"Well, do you want my advice?" Raina asked, peeking up

from her new ink - *a tiny mustache on the side of her middle finger* - with a silly smirk on her face.

A smirk that had me quick to mutter, "*Not really…*"

Of course, she gave it anyway. "I say you should go. And not only should you go, you should go and secure the bag, B. Take one for the team and make a baby with the nigga."

The fact that she remained so nonchalant had me worried she was dead serious, forcing me to squeal, "Raina! Are you out of your mind?!"

She shrugged, letting out a little giggle when she answered, "Of course I am. That's never been in question. But we're not talking about me. We're talking about you and the baby you need to conceive for the culture."

While she knew good and damn well a baby was out of the question, I also knew that wasn't the only thing up for discussion, gnawing on my lip as I quickly pushed out, "Who's to say we'll even have sex?"

The steady buzz of her tattoo gun came to a screeching halt, her face stale as if I had said the dumbest thing she'd ever heard. And she only doubled down on her expression when she huffed, "*Brooklyn*. Come on now. You really think he'd offer to fly you out without expecting a little of that *Godiva* you bragged about? And don't act like you don't wanna give it to him cause we all would if the opportunity presented itself."

She was right.

Even though I hadn't experienced his sex appeal in person, just thinking about Austin, and his slick mouth, and his muscles, and those damn dimples had me grinning with anticipation of whatever he had up his sleeve. Still, I somehow managed to play it down, telling Raina, "*Anyway*. If it happens, it happens. But I'm not showing up with any expectations other than to soak up some sun and have a good time."

Her eyes went wide with excitement, and I didn't understand why until she said, "So that confirms it then. You're going."

I shrugged, pulling my bottom lip back between my teeth to contemplate. And while there were still a few red flags - *mainly the fact that I hadn't done a thorough background check* - not even that was enough to stop me from answering, "*If he asks again…* I guess so."

"Hell yeah!" Raina cheered with a clap, doing a little dance in her seat as she sang, *"Brookie's gonna have his baby. Brookie's gonna have his baby."*

Before I could threaten her life for wishing that shit on mine, the door to the tattoo shop chimed, forcing me off the stool since I was technically supposed to be manning the desk instead of hanging out in the back talking shit with Raina. But when I made my way out to the front, there wasn't a client; instead a delivery man carrying a bouquet of flowers.

"Hi, are you Brooklyn Adams?"

"She certainly is," Raina answered from behind me, curling around to accept the flowers on my behalf while simultaneously getting her flirt on with the dude. And while I wasn't going to knock her game since homeboy was kinda fine, I was also too curious to see who the hell was sending me flowers not to interrupt their little conversation just slightly to snatch the envelope out.

I anxiously opened it and found two things; first, a plane ticket with my name on it for a direct flight scheduled for Friday afternoon to Miami, and second, a simple note written in neat handwriting.

"Be My Valentine, Brooklyn?" - Austin <3

My grin was painfully wide when I read it a few times over as if the message was going to change, the artist in me also finding his penmanship impressive. And while I already knew the answer to his question, I was glad to hear Raina agree in her own special way once she joined me to get a glimpse for herself.

"Oh, bitch. You are gonna throw every bit of that ass this weekend."

A giggle slipped from my lips as I told her, "I can't lie, this is *super* cute of him."

Raina enthusiastically agreed. "Super cute, super sweet, super... *ugh*. How is he already so bae and we haven't even met him yet?!"

"Which is exactly why we both need to chill. He could easily do this and then be on some weird, fuck shit in person," I replied, still trying to play it down so I wouldn't set myself up to be disappointed even though I really, *really* wanted to ride the high.

But I also knew it was wise to stay neutral, even when Raina said, "If he's on some fuck shit, I'm losing all hope in humanity."

Once again, I giggled just as my phone began to buzz in my pocket, pulling it out to find the heart and basketball emoji in place of Austin's name.

Okay, so maybe I was already a little too invested.

It was hard not to be with him being so... *everything*, a grin on my face when I told Raina, "This is him calling. Watch the front for me?"

"As long as you come back with details," she replied with a grin of her own before sending me to the back of the shop with a wave of her hand.

I answered the call the second I hit the hallway, trying not to sound too giddy about hearing his voice live for the first time when I said, "Austin, hey."

"What's good, Brooklyn? What you doin'?" he asked, his tone a lot warmer and deeper than the one I had heard him use in random video clips on his *Instagram*.

It was also a hell of a lot sexier, only making my grin grow even wider when I answered, "I'm at work. You know, the place you sent those beautiful flowers to."

I wasn't sure how he even knew where to send them since that wasn't something we had talked about. But I was too flattered by the gesture to ask questions, instead listening to him say, "So if you got the flowers, that means you might have an answer to my question too then, right?"

Without skipping a beat, I told him, "Not might. I *do* have an answer, and..."

"*Wait.* Before you tell me, I want you to know that I'm a chill ass nigga. So if you're comin' down with the whole, nightclub, strip club, hard drugs and heavy liquor thing in mind…" he trailed, the rest of his statement obvious without needing to speak it.

Lucky for me - *or for him* - that scene wasn't really my thing either, allowing me to reply, "I mean, I'm good without all that. But I'm also not coming down if we're just gonna be sitting in some hotel playing the staring game."

The last thing I wanted to do was travel to a city like Miami - a place I had never been - only to end up bored and trapped in a room for the weekend. But apparently, I had this whole thing all wrong when Austin asked, "Who said anything about a hotel? I got plenty of room at the crib. I mean, if a hotel makes you more comfortable, we can make that happen, *but...*"

"*Oh.* I guess I just… I've never done this before, you know," I reminded him, the idea of staying at his house exciting me and terrifying me all at once. On one hand, I was thrilled to check out his space, see how he lived, be close enough to pounce in the event that I got the urge. But on the other hand, the shit was... *risky*.

As if he could feel my anxiety through the phone, he attempted to put me at ease when he offered, "We're learning together, remember? Making our own rules." Before continuing on to say, "But I can guarantee we won't be holed up anywhere playing the staring game. I just wanted to make that clear so you won't get down here and be disappointed."

I could appreciate him being upfront, though I also couldn't help but tease, "Honesty, right? Though I really have a hard time believing you find anything wrong with a strip club, Mr. Basketball Player Dude."

Instead of laughing at my little jab, he released a heavy sigh, telling me there was definitely more to the story once he finally replied, "That whole scene is just very… been there, done that for me."

I was tempted to probe for more, but I figured I'd save my questions for later, moving on when I agreed, "Understandable. But uh… you gotta make us some plans, homie. It's only the polite thing to do when you have a visitor."

This time, he gave me the laugh I was looking for as he said, "Well damn. Okay, mama. I got you. But does that mean you're really coming?"

I gnawed on my lip, the giddiness from earlier returning as I rocked from heel to heel and teased, "I guess I'll come. I mean, since it'd be a shame to waste a good plane ticket and all."

That made him laugh even harder, a sound I was already growing incredibly fond of when he let out an astonished, "*Wowww*. Don't act like that's the only reason, baby. Cause a nigga *will* cancel and take a flight credit if you wanna play wit' me."

Since that was the last thing I wanted to happen, I quickly squealed, "I'm just kidding! I'm… really, *really* excited to meet you, Austin."

"Well as strange as it may sound, I feel like I already know you, Brooklyn," he replied, the warmth in his tone sending a rush of heat over my skin that had me wishing I could fast forward the clock. And it wasn't just his tone, but his claim as well, the instant connection he talked about feeling more and more mutual the longer we stayed on the line.

But considering I was supposed to be remaining neutral and not getting too caught up already, I decided to save my energy for the weekend, smiling when I told him, "Guess we'll just have to wait and see about that."

AUSTIN

"YOU SURE you don't want me to come with you for backup? I mean, what if she really is kinda funny-lookin' in the face?"

The question made me release a heavy sigh as I plopped down on the bed to adjust my shoelaces, wanting to be annoyed while also wondering if I should've been considering Calvin's offer. I mean, I trusted my gut that told me everything would be fine - *that she would be fine*. But I also couldn't ignore the possibility of my gut steering me wrong.

"*A little too late for that,*" I thought, standing up and dusting my hands down the front of my crewneck as I replied, "Bruh, don't wish bad luck on me like that. And even if she is kinda funny-lookin', she's just gonna be my funny-lookin' Valentine for the weekend. Now how do I look?"

With a laugh, Calvin asked, "Nigga, are you serious right now? You haven't even seen her for real yet, and you're already whipped enough to be asking *me* how you look?"

The way he asked had me releasing another sigh. "*Fuck.* I'm trippin', huh?"

"Look at my face, then decide if you want the real answer to that question," he replied, prompting me to peek his way and see his answer wouldn't have been anything more than a full-on roast. And while I couldn't exactly blame him, that still didn't stop me from moving to the mirror instead, checking myself out only to discover something was missing.

"A chain, maybe? Or how about a watch?" I asked in my head, quickly deciding on both as I moved towards the jewelry splayed on top of my dresser and admitted, "I'm just… this is different for me, man. I guess I'm a little nervous."

It was an unexpected feeling, but I suppose the whole "first-time" thing called for it since I really didn't know what I was doing. And of course, Calvin didn't really make me feel any better about it when he said, "As you should be. I mean, she could very well be coming down here to rob you blind like the City Girls taught her to."

"*Bruh…*" I groaned, this time peeking his way with a stale face that had him putting his hands up in defense.

"I'm just sayin'. You gotta be careful out here. These chicks are sneaky."

I secured my chain while also brushing him off. "*Anyway*. I'm about to go swoop her from the airport, so I'ma need you to find some business before we get back."

The last thing I needed was Calvin fucking up the vibe on some nosey shit. And I was glad he didn't fight me on it when he followed me down the stairs and answered, "You know where I'll be, boss. Good luck."

I gave him an appreciative nod as he slipped off towards the kitchen and I slipped towards the garage, trying to decide which car said I had it without doing too much. The last thing I wanted to do was look like I was trying to make a point of my wealth, even though I *did* want to make a point when it came to my good taste in automobiles.

Somehow I decided on my blacked out Mercedes G-Wagon, happy to see the tank was already full when I pulled out for the drive to the airport. But the closer I got to the terminal Brooklyn said she was waiting at, the more anxious I got, praying to God my gut had gotten this whole thing right.

When I finally spotted who I assumed was her according to the floppy black hat and leopard-print suitcase she had texted me as identifiers, I felt giddy as hell, happy to see that at least her body matched what I had seen on her *Instagram*.

"*Now let's see about that face,*" I thought as I pulled into the pick-up lane, parking illegally and grabbing the gift bag I had put together for her at the last minute before hopping out to greet her properly.

Her face was deep in her phone when I approached, allowing me to get a glimpse of just how much the pictures didn't do her any justice. And once I asked, "Can I get that bag for you, Ms. Adams?" I got the full-on view, my heart skipping a beat when she peeked up at me with her big brown eyes and red-painted lips.

Fuckin' beautiful.

She didn't say anything at first, frozen in place as her eyes gave me a quick perusal. And when she finally did speak, her voice was just above a whisper. "*Oh*… my God."

Her reaction made me chuckle as I pulled her into a quick hug, trying to keep things as casual as possible when I stepped back and asked, "How you doin', Brooklyn? How was your flight?"

Instead of answering my question, her eyes grew bigger. "Oh my God."

"Come on, baby. Don't go gettin' all starstruck and shit on me now," I told her with another little laugh, hoping that wasn't actually the case since I wasn't trying to deal with another groupie.

Thankfully, the mention was enough to snap her out of it, her lips pulled into a smirk when she replied, "No shade to your career, but this doesn't have anything to do with your stardom, Mr. Basketball Player Dude. You are just… so damn handsome. Strikingly handsome."

My eyebrow piqued. "Strikingly, huh? That's a first. But I guess if I'm *strikingly* handsome, that makes you *strikingly* gorgeous," I told her, earning myself another grin as I glanced down at the bag in my hand and remembered, "Oh, and this is for you."

While I knew how basic the whole teddy bear and chocolates thing was, Calvin had convinced me it was the gesture that counted, something he had apparently gotten right according to the huge smile that bloomed on Brooklyn's face as she dug through it and squealed, "Awww thank you! But I hope you bought all this stuff on discount. Those day after Valentine's Day sales are the best."

"*Damn.* I was wondering why this shit was so cheap. Now it all makes sense," I replied, reaching towards the handle of her suitcase as I asked, "You ready?"

I was more than ready, excited for whatever the weekend held now that we had gotten that initial greeting out of the way. But instead of agreeing as enthusiastically as I felt, Brooklyn gnawed at her lip, glancing down at her strappy-heels when she pushed out, "I mean, I'm here so..."

"That ain't what I asked you, baby," I said, hoping it didn't come off too rude. But I really needed her to be sure about what she was doing since the last thing I wanted was her to feel like I was about to hold her ass hostage, or something wild like that.

Thankfully, that didn't seem to be the case, her feelings rooted in the same anxiety I had experienced on the drive over when she replied, "No lie. I'm like… sweaty-palms nervous right now, Austin."

"Let me see," I teased, reaching for her free hand.

She immediately snatched it away, her face scrunched as she squealed, "Eww! No. That's gross."

"Just let me see, Brooklyn," I insisted, waiting for her skeptical ass to stick her hand out before I linked her fingers with my own and asked, "You ready now?"

She glanced down at our hands as if the gesture had surprised her. But when she peeked back up, the smile on her face was undeniable as she practically sang, "Sure."

With that, I felt confident leading us to my truck, her suitcase in one hand and her kind of sweaty hand in the other. But once we got there, she immediately dropped it, muttering more to herself than me, "Of course your ass pulls up in my fuckin' dream truck."

"You wanna drive it?" I asked, pulling the trunk open to toss her suitcase inside.

I could tell she wanted to answer yes and snatch the keys out of my hand, but she remained standing on the curb when she asked, "You really trust me to do that?"

"If you gotta ask, then maybe I shouldn't be," I teased with a laugh.

A laugh she joined in on even when she squealed, "Shut up! I can drive, I just…"

Instead of letting her finish, I tossed her the keys. "Have at it, baby. Just don't get us killed. This Miami traffic can be a beast."

She gave a confident shrug as she strolled past me towards the driver's side while replying, "I'm sure it's similar enough to Dallas traffic. I'll be fine. Just don't be giving me directions at the last minute; making me have to cut over four lanes of traffic and shit."

With another laugh, I told her, "I got you." Making my way to the passenger's side and pushing the seat way back to make room for my legs before climbing in. And Brooklyn was doing the exact opposite, pulling her seat way forward so that she could actually see over the steering wheel.

Instead of starting it up right away, she gripped the wheel tightly, grinning from ear-to-ear as she gushed, "*Wow*. I'm in love. I mean, it looks good on me, right?"

Truth be told, everything looked good on Brooklyn, even more so now that I was seeing it all in person. In fact, having her in front of me only made me want to touch her again and confirm she was really here, though I only nodded instead when I agreed, "It certainly does. And who knows. You play your cards right this weekend, and it could be yours."

I was only teasing and was glad Brooklyn caught on enough to easily brush me off with a giggle.

"Oh, whatever," she replied before starting up the truck. Then she gently eased into airport traffic while asking, "Okay, so where am I driving to?"

My eyes were on her as I shrugged and answered, "Wherever you wanna go, baby. You got the wheel."

She tossed me the quickest side eye without completely taking her eyes off the road, though I could still see the slight annoyance etched in her profile when she said, "You were supposed to make us some plans, remember?"

"I did. But you look like you'd rather just ride out for a minute, so I'm lettin' you do your thing," I told her, enjoying being a witness to how happy she was to be driving around in her alleged dream truck.

Her happiness only seemed to double in size once she screeched, "It just rides so smooth!"

I knew she was right, but I also knew all that smoothness hadn't come cheap, allowing me to reply, "As much as it cost me, that's the least it could do."

"I'm sure it was a drop in the bucket for you. Probably cost just as much as that *Rolex* you have on," she mentioned with a smirk that told me she was impressed. And while it was nice of her to notice since the decision to put it on in the first place was for that exact reason, it also wasn't like me not to give the full truth.

So glancing at my wrist, I admitted, "This was actually a Christmas gift from one of my teammates."

While the gift from our captain, Lamar, had surprised us all, it was easily the best one I had ever gotten. Though that only seemed to hype Brooklyn up even more as she gripped the wheel and repeated, "*A Christmas gift*? Your teammate gave you a *Rolex* for Christmas?! I can't even get a discounted tattoo out of my coworkers for Christmas! *Ugh, I'm clearly in the wrong profession...*"

I couldn't help but laugh at her little rant, the mention of her profession reminding me to ask, "Speaking of tattoos, where is all your ink at?"

The way she chose to capture her tattoos in pictures was honestly fascinating, all intimate shots that showed the little random symbols she had inked on her body without showing their exact location. And apparently that was her goal according to her teasing response of, "That's for me to know, and for you to find out."

"Oh, word? In that case, pull over," I teased right back, while also being down for a little exploration if she was really on that. But she kept the mystery alive when she only smirked instead, her eyes trained on the road as I continued, "Maybe you can tat me up one day. I'm sure you're a beast with the gun."

Her smirk fell flat, and I worried I might've said something wrong until she explained, "Oh, no. I'm not a tattoo artist. I mean, I hope to get behind the gun one day, but I just work at the shop as a receptionist for now."

"What's holdin' you up?" I asked out of pure curiosity, wanting to gather as much info on her as I could now that I had the opportunity.

Unfortunately, she didn't give me much, only shrugging when she pushed out, "I don't know. *Life*."

I could see the topic was making her a little uncomfortable, but that still didn't stop me from telling her, "Shits gonna pass you by if you don't make a move, B. You know that, right?"

"Of course!" she shouted, straightening up in her seat and tightening her grip on the steering wheel as she lowered her voice to add, "I just… get so nervous. And nerves and permanent ink don't exactly mix."

I nodded to agree. "That's true. But the only way you're gonna shake those nerves off is if you just… go for it. The more experience you get, the better you'll be. Matter of fact, get off on this next exit. I wanna take you somewhere."

The prospect of our first - *impromptu* - adventure brought her smile back as she easily maneuvered her way through traffic, my directions leading her straight to my favorite tattoo shop in the city. And while I could see the slight confusion on her face when she pulled up, she still went along with it without question, following me into the shop and instantly becoming engrossed with the environment that I imagined was similar to the one she worked in. Or maybe not, considering how wide her eyes seemed to get when she gushed, "This shop is… *everything*."

Since it was my go-to place, I had to agree, leaving her to check it out while I went to greet the owner, Greg, who wore the same slight confusion Brooklyn had a few moments before even when he gripped me up. But once he pulled back, I made the reason for my visit known, keeping my voice low to ask, "Yo, you think I can borrow your station right quick? I want baby girl to hook me up with a little somethin'."

It was a crazy idea, one I honestly wasn't even sure about

now that it had left my mouth. I mean, other than working at a shop and having some of her own, I had no clue what kind of experience she even had with tattoos, wasn't sure if she even knew how to work the machinery. But I could hear the desire in her voice to do it. And I knew if there was anything I could do to help her out, I was down for the cause; though Greg threw a slight wrench in my plans when he peeked past me and asked, "She certified?"

"Yo, Brooklyn!" I shouted across the shop, causing her head to pop up from the picture book of tattoos she was looking at so I could ask, "You got your papers?"

Her face scrunched. "*My papers*? I was born in this country!"

With a laugh, Greg stepped up to explain, "Not those kinda papers, mami. Tattoo license? Bloodborne pathogen course hours? Something that tells me I can trust you with my equipment?"

Since she wasn't aware of my plans, the confusion returned when she answered, "Oh. Uh… *no*. I mean, not yet."

Greg turned back my way with an expression that said there was nothing he could do for me, but that didn't stop me from begging, "Come on, G. I'll throw you somethin' extra. And it'll be quick. Ain't nobody even gotta know about this."

He put a hand to his chin in thought, telling me he was definitely about to try me with whatever he came up with.

"Somethin' extra? Like, courtside tickets?" he asked, his expression hopeful until I cocked my head, forcing him to change his request. "Aight, at least lower level."

With another dap, I told him, "Now that I can do. Thank you." Then I tossed over my shoulder, "Come on, Brooklyn." Leading us to the back of the shop where Greg usually hooked me up.

Once again, Brooklyn quickly became engrossed with the space, running her fingertips against the plush leather chair dominating the room as she said, "This shop is *so* much better than ours. I mean, I love my job and all. But this place is just… *inspiring*."

"Well let's see what you got. I've been itchin' for somethin' new," I told her, plopping down in the chair and rolling my sleeve up to make room for her to work.

Instead of catching my drift, she looked at me to ask, "That guy is on his way back?"

"No. You're gonna do it," I explained, watching the panic of the news flash across her face as she brought a hand to her chest.

"*Me?* But I can't… I mean, I'm not even…"

Instead of letting her ramble, I grabbed her free hand to cut her off. "I want you to go for it, Brooklyn. *I trust you* to go for it."

My support made her grin as she rocked back and forth on her heels, obviously growing more excited about the idea - *or maybe just appreciating my touch* - even when she replied, "You shouldn't be so easily trusting of strangers, Austin."

Nothing about Brooklyn read like a stranger to me, her whole vibe feeling more and more like right the longer I spent in her presence. And it wasn't just my gut telling me I was in good hands, but also the few real reasons I had gathered since she got in town; reasons I didn't mind sharing if that's what it took to convince her.

"I already trusted you to be who you said you were and that worked in my favor. I trusted you with my whip - *with my life* - and you didn't crash. And if nothing else, Greg does great cover-up work."

With that, she smirked, dropping my hand so she could rub her fingertips against the skin of my forearm - *her canvas*. "I bet you don't even know what you want."

"How about a lion's face? Right here on my wrist."

"*A lion's face*? That's *way* too hard for my first tattoo out the gate. How about… an arrow?" she suggested, my face immediately scrunching at the thought.

"*An arrow*? What's a nigga like me gonna do with a tattoo of a random ass arrow on my wrist?"

She held her hands up to defend, "It'll be small! And if its crooked and ugly, you can just wear your gifted watch every day to cover it up."

The pleading expression in her eyes told me to just go with it since this whole exercise wasn't really about me and my wants.

But considering I'd be the one with it on my body for the rest of my life, I told her, "I need it to mean something too, though."

"What does a lion's face mean to you?" she asked, the question catching me off guard since… I maybe hadn't thought about it. And Brooklyn took full advantage of my stumble, not even waiting for me to come up with some bullshit response before she said, "*Exactly*. And besides, this arrow will always mean something to you because it'll be a reminder of how crazy you were to let me do it in the first place."

"Or it'll just remind me of you," I offered, not even realizing the weight of my words until I saw Brooklyn go stiff. But then she smiled that brilliant smile of hers, and I decided a retraction wasn't worth the trouble, instead using all that energy to brace myself for whatever the hell I had gotten myself into.

BROOKLYN

"SO... HOW'D I DO?"

After spending a solid hour on the tattoo that probably would've taken a more experienced artist no more than ten minutes, I was anxious for an evaluation, gnawing on my lip as both Austin and Greg examined my efforts. Truth be told, I was more impressed with myself for not passing out before I finished it since I wasn't sure if I had even taken a breath the entire time. But now it was time to find out if that loss of oxygen was worth it, my eyes on Greg as he held a hand to his chin and studied the ink I had given Austin.

"Solid line work. Great color consistency. Symmetry is good..." he trailed with a nod before turning towards me to say, "Congratulations, mami. You've successfully lost your tattooing virginity."

My shoulders sank as I finally released the big breath I had been holding, my eyes glossy with pure exuberance when I gushed, "Thank youuu." Then I put a hand to Austin's shoulder to add, "And thank you. For taking my virginity. Or letting me take my virginity out on you. *Or…*"

He cut me off with a laugh. "Glad to be of service, baby. Still don't know what it means, but I'm sure I'll figure out something."

I nodded to agree as we both listened to Greg give the

rundown on how we had to keep the location a secret, how if anyone asked he knew nothing about this, and of course, what game he wanted tickets to. Then he left me to safely clean up the station, something I really had experience with since I had done the same thing plenty of times back home. But before I did that, I told Austin, "You know I have to get a picture, right? This is like… a monumental moment."

It was still a little crazy to me that he had even let me do it – *had been brave enough to let me do it.* And while I was more than willing to do a favor of equal or lesser value in return to show how much I appreciated him taking a chance on me, I was just happy that he seemed legitimately satisfied with my work, twisting his wrist from side to side to look at the fresh ink as he said, "You can get as many pictures as you want after you show me one of your tattoos."

"Oh, that's easy," I replied, turning my head and pulling my ear forward to show him the small heart behind it.

"I already peeped that one while you were busy concentrating on my tat. Show me something else," he insisted, licking his lips as if he expected me to show him something more intimate.

"*Maybe… definitely later,*" I thought in my head, giving him a smirk before I turned around and lifted my hair to show him the lightning bolt down the nape of my neck. "This is the newest one. Maybe three weeks old."

He stood up from his chair to examine it. "Yo, that's fire. Simple, but also dope."

With an arrogant grin, I turned back around to brag, "I like to think that's my entire persona. *Simple, but also dope.*"

He laughed, matching my grin with one of his own when he said, "Okay, one more."

I twisted my lips in thought, nearly drawing a blank on the tattoos I had in places I considered innocent enough to show him in public until I remembered the tiny anchor near my ankle. And once I pulled back the strap of my heel to give him a glimpse, he responded with an approving nod.

"You got some pretty feet on you, B."

"Thank you. Now can I get my picture, please?" I asked,

trying not to grin too hard at his little compliment as he stuck his forearm out for me. I had only been concentrating on a small part of it while I was tattooing him, but seeing the entire thing flexed with all its veins, and strength, and… *Jesus, Brooklyn. Just take the picture.*

I snapped a few from different angles on my phone before calling it good, being sure not to tag the shop's location in my *Instagram* photo when I posted one with the caption, *"It ain't nothin' like the first time…"*

"Brooklyn, that song was *not* about tattoos," Austin said from over my shoulder with a chuckle, his closeness surprising me and his smell assaulting me in the best way possible. I mean, it was truly unfair for him to look this good and smell even better.

And now he had gotten my endorphins sky high by letting me tattoo him?

Before I could respond the wrong way, my screen flashed over from *Instagram* to an incoming call from Raina, prompting me to create a little space between Austin and I so that I could take it. And even though I had stepped away, I was pretty sure he still heard her scream, "So you just out here tattooing niggas now?!"

I peeked over my shoulder to see he had *definitely* heard her according to the amused expression on his face, though I still lowered my voice to whisper, "Raina, will you chill?"

"I absolutely will not. I mean, just what kinda ass did you throw at him for him to have let you do that already?" she asked, the question making me laugh since that wasn't the case at all.

Once again, I kept my voice to a whisper when I answered, "I haven't… thrown any ass, Raina. This was his idea. I just accepted the challenge."

As if she couldn't believe it, she asked, "So this was like… a cash advance for that ass then?"

With a giggle, I told her, "I'm hanging up now."

"Wait, no. Don't hang up yet. Is he as fine as he looked on the internet?" she asked, a question I was more than happy to answer while also rushing her off the phone so I could get back to the person she was talking about.

"Yes, Raina. Goodbye now."

"*But…*" she started just as I clicked to end the call, turning around to find Austin with all eyes on me. Naturally, I wondered how long he had been looking - *and if he had heard any more of our conversation.* But instead of acknowledging either, he asked, "Your roommate, right?"

I nodded, almost ready to defend her antics until he added, "She seems like quite the character."

"She certainly is, but I love her like a sister. She's the one who did all of my tattoos. And inspired me to want to follow in her footsteps," I admitted, something I wasn't sure Raina even knew since we had never talked about it explicitly. But it was a fact I was proud to share, especially now that I had gotten my first out of the way.

"So she's the one who's a beast with the gun, huh?"

"Precisely," I answered with a grin as I double-checked to make sure I had tidied everything up before Austin led us back out to the front of the shop. And after exchanging pleasantries with Greg, we made our way back to the truck, Austin being a gentleman and opening the passenger's side door for me while asking, "You ready to get to our real plans now?"

I shrugged, teasingly gnawing on my lip when I climbed in and answered, "I don't know. I mean, spontaneous you is kinda stealing the show right now."

"Well I think you'll like both," he insisted with a smirk before closing the door behind me. And as I watched him round the front of his truck in long, confident strides, I couldn't help but agree in my head.

"*I think so too.*"

Austin was getting ready to climb in until he saw how close to the steering wheel I had moved his seat up, making him laugh as he changed the settings while teasing, "Damn, girl. You're short as hell."

"Nah, you're just tall as fuck. Long ass legs, long ass arms, long…"

With the click of his seatbelt, he cut me off. "You settin' yourself up with that one, baby. Cut it out while you're ahead."

The thought of his dick being just as long as everything else about him was enough to make me gasp, especially if it was as rich in color and veiny as his forearms. But considering that was the last thing I should've been thinking about already, I somehow found it in me to tease, "I was gonna say long ass feet, but your mind is *clearly* in the gutter."

He smirked again, even the way he eased into traffic exuding a ridiculous level of swagger when he replied, "The girl who told me she wanted to ride my face during our first conversation has the nerve to say my mind is the one in the gutter?"

"I was only being honest!" I defended with a shrug and a giggle, especially disinterested in taking my words back now that I was seeing his fine ass in person.

He only made me more eager to bring those words to life once he said, "Okay, well I'ma be honest too and tell you all that length certainly extends to places you can't see right now."

With my lip pulled between my teeth, I turned towards him in my seat to get a full view when I teased, "What? Long abs? *No.* Long… *nipples*?"

His hearty laugh filled the truck. "Brooklyn, you wild as hell. But I fucks wit' it."

I held my hands up to defend, "I'm really chill, I swear. It's just something about those dimples that make me wanna… *anyway*. Where are we going? And just so you know, Raina can track me at all times. So if you were planning on kidnapping me…"

"I actually owe her a thank you," he said, my eyebrow shooting up in surprise prompting him to continue, "For hooking me up with an address to send those flowers to."

While I was glad to know how he had gotten the information, it also managed to confuse me. "*Wait.* She knew about that? *No.* She actually kept quiet about that? What the hell kinda voodoo did you put on her? Cause that girl has never been able to keep a secret."

His grin looked borderline boyish - *hella adorable* - when he explained, "She thought it was a cute gesture. Said no one deserved something like that, or this little trip, more than you."

"So we both owe her thank yous then," I told him with a grin of my own, tempted to text her something as mushy as what she had apparently shared with Austin.

But before I could even think to get my phone out, he added, "Now to answer your original question, we're headed to one of my boys' restaurants for dinner."

I let out a sigh of relief that clashed with my stomach growling. "Oh, thank God. Cause I was surely about to dig into this box of chocolates if food wasn't on the agenda."

In fact, I still planned on digging into the box of chocolates since I wasn't sure how much longer the drive was. But the second I pulled it from the gift bag, getting ready to pop the top off, Austin teased, "Diggin' into a box of chocolate. I like the sound of that. And those are *Godivas* too, right?"

My hand went still once I caught on to his little innuendo, unable to contain the smirk that grew to my lips when I asked, "You really think you're slick, huh?"

He shrugged. "Nah. Me wantin' you ain't a secret worth keeping, especially now that you're in my city and I can actually do somethin' about it."

His straightforward attitude had me biting my tongue so I wouldn't sing his praises too prematurely. But I would've been lying if I said I wasn't completely into his confidence about… doing nasty things to me; things I was more than ready to participate in even when I told him, "Dinner first. *Then* we'll decide if you should've kept that secret."

That made him laugh. "Damn. So you doubtin' my ability to woo you in a weekend?"

The thought of him really being able to woo me in a weekend was honestly a little intimidating, especially since I wasn't sure how things between us would work beyond these circumstances. But for now, I was staying in the moment, finally popping the top off my chocolates as I answered, "Not at all. Just reminding you that I actually have standards regardless of my initial thirst saying otherwise."

"I don't see it as thirst, though. I mean, you saw something you wanted, and you weren't afraid to let it be known. It's…

refreshing. And appreciated," he said, peeking over to give me a wink that somehow made everything feel right - *and hot*.

But if there was one thing that could cool me off, it was replying, "I suppose I should thank my mother for that trait. I'm convinced she wasn't born with the ability to give a fuck."

While it had certainly been the root cause of many of our fights growing up, I had learned to appreciate my mother's blatant honesty over time, particularly after dealing with people - *men* - who treated lying like an Olympic sport. And it made sense that Austin seemed to be equally candid once he said, "Sounds like our mamas could be friends then, cause Angela Banks ain't never been with the shits either."

I wanted to laugh, but it got caught in my throat when he put his hand behind my headrest so that he could back into a parking spot; a gesture that was innocent enough while somehow also being wildly attractive. I mean, the concentration in his eyes and coolly pursed lips that made those damn dimples stand out, the extra flex in his arm, the ease at which he maneuvered his vehicle with one hand…

Girl, you are really losing your shit.

Instead of saying anything, I popped a chocolate in my mouth, hoping it would hold me over until we got a chance to order some real food. But when I peeked up to see where we had ended up at, I realized, "Wait a minute. I thought you said this was your friend's restaurant?"

"It is," Austin tossed out as he quickly turned the truck off and hopped out. And I was glad he came to open my door for me since I was a little too stunned to move, my eyes focused on the beautiful signage that said he couldn't have been telling the full truth.

I eventually accepted the hand he extended to help me out, though my eyes were still wide when I said, "It's literally named *Austin's*."

He closed the door behind me before placing a gentle hand to the small of my back to guide me inside while explaining, "Okay, so it's my restaurant. But my friend does all the important day-to-day shit, so it's really his restaurant."

"With your name on it," I added as if he had somehow forgotten that fact. But regardless of how nonchalant he was acting about it, I was beyond impressed, especially once we stepped into the charmingly intimate space that was buzzing with people. People that were obviously surprised to see the man himself step into the restaurant considering the round of applause that rang out.

While I was tickled to no end to see him in "celebrity" mode, I could tell he was trying to play off his annoyance, guiding me towards the kitchen with a little more urgency as he gave a few polite waves to his fans. And once we made it to the back, we were met by a guy who looked to already be having a long night according to the sweat pellets on his forehead that he swiped at while scolding, "Bruh, I thought you said you were coming like two hours ago. I could've gotten at least four entrees out of those reserved seats."

"Detour," Austin replied, lifting his wrist to show off his new ink - *my work* - before he introduced us. "Chef, this is my strikingly gorgeous guest, Brooklyn. Brooklyn, this is Chef Michaels. One of my closest friends and the best damn executive chef I know, even though his ass loves being stressed the fuck out over nothin'."

Chef Michaels rolled his eyes as he wiped his hands on his white coat then extended one to me, pairing it with a pleasant smile that went against his obvious annoyance with his friend. "It's a pleasure to meet you, Brooklyn. Welcome to *Austin's.*"

"Happy to be here, Chef. Can't wait to taste your cooking," I replied as I accepted his hand for a shake, ready to taste just about anyone's cooking at this point considering how hungry I was.

But I was completely caught off guard when Chef's smile grew into more of a smirk as he put a hand to Austin's shoulder and said, "*Actually*… I won't be doing the cooking for your table tonight. He will."

With wide eyes, I turned to smack a hand against Austin's chest. "Shut up! Are you serious?"

That boyish-like grin returned when he looked down at me to reply, "Being honest ain't the only thing Mama Ang taught me.

Now do you wanna hang out in here with me, or would you rather wait at the table for me to serve you?"

While being "served" sounded like a dream come true, the idea of watching Austin cook sounded just as dreamy, allowing me to answer, "Consider me your shadow. There's no way in hell I'm missing out on watching you work your way around the kitchen."

"The kitchen ain't the only thing I know how to work my way around, Brooklyn," he said with a wink, making me gasp since I knew - *and believed* - exactly what he was talking about. And apparently I wasn't the only one who had caught on since Chef Michaels made a throat-clearing noise to break some of the sensual air.

"Alright now, you two. Don't forget we still have other customers present. And let me know if you need anything, bruh," he told Austin with a dap before snapping back into Executive Chef mode, leaving Austin and I with a section of the kitchen to do whatever we pleased.

As Austin geared himself up with a black chef's jacket that had his name embroidered in beautiful red cursive, he asked, "So, tell me. What you got a taste for? We can cook up just about anything."

Seeing his fine ass in uniform had me tempted to answer that I had a taste for him. But then my stomach growled again, telling me to focus and respond more appropriately.

"Whatever you consider your specialty, I guess."

He nodded as if he already knew what he was going with before leaving to wash his hands at the sink nearby. And then he went into the industrial-sized fridge, returning with an assortment of vegetables and fresh shrimp on ice.

A man clearly after my heart.

I must've been staring at them a little too hard since Austin stopped moving to ask, "*Wait.* You aren't allergic, are you?"

"Oh God, no. That'd be depressing. But just out of curiosity, what are you making?"

He was already grabbing a bunch of different spices when he answered, "Shrimp Etouffee. It's a New Orleans dish my mom used to make all the time. That's where she's from originally."

"*No wonder she ain't with the shits,*" I muttered more to myself than him, my eyes on Austin as he glided throughout the kitchen with ease before pulling over a stool. Then he patted a hand against the wood while telling me, "Aight. Pop a squat so you can watch Daddy work."

"*Daddy?*" I asked with a giggle as I followed his directions and proudly sat my ass down. And after giving me a second to get comfortable, he slipped to stand in between my legs, resting his oversized hands against my thighs and licking his lips as if he was trying to get this whole dinner thing canceled.

"That's what I said, ain't it?" he teased, flashing me a smirk that only made me hotter.

Or maybe he just turned on the stove.

Either way, I had no problem playing along, gnawing on my lip when I told him, "You're lucky you're feeding me."

"Nah. If I'm lucky, this won't be the only thing I'm feeding you tonight."

AUSTIN

"THANK GOD I'm only here for the weekend. Cause if I keep eating like this, I won't be able to fit into any of the clothes I brought with me."

I couldn't help but laugh as Brooklyn fell back against her seat in a satiated slump, her mostly-clean bowl telling me she had definitely enjoyed my cooking without me having to ask. And while I was glad it had gone over smoothly since she was the first person I had ever tested my skills on and that roux could be tricky as hell, I was a little disappointed when I realized, "So that's a "no" on dessert, huh?"

She sat back up, resting her elbows on the table to respond, "Should it be? *Probably*. Is it? *Uhh*... I think I can make room for at least a taste."

With that, I hopped up from the table and grabbed Brooklyn's hand so she could do the same, pulling her through the now-empty restaurant towards the dessert display as she continued, "Seriously, though. That meal was *incredible*. Thank you for bringing me here."

"It was my pleasure. But the night's not over yet," I reminded her as I stopped in front of the display case to get a closer look at the different options Chef had left us.

Of course, everything looked good to me. So I let Brooklyn do the choosing, hardly surprised when she pointed her finger at a slice of the triple chocolate cheesecake.

The girl loved her chocolate.

"I have about two good bites of that dessert in me before the -itis kicks in," she warned as I opened the display case to get her cheesecake and a slice of chocolate ribbon pound cake to-go, deciding there was no need to stuff ourselves to the point of no return. But I couldn't resist grabbing one of the mini chocolate truffle cups to feed her now, loving the way her eyes immediately rolled to the back of her head after I slipped it into her mouth.

"*Oh my God*, that's delicious. We're taking a few of these with us to-go too, right? And if so, do you happen to have some *Rum Chata*? Cause that would truly make these orgasmic."

I chuckled as I packed a few in the box with the other desserts, bagging them up before I was tempted to add any more. Then I turned to wrap an arm around Brooklyn's waist and tell her, "If you're talkin' orgasms, I'll grab you a bottle from behind the bar."

Instead of taking me up on my offer, she only smirked, nodding just slightly with invitation as she slipped a little closer to me. And when she licked her lips, I licked mine out of reaction, bending my neck so she could reach them until Chef came out of nowhere to ask, "Yo, y'all… *oh damn.* My bad."

I closed my eyes with a sigh and Brooklyn giggled, pressing her forehead into my chest as if she was embarrassed about being caught. And she wasn't the only one embarrassed, Chef's cheeks flushed red when he continued, "I was gonna ask if y'all were good; if y'all needed anything before I got out of here."

"Nah, we're leaving too. Appreciate you for stickin' around, though," I told him, Brooklyn tagging on a quiet, "*Thank you*" from my chest.

"Not a problem, bruh," he replied with a nod before peeking down to tell my gir… *guest*, "It was nice to meet you, Brooklyn."

"Likewise, Chef. Those truffle cups are to die for," she said with a smile and a thumbs up, stroking Chef's ego enough to make him flush red yet again.

"Next time, try it with a shot of Rum Chata," he suggested,

Brooklyn practically jumping out of my hold to give me a look of, "*I told you!*"

Laughing together, we bid Chef a quick goodbye. Then I carried her out of the restaurant under my arm, almost stumbling when she came to a sudden stop in the middle of the parking lot.

"Oh wait! I forgot to take a picture."

Before I could ask of what, she turned to snap a quick picture of the restaurant's sign - *my name* - still glowing in the darkness, already uploading it to her *Instagram* by the time she turned back around. But when I read the caption she was adding to it, *"Say my name, say my name…"* I couldn't help but tease, "That song doesn't even match, Brooklyn."

She was quick to defend, "It doesn't have to match! It's more… *conceptual*."

Since it was her page, it was only right for me to accept her explanation, getting her to the truck and then hopping into the driver's side for the ride to my crib before I asked, "Aight, so who do you like better now? Planner Austin, or Spontaneous Austin?"

"Whichever one *isn't* talking in third person right now," she answered with a playful side eye before she turned towards me in her seat and continued, "You were right. I like both. I mean, one let me do my first tattoo on him, and the other fed me his mama's recipe done right at the restaurant with his name on it. That's like… heaven on earth. Put the two together and you'd be pretty close to perfect. So tell me. What's wrong with you?"

I couldn't help but laugh as I huffed, "*Damn.* Why somethin' gotta be wrong with me?"

"You have *all* of this amazing stuff going for yourself and somehow you're still single. *Oh no.* Please don't tell me the dick is trash," she sighed with a frown that only made me laugh even harder.

"My dick is incredible, baby," I assured her, giving her previous observation some thought before I explained, "I guess I just… live a certain lifestyle, you know. And tryna figure out who's really in it for me versus who's in it for what I can do for them is *just…* shit just gets too complicated sometimes, so I don't even bother with it."

Early on in my career, the lines had been painfully blurred, costing me more money than I could afford and a shit ton of energy I wish I could get back. I mean, sure it was fun in the moment. But the fact that all of that partying and bullshit had almost gotten me ousted from the league before I could really get my feet wet - *really make good money* - made the memories a lot less pleasant; though I was forever grateful for people like Lamar who got my head straight before it could fall all the way off.

As if she understood, Brooklyn nodded along before asking, "Well in that case, how the hell did I slip through the crack?"

"I already told you. *That ass*," I replied with a smirk that made her giggle as I continued, "Nah, being completely honest, something about you just told me you weren't on that phony shit. Like, you're impressed cause you're just naturally interested in what I have going on and it's new to you. But I don't think that's why you came out here. Am I right?"

"Nah. I literally came out here to ride your face and go," she answered, making my eyebrow pique while she sang, "*Just* kidding. Something about you just… intrigued me, Austin. The fact that you have all this and yet you're still so chill. So normal. And while I honestly had no idea who you were when you came up on my *Instagram*, I'm happy I slid in your DMs."

"I'm happy you did too. *With your slick ass*," I teased, peeking over to see the corner of her lip pulled between her teeth as she groaned, "That was *not* slick."

"Oh, it was definitely slick. "*I don't know you, but I gotta say somethin'*" knowing good and well I would want to know what the hell you were talkin' about."

"But what if that was really all I had to say?" she pressed with a smirk that told me that certainly wasn't the case.

Even if it was, I was quick to tell her, "It was still slick enough to get my attention, Brooklyn."

Since she knew I was right, she fell quiet as I pulled up to the guardhouse of my neighborhood, giving a quick wave to the security guard on duty before I continued past him to the gate as Brooklyn gushed, "*Wow.* A gated community, huh?"

With a shrug, I replied, "Yeah, people are crazy."

"So you trap yourself into a neighborhood with people just as crazy, *if not crazier*, who just so happen to have a few extra zeros in their bank account? *Got it*," she said with her usual lick of sarcasm that had me grinning until I considered her perspective.

"Well damn. When you put it like that…" I trailed, making her giggle as I turned down the private path that led to my house.

"I'm just teasing you, Austin. This is really nice. And I'm sure the privacy comes in handy too," she concluded as I finally pulled up in front of my garage, putting the truck in park before I turned in my seat to agree with her.

At least, that was the plan until I found myself lost in those gentle, brown eyes of hers, feeling a special sense of peace as I watched her sweep a piece of hair behind her ear before asking, "What?"

While I could've shared my thoughts on the whole privacy thing like I was supposed to, it felt more important to tell her, "Not a lot of people look better in person than they do on the internet, but you're for real gorgeous, baby."

In the age of filters and angles, I knew the lengths we all went through to only share our best selves no matter how many pictures we actually took to get the perfect one. But for Brooklyn, it was clear the internet was just a playground; though instead of accepting my compliment, she only giggled to reply, "Okay, seriously. You gotta stop calling me that. Cause I'm getting way too attached to hearing it, and it could very well be the thing you call every woman you come across making it not all that special."

With a little chuckle, I assured her, "Nah, it's special. I mean, I'm not saying I've never in my life called another woman baby because I'm sure I have. But it fits you. It's yours. *Baby*."

That seemed to satisfy her, an easy smile on her lips as I brushed a gentle hand against her cheek then leaned forward to press a kiss on her forehead that I planned on leaving things at for now until I saw the teasing look in her eyes.

"Your first flyout and you're already giving forehead kisses? You really *are* trying to woo me in a weekend."

Instead of pretending that wasn't true, I licked my lips to ask, "Is it working?"

The immediate smirk on her face answered yes, but I suppose she wanted more reason to give in when she leaned forward to close the space between us, stopping just short of kissing me to whisper against my lips, "I am gonna *fuck*… that cheesecake *up* when we get inside."

I started to laugh until she finally pressed on to kiss me, slowly and sweetly as if she was thanking me for bringing her when it really should've been me thanking her for coming. I mean, I could only imagine how tough of a decision it was for her, especially considering all the crazy shit that seemed to pop-up in the news about these sorts of meetups going wrong. But I suppose it had worked out for the both of us since she was proving to be exactly who I thought she was too. In fact, with her lips pressed to mine, things were working out *quite* well until I heard someone knocking on the thankfully-tinted window behind me.

"Yo! You blocked me in!" Calvin yelled, making me frown as I pulled away from Brooklyn to open the door just enough to see him.

"I thought I told you to find some business before I got back?"

"What you think I'm tryna do, bruh?" he fired back, deliberately leaning past me to see into the truck before he sang, "Heyyyy, pretty lady."

The skeptical look on Brooklyn's face in response had me quick to explain, "Brooklyn, this is my cousin, Calvin. Calvin, this is Brooklyn."

"Glad to see you really weren't a catfish, Brooklyn. Welcome to the 305," he announced, breaking Brooklyn's initial skepticism as she giggled before serving him a warm smile to say, "Thank you, cousin Calvin."

I could appreciate her being a good sport about his intrusion, but that didn't keep me from urging his ass on so I could let him out, starting my truck back up once he moved to open the garage as Brooklyn said, "He seems nice."

"A nice pain in my ass more often than not. Still my guy, though."

"Does he live here too?" she asked as I pulled over to the next slot, leaving him more than enough room to back out before turning off the truck again and answering her question.

"Only when he's beefin' with his girl. So basically, yeah."

It was honestly a shame that those two couldn't get it together long enough for him to stay out of my house permanently. Then again, I knew how annoying Calvin could be as a cousin so I could only imagine how annoying he was as a companion, grateful for Chelsea putting up with him when she did since it at least gave me a break.

"Well that's nice of you to let him stay here," Brooklyn insisted, trying to find the positive in the situation even when I groaned, "Yeah, nice until his annoying ass is interrupting us."

Reaching for my chin, she turned my head her way to say, "Don't worry, Austin. There's plenty more of where that came from." And I just knew she was about to give me those lips again when she started to lean forward, my eyes already closed with anticipation when she gripped my chin a little tighter and whispered, "*After* I get my cheesecake."

BROOKLYN

I WAS IN LOVE.

Okay, maybe it wasn't *exactly* love. But it seemed like that was the only word strong enough to correctly describe what I felt in my gut as I sat on top of Austin's kitchen island while he stood between my dangling legs and happily fed me forkfuls of cheese-cake. I had learned early on it was something he enjoyed doing - *literally feeding me* - and I wasn't complaining one bit, leaning back on my hands as I closed my eyes and groaned while he slowly pulled the fork from my lips.

"*My God.* That is some good ass cheesecake."

Blended with his chuckle, I heard the fork hit the container as Austin agreed, "It must be, cause you crushed that shit."

My eyes flew open when I realized, "*Wait.* That was the last of it? You really didn't warn me and my taste buds about the ending?!"

There was nothing worse than being unprepared for the last bite of something delicious, my eyes shooting over to find the container was indeed empty as Austin explained, "Too caught up watching you moan and groan, I guess. But we can stop by and get you some more tomorrow if you want."

His offer was tempting, mostly off the strength of getting a proper ending, but I still declined. "Nah, I really gotta chill. Getting *way* too used to eating good and being spoiled."

I hadn't even been in Miami for a full day, and yet somehow it felt like I'd been here for a week or more considering we'd been on the go since the second I touched down. But it wasn't only how much we had done in such a short amount of time, but also how quickly we had grown a liking to each other, finding an easy vibe that almost felt like a dream; especially once Austin licked his lips to ask, "What's wrong with gettin' used to that?"

It was a question I wished I didn't have to answer since there *shouldn't* have been anything wrong with it. But the truth was, "This is cute and all, Austin. But I know it's not forever. I mean, I'll be headed back to Dallas in a couple days, and you'll be resuming your season here in Miami. I'm here for a good time, but *definitely* not a long time."

"I see," he replied quietly as he stepped away, moving to discard the container in the trash then tossing the fork in the sink with an expression that almost looked disappointed as I hopped down from the island to catch him with a hand to his chest.

"Hey. What's the matter? Did I say something wrong?"

Shaking his head, he wore a semblance of a smile when he looked down at me and answered, "Nah. I'm just… sure you're tired from traveling all day and what not. Should probably get to bed so you don't fuck around and sleep your only full day here away tomorrow."

His response seemed like a cop-out, an abrupt ending to what would've otherwise been a perfect evening. But considering I wasn't sure what he had planned for us the next day and didn't want to ruin that by being a grumpy zombie or worse, I had no choice but to agree, "Oh. *Right.* I mean, I guess."

"You remember where we set you up at, right?" he asked as he led the way towards the staircase, his long strides putting him an easy three steps ahead of me by the time I answered him.

"I'm sure I can find it. And if not, I'll just sleep in whichever room I *can* find."

From the brief tour he had given me earlier, I knew if nothing else, I'd be able to find somewhere to lay my head since apparently he didn't want that place to be in his bed. But instead of letting me struggle with a search, he waited for me to hit the top of the staircase and then guided me towards the guest room I had left my things in earlier, reaching inside to flick the light on before turning my way to ask, "You need anything?"

"*Yes. You,*" was what I wanted to answer. But instead, I shook my head no, watching the slight flare in his dimples as he bent his neck to press a quick kiss against my cheek.

"Goodnight, Brooklyn."

"Night, Austin," I replied quietly as I leaned against the doorframe and watched him walk away, giving me one last peek back before he dipped into his master suite and shut the door behind him.

With a sigh, I slipped into my room and did the same, digging through my suitcase for something to sleep in as my phone buzzed next to it on the bed. And once I picked it up, I couldn't help but frown after reading the message.

"Flyout day one rating? After that tattoo shit, I'm dyiiiiing for details." - Raina

"Would've been an easy ten, but something happened." - Brooklyn

Plopping down on the bed next to the suitcase, I waited for what I knew would be a quick reply since I could see she was already typing.

"Aww damn. Dick didn't match the rest of the package, huh?" - Raina

"I wouldn't know. Didn't get it. He just sent me to my room." - Brooklyn

"Like a parent does when you get in trouble? That nigga on some weirdo, controlling shit?" - Raina

Her concern made me crack the slightest smile even though the truth wasn't exactly something to be happy about.

"No. He said something about resting up for tomorrow, but I'm not buying it." - Brooklyn

"So go talk to him, Brookie." - Raina

"Matter of fact, check the front pocket of your suitcase. You're welcome." - Raina

First, I squinted at the screen, then I looked over to my suitcase, quickly pulling back the top flap to reach the pocket she was talking about. And after carefully unzipping it, I had to hold back my squeal once I pulled out the red teddy and matching robe that I'd shown Raina online during one of our Saturday night eat, drink, and crush sessions.

I was so excited about the lingerie that I'd almost missed the card attached to it, with an envelope covered in dick doodles and a note that read:

"Because you deserve. Love you, B!" - The Best Roommate Ever

P.S.: I call dibs on being Godmom :)

With a smile, I dropped the note and picked up my phone to finally respond to her text.

"I'm not getting pregnant. But when I do, that Godmom thing is all yours! Thank youuuuuu!" - Brooklyn

"Enjoy, boo. You got this." - Raina

"*I got this,*" I repeated to myself, holding the teddy out in front of me and smiling as hard as I'd been since I got here before Austin switched up on me, knowing he wouldn't be able to deny me once I put it on.

Or maybe he'll still deny you like he did when he put you in this room in the first place.

Just the thought had me tempted to save the outfit for another time, or at least save it for an occasion that I could guarantee Austin - *or someone else* - would appreciate it. But after running my fingers against the luxurious fabric, I knew I had to at least try it on. And once I did that, there was no turning back since I looked way too good in it not to show it off immediately.

Well… show it off whenever the opportunity came for me to remove the robe I put on over it just in case Austin's cousin started beefin' with his girl again. The last thing I wanted to do was waste the first look on a *complete* stranger.

But the fact that Austin felt like the furthest thing from a stranger even though this was our first time coming face-to-face told me this conversation - *and hopefully more* - was worth having, leading me to his room where the door was already cracked open just enough for me to see inside before I entered.

His room was broken into two parts, the main portion dedicated to the normal bed, dresser, and nightstand and the additional part designed as more of a sitting area with a ridiculously large television mounted on the wall and a couch that he was lounged out on watching basketball. Or rather, studying basketball, his gaze on the screen intense as I toed over towards him and asked, "So this is why you sent me to bed early? Because you had work to do?"

Without even glancing my way, he replied, "No. I sent you to bed because I was afraid that pussy might have me thinkin' about forever. But since forever is already out of the question…"

Now it all made sense. And while I could appreciate his honesty, I also couldn't help but chuckle as I moved to stand in front of him and sang, "Ahhh, so that's what that change in energy was all about. Mr. Basketball Player Dude is really feelin' ya girl."

Glancing up at me with a smirk, he nodded. "Somethin' like that."

I was flattered as hell, suddenly finding the annoyance of him telling me goodnight to protect himself adorable as I crossed my arms over my chest and explained, "That statement was a lot more about me than you, Austin. I have to set boundaries like that for myself, *out loud*, so I don't…"

"Get too used to how good this feels? How right we already feel? *Together?*" he finished for me with hopeful eyes that gave me butterflies as he reached for my hand, then pulled me down onto his lap.

"You see this film I'm watchin'?" he asked, waiting for me to nod before he continued, "Every game, coach gives us a plan, tells us how we're gonna defend certain players, what weaknesses we're gonna attack. But sometimes, shit doesn't go according to plan. So we switch it up in the moment, do what makes sense, do what feels right, do what it takes to win."

"And you're trying to win me? That's how this whole inspirational ass *Coach Carter* speech ends, right?" I asked teasingly, making Austin chuckle as he rested a heavy hand against my thigh to say, "See why I already can't get enough of your silly ass?"

"Get as much of me as you can then," I suggested, standing

up from my spot on his lap with plans of undoing the knot on my robe; especially once I heard him use my phrase from earlier.

"Good time, not a long time, right?"

As if to answer his question, I let the tie of the robe fall to my sides, leaving it to hang open loosely as I replied, "Depends on the new game plan."

Shaking his head, he disagreed. "Nah, cause whatever you got on underneath that robe tells me you don't know how to play fair no way."

Now I was the one smirking, pushing the fabric from my shoulders as I told him, "You're right."

"*Gotdamn,*" he hissed, licking his lips as he moved towards the edge of the couch so that he could grab me by the back of my thighs, his large hands sinking into the skin just below my ass as he groaned, "You win, baby."

"Well that was easy. Guess I'll go back to my room now," I joked, pretending to tug away as he gripped me tighter.

"Nah, you ain't goin' nowhere," he slickly replied, making me grow hotter when he pulled me even closer and asked, "What happened to all that *cover my dimples with your inner thighs* energy you had in my DMs? I mean, my dimples are *right* here. And your thighs… *mmm.*"

He didn't stay there long, his hands finding their way up to the ass that had apparently gotten his attention in the first place as I pressed my hands into his shoulders and moved to straddle his lap. Then I wrapped my arms around his neck to tease, "You fed me sweets, so I guess it's only right for me to do the same, huh?"

"*Godiva* or nothin'," he replied with a smirk, leaning forward to press a kiss against my lips that I giggled into even though I had plans of giving him just that.

It was just funny to hear him use my words, flattering to hear him remember so many little details of our conversations like it really mattered to him; like *I* really mattered to him. But if him worrying about forever already being out of the question was any indication, it was clear I was more than just some random girl off of *Instagram* who he chose to spend the weekend with.

I was his first flyout, the one he cooked for, and let give him a tattoo, and fed cheesecake to. The one he trusted in his home, the one he trusted with his truck, the one he couldn't get enough of, the one he planned on wooing in a weekend.

And boy, was I wooed.

From the feel of his tongue wrestling with mine to the firm grip he had on my ass, I was beyond happy to submit to whatever he was putting out regardless of how limited our time together would be. Then again, maybe he was serious about making some adjustments to our little game plan, just the thought making me warm all over until Austin pulled back and groaned, "Fuckkk, I'm in trouble."

"What kinda trouble?" I asked, thinking he was about to announce some shit that would make our whole game plan explode. But really, it only made me explode internally with anticipation once I heard his response.

"The kinda trouble that has me wanting to spend the rest of the night inside you, Brooklyn."

With a smirk, I reminded him, "You have a very specific obligation to fulfill first, sir."

"So what you waitin' on? Bring me that pussy, baby," he insisted, licking his lips as if he was prepping them for what was to come and making my thighs tremble all at once because… *how sexy of a request?*

Honestly, I couldn't move fast enough, adjusting to a mostly-standing position on the cushions as Austin slid down far enough for his head to rest comfortably against the back of the couch. And I was just barely straddling his face when he reached between us to undo the single button that would change our dynamic forever, his immediate groan in response to coming face-to-face with my freshly-waxed pussy only making me tremble harder as he gripped into my ass to pull me down onto his mouth with a sense of urgency that completely obliterated my senses.

I mean, from his kisses alone, I already knew Austin's tongue game was solid. But nothing could've prepared me for just how good his mouth felt as he licked and sucked on my clit with the enthusiasm of a man trying to prove a point – *maybe because he was trying to prove a point* – his moans and hums only adding to the pleasure since it was obvious he was enjoying himself. And it was his personal enjoyment that encouraged me to really let go of any last bits of apprehension I was subconsciously carrying, my eyes closed and my head tilted back as I started riding his face exactly how I drunkenly imagined doing so the night I slid into his DMs.

"Dreams really do come true," I thought as Austin gave me a hard smack to the ass that confirmed this was indeed reality. And even if that wasn't enough to confirm it, the way my stomach began to coil with an impending orgasm definitely told me this was real life, my lips parted as Austin rocked his tongue in perfect rhythm with my hips to take me over the edge.

I couldn't help the way I collapsed against him, damn near suffocating him until he lowered me back down onto his lap. And instead of letting me catch my breath, he caught my mouth with a messy kiss that only sent another surge of pleasure through me before he pulled away to say, "Keepin' it a hunnid, you taste way better than *Godiva*, B."

Giggling and gushing down below all at once, I licked his chin that was still dripping with my flavor before I agreed, "You're right."

"Do that shit again," he demanded, a smirk on my lips before I gave another slow lick from the tip of his chin up to his mouth then nipped his bottom lip between my teeth. "See. That's the kinda shit that'll have a nigga ready to wife your ass up. You better chill out."

Instead of accepting his warning, I only giggled again. "If a lick to the chin has you ready to wife me up, then I'm afraid of what this pussy is gonna do to you."

"Only one way to find out," he insisted before lifting the both of us up from the couch, my legs instinctively wrapping around his waist as he carried me over to the bed. And after depositing me onto the mattress, he made quick work of removing his t-shirt and basketball shorts, the glow from the TV in his sitting area providing just enough light for me to see how damn immaculate his body was as I propped myself up on my elbows to watch him.

Thick biceps, stacked abs, muscular thighs with a dick between them that ended up stealing the show; especially once he started stroking it in his hand on his short walk over to the nightstand for a condom to put on. And the view of him from behind was just as impressive, complete with a strong back and an ass that told me he didn't skip the squat rack on leg day.

"Do they even have leg day in the NBA?" I wondered, apparently still wearing the question on my face when Austin turned back around, prompting him to ask, "Everything okay?"

"Everything is fine. I was just, *and don't take this the wrong way*, but you have a really nice ass."

From the way his eyes immediately tightened in response, I could tell my words hadn't been received as intended. Though I still couldn't help but laugh as I whined, "It's a compliment, Austin!"

"If you say so," he replied, grabbing me by my ankles to pull me towards the edge of the bed as he continued, "But for the record, yours looks way better."

My response got caught in my throat once Austin glided into me with a slow plunge, my legs resting against his shoulders as he groaned, "*Gotdamn*. What kinda rings you like?"

I wanted to laugh, but could only moan as he went even deeper with a second and third stroke, squeezing my ankles to keep my legs in a V-formation as he started fuckin' me faster and asked, "How many karats you want, baby?"

Again, the humor got lost in the pleasure as the smacking of our skin and our shared moans dominated the soundwaves in the room, my shriek interrupting what had become a steady murmur when Austin leaned into me to go even deeper. In fact, I found myself scurrying away from him on the mattress until he climbed on to join me with a laugh.

"*I know your ass ain't runnin'...*" he teased with an arrogant smirk before gliding back inside of me with a stroke that only had me reaching between us in an attempt to keep him – *and his dick*- at a reasonable distance. But instead of letting my hands dictate anything, he pinned them over my head and said, "Take it all, B," intertwining his fingers with mine as he slowed his strokes to a pace that was somehow even more intoxicating than before. Or maybe it was just the fact that it felt so much more intimate,

Austin burying himself as deep as my body would allow and creating a pleasurable friction against my clit that had those stomach coils returning in record time.

He knew it too, his arrogant smirk back as he continued to drive into me and urged, "Let it go, baby. Let me hear it."

You would've thought those words were some secret password to unlock the scream of ecstasy I belted and the waves of satisfaction that immediately coursed through me in response, my nerve-endings tingling and my voice hoarse by the time I finally settled with Austin still wedged between my thighs. And while I expected him to at least give me a few moments to recover, I quickly learned that wouldn't be the case at all, Austin only pulling out long enough to flip me onto my stomach before plunging into me again; this time from behind.

"Arch that back for me," he requested, my body granting his wish before my brain could even process. And though I didn't have much left in the tank, I gave everything I had when I pressed my fingers into the mattress for leverage and threw my ass back at him, making him groan, "*Definitely got the better ass,*" as he dug his fingers into my hips and met me with strokes that had me seeing blue and pink stars with how tightly I had my eyes closed.

It wasn't long before Austin was warning me about his approaching nut, only encouraging me to go harder so he could experience what he had already done for me twice. And somehow, me going hard turned into a third orgasm that left me beyond depleted as I collapsed onto the bed while Austin cussed through his own before collapsing next to me.

My face was happily buried in the mattress until I heard him ask, "You got a lot of family back in Dallas?"

"*Huh?*"

Turning my way, he explained, "Your family. Is it big? I'm tryna price out this wedding ceremony in my head."

"*Boy…*" I groaned with a laugh that made him laugh too as he climbed up from the mattress and said, "Let me go take care of this rubber." Then he rushed off to the bathroom as I laid there with a satiated smile, letting the life come back to my limbs as I grew a better understanding of exactly why he considered not crossing this particular line tonight.

I mean, how in the world was I supposed to experience this – *experience him* - for only a couple of days? How did this already feel like so much more than just instant attraction and bomb ass sex? And most importantly, how much was I willing to do to make it a good time *and* a long time with Austin?

Instead of worrying myself with a search for answers, I shimmied towards the headboard for a pillow, not even bothering to get under the covers since I just needed a second to close my eyes and gather myself before I went back to my room to wrap my hair. But of course, plans quickly changed once my head hit the pillow that felt like a literal cloud, sending me to dreamland before the man of my dreams could even return from the bathroom.

AUSTIN

SHE WAS SLEEPING SO PEACEFULLY that I hated to wake her. But the fact that I'd already worked out, showered, and had a light breakfast meant it was past time for her to get up; especially since we had somewhere to be.

It was a destination I wasn't sure how she'd feel about, a place I knew could be an absolute hit or a total miss depending on if she was into being outdoors or not. But I was hoping for the best as I gently started shaking her shoulder, chuckling at the way she immediately moved to bury her head in the pillows until I pulled one of them away from her and urged, "Brooklyn, wake up."

"No thanks," she replied groggily with her face still smashed against the pillow I hadn't taken, only making me laugh harder before I tried another approach.

"Come on, baby. We gotta get going so we don't miss our scheduled appointment."

Even though I was sure I could pull some strings in the event that we really did miss our appointment, I had a feeling Brooklyn would be more interested in the fact that I had made plans for us. And luckily, that seemed to do the trick, at least enough for her to slowly sit up and ask, "What time is it?"

"Almost ten. Now go get dressed. We have about a thirty-minute drive without traffic and our appointment is at noon."

Her face scrunched when she repeated, "*Noon*? If that's the case, I can go back to sleep."

Then she moved to pull the cover over her head until I caught it and explained, "Nah, traffic is too unpredictable to risk it. And I don't know if you've seen your hair after last night, *but...*"

"*Oh, God...*" she groaned, dropping the cover to sit back up and assess the damage we'd done to the hairstyle I was sure she had just gotten done before she left Dallas.

Between the rounds of sex we'd had and how wild of a sleeper she was, that shit honestly didn't stand a chance. Though her little panic only made me smirk, admiring how the wild hair added to her appeal when I found a spot next to her at the edge of the mattress and told her, "Nothin' to be ashamed of, baby. Just means I did my job."

Since she knew it was true, she could only toss me a side eye before she sighed, "*Anyway*. Exactly what kind of appointment do we have?"

"It's a surprise," I replied with a grin that only grew wider once I saw Brooklyn's face turn more skeptical.

"If it's a surprise, how am I supposed to know what to wear?" she halfway whined, tucking a piece of hair behind her ear that almost immediately disobeyed by flying back into her face.

So this time, I did it for her, brushing a hand against her cheek in the process as I suggested, "Just dress casual, Brooklyn."

My assumption that my advice would somehow make things easier for her quickly proved itself wrong according to the flat look on her face when she replied, "There's levels to casual, Austin. I mean, there's brunch casual, mall casual, *beach casual...*"

"Aight, somewhere between mall casual and beach casual. Something comfortable and fit for outdoors that you wouldn't mind getting dirty, and possibly wet."

I was trying to explain as best as I could without completely giving the surprise away, incredibly pleased to see Brooklyn's flat expression turn intrigued when she repeated, "*Dirty* and *wet*? I'm into it."

"So I've learned," I teased, leaning towards her for a kiss that she dodged with her hands pressed into my shoulders.

"Lips to yourself, Mr. *We-Gotta-Get-Going,"* she giggled, moving to climb off the opposite side of the mattress until I pulled her back to the middle from behind.

"Nah, we always got time for that."

My lips were at her neck as she groaned, "Austin, quit it. Cause I need all the time I can get to work some magic on this hair."

Suddenly, I wished I would've never mentioned it, nipping at her ear before I suggested, "Just slick that shit back into a ponytail and borrow one of my hats."

"And look like someone's bad ass little brother in all of my pictures for *Instagram*? No, sir. Not gonna happen," she replied with another little laugh even though I could tell she was serious since she continued to pull away from me in pursuit of the robe I had left at the foot of the bed – yet another thing I wished I wouldn't have bothered with since it ended with her covering up that glorious body of hers.

She was already knotting it closed by the time I asked, "So it's all about the 'Gram, huh?"

While I considered myself more of a casual user of the app, refusing to get caught up in that shit too heavily since I knew how much trouble it had caused for some of my peers, I also knew some people lived for the likes. And I could only hope that wasn't the case with Brooklyn considering how easily addictive it could all be; though I shouldn't have been surprised when she slickly fired back, "*Instagram* is how I got your fine ass, remember?"

With a smirk, I agreed, "Good point. Go do what you gotta do, baby. You got an hour."

Serving a little extra in her hips, she left the room, leaving me to figure out how to waste time until she was ready. And I bet you can guess where I ended up first - *Instagram.*

I started with a few scrolls of the people I followed, giving likes to all the pictures of my teammates either on vacation with their families or doing work in their communities. Then I moved to the *Explore* page, giving likes to all the pictures from the first night of All-Star Weekend that included the celebrity game and a game between the younger stars from the USA and the World. And I was just getting ready to hop over to another app when a direct message popped up at the top of the screen from a familiar username, the little bit I could see immediately making me frown before it disappeared.

"What the fuck does she want?" I thought, clicking over to my inbox to open the full message.

@EspressoEstelle : "Was hoping to run into you at All-Star, but I see you really are avoiding me. I guess I'll just have to make my way down there for us to make up properly ;)."

Why she thought the two of us "making up" was even a possibility considering it had been a few months since we last interacted, I wasn't sure.

Actually, I knew the reason. There was something about Estelle that I had always struggled to shake in the past, creating a confidence on her end that no matter what, she could get me back.

Not this time, though.

In fact, I felt more confident than ever as I typed out a response.

@ABTreyTwo: "Save yourself a trip. It's not gonna happen."

I could see the exact moment she opened the message to read it, quickly responding from the same arrogant place from before.

@EspressoEstelle: "You talk a big game over these messages, but I know you won't be able to resist me in person, Austin."

Once upon a time, she wouldn't have been lying. It had always been our thing; showing up to the same places like we didn't fuck with each other, like we didn't know each other would be there, then leaving separately with the same destination – typically my bedroom.

In the beginning, it was fun as hell; the thrill of keeping it all a secret and the crazy sex we'd have whenever we successfully completed the mission. But admittedly, I grew tired of the dynamic, began to desire something more solid than just fucking around. And since Estelle wasn't interested in me for anything beyond sex, I moved on from that situation – *mostly*.

I assumed the few times I doubled back when she visited the city was the reason she decided to send me a sexy picture when I didn't respond to her message right away, almost as if she was trying to remind me of what I'd be missing out on by putting an official end to our little game. And though the picture was indeed impressive, I lowkey felt guilty for even looking at it with Brooklyn on my mind – *and in my house*.

While Estelle was a good time, Brooklyn already felt like that and more, a breath of fresh air and possibly that something solid I'd been looking for if day one was any indication. And since the last thing I wanted to do was fuck that up before it could really blossom, I didn't bother responding to Estelle, instead blocking her from being able to send me anything else and then doing the same on my phone since I was sure that would be her next move.

Somebody somewhere was proud of me. But I couldn't get to that point myself, too shook by how easy it had been to wipe my hands with that situation on the pure strength of the possibility of something real with Brooklyn as if she wasn't the one to acknowledge "forever" being out of the question from the jump.

Maybe last night had really changed things for us. And I suppose I was anxious to find out since I made quick work of changing into something light for the day before I left my room in pursuit of the one she was keeping her things in.

Giving the guest room door a knock, I asked, "Can I come in?"

"Yeah, I'm almost ready!" she shouted back, prompting me to

enter the room where I found her in front of the mirror perfecting the bun she had managed to whip her hair up into. But the bun was really the last thing I could focus on, the tank top and daisy dukes she had chosen for the occasion damn near making my mouth water with how good her ass looked in them.

"So I see you *do* know what casual means," I commented, watching the little smirk she gave me through the mirror before she replied, "Your clues might've helped a little bit, even though I still don't know where we're going."

With a shrug, I insisted, "That's the fun part, B. Now let's get outta here before we miss our boat."

I tried to slip in the single word hint nonchalantly. But of course, it was still enough to capture Brooklyn's interest, her eyes twinkling with excitement when she repeated, "Boat?! We're going on a boat? What kinda boat?"

"Can't tell you all that," I answered, making Brooklyn grunt before she started throwing out guesses anyway.

"So a speedboat? Or no, a yacht? What about a canoe? I'll even take a paddleboat."

For whatever reason, the last guess made me chuckle as, *instead of confirming anything,* I replied, "I've already said too much."

"And now the suspense is killing me," she groaned as she plopped down on the bed to put her sandals on, the fact that she really seemed pressed about our destination only making me want to tease her even more.

So that's what I did, approaching where she was seated to ask, "You really want me to tell you, baby?"

"Yes!" she squealed, quickly securing the latch on her sandal so that she could stand and face me straight up; though our height difference forced her to tilt her head back so she could find my eyes.

Still, no matter how much her orbs begged me to give her the answers she was looking for, the only response I planned to give was, "Too bad."

With another grunt, she stepped away to grab her wallet and phone as she muttered, "*But I'm the one who doesn't play fair…*"

"Guess I learned a little somethin' from you last night," I

replied playfully, catching the smirk on her face when she headed back my way.

Stopping right in front of me, she ran a finger from my chin straight down to my dick before asking, "*Just* a little somethin', Austin?"

Instead of answering her question, I urged, "Come on before I take you up on what your hands are tellin' me you want."

Shrugging, she blew past me out of the room while tossing over her shoulder, "Who knows? Maybe the boat you're taking me on will have a room for that."

"Nah, it's not that kinda… *wait.* You really think you're slick, don't you?" I asked, shutting down Brooklyn's attempt at getting more information out of me about our water ride.

Since she'd gotten caught, she could only giggle as she admitted, "It was worth a try," before making her way down the stairs and out to my truck for the drive out to the Everglades - *because that's where we were going.*

Considering Brooklyn knew nothing about Miami, she was clueless of our destination the entire ride, using the little bit of traffic we hit to snap a picture of herself in the side view mirror that she posted to *Instagram* with the caption, *"305 to My City. I get it, I get it…"* And I was quick to clown her about using a Drake lyric instead of lyrics by an artist who was actually from the city, leading to a playful argument about how Drake was the nomad of hip-hop that lasted until we pulled up to where Lamar, his wife Kaylin, and their friends Guy and Nova* were waiting on us.

I was already out of the truck when I realized Brooklyn hadn't budged, practically frozen in her seat when I made my way over to open the door for her. And even then, she didn't move, her eyes wide as she stared at the sign in front of us.

"Brooklyn, what's wrong?" I asked, hoping to break the seemingly-stunned expression on her face.

Not only did my question break it, it made her hysterical when she turned my way and shouted, "Alligators! That's what's wrong!"

While her reaction should've been alarming as far as getting this whole "making plans" thing right, I could only laugh as I assured her, "We'll be in the boat, B. They're not gonna mess with you there."

"Says who? *You*? Are you an alligator-whisperer, or somethin'? Cause if not, your words mean nothing," she insisted, only making me laugh harder as I leaned against the door and reminded her of her one request for this trip.

"You said you didn't want to be holed up in a room staring at me all day."

"Compared to coming face-to-face with an alligator, that actually doesn't sound so bad," she replied with a frown, crossing her arms over her chest in a pout as I felt a gentle hand against my back.

"Hey, Austin! Everything okay?" Kaylin asked, looking between Brooklyn and I for an answer that I was sure became obvious even before I explained, "Yeah, Brooklyn is just being scary."

Of course, Brooklyn only frowned harder at that, Kaylin moving to take my place against the door when she said, "Hi, Brooklyn. I'm Kaylin, Lamar's wife. I know you don't know me yet, *or him*. But formerly-terrified black woman to currently-terrified black woman, I promise it's not as bad as you think."

"So you've done this before?" Brooklyn asked with softened eyes, the crack in her demeanor making me hopeful as Kaylin continued her convincing.

"This exact one? *No*. But I've done them in other cities and had a blast after getting past the *"fuck that tiny boat and those human-eating gators"* stage you're probably in right now."

"That's exactly what it is," Brooklyn agreed with a little chuckle before releasing a heavy sigh. "Fine. I'll go. But I swear to God if I die because an alligator wants to eat me for lunch…"

"*Shit*. I can't even blame him there," I joked, making Brooklyn smirk and Kaylin mutter, "*I know that's right…*" as she made room for Brooklyn to climb out. And after introducing her to the rest of the folks waiting on us - *including a slightly-awkward introduction to Guy since I'd gone out on a date with his now-wife a while back* - we made our way out to the swamp, Brooklyn holding onto me for dear life as I helped her across the dock and then onto the airboat where she sat as close to me as she could while the tour guide gave us instructions.

"*A definite perk of this activity choice,*" I thought as Brooklyn squealed and held onto me even tighter in response to the tour guide's suggestion that the gators could jump. But a quick kiss to her temple and a smooth takeoff was enough to calm her down, eventually agreeing that it wasn't so bad by the time we came up on our first alligator that was far enough away for Brooklyn to acknowledge how pretty it was.

The second one was a little closer, but small enough for her to think it was cute. And then we saw two together that she assumed was a mom and her baby, making her really find the creatures adorable as she leaned close enough to the edge to get a good picture that I read the *Instagram* caption for over her shoulder once she snuggled back up under me.

"*Alligator seats with the head in the inside?* Really, Brooklyn?" I asked with a chuckle, finding the Big Tymers shoutout a little inappropriate considering we were currently at a gator sanctuary.

Shrugging, she replied, "It was all I could think of. I mean, it was either that or a line from *Alligators* by Gucci Mane which is about shoes looking like alligators, so…"

"*Still Fly* it is," I concluded, settling in for the rest of the hour-long tour that ended with Brooklyn being all about the swamp life now that her first experience had gone safely.

At least, that's how she was acting until the mention of us all taking a picture holding a baby gator, something that excited the rest of the group while also making Brooklyn's new ego disappear.

"*I'm good,*" she continuously insisted as we watched the other couples get their photo op with the gator that couldn't eat Brooklyn if it wanted to considering its mouth was taped shut. And I suppose I was trying to guilt trip her a little bit when I asked, "You really gonna make me be the lame nigga taking a picture by myself?"

"If you want a picture with the gator, then yes," she replied, even holding out her hand to offer, "Want me to get one on your phone too?"

Shaking my head, I wrapped an arm around her shoulder and

pressed, "Come on, Brooklyn. I let you give me a tattoo. So do this for me. *Please*."

Instead of immediately granting my wish, she turned in my hold to say, "*Correction*, you peer-pressured me into giving you a tattoo," releasing a heavy sigh before she continued, "*But*, because I believe in fairness, I'll take the stupid picture with you."

My excitement only made me squeeze her tighter as I guided us towards the photo station while asking, "Since when do you believe in fairness?"

"Since right now. And it expires in five minutes, so let's make this quick," she urged, making me laugh as Lamar and Kaylin gently handed the gator back to the trainer. And after giving us a look to ask if we were sure we wanted a turn since Brooklyn was visibly nervous, the trainer showed us exactly where to hold the gator safely before handing it our way, Brooklyn holding her breath when she smiled as if that was somehow going to keep it from going after her during the thirty seconds the moment lasted.

Even though it went quick, it was still long enough for Kaylin to gush, "Awww! You two are so cute!" Turning towards her husband to ask, "Aren't they cute, babe?"

"Yeah, looks like little bro finally got him one," Lamar agreed with something like a proud nod, making me feel a way as we handed the gator back over to its trainer. And while I thought I was the only one paying attention to the comments they were making about us, I quickly learned that Brooklyn had been too, a pleased grin on her face when she wrapped an arm around me to ask an important question.

"So… what's next?"

BROOKLYN

IF YOU WOULD'VE TOLD me I'd spend the day enjoying alligators in multiple forms - *first looking at them in their habitat and then eating them in fried bites for a late lunch at the beach* - I wouldn't have believed you. But that was exactly what had happened, and I couldn't have been more grateful for Austin pushing me out of my comfort zone on both accounts, his confident energy making it easy for me to trust his judgment and fall more in... *like* with him overall.

I mean, there was really nothing for me *not* to like. He was fun to be around, attentive, touchy and affectionate without crowding me, easy to talk to, and finer than fine; practically perfect except for the fact that I'd be thousands of miles away from him starting tomorrow afternoon. But I was trying my best not to focus too much on that part yet, instead enjoying the feel of just having him around as I laid between his legs on the couch while we watched different NBA players - *his friends* - participate in the All-Star Weekend Three-Point Contest.

Draping an arm around me, he planted a quick kiss against my temple before asking, "Are you sure you're good with this, B? I mean, if you really wanna go out and see more of the city, we can."

"After being out in the sun all day, this is *just* what I need," I told him, snuggling in a little closer as we watched the second round of shooters. At least, we were supposed to be watching the second round of shooters, my eyes drifting closed until I felt my phone vibrating in my lap.

One glance at the screen had me wide awake as I started to move away from Austin to answer the *FaceTime* call until he caught me by the arm to say, "*Wait.* I wanna talk to her too."

My smirk twisted on its own as I was faced with the decision to take him up on his request or to leave knowing Raina was a loose cannon and could very well say something not meant for his ears. But after another buzz, I decided to go for it, plopping back down into my spot between his legs before pressing to accept the call.

Of course, once Raina picked up on our semi-cuddled position, she couldn't help but tease, "Well don't you two look cozy as hell."

Instead of indulging her, I only smiled before I asked, "What do you want, Raina?"

"I was just calling to confirm your arrival time tomorrow so I can make sure I'm there to pick you up."

If it was someone else calling, I might've believed the claim. But considering Raina's eyes were clearly trying to explore everything in my background, I could only shake my head as I replied, "I'm pretty sure I emailed you my flight itinerary. And if I didn't, you could've just texted me and asked."

With a sneaky grin, she admitted, "Okay, so maybe I really just wanted to see your face when I asked how everything was going down there. And now I have an answer. Hey, Austin."

I tilted the phone just enough for her to see his face when he said, "What's good, Raina? Your girl is over here fallin' asleep on me. I must be boring her."

"*That's not true...*" I started before Raina interrupted to explain, "Nah, she's just a sleepyhead. Good cuddles or good dick always does the trick."

"*So I've learned,*" he muttered with an arrogant smirk that made me playfully roll my eyes at him through the screen as I groaned, "*Anyway*. I land at 3 PM. Anything else?"

"One more thing. It's y'alls last night together and y'all really still have on clothes right now?"

"*There's that loose cannon,*" I thought, rushing her off the phone with an annoyed, "Goodbye, Raina!" that had Austin chuckling right against my ear. And after I tossed my phone to the opposite end of the couch, he pulled me back even closer, nipping my ear with his teeth before he groaned, "Your friend had a point."

"My friend needs to mind her own business," I replied with a chuckle that got caught in my belly once I felt Austin's hand slowly dragging towards that same direction. But he didn't stop there, pushing past the pajama shorts I had put on into my panties where he started rubbing lazy circles against my already swollen clit.

My eyes were already drifting closed for new reasons by the time he asked, "Does that mean you won't appreciate me doing this?"

"I… didn't say that," I pushed out, the thickness of his fingertips working magic that had me panting and grinding back against his hand as I became more and more sensitive to his touch.

In fact, I felt like I was going to combust when he asked, "You been this wet for me all this time?"

With the slowed pace of his strumming, I found enough breath to admit, "I love the way you smell fresh out of the shower."

It was intoxicating, honestly; only adding to everything that was already too good to be true about Austin. But my mention of the shower only encouraged him to press, "You mean, the shower you should've joined me for?" before he pulled his fingers out of my panties and slipped them between my lips so I could taste my flavor, my arousal making me moan as I gleefully licked his hand clean.

Between that and how hot he had me, it made sense for Austin's dick to practically be stabbing me in the back by the time I answered, "Nah, I needed to be able to focus on a good scrub without you distracting me. You know, wash off that combination of swamp and sand from today."

"Well thank you for being such a good sport, baby," he sang, wrapping me in a tight hug from behind and pressing a kiss against my cheek that added a layer of warmth and fuzziness to the moment even though that didn't exactly align with what I now had in mind.

Because, yes.

My friend Raina did *have a point.*

Pulling myself out of his hold, I turned to face him, sitting up on my knees when I admitted, "You have a way of bringing that out of me, Austin. Pushing me *just* enough. Really, I should be thanking you. Let me… *thank you.*"

If he didn't catch my drift right away, I knew he would once I started tugging at the waistband of his basketball shorts, his lifted hips giving way to the dick that had my attention long before I even had my eyes on it. But now that I did, I couldn't get my hands on it fast enough, fascinated with its smoothness as Austin scolded, "Nah, don't play wit' it, B. If you want it, take it."

Apparently he didn't know what he was getting himself into by applying pressure when it came to this, but he learned his lesson once I got myself in position to swallow him whole, his quads flexed as he groaned, "*Ohhh shit,*" while I sucked and stroked him senseless.

The more he groaned, the wetter my mouth got, creating a mess of saliva that I used to massage his balls with when I finally came up for air. But my breath was quickly taken away when Austin grabbed me by the chin to pull me up for a sloppy kiss, tonguing me with a purpose before guiding my face back down to his dick that I was now even more eager to leave my mark on.

As if I hadn't already.

Still, I accepted the personal challenge of making him completely weak with my mouth, double-fisting his shaft as I licked his balls before tonguing my way back up from the base to the tip of his dick where I looked him in the eyes and asked, "I guess I took it, huh?"

Before he could even answer, I swallowed him again, his grunts of pleasure coinciding with his dick repeatedly crashing into the back of my throat. But it was a feeling that I relished, along with the soreness in my jaws and the mess on my face because it equated to a very satisfied Austin who had carved his own little special place in my heart in the matter of a few nights.

He deserved.

When he warned me about his nut, I took it in the stride, swallowing every drop including the second wave that I stroked out of him when he begged me to "*stop playin*'". But I had to take my moments of advantage when I had them since I knew there would be nothing light about Austin taking charge, an excited smirk on my face as I watched him - *and his dick* - slowly come back to life.

Once he started stroking it in his hand, I knew it was game on; though I still couldn't help teasing him when I suggested, "Don't you wanna watch the dunk contest?"

Shaking his head, he coolly replied, "Nah, I'll catch it later. Right now, I wanna watch you bouncin' on my dick."

"Like… *right*, right now?" I asked playfully as I stood up from the couch so that I could step out of my shorts and panties, the sight of my naked lower half only making Austin's wants more urgent.

"*Right*, right now, Brooklyn," he growled, grabbing me by the hand and pulling me onto his lap where I hovered to align us before gliding down onto his dick with a satisfied hum.

"God, you feel so good," I groaned as I pressed my hands into the back of the couch and slowly found the rhythm in my hips, Austin leaning forward to swallow my praises with kisses that I couldn't get enough of.

I mean, between the way his fingers were gripping my ass, the feel of his tongue diving in and out of my mouth, and the fullness of his dick inside of me, I was in total heaven, not even stopping when I realized, "*Shit.* We should probably be using protection, Austin."

"You're right," he agreed though he didn't stop either, instead holding me closer so that he could kiss on my neck before insisting, "I'll go upstairs. Get a condom. *If you want.*"

Before I got here, it wouldn't have even been a question. But admittedly, the moment - *Austin, period* - had me completely caught up, consequences quickly becoming an afterthought when I told him, "Next time."

"*Next time*?" he repeated, stopping all motion to look me in the eyes for true confirmation.

While I appreciated him trying to be more responsible about this than I was, I was already in too deep, wrapping my arms around his neck to answer, "Next time."

"Cause there will be a next time?" he pressed with a glimmer of hope in his eyes as if there was still some uncertainty about our future beyond this weekend.

Again, before I got here, I would've understood his concern. But I was happy to kill that knowing my original game plan coming into this whole thing had been changed completely, resting my forehead against his when I whispered against his lips, "Most definitely."

"You promise, baby?" he asked as he moved us towards the edge of the couch and started stroking me from below, keeping me close with a hand wrapped tightly around my back as I struggled to respond.

"*I…* fuck*… I promise,*" I hissed. And thankfully, that was enough to keep him from asking me any more questions since I could barely breathe, let alone think about answers with how damn good he felt.

Honestly, the fact that we lived so far apart was already starting to feel like a punishment since that meant I wouldn't be experiencing this again soon enough. But I'd deal with that when I was back in Dallas, right now my focus solely on receiving every ounce of pleasure Austin was dishing out until I collapsed against him with an orgasm that left my heart pounding and my pussy throbbing.

My head felt like it was in the clouds even though it was really just resting on Austin's shoulder when he hissed, "*Shit. Hop up.*" And thankfully my body knew what to do without my brain having to think twice, getting me off of his dick in time for him to nut in his hand instead of inside of me even though I was still pretty much in his lap.

His grunts as he stroked himself empty were like music to my ears as I smiled to myself, grinning even harder once he admitted, "Flying you out for the weekend was the best decision I've made in a long ass time."

Regardless of whatever questionable decisions he'd made in his past, I still felt confident replying, "I'd have to agree with you there, Mr. Basketball Player Dude."

"*I bet you do,*" he teased, chuckling when I snuggled closer even though I knew we both needed to clean ourselves up. But I just needed a second, or maybe more than a few seconds since I wasn't sure how much time had passed when Austin asked, "Brooklyn, you sleep?

AUSTIN

I NEVER THOUGHT I'd say this, but the drive to the airport wasn't long enough.

Between the morning sex, the breakfast she cooked but let me feed her, and then the mid-morning wet and wild action in the shower, I thought for sure I had filled my reserve with enough of Brooklyn to last me until whenever we'd see each other again. But really, it had only made things worse, only made it that much harder for me to not be annoyed by the lighter than usual traffic and the open parking spot in the drop-off area at the airport.

"Since when is the drop-off area light on a Sunday afternoon?" I thought, putting the truck in park as Brooklyn let out a heavy sigh. And I was just getting ready to ask her what was wrong when she turned my way to say, "This trip was… absolutely amazing, Austin. *Seriously*. Thank you for flying me out and making this the best lovers' weekend with a stranger ever."

While I couldn't have agreed more with the weekend turning out even better than I could've imagined, I was more intrigued by her mention of what she had coined as lovers' weekend, leading me to glance at my wrist when I muttered more to myself than her, "*I finally figured it out.*"

Her piqued eyebrow prompted me to explain aloud, "The

tattoo. Your fine ass came down here and shot me with cupid's arrow. Tattooed that shit on me and everything. *Wowww.*"

Brooklyn immediately started giggling, quick to defend, "If that's the case, I should've gotten one too! Cause, *shit…* I like me some you, Mr. Basketball Player Dude."

"The feeling is beyond mutual, B," I told her, brushing a hand against her chin before I urged, "Now come on, cause I'm already thinking of ways to convince you to miss this flight so you can stay a little while longer."

"No, sir," she sang, moving to open her door as she continued, "You might be rich, but some of us have jobs to be at tomorrow."

"I respect it," I told her before she finally climbed out and I did the same, grabbing her bag from the trunk and sitting it next to where she was standing on the curb so I could pull her in for a hug.

"Now don't you get back to Dallas and start acting like a real stranger," I warned teasingly after pressing a kiss against her neck, making her giggle as she pulled away.

"I should be the one telling you that. I mean, I'm sure you'll get busy with the season and forget about little ol' me in no time," she insisted, crossing her arms over her chest with an exaggerated pout.

Shaking my head, I assured her, "Nah, that'll never happen. I always got my reminder with me right here."

Then I flashed my wrist like I was showing off the band of my *Rolex* or some shit, breaking her frown when she giggled and sighed, "*Damn, I'm gonna miss you.*"

"Well I'm already missin' you, B. *And* that *Godiva.* You sure you ain't tryna catch a later flight?" I asked, making her giggle again when I pulled her arms apart and wrapped them around my body in another hug.

Tilting her head back to find my eyes, she replied, "I have to go, Austin. But I promised you a next time, and I keep my promises."

"You better," I pressed, kissing her forehead, then her nose, and then finally her lips that I lingered at for a few extra seconds before pulling away with a quiet goodbye.

Grabbing the handle of her suitcase, she replied, "See you later, alligator," serving me a smirk before heading into the airport.

With the drop-off area beginning to fill up the way I expected it to be, I knew I had to get going before the patrol got on my ass about making room for more cars; though I shouldn't have been surprised when I got to the freeway and hit standstill traffic.

"Now everybody and they mama wanna be on the road," I groaned, peeking ahead to see there had actually been a pretty bad accident which meant I'd be stuck for a little minute. And while I probably should've been staying alert regardless, I couldn't help pulling out my phone to pass the time, stopping at *Instagram* first and grinning hard as hell when the first picture that popped up on my timeline was one that Brooklyn had posted with the location tagged as the airport even though she'd taken it the night before at my house.

It was a close-up shot of the two of us cuddled up on the couch, though my face was cropped in a way that you couldn't necessarily tell who I was. But I knew who I was, and I knew the caption was a lyric that related to the picture in some way; though I couldn't place it right away.

"I've got a fear of flying high, but I'm prepared to spread my wings…" I read out loud, doing a quick *Google* search of the line to discover it was from an old Mya song. And once I clicked to play it through my car speakers, I found myself smiling even harder as I realized what Brooklyn was talking about.

The way we fell for each other so hard and fast scared her the same way people were scared of planes, but she was ready to give us a go anyway - *was prepared to spread her wings and face that fear of flying anyway* - which explained the location tag.

After "liking" the picture, I commented with an airplane emoji and a heart before moving to post a picture of my own. It was one I had taken of Brooklyn mid-laugh when we had lunch at the beach the day before, her pure exuberance in combination with the sunshine creating a perfect glow that I left filterless as I came up with the perfect caption.

"I wanna be the reason you smile…"

By the time I shared it, traffic had finally began to move again which meant I couldn't check for a response until I made it home almost an hour later. But once I pulled into my driveway, I was on it, scrolling until I found the comment - *or comments* - I was looking for.

@B_AdamsFinest: Come through, G-Unit. Real ones know what's up.

@B_AdamsFinest: Also *smiling hard AF :)*

Smiling back like she could see me, I "liked" both comments before making my way into the house, the fact that the lights were already on making it less of a surprise when I found my cousin Calvin on the couch.

Shaking my head, I joked, "Damn, bruh. What you got, surveillance on my crib or somethin'? How'd you know it was time for you to come back?"

He didn't even look my way when he shrugged to answer, "I got connects around here. And the hotel I stayed at last night didn't have late check-out."

My face scrunched as I repeated, "*Hotel*? I thought you were staying at Chelsea's?"

"I was… until we got into it. And usually I come here, but *clearly* that wasn't an option," he answered, tossing a side eye my way before he continued, "But anyway, enough about my shit. How did things go with ol' girl?"

Plopping down on the couch next to him, I started replaying the weekend in my head, an easy smile on my lips by the time I finally admitted, "*Honestly*? Baby girl got me feelin' shit I haven't felt in a long ass time; if ever."

It was crazy how quickly everything had happened, crazy how strong my feelings for Brooklyn already were. But there was no denying the truth, even when Calvin replied, "Damn. It was like that?"

"Like, I don't even know when I'll be able to see her again, and somehow I'm already countin' down the days," I told him, fully expecting him to clown me for being so caught up.

Surprisingly enough, he didn't, only nodding as he said, "That's what's up, bruh. I'm happy everything went well."

"Yeah. I just wish we ain't have all this distance between us. I mean, I'm sure we can make it work, *but...*"

"Go see her."

"*What?*"

"You still got a couple of days before practice and shit starts back up, right?" Calvin asked, watching me nod before he repeated, "So go see her."

"*Already*? I mean, I don't want her to feel like I'm doin' too much."

"Okay, so consult with her homegirl first," he suggested, making more sense than usual when he explained, "If she thinks it's a good idea, you can fly out in the morning. Spend a day or two in her city and make it back in time for the first whistle at practice."

"That's... actually not a bad idea," I agreed, pulling out my phone to send Raina a message on *Instagram* as I told Calvin, "Good lookin' out, man."

With a proud smirk, he fell back against the couch and replied, "Not a problem, cuz. It makes me happy to see you happy, and it's obvious this chick makes you happy. And besides, I'd do anything to get the house to myself for a few days."

"*Should've known your ass had an ulterior motive,*" I muttered, shaking my head as I typed out my possible plans for Raina's input. And when she responded with enthusiastic approval along with insight on how Brooklyn apparently hadn't stopped talking about me since she got back in town, I couldn't get my flight reserved fast enough, even going as far as packing my bag that night instead of waiting until the last minute like usual.

Yeah, I was *that* pressed.

With Calvin giving me a ride to the airport the next morning, I made it through TSA with plenty of time to spare, using my phone to watch highlights from the three-point and dunk contest that I had missed thanks to Brooklyn to pass as much of it as I could before it was almost my turn to board. But I should've known I wouldn't be able to pull off my little impromptu trip without at least one hiccup which explained Estelle deboarding the same plane I was getting ready to get on.

Once she saw me waiting at the gate, a sinister grin grew to her lips, her whole approach oozing with arrogance as she heeled over to me to ask, "Did you really think a petty block was going to stop me from coming to see you, Austin?"

Rolling my eyes, I was beyond annoyed when I told her, "It should've. But if it didn't, the fact that you just landed and I'm still leaving should make it very clear that I'm done fuckin' with you, Estelle. Take a hint and move on."

Instead of accepting my suggestion, she pressed, "Does this have something to do with that girl you posted on your *Instagram*?"

"The *Instagram* that I blocked you on?" I countered even though she was quick to brush me off with a wave of her hand.

"You knew good and damn well that picture was going to be everywhere. Everyone wanting to know more about Austin Banks's new boo like her basic ass is…"

Holding up my hand, I cut her off. "Nah. See what you're not gon' do is sit up here and start talkin' shit just cause you're jealous. You had your chance, Estelle. Now take your L and go enjoy your time in the city. I'm sure you won't have a problem finding somebody to entertain you. It just won't be me."

"But I want..." she started to beg before I cut her off again.

"*Estelle.* All this whining shit is mad extra," I told her, her pouty lips doing nothing to stop me from continuing, "Now I got a plane to catch to go and surprise someone I know really fucks with me. Maybe one day you'll find the same."

Brushing a hand against her shoulder, I dismissed myself to board the plane, grateful to be leaving Estelle behind in an even more permanent way when we finally took off. And by the time I made it to Dallas, all of my annoyed energy was replaced with excitement to see Brooklyn, the *Uber* ride from the airport to the tattoo shop she worked at only making that excitement skyrocket as I braced myself for her reaction to seeing me.

"*I hope Raina was right,*" I prayed as I climbed out of the car, taking a deep breath before I entered the shop. And it felt like fate that Brooklyn's back was towards me, giving me a few extra seconds to admire her from behind as she slowly turned around and started, "Hi, can I… *Austin?*"

Her jaw dropped, and I could only smile as I used the same line from the first time we saw each other in person. "Come on, baby. Don't go gettin' all starstruck and shit on me now."

Bending around the desk, she jumped into my arms and squealed, "Oh my God! What are you doing here?!"

Hugging her back just as tightly as she was squeezing me, I explained, "My cousin reminded me that I still had a few days left of my break. And I know you had to get back here to the shop, but that didn't mean I couldn't come to you. Even if it is the lesser city."

Of course I couldn't help sneaking in a Houston vs. Dallas jab, though Brooklyn wasn't fazed when she replied, "You can hate all you want to. I'm too happy you're here to care." Then she pulled my face down to hers for a kiss that turned into an assortment of kisses until a relatively familiar face appeared from the back and cleared her throat to get our attention.

"Oh, what a surprise," Raina sang sarcastically since she'd had a hand in orchestrating the whole thing, Brooklyn tucking herself under my arm as I moved to greet her friend.

"It's good to finally meet you in person, Raina. And thanks for your help."

"Any time," Raina replied with a proud smile, shooting a wink Brooklyn's way that made her squeeze me even tighter before she shared, "So I'm not technically off of work for a few more hours, *but…*"

"I'll cover for you!" Raina interjected, crossing her arms as she insisted, "Mondays are usually pretty slow anyway."

"Are you sure, Raina?"

"Absolutely. Go have fun, girl. I know I would if I were you," Raina answered with a giggle, practically kicking us out when she started guiding us towards the door.

"Then it's settled. Time to show you around my neck of the woods," Brooklyn bragged, doubling back to grab her purse before leading us out onto the sidewalk where she asked, "So, what should we do first? Are you hungry? We can go grab something to eat if you are. Or just grab a drink while we figure out what we wanna do."

Wrapping her in a low hug, I admitted, "I honestly don't care what we do, baby. I just wanna be with you. I came all the way here *just* for a little more of you."

I might've been laying it on thick, but I didn't even care. Cause just like I supposedly had a way of challenging Brooklyn just enough, she had a way of turning me into a lovey-dovey ass nigga.

A proud one though, with no shame in my game when it came to being completely infatuated with the woman in front of me, grateful for her bold move of sliding in my DMs on a dare along with her ability to read my mind when she licked her lips to say, "Well then, I think I know *exactly* where to start our little tour of the city. First stop: *my place.*"

The End

EXTRAS

Enjoyed this book?
Please leave a review on Amazon or Goodreads!

To stay up-to-date with all of Alexandra Warren's happenings including samples and excerpts, visit actuallyitsalexandra.com, like her Facebook page, or sign-up for her newsletter!

Also, be sure to check out the playlist of all the songs mentioned on Brooklyn's Instagram on Spotify!

FEATURED TITLES

Read all about Guy and Nova, along with Austin's introduction in, *If Only for the Summer

School may be out, but class is still in session...

After a hectic school year with her classroom of first graders, Nova Grant is desperate for a break. So when her best friend invites her to spend the summer down in Miami, taking the vacation is a no-brainer. The only thing is, her best friend's husband had the same idea, inviting his friend Guy Thompson to stay in the condo Nova was already guaranteed.

Set up or accidental... Fate or coincidental... the attraction between the two is undeniable from day one. But with their days under the sun numbered and plenty of lessons to learn between them, Guy and Nova still find themselves teetering the line of lust and love, even if it's only for the summer…

ALSO BY ALEXANDRA WARREN

Attractions & Distractions Series
Getting The Edge
An Unconventional Love
The PreGame Ritual
Distracted
The Real Deal
A Rehearsal For Love
An Encore For Love
Love at First Spite
In Spite of it All
Accidental Arrangements
Heated Harmonies
If Only for the Summer
In His Corner
The Games We Play (FWB Book 1)
The Lessons We Learn (FWB Book 2)
Win & Losses
Building 402 Series (Book 1-3)
A Tale of Two Cities Holiday Collection (Individuals)